THE SWINGER'S FILE ON
UP AND COMING ATTRACTIONS

*Can you decipher this code for big-city
swingers only? Iris did. But of course
she had one very definite advantage—
her own willing body. . . .*

"Sassy and sexy!"
—PATRICIA BOSWORTH,
Critic and Journalist

Other SIGNET Books by Joyce Elbert

THE
THREE
OF US

Joyce Elbert

A SIGNET BOOK
NEW AMERICAN LIBRARY
TIMES MIRROR

SIGNET TRADEMARK REG. U.S. PAT. OFF. AND FOREIGN COUNTRIES
REGISTERED TRADEMARK—MARCA REGISTRADA
HECHO EN CHICAGO, U.S.A.

SIGNET, SIGNET CLASSICS,
MENTOR, PLUME AND MERIDIAN BOOKS
are published by The New American Library, Inc.,
1301 Avenue of the Americas, New York, New York 10019

FIRST PRINTING, JULY, 1974

1 2 3 4 5 6 7 8 9

PRINTED IN THE UNITED STATES OF AMERICA

To Jake

PART I

Chapter One

"It's been an awfully long day."

"It's been an *awful* day."

"It most certainly has."

"What the three of us need to do, more than anything else," he said, "is just plain relax. Do you think a glass of champagne might help?"

"A glass of champagne sounds like a marvelous idea."

He opened the champagne bottle, and poured three glasses full. "I propose a toast to—"

"The three of us," both women said in unison.

The camera came in for a closeup of their smiles, their three glasses touching, as the sound of organ music grew louder and the soap opera was off the air, to be continued the next day.

Before switching off the set, Iris watched the credits on the television screen and felt the usual touch of jealousy when it said that the part of Elizabeth was being played by Elizabeth Small. It seemed to Iris, who watched "The Troubled Heart" religiously every weekday afternoon, that her sister became more beautiful, more glowing with each turgid performance. Sometimes it was hard for her to believe they *were* sisters, they were so different, not merely in looks, but in temperament, inclination, desires. They always had been right from the start. Not that Iris could remember that far back, of course, but their mother never let them forget the chasm of personality that lay between them, according to her, since the day they were born. Ginger was remarkable when it came to conjuring up early memories of her daughters, and at moments Iris suspected that she had taken a tape recorder and camera with her when she went into the delivery room, both times.

"Even your styles of being born were different. Elizabeth came roaring out, red faced, screaming, kicking. The doctor said he'd never seen a baby so anxious to begin life. But you, Iris, well, you were another story altogether. I was in labor for seventeen hours with you; you didn't want to be born at all, you bad girl, and when you did finally emerge, you were barely breathing. We had to put you in an oxygen tent first thing. The doctor said it was a miracle you ever survived."

With the television set turned off, the house was very still, shaded. Iris had drawn the heavy beige drapes, shutting out the California sun, which otherwise would have flooded the rooms with its persistent, luminous warmth. In the dining room, a clock chimed four. Iris sat cross-legged on the cocoa brown sofa, the TV remote control still in her hand, her eyes barely moving. Like the house, there was an air of expectancy about her, as though she were waiting for someone to come along and pierce her calm detachment.

After a moment she reached over to the lacquered coffee table, poured herself another Bombay gin, straight, and drank it down in one long swallow. Tepid. Smooth. Nauseating. It was the story of her life, except for the one not-so-smooth incident of Bob's unlikely death over a year ago. Yes, that most certainly was outside the dull pattern she had come to recognize as her own. A smile twisted Iris' lips into a line of humorless derision. Bob himself had been outside her pattern. In life, as well as in death. He was still so vivid to her—tall, athletic, deeply tanned, bursting with energy, a real technicolor advertisement for all the advantages of living in the land of oranges and sunshine.

It was only in the last year that Iris had begun to admit to herself the ugly reasons for his having asked her to marry him and his subsequent and almost immediate infidelity that lasted until the very end. Those did not fit into the advertisement; they had to be darkened, blacked out. She flicked the remote control switch on and off. The television screen lit up for the barest of seconds, then died. The screen was like a window to the world of warmth, humor, human exchange. Without it, the living room dwindled into four walls, just as without Bob she had dwindled once more into the lonely person she'd been before they met.

In one sense, Iris was glad she didn't know who the other woman was; it made it easier for her to bear. The only thing she would have wished was that Bob had been alone at the beach house when the fire broke out. Foolish. What difference did it actually make if the woman had been there or not on that last, fatal day? But it did make a difference. Without her presence, Iris might have been able to delude herself that the affair between them was finally over, that Bob had ended it, that he was coming back to her to really begin their marriage.

But the woman had even cheated her out of that one last consolation. Like the mysterious figure she had always been, she disappeared into the Malibu night before the police and firemen arrived at the burning house. No foul play was suspected, and when Bob died at the hospital hours later, the only words he murmured were, "Sex says good-bye." At least, that was what it had *sounded* like to Iris' dazed ears as she leaned over the bed, praying for some kind of last-minute reprieve—a message of hope from the husband who had abandoned her almost immediately on marrying her. She could not cry, she remembered. Her parents cried, Elizabeth cried, even one of the nurses burst into sudden tears, but not she. Dry-eyed and empty, she had walked out of the hospital and had driven back to her house in the Hollywood Hills, wondering how she would get through the rest of her life.

Iris poured herself another drink and noticed that the gin bottle which had been full that morning was now half-empty. She started drinking right after lunch these days. Since Bob's death her taste in food had become disgustingly repetitive, and for the last several weeks lunch had consisted of peanut butter sandwiches on white bread. Before that, it had been Spanich rice out of a can, and before that frozen fish sticks, and so on, day after day, until she'd found she couldn't look at the particular food without gagging. Only the drink in her glass had remained consistently spectacular: Bombay gin with ice, although as the afternoons wore on and proprieties wore off, she'd stopped bothering with ice. It didn't seem worth the effort to walk the few steps to the well-stocked bar, and by the time "The Troubled Heart" came on the air at three-thirty, she was down to straight Bombay. Why dilute good stuff, anyway?

Her parents, not unreasonably, had become worried about her drinking. Ginger telephoned regularly to find out how she was, and invariably asked what on earth she was doing home on such a beautiful day. It seemed useless to answer that except for brief rainy spells it was always a beautiful day in Los Angeles, sunny, mild, coquettishly inviting. How *can* you stay indoors, Ginger would want to know, when there are so many *things* you could be doing? Her mother had an unfortunate habit of talking in italics, as though she didn't trust the inherent importance of what she was saying to speak for itself. A bothersome trait, which had driven Iris crazy as far back as she could remember. Apparently her father had gotten used to it, because she'd never heard him mention it, never seen him disturbed by the quality she found so grating. But then, he had been married to her mother for twenty-nine years. After so long a period of time, one probably got used to such things, one adjusted. Either that, or one went crazy.

Sometimes Iris wondered what would have happened if Bob had lived. Would she have adjusted to his pecadillos? She doubted it. She also doubted that she would have gone crazy. Probably she would have done exactly what she was doing now, without him, drinking herself to death. It sounded so melodramatic, archaic too, since practically nobody she knew drank much. Alcohol was unfashionable, adherence to it a sure sign of being part of an older, moldier generation. Even her own parents smoked grass from time to time, as though trying to prove their youthful outlook and contemporary inclinations. Besides, as Ginger was fond of pointing out, marijuana was organic *and* noncaloric. Iris didn't give a damn about calories, organic foods, or the brand of healthy California living that was constantly being touted to her wherever she turned. She had used her swimming pool exactly twice since moving into the house four years ago, when she was nineteen. It lay outside now with a thin film of gook covering it, neglected and dirty, unlike the pools of her hillside neighbors which reverberated with sounds of splashing water and exuberant cries of happy sun-worshippers. Fuck them all, was how Iris felt about the whole wholesome business, wondering what her next luncheon menu would consist of. Canned ravioli, no doubt. How low could you get?

When the telephone rang a few minutes later, she knew it was her mother, who had gotten into the habit of calling shortly after four o'clock, by which time Iris' television day had come to an end. In addition to "The Troubled Heart," she watched three other soap operas that preceded it on the same channel. In the evening she read. Evening TV, she had long ago concluded, was for the violence and sitcom idiots who had elected Ronald Reagan governor.

"Your father and I want to have dinner with you this evening," Ginger said. "Are you *free*?"

"No, I have a date with Ryan O'Neal."

"You *do*?" Then her mother realized she was being put on. "I don't think that's so funny. Frankly, I don't like Ryan, but at the rate you're going . . ."

It was another bothersome trait of Ginger's that when she was not italicizing she had a tendency to leave sentences dreamily unfinished.

"Where shall we meet?" Iris asked.

"Your father and I thought it might be nice to go to the Polo Lounge for a change. We haven't been there in *months*. Is that all right with you?"

"Ugh."

"What?"

"The Polo Lounge is fine." Her parents would probably order the McCarthy Salad with Thousand Island dressing, and out of apathy she probably would, too, despite the fact that it looked like premasticated baby food. "What time?"

"Eight?"

"Eight, it is." Four more hours. She was bound to be smashed by then.

"Iris, have you been out at all today?"

"Yes. I went to the supermarket."

"Well, I suppose that's something. I mean, just as long as you get out of that gloomy house even *occasionally*. What did you buy?"

"Canned ravioli."

"That's *disgusting*. I'm sorry, dear, I know you haven't been yourself since poor Bob died. Did I tell you that we had a very interesting inquiry regarding his bagel sculpture, just the other day?"

"No."

"We'll tell you all about it at dinner. I'm looking forward to seeing you, dear. So is your father. Please don't be late. You know how your father is about punctuality."

"Yes, I know. See you at eight."

"Good-bye, dear. I hope you're not . . ."

"Good-bye, Ginger."

Drunk was what her mother wanted to say. But she was drunk, she'd been drunk every day since Bob died, and for all she knew she might be drunk every day from then on until the end of her life. What difference did it really make? Her drinking didn't interfere with anything, for the simple reason that there wasn't anything she particularly wanted to do. Unlike Elizabeth, who had seemingly been born with the desire to become a famous actress, Iris had never been conscious of any career ambitions of her own. Since childhood, her singular goal had been to fall in love and get married, which, miraculously, she had done barely a week after she met Bob at a chili place on the Strip. What she hadn't counted on was his death's robbing her of the only thing she had ever wanted.

Glass in hand, she got up from the sofa and unsteadily made her way into the darkened bedroom. Perhaps if she took a little nap, she could sleep off some of the gin before it was time to shower, dress, and go meet her parents at the Polo Lounge. As she lay her head on the soft pillow, Bob's last words once more danced across her mind: *Sex says good-bye.* Iris smiled to herself. As far as she was concerned, it had never said hello . . .

When she arrived at the Beverly Hills Hotel, it was twenty past eight and she felt almost human. The nap had sobered, if not refreshed her and she wished she were back in bed reading a Françoise Sagan novel, a glass of Bombay gin at her side. She chatted amiably with the man who parked cars before giving him the keys to her Jaguar, then walked unhurriedly up the red carpet and into the sleekness of the celebrated Polo Lounge. Although Iris lived by few rules of any kind, she considered it ridiculous to rush if one were late already. Despite the dim lighting, she spotted her parents immediately. They were at one of the corner booths, stretching their necks like cranes, looking, peering.

"We thought you might have an *accident*," her mother said, as Iris kissed them both on the cheek. "Drinking and driving, you know . . ."

"I knew better," her father said, as she sat down opposite them. "Iris is always late, just as Elizabeth is always on time. She can't help it. It's her nature."

"Of course she can help it, Harvey. Anybody can help anything they want to. Dr. St. James says that in the ethics of The New Realism all those secondhand excuses have to be completely dispensed with."

"What's The New Realism?" Iris asked.

"It's the newest pile of crap," her father replied. "But what's the difference? If it's not one charlatan, it's another. Ginger can't stop herself from being attracted to these cultists' bag of tricks, any more than you, Iris, can stop being late. Would you like a drink?"

Ginger gave her husband a formidable glance, and Iris could well imagine the reason for it. Her poor father. He had undoubtedly been warned not to encourage her drinking, and undoubtedly he had forgotten. Either that, or he thought her drinking was inevitable anyway. What a peculiar pair they were, her father with his stubborn, fatalistic bent, her mother just as stubbornly convinced that all things could be changed by one system or the other.

"I'd like a martini, with Bombay gin. Please."

Both her parents had fishbowls in front of them, filled with some sort of glistening fruit punch. Just the thought of the sickly sweet contents made Iris ill, and she tried to wipe it away with a taste of the guacamole dip that the Polo Lounge was famous for. It was all right, if you hadn't spent twenty-three years of your life eating avocados in one form or another. She took a pack of cigarettes out of her shoulder bag, hoping that her mother would not go into one of her militant speeches about the hazards of nicotine. She was tired of being lectured. Do this, don't do that, or that, or that, or *that*. She had listened to all the warnings a million times over, and noticed now that her hand trembled as she lit the cigarette. Nerves. Dissipation. Bad habits. Invincible evidence of her lifelong disobedience to her parents' wishes. And yet the irony was that she did want to please them, wanted them to approve of her, love her, damn it, the way they did Elizabeth. No, that wasn't exactly true. Elizabeth was someone else, with different qualities. Iris wanted her parents to love her as she was, without change, without compromise, simply and just because she was herself.

"Did you really buy canned ravioli at the supermarket today?" she heard Ginger say, to her surprise.

"No, I didn't."

"I don't understand you, Iris. What *did* you buy, in that case?"

"Nothing. I didn't go to the supermarket."

"But on the telephone this afternoon, you said . . ."

"I know. I was lying."

"What a strange thing to lie about. Imagine, Harvey. The supermarket."

Her father shook his head, as though it were quite beyond him.

"I thought it would make you feel better to know that I'd gone out and gotten some air."

"Then you were home all day."

"Yes. Eating peanut butter sandwiches, and watching soap operas. Elizabeth gave a sparkling performance, I might add."

"If you ate a decent lunch, perhaps you wouldn't drink so much," Ginger said. "As for Elizabeth, she *always* gives a sparkling performance. She works at what she does."

Mockingly, Iris raised her glass. "I work at what I do, too."

Her parents exchanged glances.

"I mean, being an unhappy young widow. It takes practice. Cheers."

Her parents sipped their punch like children, through long colorful straws, but there was a pensiveness about them that Iris could not fathom. Had something upsetting happened, something she didn't know about? Even in their most disapproving moments there was an underlying note of lightness that they tried to submerge. Now it was strangely absent.

"Iris, we've been worried about you," her mother said. "It's been more than a year since Bob died and, frankly, you don't seem to be snapping out of the initial shock. If anything, you seem more depressed as time goes by. And there's the drinking. And your being holed up by yourself in that gloomy house, day and night. It's unnatural, unhealthy. You don't go anywhere, you don't do anything, you don't have any friends. You've lost weight, and you don't look well. We thought a change might be good for you."

The restaurant was too noisy, the people too loud, with the exception of three call girls at the next table. Very carefully dressed and made up, they sipped frozen daiquiris and ignored each other's presence, their eyes vigilantly floating around the room as though expecting someone (little did Iris guess that before long she was going to join their professional ranks).

Iris heard her own voice, weak and faint. "What kind of change?"

"A change of scenery," her father said. "You know, to get you out of that house and into a different environment where you'd meet new people, be under new influences. It might be just the ticket. That's what we decided, your mother and I, before we called Elizabeth."

"What does she have to do with it?"

"She lives in New York," her father said, "and she is your

sister. She's concerned about you, too. We spoke to her and explained the situation, asked her if she could get you an apartment there. Maybe someplace near where she lives. Asked her if she could introduce you to some of her friends, she must know a lot of people by now. You know how gregarious Elizabeth is. Makes friends faster than anyone I've ever seen. She's probably on talking terms with half of New York."

He continued to ramble on, but Iris had stopped listening. New York. They wanted her to move to New York, a city she had never even visited, let alone lived in. Except for Elizabeth, she didn't know a soul there. She was California born and bred, and despite her indifference to many of its widely publicized virtues, it was the only place she knew. It was home. And they wanted her to leave it. The martini suddenly tasted bitter in her mouth, and she put down the glass. Liquor was really revolting, she didn't know how she went on drinking it.

"But I don't want to go to New York," she said, feeling more childish than ever.

When she was about ten years old, her parents had announced that they were taking her and Elizabeth to Palm Springs for the weekend, and her response had been as negative then as now. She had gone regardless and been perfectly miserable, unlike Elizabeth, who had thoroughly enjoyed the experience. Elizabeth had always been the adventuresome one, ready to try anything new and unexplored, ready to go anywhere. Since moving to New York about a year ago, she had written to Iris only a few times, but the letters clearly spelled out her enthusiasm. Iris remembered her last words: *I'm enchanted with New York. It's so different from L.A. Really worlds apart.* That was what bothered Iris the most. From everything she had read about New York, from all the movies she had seen, she could not imagine living in that cold, crowded, claustrophobic city. She was used to palm trees and open spaces, the proximity of the ocean, pastel stucco houses, and people with year-round suntans. She was used to the casualness of Southern California, its informality. To her mind, New York meant granite, cement, and tall, colorless buildings through which millions of scurrying strangers came and went incessantly.

". . . this perfectly nice, young couple that Elizabeth knows," her mother was saying, "and by one of those odd coincidences they're coming out here. So, providing you agree, what we've arranged to do is have you swap places to live. They'll sublet your charming little house, and you'll sublet their apartment, which Elizabeth says is quite attractive, and not at all far from her own apartment. That way, you won't have to be bothered buying furniture, or cooking utensils, or any of those boring things. Your father and I think it's a splendid idea, and so does Elizabeth. She was quite enthusiastic, in fact. What do *you* think, dear?"

"A few minutes ago you said my house was gloomy. Now all of a sudden it's charming. How come?"

"What I meant, dear, is that it *could* be charming if you let a little sunlight in, instead of keeping the drapes drawn all the time. Also, it could use some colorful touches, but let's not get sidetracked. The point is, what do you think of the idea of moving to New York for a while?"

She felt tears come to her eyes. She was so damn alone. It was as if, by dying, Bob had abandoned her once more to the omniscient tyranny of her mother and father, and she felt the old sense of helplessness she'd had as a child whenever she disagreed with their demands. But she was no longer a child, she reminded herself, she was tweny-three, grown up, a widow. She could do as she pleased. They wouldn't like it, but what had she ever done that they'd liked, aside from marrying Bob? Nothing. Yet that one act had distinguished her in their eyes, they'd looked at her differently then, secretly trying to discover the qualities he found in her that they, her own parents, who should have known her best of all, had somehow neglected to see. But since his death they had gradually slipped back to looking at her in the same old disapproving way as before, almost as though nothing at all had happened to her in the interim. By dying, Bob had not only removed himself, he had also removed the more appealing person she'd become as his wife.

"I think it's a lousy idea," she said, swallowing the rest of her martini and signaling the waiter for another. "You might almost say ghoulish."

"Ghoulish," her father repeated. "But how?"

"Because you know perfectly well that I don't like new places, that I'm not a traveler, that I don't . . ." She could not keep the tears from streaming down her checks. "How could you have done this, without even consulting me?"

"Now, dear, there's nothing to cry about. It's not as though we were sending you to Siberia," her mother said.

"As far as I'm concerned, it might just as well be Siberia."

"I was afraid this would happen," her father said. "Remember, Ginger? I said she might take it badly."

"Now let's not get excited. It's just come as a surprise to her. That's all. She'll get used to the idea soon enough."

So they had decided for her.

"Stop talking about me as though I weren't here."

Thank God for alcohol, she thought. It dulled the pain most of the time, made it possible for her to get up each morning without blowing her brains out, made it possible for her to sit here without exploding. What did her parents know about such things? It was odd, their degree of insensitivity. And yet they had created one of the most successful avant garde art galleries in Los Angeles. They had to possess a sensitivity of some kind, but unfortunately it did not seem to extend to their children. Only to their artists. They had treated Bob like a son—indulged him, pampered him, understood him. Loved him, goddamn it, and he'd been happy in the midst of that loving warmth. It suddenly struck Iris that she'd never been happy in her life. Never. At times she had come close, like when she was marrying Bob, but that was only the anticipation of happiness, not the state itself. What if that's all there was? What a weird possibility. What if she'd been knocking herself out all these years for nothing? Just as abruptly as she had started to cry, she now started to laugh. The three carefully made-up call girls at the next table looked at her for a moment, without interest, then resumed their floating, vigilant watch.

"A dull evening," one of them said.

(Exciting evenings awaited Iris, if only she had known it then.)

Seconds later the waiter appeared with Iris's martini, and she stopped laughing. Her mother was wearing a two-piece yellow Shantung dress, with a high Mandarin collar. Her father was wearing a handsome sport shirt open at the neck to accommodate an equally handsome ascot. *They protect their necks*, was the thought that made her stop laughing. She never had.

"Is anybody hungry?" her father asked. "I'm going to have the McCarthy Salad with Thousand Island dressing."

Chapter Two

When it came to love, Elizabeth had a survival theory: as soon as she felt herself sinking into that delicious but perilous maelstrom, she immediately found another man to take the edge off her emotions. It didn't matter who the second man was, just so long as he kept her sufficiently distracted in between the times she saw the first man. That way she never became too desperate, or did anything too hysterical to frighten off the man she really wanted. It was astonishing how easily men were frightened by an intensely-in-love woman; they ran away like rabbits. The only trouble with her theory, which she'd long considered ingenious, was that it stopped working the day she met Jamie Mann.

"Hey," he said, tickling her on the back of the neck, a particularly vulnerable spot. "Wake up. I'm ravenous."

She turned over and smiled at him, eyes still closed. "What for?"

"Food."

"That's boring."

"Not when your stomach feels like mine. Come on, Liz. Aren't you even slightly hungry? I'll call the Stage Deli. Bagels, cream cheese, smoked salmon, anything you want. It's Sunday."

"I want you."

She heard him sigh and knew she shouldn't go on in this vein; it was disastrous. They had made love last night, and as usual it was marvelous. But now she wanted to again. No, it wasn't that she wanted to, she *had* to. It was the only time she felt really safe with Jamie, really secure, when he had his arms around her, his mouth pressed to hers, his body reassuring her every second that he found her desirable and had not yet tired of her. But as soon as it was over, all of her doubts came up again, even more intensely than before, as though the love-making were only a sham to camouflage his growing indifference.

"Liz? Say something."

"I just did."

She turned toward him, discreetly allowing the covers to slip from her shoulders, revealing her bare breasts (an actress was always auditioning). Whenever she slept over at his place, as she had done last night, they'd gotten into the habit of sharing his one pair of beat-up pajamas. She wore the bottoms, and he the tops. It was one of those foolish lovers' rituals that had begun the first night she stayed over, and then—more on her insistence than his—they subsequently repeated it. The Pajama Ploy. Jamie claimed it was a bit of business from an old Claudette Colbert/Gary Cooper movie, and maybe it was. All Elizabeth knew was that it gave her a sense of sharing, belonging, a needed sense of continuity, for there was nothing about Jamie's attitude that led her to believe in any continuity at all. Although they had been together more than six months, Elizabeth wondered each time she saw him whether it might not be the last.

"You're insatiable."

But he was not angry; would any man be? No, he was flattered that she found him so irresistible. Sometimes she wondered whether it ever occurred to him that her exorbitant sensuality was partly a cover-up for her exorbitant insecurity. It gave her an uneasy feeling to know she was such a fraud, for she was certain that if Jamie should ever commit himself to her, truly commit himself, her super-sized libido would shrink to normal size overnight.

"Jamie?" And now she opened her eyes. "Kiss me. I feel the need for a Sunday-morning kiss in the most desperate way." If she kept her voice light, teasing, it was okay, non-scary stuff. God, how one had to cater to their fears, she thought, despising him in that one second, as a second later she responded to his kiss with all the residual passion of last night. "More." She put her arms around him, her legs, and felt herself grow hot, moist. "Please, Jamie. I'm so excited." And almost to her surprise, it was true. Tap. And she was turned on again, felt him unbuttoning his pajama top, removing it, sliding her pajama pants down her legs, down and off, onto the floor. He was turned on, too. "Hit me a little." He struck her lightly across the face. He was getting used to it but didn't much like it, was as baffled as she by this latest re-

quest of hers which had sprung from nowhere, for violence
had never been part of her sexual agenda. "Once more." This
time he smacked her on the ass, he was experimenting with
it, and she could tell he hoped that she didn't go too far in
her demands, or it would be all over between them. "Merely
love pats." That was so he wouldn't think she was some sort
of S-M freak. Or was she? She had never requested this before, not from anyone, not ever—the idea had always re-
pelled her whenever she'd heard it mentioned. Demented
people did such things, sick people. But it didn't hurt, he was
gentle, careful. Perhaps it was the gesture that she wanted,
maybe that was it, but why? "Oh, Jamie, darling." Now they
were lying on their sides, facing each other, touching each
other, and the excitement was building deliciously. He was
slow and unhurried, he knew not to rush, he was confident
of his hold on her and could take his time, there was so
much time, she loved waking up like this. "I love it." He
was holding her everywhere, all bases covered, and quite
suddenly a desire to go down on him came over her; she
resisted for a moment, not wanting to break his hold; she
would wait and see if the desire persisted. Yes. But still she
did not break away, luxuriating in the many quick sensations
that he slowly drew from her, bathing in them until she
allowed her own resistance to die. "I want to." She slid
down the campy black satin sheets that he had bought for
his previous girlfriend, a shimmering blonde number. But
she didn't want him to come that way, no, she would have
to be extra careful, morning-careful not to go too far or
it would all be over, and she wanted it to last. She was
good at it, but had to be really excited to do it, some
men never excited her that way—she didn't know why—
they just didn't arouse the desire, and she refused to
pretend. But with Jamie it was natural and satisfying. "That's
all you get." Sliding up and under him. They were more con-
ventional in the morning, she had noticed some time ago with
amusement, and she was usually underneath him then—although not always, but usually—whereas at night they played
around more, experimented with angles, shadings were more
subtle and more violent. And at last he was inside her, his
face flushed. She tried to look in his eyes, but he looked
away, not wanting to be diverted from himself, and soon she
closed hers and let her body ride with him wherever he took
it, however he went, faster, slower, wildly thumping, then

easy, teasing, sweating, she was drenched. "I'm going to come." He picked up then, knew her beat and really gave it to her as she felt the immense waves start up from her toes and finally drown her in shuddering, spastic delight.

Then, like all Sundays, the day progressed in funny unrehearsed stages, the only cue being that Elizabeth had a show to do at nine o'clock that evening She had just gotten the part, replacing an actress who was going to have a baby. The play was one of the off-off-Broadway minor successes of the season, and in it Elizabeth was supposed to be a Vassar girl turned prostitute. For close to two hours she paraded across the stage, wearing only a slinky kimono which slopped open at the right times to reveal interesting expanses of legs, thighs, breasts—whichever private parts she most felt like making public that particular evening. It was a serious professional problem, though, doing this play at the same time she was portraying a goody-goody-secretary-slave five afternoons a week on "The Troubled Heart." AFTRA had inserted its usual morals clause in her contract, which gave the network the right to dismiss any actor who simultaneously appeared in another theatrical production in a role that could be considered morally questionable.

The mentality of soap-opera sponsors was truly fascinating. Because she played a nice, virginal girl on "The Troubled Heart," she was expected to project that nice, virginal image in the public eye at all times, in both her personal and professional lives. So far nobody connected with the soap opera (except Jamie, of course) knew about the play, or the network would have fired her instantly. And she didn't want to be fired. Soap-opera money was just too damned good, but so was all that invaluable stage experience every night. It was a nerve-wracking situation for Elizabeth, wondering when somebody would catch on to her and gum up the works. Jamie had said that it was a ridiculous situation as well, and he was right:

"The irony of it all is that the average housewife watching 'The Troubled Heart' in Des Moines or St. Louis isn't about to come to New York and buy a ticket to your play, anyway. So odds are one in a million that she'll ever see you parading around in that wicked kimono. But try to tell that to Mr. Soap Sponsor and he'll tell you he can't afford to take chances."

"What would people in Des Moines think if they could see me *now*?" she said to him.

He was eating sturgeon and cream cheese on a bagel, and had just bitten into one of the black-olive accompaniments

"They'd envy me."

He had gotten to the theater section first, and was skimming News of the Rialto. Even though Elizabeth had offered to make breakfast for the two of them, he'd called the Stage after all. She always offered, and he always refused. The Stage, Zabar's, Fine & Shapiro, it didn't matter to him, just so long as the food was prepared and assembled by impersonal hands, and delivered just as impersonally in stapled white bags. Although Elizabeth had been in New York for only a year, she'd come to realize that most men here didn't like you to cook for them. Not even the simplest things. It was weird. Scramble a lousy egg, and they thought you were ready to drag them off to the altar. Quite unlike L.A., where cooking at home was a big thing for both sexes and didn't seem to carry with it any ominous marital threats.

"Plaids are in," she announced, without looking up from the fashion pages in the magazine section.

After her bath she'd put on his pajama bottoms again, those and her tortoise-rimmed glasses. Her eyesight was impossible, she had to wear contact lenses on "The Troubled Heart" or she would never be able to see the teleprompter. In the off-off-Broadway play (aptly named *Off Balance*), she once forgot to put in the lenses and nearly walked clear off center stage and into the pit below. Iris was the one with perfect vision. It figured, Elizabeth thought for the millionth grim time, since if there was one thing Iris didn't particularly need, it was twenty-twenty eyesight.

"What for?" Elizabeth had said to Robert, months before his death. "So she can catch the two of us at it?"

Fortunately, Iris' husband was as mordant as she. "People see what they want to. Even if Iris walked in while we were in bed, she'd decide it was some new kind of Hollywood psychotherapy."

"My sister may be naive, but she's not an idiot."

"She's a frightened little girl," was his answer.

"And what am I?"

"At the moment, coy."

"Does that irritate you?"

"Nothing about you possibly could. There are just some things I like better than others."

"Such as?"

He took her hand. "Your calling me *Robert*. Nobody else does. Not even Iris. Nobody ever has. I wouldn't let them. Before you, I never much liked the name, it seemed too stiff, too formal. But now it's taken on a whole other meaning."

"A *private* meaning."

"That's what's so nice about it. It's your name for me."

They'd been dining at the Chart House, which was perched on a knoll overlooking Malibu. It was one of their favorite places. Something about the dark expanse of ocean below, the candlelit tables, and the recurrent sounds of surf, all mingled together to create an atmosphere that suited them both. Mystery. Secrecy. Strong but unseen. Like their love for each other. Was that why it had appealed to her so? The lure of the forbidden. Particularly, when in this case the forbidden was even doubly so, since she had stolen not just another woman's husband, but her own sister's. Elizabeth often wondered what would have happened if Robert hadn't died in that grotesque fire. Would he eventually have left Iris, figuring he could marry her? But that was the funny thing: she didn't want to marry him. She wanted him, them, exactly as they were. Sneaks in the night, defying an innocent person so close to them both, so unsuspecting, so unhappy in her confusion.

"And yet I love Iris," Elizabeth used to say to Robert. How many times had she said it?

"I love Iris, too. In my own way."

They both loved Iris so much they were doing everything they could to make Iris perfectly miserable. Robert at least had the vague justification that his need for Elizabeth was so overwhelming he couldn't help himself. Elizabeth did not even have that. For her it was a convenient love, a reassuring love, ego-enhancing, and bitchy. It was, in fact, everything that her love for Jamie was not. She was as consumed with love for Jamie, as Robert had been for her. Which was why she tried to treat Jamie so casually. If she couldn't subdue her feelings, the least she could do to protect herself was subdue her tactics. Poor Iris had never been able to do either. She used to wear her heart *and* her head on her sleeve, when she was married to Robert.

"Another Ionesco play is scheduled to open," Jamie said, putting down his half-eaten bagel and lighting a cigarette.

They were eating off the coffee table downstairs in his wood-paneled living room. If there were two things the Des Artistes could boast about most of their apartments, it was an astonishing preponderance of duplexes and an equally astonishing lack of plaster walls. The first time Elizabeth had seen Jamie's place, all she could think of was what a haven it would be for termites. The first time she'd seen Jamie, she didn't know what to think, having always imagined that writers of television soap operas were little old ladies with blue hair and DAR carrying cards. She had been working on "The Troubled Heart" for several months before they came face-to-face, which was not unusual since actors and writers rarely had reason to meet. But Jamie had gone down to the studio one afternoon to see their producer and, while waiting, had dropped into the control booth to watch the taping of next day's show. He saw her on all fifteen monitors at once, speaking words he had written, and when her episode was over, the director introduced them. Her first impression was of a magnificent monochrome: sandy eyes, hair, soul. Then he spoke, and something more intricate, more intimate, revealed itself: he was not mean, but would like to be. She guessed she fell in love with him instantly.

"Aren't you going to finish that bagel?" she asked.

"No. Do you want it?"

All she could think of was Robert's famous bagel sculpture that dominated her parents' gallery. "Yes, this omelette is very boring."

"Of course it is. Who would order a Western omelette from the Stage Delicatessen?"

"A Westerner, like me."

But he had turned to the television page, and was no longer listening. Besides, having grown up in some remote part of New York City that she'd never heard of, he thought he knew everything. Or at least that was the way he acted a lot of the time. Elizabeth didn't mind. She rather liked his casual arrogance, because it was so fake. The first night they made love, he had held her wrists very tight while moving inside her, daring her to unclasp herself. But she knew better than to try. He wanted her to appear helpless, to not challenge any of his actions, to be his willing victim. And as soon as she allowed herself to be that, he was so sweet and considerate of her pleasures, he would have done anything for her. He objected only when she smiled with gratification.

"You're smiling."

She felt glowing, radiant. "It feels nice."

The logic was lost on him, would always be. It was a silent battle of control he wanted; smiling ruined his fantasies, and from then on she tried not to. But lovers can't be fooled. That was why he hadn't fallen head-over-heels: she would never be sufficiently afraid of him, no matter how much she pretended. But at least he had one consolation, a fair degree of professional control, since virtually every word that came out of her mouth on "The Troubled Heart" had been written by Jamie Mann. She felt sure that that made up for quite a lot of things that didn't hit the mark when they were in bed. Maybe not everything, but a lot. Control, control. He must have had the kind of mother who, to his humiliation, sent him to the drugstore for Kotex when he was twelve years old.

Elizabeth had gotten her period when she was twelve. It came on during a plié at her dance class; she felt something very strange and wet, and asked to be excused. Luckily she was wearing panties beneath her black leotard, and the blood did not have a chance to run out before the maid had driven her home. According to her mother, twelve was the average age for an American girl to begin to menstruate, and Ginger seemed very happy that her daughter had turned out to be so average. One of her daughters anyway, for Iris was fifteen before she'd reached the state of womanhood. And even then, she had a strange reaction to it.

"I'm so happy," Elizabeth remembered her sister saying, and there were tears of excitement in Iris' eyes, as though she'd been afraid this day would never occur. But then, Iris had strange reactions to just about everything.

"I wonder how New York will grab her," Elizabeth said.

"What?"

"My sister. I told you. She's due in tomorrow. I wonder if she'll like New York."

"From your description of her, she doesn't seem to like very much of anything."

It was true. Iris was the most unhappy person she knew, and Elizabeth had never been able to understand why.

"Darling," she said, "I have a favor to ask of you."

Jamie looked up, instantly alert.

Don't cook for them. Don't ask them to do you favors.
The two unspoken rules. Well, thank God she still had some
California spirit left and hadn't become completely brain-
washed by the mores of men in this exciting but inexplicable
city.

"Her plane gets in at three, and I'll be at the studio. Would
you mind very much?"

"Meeting her at the airport." He shook his head in dismal
resignation. "Yes, I would mind, if you want the truth. I've
got a week's worth of scripts to catch up on."

"But you'll do it anyway."

"I'll do it anyway."

"Will you, Jamie?"

"Jamie will."

Elizabeth got up and kissed him on the cheek, her breasts
brushing his neck. "You can be very sweet, when you want
to."

"That's true."

And then for his sake. "But you can also be an impossible
bastard."

"True, too."

"She's coming in on United's flight 304."

Jamie smeared some cream cheese on her left nipple, and
began to lick it off. "It tastes better with sturgeon."

Chapter Three

Elizabeth had begun to get on his nerves. Jamie could always
tell when the beginning of the end was near: if a woman
went down on him and he'd rather be figuring out the *New
York* magazine puzzle, it was time to call it quits. And in the
past he would have done just that. *Sorry, baby, but this is the
end of the line.* Yet somehow, he couldn't bring himself to
say it to Elizabeth, and even worse, he couldn't understand
why.

He had called it quits with Gina, Elizabeth's predecessor,

who'd taken it very badly indeed. Maybe that was why. When he told Gina that he was afraid the masquerade was over, she promptly picked up his cast-iron skillet and tried to hit him over the head with it. Thank God he had fast reflexes and ducked at the right moment or he undoubtedly would have suffered a brain concussion. Then she collapsed in tears and refused to leave his apartment. He finally got rid of her four days later, only because she had to go home to take a shit. Gina was one of those women who couldn't shit in any bathroom except her own, for reasons that five analysts still hadn't figured out. Yes, nature had saved him that time, and he also learned an invaluable lesson, namely, never get rid of a woman in one's own apartment. He'd been thinking a lot about that lately. Probably a restaurant was best, someplace French, expensive, and well lit, so she would be too embarrassed to make a scene. Lutèce or Périgord Park. They would start with crèpes farcies . . .

He stopped for a light and noticed that it was ten past two. If traffic didn't get heavy, he'd be a JFK in more than plenty of time to meet Little Sister's plane and guide her back to the apartment she was going to sublet from Elizabeth's friends the O'Reillys. Elizabeth had given him the keys to the place, as well as careful instructions what to tell Iris to feed Bergdorf, the Yorkshire terrier, who, it seemed, went with the apartment.

"How come?" Jamie asked, when Elizabeth explained the apartment arrangements. "Why aren't they taking the mutt with them?"

"Because after they had him awhile, Sheila discovered that Tom was allergic to Yorkshire terriers. He broke out in a rash if Bergdorf was anywhere around, so they had to dump the poor little fellow. I hope Iris doesn't mind. According to Sheila, Bergdorf will eat only steamed organic carrots and lightly broiled calves' liver."

"No wonder he's called Bergdorf."

The dog, who was on the seat beside Jamie, chose that moment to start barking. If it could be called a bark. He was so tiny, a yelp or a squeal would be more like it, pathetic, really, no dog should be so small and overbred. Jamie patted him on the head just as the light turned green, and Bergdorf looked at him with moist and confused eyes, no doubt wondering what had happened to his beloved owners.

"They're winging their way west to Hollywood," Jamie said, "to be in motion pictures. May heaven help them."

The car in front of him, a dusty Plymouth, suddenly stopped short, and again Jamie thanked his quick reflexes as well as the masterful Porsche engineering for averting a traffic calamity. It was really a great car and worth every cent of the fifteen thousand dollars he had bravely paid for it last Spring.

"No, no financing," he told the gray-haired salesman, giving it the whole Gene Kelly bit. "Cash and carry, that's my motto."

Since the salesman was easily twenty years his senior, he shot Jamie a look that could have withered a cactus, and Jamie thought of his father, who was about the salesmen's age and still not pulling in more than twenty-five thousand a year. It was all so cockeyed, this whole money-and-age business. At thirty, Jamie made fifteen hundred dollars a week for writing "The Troubled Heart." Normally. But since his partner had died a couple of months ago and had still not been replaced, he was temporarily earning twice that much. Three thousand dollars every goddamned week for tearing at the heartstrings of housewives throughout the United States.

It was more than a sobering thought; it was absolutely mesmerizing. No wonder women hit him over the head with cast-iron skillets when he tried to get rid of them. How many guys were there like him around? Good-looking, heterosexual, and loaded with dough. Considerate, too. Well, most of the time. Like thinking up the idea of taking Elizabeth to Lutèce to break it off. Or what he was doing right now, when he should be back at the Des Artistes grinding out the next batch of scripts. Money or no, it was rough without another writing partner to help share the burden, it was murder carrying all that workload yourself, exhausting. He couldn't remember the last time he'd had a good night's sleep, and if it weren't for Dexamyl, he probably would have collapsed two weeks ago.

At the next stoplight, Jamie took a green rubber band out of the glove compartment and wound it around his left index finger. That was to remind him to definitely speak to Derek as soon as he got back to the city, to find out what, if anything, was happening in the replacement department. Much as Jamie liked making three thousand dollars a week, there were other things he liked even more, such as being alive to enjoy it.

It was a beautiful October day, crisp, clear, an unusual day for New York, and he had put the top of the car down to make the most of it. The wind brushed his hair. Super sunglasses shielded his eyes from soot and glare. A Swedish turtleneck sweater was cool. Wow. And Frank Sinatra belting it out on the radio. *When I get you up there where the air is rarified, we'll just glide, starry-eyed.* The fact that Sinatra belonged to his parents' generation was one of the reasons Jamie liked to listen to him, to the words of the songs he sang with such sentimental conviction. *Boozy romanticism* best described that generation, which Jamie felt he understood far better than his own, with its free-wheeling hedonism and still-unresolved direction. The past was always safer, no question about it, and there was no past quite so safe as that conjured up by the slow-moving entanglements on "The Troubled Heart." Emotionally, the soap opera world had not advanced beyond 1950, no matter how hard it tried to deal with timely problems like drugs, illegitimacy, abortion and, of course, adultery, long one of the mainstays of daytime television but treated more openly, more courageously in recent years.

Another rubber band, red this time. Another reminder. He had a potential adultery situation on "The Troubled Heart," and so far neither he, nor Derek, nor the sponsors had been able to decide whether to make it materialize or not, and they were going to have to. And soon. The situation involved Elizabeth and the man she worked for, a suave, bigshot politician, with (what else?) an invalid wife. The politician was amorously interested in Elizabeth and she was attracted to him, they had established that much, but still undecided was whether she would succumb to his charms. It could go either way, depending upon:

1. Whether they wanted to build up Elizabeth's part by involving her in an adulterous affair;
2. Whether they thought the audience would accept her as changing from virtuous to adulterous;
3. Whether they could sufficiently motivate the change (perhaps a parent's sudden death, or serious illness);
4. Or whether they should merely use Elizabeth to dra-

matize the politician's latent corruption, without allowing her to become personally involved with him.

There was a fifth and important consideration: mail from viewers. So far it had not been too heavy regarding Elizabeth, not too interested in the character she portrayed, or, to be more precise, not too *excited.* That was always a sign of having struck home, when the mail became emotionally loaded, when it showed that viewers cared about one of the characters, and cared violently, one way or the other. Every once in a while fan mail surprised even diehards at the network. Like the time they'd hired a rather plain-looking actress for a brief stint, but something about her caught the audience's fancy and the letters in her favor had been so overwhelming that she was ultimately written into the show as one of the regulars.

Soap-opera audiences had an emotional mind of their own, and you never knew how they were going to respond to any given character. Jamie would have liked to think that the reaction depended mostly upon the way the character was *written,* but he knew only too well that it very often depended upon the way the particular actor or actress playing that character *looked.* A curve of the lip, an expression in the eyes, an appealing (or nonappealing) voice, and an entire plot line had been known to depart from its original intention. Even more mysterious was the uncanny eye of the camera; it was often hard to tell just which specific facets it might pick up.

That Elizabeth was a competent actress nobody connected with the show had ever denied, but something was wrong. With her? Or was it the undimensional role she'd been given? Jamie himself wasn't sure, and more than anyone he realized he was the most inclined to subjectivity. Still, he couldn't help feeling that whatever Elizabeth's defects as a woman, she was abundantly talented as an actress. And talent had always impressed him. Was that why he found it so difficult to break up with her? Or was it just vaguely possible that he was far more involved than he cared to admit? Of the two explanations, he much preferred the former, which automatically made him think the latter was the correct one.

JFK was an even worse mess than he had remembered. Frantic, noisy, overheated, confusing. And Jamie hated it. Airports made him anxious. His father, who had been a fighter pilot during the Second World War, was in love with planes and had pushed Jamie into becoming a science major. His father's plan was for Jamie to be one of the first geniuses in the United States aerospace program, but Jamie fooled him. After winning a scholarship to M.I.T., he dropped out in his third year, writing FUCK YOU across a physics textbook and handing it, wordlessly, to the startled professor.

Today, Jamie's airport anxiety was heightened by an extreme sense of restlessness. After all the past weeks of being cooped up with only a typewriter, his imagination, and Elizabeth for company, he felt like breaking out. But how? He toyed with the idea of latching onto the nearest available stewardess and taking her back to the Des Artistes with him, after he had dropped off Little Sister. He hadn't been with another woman except Elizabeth for so long that it was positively indecent. Maybe he and the stew could hole up for a few days, shut the blinds, stop the clock, order champagne, and obliterate themselves from the cares of the world in each other's loving arms. That was what he needed. A good, old-fashioned, uninvolved, uninhibited, unsentimental fuck. And brother, he needed it badly.

"What a darling little dog."

A pretty red-haired stewardess was smiling at him, patting the dog. She even had freckles on her exquisite nose, good legs, the works. Jamie stared at her as though she were the proverbial mirage in the desert, and found himself speechless.

"Does it have a name?"

"Bergdorf."

She smiled again, waiting for him to say something, do something. He cleared his throat.

"Could you please tell me where flight 304 will be landing? I'm meeting someone."

Her smile faded and she became professionally helpful, pointing out the information desk. *Fool,* he said to himself, *klutz, schmuck, idiot, moron, jackass, jerk, it's still not too late, say something, say you're meeting your grandfather.*

"Thank you very much," he said.

They walked off in opposite directions, Jamie still calling himself every foul name he could think of. His stomach began to ache. The girl dispensing flight information was not as good-looking as the stewardess, but she wasn't bad either. Maybe her shift would be over in a few minutes. Maybe it still wasn't too late to get on the ball.

"Flight 304—" he began.

She smiled much as the stewardess had: beyond the call of duty. "It's just landed, sir."

"Would you please page a Miss Iris Barnes?"

"Gladly, sir."

As soon as the announcement went out over the loud-speaker, she said, "That's a cute little dog you have there."

Instead of acting like George Peppard about to complete a very successful rescue mission, he said, "I can't stand little dogs." Then he stepped quickly aside. Something was definitely wrong with him. Perhaps he should phone Dr. Williams and make an appointment, but he had tried all that therapy stuff a couple of years ago and nothing much had come of it. Besides, he didn't have the time these days to lie around on analysts' couches, plumbing his past. Between making love to Elizabeth and keeping "The Troubled Heart" going five days a week, he had his hands full, more than full, they were practically dropping at his sides from sheer exhaustion. Outwardly, he looked the picture of vibrant health, but inwardly he felt ancient. He remembered reading that when Byron died in his early thirties, an autopsy was made on his body, and the doctors discovered that the poet had the innards of an eighty-year-old man. Well, Byron had nothing on him. His innards would be ninety, if they were a day. Maybe a hundred. His innards would make headlines in weighty medical journals, doctors would be stunned.

Jamie clutched his stomach and nearly dropped the dog. He'd been feeling pretty queasy in that area lately, pains, discomfort, was it possible he was getting an ulcer? Of course it was possible, any ailment was possible, considering the amount of pressure he'd been under. Actually, an ulcer would be mild; it might be something much worse than that. He thought of his poor partner who had just keeled over one day, after finishing the dialogue of a tantalizing Friday episode, and died a few minutes later of what was diagnosed as cardiac arrest. When Derek called Jamie to tell him the terrible news, all he could think to say was, "How far did he get?"

Derek had not understood. "Far? What do you mean? He was at home, in his den."

"No, no. I mean, how far in the writing? Which episode was he up to?"

Derek was shocked by his callousness. "Really, old boy, that's a hell of a thing to think of at a time like this."

"I know it is, but it's what I'm thinking. Did he finish episode 1102? The one where Susan announces she's leaving her husband? Do you know that?"

"I'm afraid I don't."

"Oh shit, this was all I needed. I'll be right over."

"But, but," Derek said, "the funeral isn't until tomorrow."

"I'm not talking about the funeral. I want to get a look at the last page in his typewriter."

Derek had regarded him very cautiously since then, and in one sense Jamie could hardly blame him, but Derek was only a producer and didn't really understand what kind of pressure writers of soap operas were up against. It was the terrible day-in, day-out grind of just plain turning it out, keeping it going, the old story line, complications, misunderstandings, recriminations, forgivenesses, tragedies, infidelities, reconciliations, murders, marriages, divorces, funerals, births, illnesses, operations, recoveries, it was too much like life, it was bigger than life; life took a holiday now and then. The only holiday that soap writers had was when they dropped dead. At least his partner had had the wherewithal to finish the episode he was writing before calling it quits. A real pro, that guy. Jamie had to hand it to him. Few people knew how to go out in style any more.

"Hartz Mountain Bird Seed."

Jamie turned around. "What?"

For one deranged moment he thought that perhaps the red-haired stewardess had returned. But no. And it wasn't the information girl either. It was another girl, a traveler with matching Gucci luggage, a lemon yellow pants suit, and a white raincoat over her arm.

"You are Jamie Mann, aren't you?"

"Yes, but how did you know that I'd be—?"

"Elizabeth telephoned me this morning."

"So you're Iris."

"Remember what Fred Allen said."

"What?"

" 'If I had my life to live over, I'd live over a delicatessen.' "

"I don't get it."

"You will."

She was not unattractive but she was definitely out of another era; somehow she reminded him of Priscilla Lane in an old John Garfield movie (why couldn't he get his mind off movie stars today?). She had blonde hair, curly, bouncy; Priscilla's same, square jawline and disconcerting violet eyes. He thought of Elizabeth's dark eyes, and her dark hair that fit her head like a beautifully sleek cap, and could not imagine two more dissimilar-looking people. And it wasn't just the coloring; the shape of their faces was completely different. Fascinating.

"Why did you say Hartz Mountain Bird Seed?"

"Because of the man I sat next to on the plane. He was reminiscing about the Thirties, and who was making money and who wasn't."

Jamie waited for her to continue, but she seemed to have ended her story.

"Well, go on."

She began to laugh. Her laugh was like her eyes. Disconcerting, disconnected.

"He said that one of the big money-makers during the great depression was Hartz Mountain Bird Seed."

"I like the Fred Allen line better."

"No! No!" Her laughter had become more jagged. A few people turned around to look at her. "Don't you understand? Don't you get it?"

"I guess this just isn't my day."

"Because everyone was buying canaries!"

"I think I'm going to kill myself," Jamie said, motioning to a porter. "Screw 'The Troubled Heart.' Let Derek figure out what happens in the next thrilling episode, if he thinks it's such a breeze."

But it was not until they were in his Porsche, driving toward New York, that he realized the girl beside him was dead drunk. He'd forgotten that Elizabeth said her sister had a drinking problem. Nothing really seemed to register upon Iris. When he told her that Bergdorf was going to be her responsibility from then on, she said maybe she could feed him Hartz Mountain Bird Seed. Then despite innumerable corrections on his part, she kept calling the dog Bendel, kissing him, and mumbling to him in what sounded like some sort of demented Spanish.

"You must have had quite a bit to drink on the plane."

She waved her hand in a flippant gesture, inadvertently hitting the side window. "You know how it is when you go first class. Those eager stewardesses just keep on filling up your champagne glass. I don't even like champagne. Do you like champagne? I like Bombay gin."

Although Jamie made three thousand dollars a week, he was still impressed by people who flew first class on their own money. It was the kind of happy self-indulgence he admired. But of course the family was loaded, Elizabeth had told him about her parents' Bel Air mansion with the Jacuzzi whirlpool bath and Japanese gardener. And all of it was due to the highly lucrative dealings of their art gallery. The most recent story was that they'd been offered an immense sum of money for a bagel sculpture done by Iris' late husband. According to Elizabeth, it was a ten-foot steel bagel with one bite taken out of it. Jamie couldn't imagine who would want the damned atrocity, it sounded hideous, moronic, but apparently there was a buyer for everything. It was like love. After all, Jane Withers had found a husband, two husbands, hadn't she? (If he didn't get his mind off old movie stars, he would go nuts.)

"At the airport you mentioned something about 'The Troubled Heart,' " Iris said suddenly. "That's the soap opera my sister is in."

"I know."

"Oh, of course you would know. What am I thinking of?"

He wondered how much Elizabeth had told Iris about their personal relationship. "Your sister is a fine actress."

"And I'm a fine widow."

It occurred to him that they hadn't had a good juicy death on the show for a long time. "What's that supposed to mean?"

"Nothing. Don't mind me. But I'll bet you think soap operas are for the birds. All men think that."

"Oh, do they?"

"Sure. They figure it's just a bunch of sob-sister crap. Do you ever watch 'The Troubled Heart'?"

"I not only watch it, my dear, I write it."

"Well, well." There was sarcasm in her tone, but admiration too. "I took a couple of TV writing courses at UCLA. But I wasn't very good. In fact, I was plain lousy."

"Maybe it's not your thing."

"Bombay gin is my thing. But let's not get into that. Anyway, I absolutely adore soap operas. I watch them every day. I'm hooked on them. They're real folk art, they're . . ."

She fell asleep in the middle of the sentence, and did not

wake up until Jamie pulled into the circular driveway of a gleaming, high-rise apartment building in the East Eighties. A doorman who looked like an ex-Boston cop came out to open the door for Iris.

"Are we here?" she asked.

Through the window on her side part of the lobby could be seen, revealing a fake waterfall dripping on artificial red and yellow tulips.

"This is it," Jamie said.

"It looks absolutely awful. Who designed this building? The Marx Brothers?"

"Probably. But I understand that your apartment is quite nice. At least that's what Elizabeth said. I haven't seen it. Would you like me to take the suitcase up for you, or would you rather the doorman got someone?"

She turned and smiled at him for the first time, and he realized that the nap had sobered her. She seemed very young, defenseless, and, unless he was imagining it, more than a little unnerved by her new surroundings.

"I'd rather you took them up." Even her voice was softer, all vestiges of flippancy and sarcasm gone. "That is, if it's not too much trouble."

"No trouble at all."

He was not imagining it. She *was* frightened. Jamie liked that.

Chapter Four

The apartment was on the twenty-second floor.

"I think my nose is bleeding," Iris said, as Jamie unlocked the door with keys that Elizabeth had given him. "I've never been this high up in my life."

The liquor had worn off and she felt a little shaky, more than a little apprehensive as she viewed her new home. It wasn't bad, it wasn't terrible, but . . . well . . . calm down, she told herself, trying to be objective. The floors were nice, shiny parquet, and the furniture that the O'Reillys had left behind was unobtrusive in the kind of modern, streamlined way she did not particularly favor, but at least could live with. Then she saw the paintings on the walls. There were quite a few of them and each was of a different animal—a cat, a zebra, a kangaroo, a pelican, a turtle—and each was painted in the same flat, childlike, undimensional style, so much so that Iris couldn't help wondering whether there was some new, esoteric art movement afoot in New York that her parents had not heard about. Either that, or the O'Reillys had a three-year-old nephew who was studying to be Rousseau.

"It seems so *small*," she said, finally, poking around the closets.

"Small?" Jamie was surprised. "Are you kidding? For one person? For New York? Honey, I've got news for you. There are apartments like this all over the city being occupied this very minute by four, count them, four young ladies who think they're in heaven. No apartment in New York that has a separate bedroom is small. Remember that."

Was he kidding her? A separate bedroom. It sounded so funny. She felt like saying, separate from *what*? Her own house in the Hollywood Hills had three bedrooms, her parents' house had seven, even Elizabeth's funny old place in Laurel Canyon with the wobbled windows boasted two, and by no stretch of the imagination could be considered large. But of course that was according to California standards, she reminded herself. Obviously, the housing situation was different here.

"And you have a view," Jamie pointed out.

Grimy rooftops. "You sound like a struggling real estate agent."

Solicitude turned to anger. "Look, Iris, frankly I don't give a damn—"

"I'm sorry. I know you're trying to be nice. It's just that I'm . . ." Was she getting to be like her mother, leaving sentences in midair? "I'm a little disoriented, that's all. The plane ride. A new apartment. New York. I've never been here before, you know. I guess I'm still in a state of shock."

He seemed immediately placated. "I didn't realize this was your first trip east. You must be tired."

"Yes, I am."

But she wasn't tired, not really, she was on edge and dying for a drink, ten drinks, a hundred, a million. Her heart felt like it was pounding in her throat, a familiar symptom that set in between the time the last vestiges of alcohol had worn off and a new supply could be consumed. At home, that time period did not last very long. She did not allow it to, for as much as Iris was appalled and frightened by her drinking habits, she was even more frightened by the galloping anxiety that she felt without alcohol.

"Let's have a drink. I've got a bottle in my suitcase." She pointed to the smaller of the two Gucci bags. "That one."

Then she sat down on the sofa, a teak Danish thing, and watched while Jamie opened the suitcase. It made her feel a little less guilty if someone else mixed the drinks, yet on the other hand they never made them strong enough. The drinkers' dilemma. In a moment he had pulled out a full quart of Bombay gin and was studying the label, with the famous picture of Queen Victoria on the front.

"How would you like it?"

Stiff. "On the rocks, if there's ice."

"I'm sure there is." ·

He disappeared into the kitchen and she could hear him loosening ice cubes, getting glasses, pouring the wretched-wonderful stuff. On the side of the Bombay bottle it said: WHAT IS GIN? GIN IS A STATE OF MIND. Iris knew the label by heart.

"Here we go."

He handed her a fair-sized drink, and she noticed that he had made a much smaller one for himself. He was watching her without appearing to, oh, she knew the way people who didn't particularly drink themselves liked to watch people who did; they were curious, sometimes fascinated, often revolted—but interested. They couldn't understand what it was that drinkers sought in alcohol, what they ultimately found, it was a complete mystery to non-drinkers. She wondered how much Elizabeth had told him about her sister's growing addiction, and more importantly, in what tone? Contemptuous? Concerned? Confused? Or, perhaps, merely indifferent. It struck Iris again, as it had so many times in the past, how little she really knew about Elizabeth's true feelings on the most elementary subjects.

"But what can you expect?" Iris' husband said to her once. "Elizabeth is an actress. She doesn't have feelings like ordinary people."

Although it gratified her to hear Elizabeth demeaned, she

guiltily felt compelled to rush to her defense. "That's an insulting thing to say. What do you mean, she doesn't have feelings? Everyone has feelings . . . of one sort or another."

"What I mean," Bob had persisted, "is that Elizabeth's feelings are as changeable as her theatrical role of the moment. She's a chameleon. Like all actresses."

Bob and Elizabeth had never gotten on together; their mutual antipathy was apparent right from the start, a situation which had both pleased and disturbed Iris during the brief year of her marriage. Whenever the family got together (which, fortunately, was not too often) there was always that uneasy undercurrent of dislike and distrust between her husband and her sister. Conflict. It was something that Iris had never had much tolerance for, it frightened her too much whenever and wherever she encounted it—the fear of its possible, eventual explosion, the knowledge that she would be helpless to deal with any display of brute emotion.

"*A votre santé*," Jamie said, raising his glass to her.

"Cheers," she was about to reply, as in the next apartment somebody slammed a door so hard that she almost dropped her drink. Then the sound of flushing water could be heard, followed by another stupendous door slam. Overhead a woman walked across the room—the click-clack of her heels was muted but unmistakable.

Jamie smiled at her bewilderment. "The acoustics in these new buildings are pretty terrible, but you'll get used to it. They say that people do. I don't know. It would drive me clear up a wall."

Iris thought of her quiet, quiet house in California, her quiet, quiet life there, and wondered how she could have ever allowed her parents to talk her into making this ludicrous, nonsensical move. "Where do you live?"

She had finished her gin in two discreet gulps and was debating whether to ask him for another, or just get up and make it herself. Maybe she should wait a minute or two, so as not to seem too eager.

"Across town, on the West Side. In a very old, very unique building."

"What's so unique about it?"

"Several things. First, it hasn't been torn down yet. Second, it has some great Howard Christy murals in the lobby. And third, it's extraordinarily soundproof. I can't stand noise when I'm writing. It's hard enough to concentrate as it is, without worrying about interference from neighbors. I work at night a lot, and my typewriter is pretty noisy. It's a vintage Smith-Corona. I can't get used to the electric kind. . . ."

Iris was not listening to a word. She had tuned him out. She did not give a damn about his writing habits, his West Side apartment, she had never heard of a painter named Howard Christy (was Jamie trying to impress her on the art level, because he knew of her parents' gallery?), all she could think of was getting another drink. And *now*. Before her heart jumped right out of her throat and writhed to death on the O'Reillys' tan shag rug, while the two of them watched it in glazed disbelief. God, but she felt awful. And on top of everything, her head was starting to throb, as though to pay her back for having scarcely touched her lunch on the plane. It had been some terrible-looking chicken thing smothered in a white sauce, surrounded by small, unhealthy potatoes and glaucous green peas.

"I think I'll make myself another drink," she said, getting up before he could volunteer.

In the kitchen, which had another animal painting on the wall (an elephant), she gulped down as much gin as she could straight from the bottle, without gagging, then poured herself a respectable drink over a tall glassful of ice cubes. Before going back inside, she drank half the gin in the glass, replaced it, and, starting to feel fortified, at last returned to the living room, ready to face the attractive Mr. Mann. With the clarity of alcohol, she was just beginning to really notice him, to see what it was that Elizabeth saw in him: a boyish self-assurance laced with a not-so-boyish sensuality. They both began to speak at once.

"How come you don't have a suntan?"

"Are you in love with my sister?"

Before either could answer, the doorbell rang. Jamie jumped up to get it, and in walked an attractive middle-aged woman followed by a dog that looked like an alligator. Bergdorf, whom Iris had completely forgotten about, came running out from under the sofa and the two dogs started to bark and bite each other. At least that's what appeared to be happening. Iris could not tell for sure, it had happened so fast, was still happening, perhaps they were only playing, but it certainly seemed ferocious to her.

"Stop it immediately," the middle-aged woman commanded. The dog that looked like an alligator was trying to bite

Bergdorf's nose, while Bergdorf, being much smaller, was whirling about as fast as he could, skidding on the waxed floor, aiming for the other dog's hind legs. Thankful for this opportunity to enjoy her drink in peace, Iris sank into the teak sofa and watched the animal fight with bland interest. If she were any judge of it, Bergdorf was definitely winning despite his inferior size.

"Go on, Bergdorf," she called out. "Go get him."

"It's a *her*," the middle-aged woman said. "And how cruel of you to encourage them."

Nobody had ever called Iris cruel in her life. She was starting to feel vaguely, drunkenly important. Maybe New York wouldn't be so bad after all. Maybe she would develop a fascinating new identity here. It was a thrilling thought.

"Bite *her* ear," she said to the Yorkshire terrier. "Hard. Remember, *she* started this."

"They both started it," the middle-aged woman said. "And frankly, I don't understand your hostile attitude at all."

She was wearing a dark, long-sleeved, monklike robe that came to her ankles, and was cut in such a way that it was very difficult, if not impossible, to tell what was going on underneath. Not fat, Iris thought, but probably flabby, and clever enough to know how to conceal it. The woman's hair color was another clever stroke: an imperfect auburn (perfectly dyed), pulled back into a soft chignon, with a few wispy strands ingeniously curling about her forehead to offset any effect of harshness. She was nobody to be trifled with, Iris could see that, even through her gin-soaked haze. There was something oddly familiar about the woman, she reminded Iris of someone, but who?

"What are you going to do?" The woman was clearly alarmed as she saw Jamie emerge from the kitchen, carrying a large enameled pan. "What do you have in there?"

"Water."

Before the woman or Iris could protest, he poured the water over both dogs' heads, and they leaped apart, stunned, howling. Then the alligator dog made a lunge at Jamie's left hand, grabbed it in his teeth, and drew blood.

"That's my typing hand," Jamie shouted, kicking the dog.

"I am Mrs. Richmond," the middle-aged woman announced, the hem of her monk's robe trailing in water, "and I live next door. I came in here to meet my new neighbors and welcome them to Picasso Towers, but of course I had no idea that Bergdorf and Bettina would get into such a violent fight. It's very strange. They're old, old friends. I knew the O'Reillys quite well, you see." She started at Iris. "Particularly Sheila O'Reilly."

"I am not one of your new neighbors," Jamie said, sucking the blood from his hand. "I was merely helping Mrs. Barnes get settled. She's just arrived from California."

"Nor did I have any idea," Mrs. Richmond went on, "that I would encounter human as well as animal cruelty, when I rang the bell." She stopped suddenly. "Did you say *Mrs.* Barnes?"

"That's what I said," Jamie said.

"Oh." She smiled at Iris, but it was not a smile that Iris liked. "Then you're married. Like Sheila."

"I used to be. I'm a widow."

"I'm sorry, my dear. And you're so young. How long ago did it happen?"

"A little over a year."

"I won't ask you any more questions now. But you must drop into my apartment some afternoon. We'll have a cup of tea and talk. I'm in 22-H. The doctor isn't there in the afternoon."

Iris finished her drink. "I'm always looking for a good doctor."

"Sometimes it helps to have a cup of tea and talk."

"I hope you use Red Rose," Jamie said. "According to the television commercials, it's supposed to be a pretty potent brew."

"Men are supposed to be potent, not tea," Mrs. Richmond said. "Besides, I use Lipton's. I never heard of the other brand."

"It's a man's tea."

"Good. Then you drink it." Mrs. Richmond turned to Iris. "I assume that you're a friend of the O'Reillys. Since you have their dog, that is."

"No, I've never even met them. They're friends of my sister. She's an actress. She's on 'The Troubled Heart.' "

"I write 'The Troubled Heart,' " Jamie said. "That is, I used to write it. When I still had a hand I could type with."

Mrs. Richmond seemed suddenly and totally disarmed by this piece of information. Her manner changed, the phony archness giving way to phony concern.

"I'm terribly sorry that Bettina bit you. She must be going

into heat. If the doctor were in now, I'd have him take a look at your hand, but he's operating this afternoon. He's a bone surgeon. Oh, never mind about the doctor, we can talk about him another time. I find this much more exciting, that you write 'The Troubled Heart,' I mean. It's my favorite soap opera. Tell me, is that nice girl Elizabeth going to give in and have an affair with that awful, married politician?"

"Tune in next Friday and find out," Jamie said.

"I can't. Friday is the one day that, much to my regret, I don't watch it."

"But that's the best day," Jamie said. "That's the cliff-hanger. That's the consternation fade-out. How come you don't watch on Friday?"

"It's my charity day. I work at Bellevue. The alcoholic ward. It's really something, let me tell you." Mrs. Richmond produced a leash from her pocket. "Well, I must be going now. I have to walk Bettina. It was very interesting meeting you both, very interesting indeed. Don't forget, Mrs. Barnes, 22-H."

"Charity begins at home," Iris said, inadvertently knocking her glass on the floor.

A second later she realized who Mrs. Richmond reminded her of: her mother.

Chapter Five

At 3:45 P.M., as Jamie was unlocking the door to Iris' new, high-rise apartment, Elizabeth stood at one end of a huge television studio, blotting her 7A Pan-Stik forehead with a Kleenex and mumbling bits of dialogue to herself.

Act III of "The Troubled Heart" was almost over, thank God, she couldn't wait for today's taping to end. Half an hour ago, following dress rehearsal, the air conditioning had been shut off as it always was (noise interference), so that on warm days like this everyone in the studio simply suffered and prayed that their antiperspirants were working. It was hard on the grips and technical crew, but much harder on the actors who had to contend with the heat blast from all those sizzling overhead lights.

Elizabeth felt wet and sticky, and silently cursed the Ban-Lon dress she'd been told to wear for Act IV. It was a lovely gold-and-brown print, flattering colors because of her hair and eyes, but unfortunately it had long sleeves, a Mandarin neckline, and clung in all the wrong places. Like at her hips, which were still one inch too wide, despite her daily exercise routine. She made a mental note to up the hip exercises to fifty the first thing tomorrow morning.

On the Act III set (Jeffersonville General Hospital), two actors who played doctors in the series were winding up their solemn, medical exchange.

1st DOCTOR: In this case, exploratory surgery could be dangerous. Don't forget, the patient has a coronary condition.

2ND DOCTOR: It could be dangerous if you don't attempt exploratory surgery, Sam.

1ST DOCTOR: But he might have a ruptured appendix. His white count is high, and he's running a fever.

2ND DOCTOR: Okay, Sam, what's your tentative diagnosis?

1ST DOCTOR: Pancreatitis. As you know, it doesn't call for surgery. Let's treat him with anticoagulants and antibiotics. If he doesn't respond within twenty-four hours, then I'll agree to exploratory surgery.

2ND DOCTOR (grimly): We'll do it your way, Sam, but remember, I warned you.

1ST DOCTOR: Warned me?

2ND DOCTOR (even more grimly): He might not be *alive* in twenty-four hours.

The red eye of the camera went dead, organ music came up, and the stage manager waved his script at the two actor-doctors who walked off the set, talking about a play that had just opened. Act III was over. There was a one-minute commercial break.

"Act IV is the restaurant," the stage manager announced, adjusting his headset. "Let's keep it moving, kids."

The restaurant set, which had been assembled that morning, occupied the partition space directly next to the hospital set. Elizabeth and the actor who played her corrupt political boss were seated at a small, round table in front of the three cameras and boom mike. Several extras were seated at tables behind them, ready to begin their low-keyed dining conversation as soon as they got the cue. Elizabeth hoped they didn't talk too loud, or say anything interesting. Once, in a previous restaurant scene, she had become so distracted by an exchange between two extras that she momentarily forgot her lines and had to resort to the teleprompter. Luckily, she was wearing her contact lenses that day.

"Ten seconds," the stage manager called out.

Elizabeth tested her smile. The first line of dialogue was hers. Five seconds to air, four, three, two, one. She was ready.

"This restaurant is lovely, Mr. Crawford. I've never been here before."

"I'm glad, Elizabeth."

"Glad. But why?"

"At the risk of sounding immodest, I like to be first. Not just in elections. First in *everything* . . ."

Five minutes and nine pages of dialogue later, Act IV was over and so was Elizabeth's part for the day. Act V did not include her. It would be played between the first doctor and his patient's wife, who had to be told that exploratory surgery was not going to be performed on her husband, at least not for the next twenty-four hours.

"Okay, kids, we're going into the windup," the stage manager said. "Places, please. And keep the ball *moving*."

Elizabeth hurried out of the studio and went across the hall to the control room, where a cake-mix commercial appeared simultaneously on a long row of monitors, most in color, a few in black and white. Lined up in chairs facing the monitors were the director of "The Troubled Heart," the assistant director, production supervisor, audio engineer, and video man. Several visitors stood behind them, commenting on the extensive, intricate panels of electronic equipment. In contrast to the hot, tense, brightly lit studio, this room was dark, flowing with talk, and beautifully, exquisitely air-conditioned.

Elizabeth found a place against the wall and leaned back, letting the cool waves of air invade her body as quickly as possible. It was not until her stickiness had begun to evaporate that she spotted Derek. He was standing at the far end of the room, motionless, his eyes fixed upon a monitor screen. Everyone in the room was silent now, as Act V rapidly drew to a close.

"We're doing everything we possibly can," the first doctor said to his patient's wife. "Why don't you go home and try to get some sleep? You look exhausted."

The actress who played the wife opened her mouth as though to speak, then swallowed. One of the cameras came in for a closeup of her worried, haggard face.

"And fade-out," the director instructed. "Theme music. Last commercial. And credits."

Another episode of "The Troubled Heart" had been successfully completed, and everyone in the control room seemed to burst into a relieved crossfire of talk all at once.

"Derek," Elizabeth said, moving quickly toward the tall, fair-haired man. "I'd like to speak to you."

It took him a moment to acknowledge her. His eyes were like transparent blue glass, behind which only a void could be seen.

"I'm in a bit of a rush, love."

His British accent never failed to surprise her, it seemed so jarring in an American television control room. Derek himself had always seemed out of place to her. Rumor had it that his wife, who had chosen to remain behind in London, was a favored niece of the sponsor of the show. But rumors were unreliable in an industry where rivalry, jealousy, and fierce competition were as commonplace as coffee and Danish during morning rehearsals.

"Please," Elizabeth said. "It won't take long. And it's rather important."

Derek gazed down at her from his six-foot, three-inch spot on the universe. "Very well, love. Why don't you go on to the small conference room? I'll be there in a moment."

"Thank you."

Elizabeth slipped past the others and walked down the long, cheerless hall, her heart beating with determination that had been building and festering for weeks now. She was tired of being given the run-around. By Jamie, by the directors of the show, by Derek himself, who so far had neatly managed to avoid any confrontation with her. Derek Christopher. She remembered the first time she ever laid eyes on the kinky son of a bitch.

It was the day she came to audition for the part of Elizabeth on "The Troubled Heart." Sheila O'Reilly, who was then playing a nurse on the series, had phoned to tell her about the upcoming audition and the kind of girl they were looking for.

"I saw the breakdown sheet," Sheila said, trying to keep the excitement out of her voice, "and you'd be perfect for what they have in mind."

"What do they have in mind?"

"Don't sound so enthusiastic."

"I'm sorry, Sheila. I know you're trying to help, and I appreciate it, but—"

"You're damn right I'm trying to help. Do you realize how many unemployed actresses would give their eyeballs to get steady work like this? Scale is two-ten a day. Two-ten. Every time more than five lines of dialogue come out of that beautiful, crazy mouth of yours. Two-ten!"

Elizabeth made it a point never to tell other people in the business that she had a private income; they would have resented her for it.

"I agree that the money is good, Sheila, and I'm not knocking soaps. I realize they have a very large audience, but—"

"A very large audience, she says. Ten million people watch the show every week. Elizabeth, you would have to be in a play for something like twenty years to be seen by as many people as will see you in 'The Troubled Heart' in one lousy *week*."

Ten million. She was stunned. "I had no idea it was as high as that." Her face would be seen by ten million strangers. It was more than a sobering thought, it was electrifying. "What's the girl supposed to be like? The one you want me to audition for?"

Sheila let out a relieved, triumphant laugh. "That's more like it, you snob. Okay, here's the rough description. First off, her name is Elizabeth which I think is pretty funny. She comes from a good family, not rich, but solid, professional, upper middle class. The girl herself is young, and pretty in a quiet, sensitive sort of way. She has a strong moral character and at first glance might even be a virgin, but later it's learned that she was married, tragically, at an early age and has been divorced for a few years. There are hints of sensuous depths, as yet unrevealed." Sheila paused, letting the description register. "What do you think? I say you could do it with the right clothes and makeup, tone down the glamor stuff a bit. And I think they'd go for you. Especially Derek."

"Who's Derek?"

"Our producer. But he's not the only one you'll have to impress. The executive producer will be there, men from the agency, oh, a raft of people. They'll give you the script about an hour before they want you to read. Memorize as much of it as you can, but don't worry if you get a line or two screwed up. They don't expect you to be letter perfect. The main thing is whether you come across like the girl they have in mind. Whether you project the right emotional quality."

"Will I read with someone?"

"Oh, sure, but it won't be an actor. They never use other actors for these auditions."

"Why not?"

"It's harder that way, for the person being auditioned. Probably Derek or one of the directors will read with you, but whoever it is, you can be certain of one thing: he'll read his lines like a wooden dummy, so don't expect any help from the other side. You're going to have to pull the characterization together all by your own sweet self."

"I guess I'd better phone my agent."

"Absolutely. Get him prepared to start contract negotiations."

She was impressed by Sheila's faith in her. "You are optimistic, aren't you?"

"Call it ESP."

"Come to think of it, why didn't my agent tell me about this part? What am I paying him ten percent for?"

"He doesn't know about it yet, that's why. I just found out myself. You see, they thought they had someone for the part, good actress, I worked with her once at La Mama, but she called up today with commiserations and champagne regrets. It seems the lucky girl landed the lead in a new Otto Preminger movie, and is on her way to Spain and higher achievements."

The morning of the audition Elizabeth drank two cups of Sanka, smoked four cigarettes, and slipped into her Aquascutum raincoat, a meticulously tailored, discreetly expensive, newly purchased self-indulgence. It was exactly the kind of coat that a girl with strong moral character and unrevealed sensuous depths would wear. Elizabeth was certain of that, just as she was suddenly certain she would get the part of Elizabeth. Could it be mere coincidence that their first names were one and the same for no good reason? Or, as she said a couple of hours later to the seven men and one miniskirted casting director assembled in an executive conference room:

"Good morning. I am Elizabeth . . ." Pausing, smiling. "Elizabeth Small. I'm ready to audition."

The scene they had chosen was supposed to take place in the politician's office, and it was indeed Derek who would read with her. According to the script, Elizabeth returns from lunch one afternoon and finds her boss in a state of barely controlled rage because his wife, a chronic invalid, has just refused to let him institutionalize her. As the scene unfolds, Elizabeth's ambivalence mounts: the man she has always admired and respected now displays a callous side to his nature that she was never aware of. How Elizabeth (the secretary) reconciles her feelings in light of this new, unpleasant knowledge is the basis upon which Elizabeth (the actress) will be judged.

One thing immediately occurred to her. Since she was supposed to be returning from lunch, she could play the brief scene in her Aquascutum raincoat. The more she thought about it, the more she realized what a stroke of genius and good luck it was to have worn that particular coat on this particular day. Not only was the coat stylishly understated and ridiculously flattering, it was also made in England. Derek spotted it at once.

"Lovely," he said. "And very fitting for the role."

He read his lines just as Sheila had predicted, like a wooden dummy, but nothing could throw her at that point, she felt too widely self-confident. And her self-confidence grew with each exchange of dialogue. She understood the girl she was playing, her naiveté, her idealism, her careful background, her not-so-careful marriage. It wasn't because she identified, no, not at all, she understood because the girl was so much like Iris.

When the scene was over, Derek dismissed her with a handshake and went to join the others. There were a few hushed comments up and down the long conference table, the whispered power of dark-suited men with impassive faces. Then the casting director politely thanked her for her time and said they would be in touch with her agent. But when the call came late the following afternoon, it was from the casting director's secretary who sounded as though she were about to explode with excitement.

"Your agent has left for the day, but we thought you'd want to know as soon as possible. Congratulations, Miss Small. You've been chosen to play the part of Elizabeth on 'The Troubled Heart.' The agency would like to send over a batch of scripts right away. Will you be home?"

Elizabeth kept her voice courteous, but crisp. "No, as a matter of fact, I won't. I have an appointment at the masseuse. Would you please arrange to have the scripts left with my doorman?"

"Yes, yes of course."

"Thanks. Bye-Bye."

She hung up before the bewildered girl could say anything else. Then she dialed Sheila's home number.

"O'Reilly's Bar & Grill."

"Sheila?"

"Oh, it's you." Sheila's tone was strangely defiant, unfriendly. "Hi."

In the background Ray Charles was singing something soft, and a man's voice called out, "Hey, that's not fair," but it didn't sound like Tom. For a moment Elizabeth was caught off guard, then she found herself smiling. So Sheila played around. She never would have suspected. And she thought of Robert, of Iris, of how little Iris suspected right up to the end, in that grim hospital room. *Sex says good-bye.* Iris had even gotten Robert's last words wrong, but Elizabeth understood them exactly as he knew she would. *Essex says good-bye . . .* to Elizabeth, his love, in their own private code.

"I guess I look like a girl with strong moral character and unrevealed sensuous depth," Elizabeth said to Sheila. "I got the part. Do you know a good masseuse?"

Derek Christopher closed the conference room door behind him and sat down on one of the tan leather chairs, facing Elizabeth.

"Now, love, what can I do for you?"

"It's about my part."

He took out a cigar and lit it. "What about your part?"

"It's not going anywhere." She couldn't stand cigar smoke, and Derek knew it. Was this his way of warding off temperamental complaints from ungrateful actors? "What I mean is, nothing seems to be happening to me in terms of the story line."

"I wouldn't say that. We're establishing your character."

"You've been establishing it for months now. The question is, do I or do I not screw my boss, or have I just been written in as a foil? I read next week's scripts and about all I do for a change is say good morning, and serve coffee, and answer the telephone, and look pensive and virtuous. There aren't any new plot developments that include *me*."

"We're working on it, Elizabeth. We're not unaware of the situation. We'd like to get you sexually involved, it would lend spice to the show, but it's tricky. The sponsor isn't completely certain whether the audience will accept you as going to bed with a married man, particularly an unscrupulous, older, married man. I have my doubts, too. Your character so far wouldn't indicate that you'd ever do such a thing."

"But I'm not supposed to know that he's unscrupulous, at least not yet. I'm taken in by him. I respect and admire Mr. Crawford. And don't forget, I'm attracted to him, we've already established that."

Derek gazed down at his gray pin-striped suit, his splashy tie. "Respect, yes. Admire, yes. Attracted, yes. But bed? The writer isn't sure."

"The writer?" Jamie had assured her for months now that he was the only one fighting to get her part built up. "I don't understand."

"The writer of 'The Troubled Heart,'" Derek said patiently. "Jamie Mann. Why do you look so surprised?"

Neither Derek nor anybody else connected with the show had the faintest clue about her and Jamie. They had both gone out of their way to keep the affair as quiet as possible, and up until now they'd succeeded. Elizabeth did not intend to give away her secret, certainly not at this point, and certainly not to Derek Christopher. It would be an embarrassing admission under any circumstances, but especially embarrassing if Jamie were trying to sabotage her part. How Derek would laugh.

"The reason I'm surprised," she said, "is because you've just contradicted yourself. A minute ago you claimed it was the sponsor who couldn't decide whether I should go to bed with Crawford. Now you're saying it's the writer."

Derek tapped his fingers on the table, patience starting to wear thin. "Please don't split hairs, Elizabeth. What difference does it make who it is? Both the sponsor and the writer are highly influential, both have their say-so in determining the way the plot will go. All I can tell you is what I have already said: we don't *know* how it will go. And until we do, I'm afraid you'll just have to sit tight and hope for the best. Okay?"

She felt like stabbing him. That smugness, that self-satisfied air of superiority. Who did he think he was? Another rumor about Derek Christopher was that he had antagonized so many people in England, the only job he'd ever be able to get there was as a janitor.

"While I'm sitting tight," she said, "and hoping for the best, do you think something can be done to give my part a little zip? A little spirit? So that the audience doesn't die of boredom every time they see me on screen?"

"I'm glad that you mention the audience. Another influential factor. Your fan mail to date hasn't been too enthusiastic, our viewers don't seem to be especially interested in Elizabeth, and as you know we have to take their response into careful consideration."

No, she wouldn't stab him, she would poison his afternoon tea. Neater that way. She forced herself to smile.

"Of course they're not interested, Derek. How could they be, the way my part's been written up until now? I'm so sweet and pure, it's enough to nauseate even the most puritanic housewife in Lafayette, Indiana."

"Bad market, Lafayette," Derek mumbled. "One of the worst."

"Can't something catastrophic happen to me, maybe some sort of family tragedy that jolts me out of my dull existence? How about one of my parents suddenly dying in another city, I go out of town to attend the funeral, and when I return to Jeffersonville I'm a different person? More cynical, more worldly, more susceptible to the wicked Mr. Crawford."

"I do believe you were hired as an actress, not a writer." Derek stood up, signaling the end of their conversation. "You're a good actress, you've been doing a fine job. Let's keep it at that, shall we?"

Elizabeth stood up, too. They were awkwardly close. She could smell his after-shave lotion.

"What choice do I have, Derek? You're the producer."

"So good of you to finally remember it. Now be a good girl and run along to the reading for tomorrow's show." He glanced at his watch. "I must go, too. I'm late for an appointment."

Appointment with whom? Elizabeth felt like asking. She

wondered how she could have ever found him attractive in the beginning, how she could have ever gone to bed with him, but most of all she wondered about his success in finding women to do what she'd refused to do during their one and only intimate encounter. As a result of her flat refusal, he had never asked to see her again. Then she became involved with Jamie and stopped thinking of Derek, except in the strictest professional terms. Would she soon be thinking of Jamie in those same terms? It was a sickening possibility, but one that she now had to consider.

"Cheer up," Derek said, as he followed her out into the hallway. "It's always darkest before you-know-what."

"Disaster."

Then she turned right and headed for the rehearsal room, where the director and cast were assembling to read and time tomorrow's script. Later she would call Iris and make sure she had arrived safely. The three of them would probably have an early dinner after the rehearsal, she, and Iris, and Jamie. No, Elizabeth decided, she would not beat around the bush.

"Darling, are you by any chance trying to get me written out of the 'The Troubled Heart'?"

That was what she would say to the suspected saboteur. But definitely.

Chapter Six

Elizabeth had taken a table at the restaurant and was not-so-patiently sipping a parsley juice cocktail, when Jamie arrived with a drunken Iris at his side. Iris' pants suit looked as though she'd been sleeping in it for days.

"We're here at last," he said to Elizabeth's smile of grateful relief. "She's your responsibility now."

For a while there he didn't think they were going to make it, and he was infuriated with Elizabeth for having pushed Iris off on him, infuriated with himself for letting her get

away with it. The taxi ride calmed him down somewhat, but
a smoldering glare of resentment still remained. Jamie did
not like unfamiliar situations, in which he felt loss of control.
Not a drinker, he found it hard to gauge the degree of another person's drunkenness, and even though experience
should have warned him that he tended to overestimate everyone's capacity for alcohol, some brand of naiveté or will-
ful illusion continued to lead him astray. It was only after
Mrs. Richmond left, taking the alligator dog with her, that he
saw how smashed Iris was. She could barely walk; one lurch-
ing trip to the bathroom made it plain that the last thing in
the world she needed was another Bombay gin which she
then began to insist upon.

"Really, Iris," he said as firmly as possible, "I don't think
it's such a good idea."

He waited for her rebuttal, but she was now staring
straight ahead, an adamant statue.

"No, I don't think it's a good idea at all, not in your
present condition."

The statue waited.

"I know it's none of my business, but I'm only trying to do
what I consider best for you."

The statue's eyelids fluttered, signs of burgeoning life.

"If you think I like this role I've been forced into, you're
even crazier than I think you are."

The statue was silent. Jamie couldn't stand silence, he lived
in a noisy world. His typewriter banged and clicked away
much of the waking hours, banged and clicked out every
emotion known to the human race since the start of time,
and that noise was comforting: when Jamie wrote, he listened. Now there was nothing but the terrible, unfamiliar
sound of no words. Still he refused to be so cheaply threat-
ened.

"Iris, don't you think you've had enough?"

The statue crumbled, and Iris gave him the kind of look
that he felt certain she had given others before him, and
what was worse, he, they, all of them, deserved it. Only stupid people asked stupid questions, but the more stupid they
were, the longer they insisted upon an answer. Hoping to sal-
vage a shred of pride, he went into the kitchen and began to
pour from the Queen Victoria bottle. (But what about Iris'
pride, he asked himself, struggling with ice cubes, why didn't
she care that she was plastered and making a fool of herself?

Nobody answered.) Elizabeth should see him now, he thought with perverse satisfaction, Elizabeth, who, despite her reputation for being difficult, tried her best to remain reasonable when they were together so as not to antagonize her temperamental lover. Maybe that was it, maybe it was her goddamned uphill attempts at steadying the boat that had started to irritate him so much. Yet that was what he told her he wanted, right from the beginning, a steady boat. She was a fool to have believed him, though; like most people she'd fallen for the defense. He'd fallen, too, the worst fall of all; he believed himself.

"Here you are, madam."

Iris grabbed the glass and belted down half the contents, then looked at him through hostile, faraway eyes. "Did you know that I was a virgin when I got married?"

Jamie returned to the tubular, chrome chair he'd been sitting in. "I don't know anything about you."

"Virgin. That is correcto. And I was twenty-one when Bob and I got married. Twenty-one. That's practically ancient these days. How old are you?"

"Thirty. Doddering."

"I'll tell you something even more surprising. I've never been to bed with another man in my life. Never. Not before Bob, and not since. Only Bob. Isn't that wonderful?"

He couldn't tell whether she was being serious or sarcastic. "Let's just say it's rather strange."

She finished the rest of the drink and stood up. "Strange. Okay. Call it anything you like, but I say it's wonderful. Know why?"

"Why?"

Her laughter was eerie; it sounded as though it came from another person buried deep within her. "Because it makes me seem romantic." She looked around. "Where's my coat?"

Jamie looked around too, vaguely recalling something white slung over her arm when they met at the airport. "Maybe you left it in the bedroom."

She laughed again. At herself? The world? "Oh yes, the *separate* bedroom. There's a painting of an antelope over the twin bureaus. That's where it must be."

"I'll get it."

She sat down, collapsed would have been more like it, and barely seemed to notice as he returned with the coat and put it around her shoulders. To his surprise, her skin was cold despite the mild weather.

"Bergdorf was sitting on it. Which reminds me. I'd better feed him before we leave."

In the cupboard was a can of Alpo Beef Parts. Jamie opened it and poured half the contents into a Limoges dish, and set it on the floor next to the stove. Beside it he put another Limoges dish of water. The Yorkshire terrier started to eat quickly, eagerly.

"I thought he only liked steamed carrots and lightly broiled calves' liver," Iris said, astonishing Jamie with her peculiarly selective memory. "Isn't that what you told me in the car?"

"That's what Elizabeth told *me*. Maybe it's the china that he likes. Anyhow, if you're ready, let's go. We're late."

"That's okay. I'm always late."

"Well, I'm not."

"I'm always late, and Elizabeth is always on time. She'll understand. It's always been that way."

They were some pair, these sisters. "It sounds pretty boring. Everybody always doing the same thing."

"It is boring, but we do it anyway." She winked suddenly, a glittering, inviting flash of violet. "We're idiots, Elizabeth and I. We go on doing the same thing because we don't know how to do anything else."

"I hope you know how to walk a dog. Because if you don't, you're going to be in a lot of trouble."

"Not really," she said, as they went out the door. "That's what money is for. To pay people to do all the unpleasant things you don't want to do."

Jamie thought of her parents' three-hundred-thousand-dollar Bel Air estate and all the hired help and trimmings that went with it. Then he thought of how he had grown up, in a three-room apartment in Morningside Heights with a cleaning lady who came in half a day a week, and an electric fireplace that made revolving shadows on the living-room wall.

The two sisters embraced with a self-consciousness that Jamie found utterly touching, at the same time that he found it, somehow, utterly unconvincing. It reminded him of a scene between Bette Davis and Miriam Hopkins in a vintage Warner Brothers movie (good God, was he back to old movie stars again, or had he never gotten them off his mind?).

"Darling," Elizabeth said, auditioning for the part of the

superior sister, "it's marvelous to see you again. I've missed you like mad. How long has it been?"

"A year." Iris plopped down between the two of them. "A rotten year."

"I know. That is, I can imagine how rough it must have been."

"Can you?"

"Of course I can. I'm your sister."

"What does that have to do with the price of anything?"

"Just that I've thought of you a great deal this past year. It had to have been a terrible time, but all that's over now. That's all in the past."

"Is it?"

"Of course it is. Which is precisely why I'm so glad you decided to move to New York. I know you'll love it here once you get settled."

Elizabeth was wearing one of Jamie's favorite outfits, a three-piece tangerine jersey. The brief jacket was slung over her shoulders, revealing a sleeveless print blouse. As usual, she looked her attractive, well-groomed self. Jamie admired that quality of self-care, self-esteem, Elizabeth would never be publicly caught dead in a state of dishevelment. Even her fingernails, long and gracefully tapering, had been painted a complimentary shade of tangerine. Iris', he noticed for the first time, were short and cut straight across like a child's.

"How are Mom and Dad?" the auditioner asked.

"Ginger and Harvey are fine. Where's the waiter? I want a drink."

"The only kind of drink you can get here," Jamie said, "is fruit or vegetable juice."

"What?"

"There are a number of delicious varieties," Elizabeth said. "Unusual ones, too. You might want to try the Spring Cocktail. It's made with rhubarb and fresh strawberries, flavored with honey. I've been told it's served with great success at Elizabeth Arden's health farm in Arizona. The Main Chance."

"I had my main chance when I married Bob. I want a martini."

"There are no alcoholic beverages served here, no food that's been treated with poisonous chemical sprays, nothing but good, wholesome, delicious, organic meals."

"You sound just like Ginger. I tell you, I don't want an organic meal. I want a martini."

"That's the same as drinking poison."

"It's my stomach. Where am I, anyway? What kind of place is this?"

"It's one of our favorite restaurants. Didn't you notice the name when you came in? 'Nature's Oasis.' Now don't be difficult, Iris. You know one of the reasons you left Los Angeles was to get out of the martini rut."

"It wasn't my idea to leave. I only did it under duress. God knows why I ever agreed to go."

Elizabeth tried to look cheerful. "Nonetheless, here you are, and I am somewhat responsible for you. I promised Mom and Dad to keep an eye on you and that's precisely what I intend to do."

"I wish you'd stop calling them Mom and Dad. It sounds so phony."

"Ginger and Harvey. Very well. Now shall we order?"

Elizabeth's breasts were larger than Iris's, Jamie thought, Elizabeth was better-looking, more mature, more talented, more pulled together, more everything. Then why did he want to get rid of her?

"Let's see now," Elizabeth said, consulting the menu even though she knew it by heart. "How about the Spring Cocktail, eggplant loaf with fresh tomato sauce, a bean sprout salad, and some nice, refreshing verbena tea. How does that sound?"

"I want a martini, steak and french fried potatoes, and afterward I want coffee with cream and sugar, and a chocolate sundae. How does *that* sound?"

Jamie was giddily about to say he thought it was a swell idea, but Elizabeth had already motioned to the waiter. The meal ordered, an uncomfortable silence settled upon them, broken sporadically by bits and pieces of forced conversation.

ELIZABETH: How do you like your new apartment?
IRIS: It's okay. Who did all those dumb animal paintings?
ELIZABETH: I haven't the slightest idea.
IRIS: Where do you live?
ELIZABETH: Not far from you. In the East Seventies.
JAMIE: I'm the only person who lives on the West Side.
IRIS: I met my next-door neighbor. A Mrs. Richmond. Do you know her?

ELIZABETH: Nobody in New York knows their neighbors. How did you meet?

JAMIE: She came barging in, while Iris and I—

IRIS: Were having a drink. And it wasn't a Spring Cocktail.

ELIZABETH (giving Jamie a dirty look): Is she nice?

JAMIE: Terrible.

IRIS: She reminds me of Mom.

ELIZABETH: Ginger.

Fortunately, the waiter arrived with their food at that point and the meal began. Jamie gulped down his celery and apple juice, and said, "I think I have an ulcer. I'd like to check into a hospital and get that G.I. series, and find out for sure, but I can't spare the time."

"Maybe you could take your typewriter along." Elizabeth was eating her baked, stuffed heart with obvious enjoyment. "It's not as though you would be too sick to work."

"Sympathy. That's what I love."

"But I'm sympathetic, darling. I think it's cruel that they haven't hired another writer yet. I don't know how you do it, turning out all those scripts, day after day."

And making love to you the rest of the time, he thought. "I don't know how I do it either, but I'll tell you something. I can't go on doing it much longer. I'm a wreck. I'm a physical wreck. I can't sleep, my stomach hurts, and my head is filled with names of old movie stars. It's not a normal way to live."

"Which old movie stars?" Iris asked, taking a cautious bite of the eggplant loaf. "Name a few."

"Jane Withers, John Garfield, Miriam Hopkins."

Iris put down her fork. "This thing is inedible."

"Take a few more bites," Elizabeth urged her. "It's an acquired taste."

"So are martinis. I wish I were back at the Polo Lounge. I didn't know when I was well off."

"Gene Kelly, Bette Davis, Priscilla Lane. You look like her."

"I do?"

"Sure. Didn't anybody ever comment on the resemblance?"

"I don't even know who Priscilla Lane is. Was she nice?"

Jamie dug into his cheese-and-rice roll, feeling positively ancient. "She always played the sweet young thing, if that's what you mean."

"The sweet young thing," Iris said in disgust. "That's me. Did you know I was a virgin when I got married?"

"You've already told me."

Elizabeth looked at him. "My, my, you two sure have covered ground in a hurry, haven't you?"

"What was I supposed to do?" he asked. "Gag and bind her?"

"I not only was a virgin—"

"Iris," Elizabeth said, "I'm sure that Jamie isn't interested in hearing any more details of your unfortunate sex life."

"What you mean is, you're not interested. Why should you be, Miss Hot Pants of Beverly Hills High? Unfortunate is right."

"Iris, please. Try to pull yourself together. You're behaving like a fool. Don't you have any pride?"

"Don't *I* have any pride? That's a good one. I didn't go down on the whole football team in one afternoon, and then gargle for three days with Listerine. I used to hear you in the bathroom. Besides, Buddy Janis told."

"All I can say to these ridiculous accusations of yours is that you lead a rich fantasy life. You're in even worse shape than I imagined."

"With a sister like you, who needs fantasies? Your exploits are famous in Southern California. Maybe Northern California, for all I know."

Elizabeth shook her head, dazed. "I can't believe my ears."

"It's your mouth we're talking about, not your ears. Buddy Janis said you bit him. He had to wear a band-aid on his penis until it healed."

"You're not only an alcoholic, you're a pathological liar."

"And you're a pathological cocksucker."

Jamie felt like a spectator at a bad tennis match, it was embarrassing to observe—this grotesque sister rivalry—yet intriguing at the same time. The most intriguing part was that he wasn't sure who was telling the truth.

"I can't eat this crap any longer," Iris said, pushing her plate away. "Excuse me. I'm going to the ladies' room to throw up."

Jamie didn't know what to do, except get them both out of there as quickly as possible. Iris' behavior was inexcusable, there was no doubt about that, yet at the same time he felt sorry for her. She must be very jealous of Elizabeth to attack her so viciously. But he felt even sorrier for Elizabeth to have been subjected to such humiliating accusations in his presence. He had never felt sorry for Elizabeth before. Maybe the auditioner wasn't as sure of herself as she pretended, as he had always believed. It made Jamie like her all over again (love her?), she seemed so incapable of defending herself in the face of Iris' wild remarks; she seemed so vulnerable.

Vulnerability. It always won the day on soaps; everybody identified with the loser. Elizabeth was losing on two scores, here with her unpredictable sister, and on "The Troubled Heart." If they didn't build up her part, and *soon*, she would have to be written out, and he couldn't bear to be the guy to do it. The heavy. Edward G. Robinson, James Cagney, Bela Lugosi. Mary Astor, too, when she played the concert pianist reluctantly pregnant with George Brent's baby. Maybe the thing to do was make Elizabeth go to bed with Crawford, and get pregnant. Instead of having an abortion (which had recently become an accepted, although highly condemned, act on daytime television), she could give birth to Crawford's illegitimate child. Just the way women used to in the old movies.

"Look, Elizabeth, before Iris gets back, I want to tell you that I've been thinking a lot about what we're going to do with you on 'The Troubled Heart.' The fact is there's a story conference coming up next week, and we're definitely going to decide upon it then. One way or the other."

"I was wondering what that green rubber band on your finger was for."

Not only did she know his habits, but she had miraculously pulled herself together from the confrontation with Iris, and was once more the controlled, professional actress.

"It's not the green one that concerns you, it's the red. The green is for something else."

"Green, red, who cares? But speaking of conferences, I think there's something you should know. I just had a small conference myself. With dear Derek."

"Really? Tell me about it. What happened?"

"He put the blame on you. He said it was you, not the sponsor, who's been stalling about what to do with my part."

Intrigue, one-upmanship, passing the buck. It was so typical of so many people in television. He wished Derek hadn't done it, it only created unnecessary tensions and hostilities. On the other hand, how did he know that Elizabeth was telling the truth? Maybe she had gone down on the whole football team.

"How would you like to get knocked up by Crawford and have the baby? With a development like that, you could be on the show for another year, maybe more, depending on how things go. I shouldn't even be telling you this, but it's one of my ideas."

"Oh, Jamie, that would be wonderful. Why did Derek say—? Never mind. Do you think the others will go for it?"

"I don't know. It will just have to wait until next week. The cake mix guys might not buy it. You've been so pure and virginal up until now."

Iris came toward them, paler than before. "She hasn't been a virgin since she was fourteen."

"That's enough," Jamie said, "and I mean it, Iris. You've had your fun for the evening, if that's what you call it. Now drink your damn tea and shut up."

His stomach hurt so badly that he didn't know how much longer he could go on sitting there. The prospect of that G.I. series didn't appeal to him either, but if he had an ulcer he had better do something about it. Elizabeth's part wasn't the only thing he was going to talk to Derek about, there was still the green rubber band. A second writer was what he needed, he hated to part with the extra fifteen hundred dollars but he needed writing help, it was an emergency. With another writer, he could check into Doctor's Hospital; the strain was simply too much, it was inhuman. All the soaps had two directors and usually more than two writers. If he went on at this rate, he would be the only person in the business turning out seventeen thousand, five hundred words a week, two hundred and sixty episodes a year! No wonder his stomach hurt.

"It didn't do me any good being a virgin." Iris had begun to cry. "Bob started having an affair with somebody right after we got married. He thought I didn't know, but I knew. I just didn't know who the woman was. I didn't want to know."

The other woman. If Elizabeth went to bed with Crawford, all the viewers would identify with his poor, invalid wife. They would be intrigued by Elizabeth, but she would have to be punished. The other woman was always a good part, the bitch was a juicy role; all the shut-ins who watched "The Troubled Heart" could live more than vicariously. Or, as he had said at the last story conference, "There are certain given situations in which you can have your cake and eat it, too." That went over big with the guys at the agency, who, three days later, would think they had said it themselves.

"Iris, please don't cry," he heard Elizabeth say in her gentlest voice. "I know that you're upset or you wouldn't have said all those dreadful things to me. I know you don't mean them. It's the trip, being in a strange city, the past year, Bob's unfortunate death, but you've got to stop feeling sorry for yourself."

"How can you be so kind to me?" She was crying even harder now, the sobs coming out of her throat in choked, garbled sounds. "After how nasty I've been?"

"Because I understand you, darling, I really do. When you drink, you become belligerent, hostile, cruel. I know that you're not any of those things. It's the alcohol. You simply have to stop drinking."

"I've tried, but it doesn't work."

"Well, I have a suggestion. You must get a job, it's the only answer. Is there anything at all you'd like to do, anything you think you might be interested in?"

Iris drank her verbena tea, the tears subsiding. "I'm not trained at anything. I'm not talented. I'm not like you, Liz. You're lucky, you always knew what you wanted to do right from the start. I remember when we were children . . . the dancing lessons, the singing lessons, the acting lessons, the devotion. And what was I doing after school? Sitting out by the pool, reading the entire Nancy Drew series. Remember what Ginger used to say?"

"No. What?"

To Jamie's amazement, they were both smiling now, sharing early childhood memories, and he was jealous. He had been an only child in a lonely, grownup world, studying to be a great chemist at the Bronx High School of Science. Chloral hydrate was a good way to knock off people on soaps. Maybe someone could use it on Crawford when the time came to get rid of him. The stuff had been invented in 1832 by a German named Liebig, and the killing dose was twenty-five grams. How could he have remembered that after all these years?

"Ginger used to say that if the house burned down, I'd sit there reading a book."

The minute Iris said it, both sisters looked at each other in sudden dismay. Jamie could not keep up with their shift of mood.

"What is it?" he said. "What's the matter? The two of you look like you've just seen a ghost."

"It's the way Bob died," Elizabeth said. "He burned to death in their house at Malibu. One of his welding tanks exploded. It was a ghastly accident."

"It was the accident that ruined my life," Iris said. "The only thing I ever wanted to do was be married, and be happy. A wife. That was what I wanted to be, and I didn't even do that right."

"You can't blame Bob's infidelity on yourself. He probably would have been unfaithful, no matter who he married. He was a born cheat. And to think that our own parents gave him his first big professional break."

"You always hated Bob, didn't you?"

"I didn't hate him, Iris. I just didn't particularly like him."

"Sex says good-bye."

"What?" Jamie asked.

"Those were my husband's last words, and I still don't know what the hell they mean. Sex can say goodbye forever, as far as I'm concerned. What has sex ever done for me?"

Fortunately Elizabeth had to go to her off-off-Broadway theater or the evening might have dragged on indefinitely, and Jamie didn't think he could take much more of the emotional pyrotechnics of the past few hours. Had it only been that afternoon that he'd picked Iris up at the airport? It seemed like weeks, months ago. Upon Elizabeth's urging, he agreed to take Iris home. He further agreed that if there were any Bombay gin left he would pour it down the sink.

"Will I see you after the show?" Elizabeth asked him when they were out in the street getting taxis. "Or will you be busy working?"

"Why don't you call me?"

"Okay, darling."

She lifted up her face to be kissed, which Jamie dutifully did. She really was lovely, and he became conscious of her perfume for the first time that evening. Joy. It pleased him to know that it was the most expensive scent in the world.

"Give a good performance," he said, suddenly wanting to make love to her.

"I'll try, darling."

The doorman shift had changed when he and Iris got to her building, the ex-Boston cop now replaced by a man with a moustache and an English accent. To Jamie's ears he sounded just like Derek.

"Good evening, sir. How have you been?"

"Fine," Jamie said.

The Englishman held the inside lobby door open, and smiled politely at Iris. "It's nice to see you again."

The elevator had Muzak.

"I wonder who he thought we were," Jamie said. "Look, as soon as we get upstairs, I'm going to pour out the gin, and then I'm going to walk Bergdorf. Tomorrow you can make your own arrangements. Okay?"

"You really are very nice. I'm sorry that I've been so impossible, but I promise to improve."

Jamie took the Yorkshire terrier for a fast trot around the block, exchanged a few more friendly words with the English doorman, who wanted to know if he had had a nice time in Zurich (Jamie said yes), and found Iris in the bedroom when he returned. She was unpacking her suitcases, putting sweaters, scarves, belts, and pantyhose into bureau drawers at a diligent rate of speed. He was just about to tell her that he was going home, when the telephone rang. She picked up the wall extension.

"Hello."

There was a pause.

"Hello," she said again.

There was another pause.

Then, "No, this isn't Sheila. She's moved to Los Angeles. I have her—"

Jamie could hear the dial tone.

She replaced the receiver. "Whoever he was, he hung up. I was going to give him my number in L.A." She shrugged, and opened another bureau drawer.

"Bergdorf has done his business," Jamie said. "I've poured the rest of Queen Victoria down the sink, and I'm going home. I hope you—" He was about to say, "sleep well," but there was such a strange expression on her face that he said, "What's the matter, Iris?"

Only then did he notice the piece of paper she held in her hand. There seemed to be some writing on it.

"It was in the bureau drawer," she said. "I guess the O'Reillys left it behind."

"So? Mail it to them, if you think it's important."

"Yes. Of course."

He was anxious to leave, get back to his own place, sit down at the typewriter and do some work, and later, well, later Elizabeth would call. He remembered the scent of Joy when he had kissed her. Tantalizing. The evening might turn out to have its rewards, after all.

"I'll talk to you soon, Iris. Try to get some sleep."

"Yes."

She still had the piece of paper in her hand as she walked him to the door and said good night.

PART II

Chapter Seven

The handwriting on the paper seemed to be that of a woman, Sheila O'Reilly, no doubt, but Iris could make nothing of the contents. It was a list of some kind.

Tutti Frutti	Harold
Yellow Dragon	Ken P.
Strawberry Flip	Derek
The Storm	Larry
Black Butterfly	Pete
Nebraska Tailspin	Rudolph
Six-Love	Freddie
The Screamer	MM
On-the-Rocks	Ernie
Wedding Ring	Alan
Bubble Bath	Charles

The list went on, but Iris did not. What was the point? None of it made any sense, and she thought of what Jamie had said about sending the piece of paper to the O'Reillys if it seemed important. Something told Iris that it *was* important, but something else told her not to send it anywhere, to hang onto it instead. Acting on an instinct she did not understand, she slipped the paper beneath a pile of cashmere sweaters in the top bureau drawer and continued to unpack the rest of her clothes. When she was finished, she took a shower and put on an old but expensive pair of silk violet pajamas, almost the same color as her eyes. They had been a birthday gift from her parents when she was nineteen. Four years ago, just before she left home to take her own house in the Hollywood Hills, before she met Bob. On the pocket over her right breast, her mother had had her initials monogrammed: ILS. Iris Lily Small. Irises and lilies were Ginger's professed favorite flowers.

65

"They're so much like you, dear," she recalled Ginger saying to her. "Delicate, fragile, tender."

Iris turned out all the lights except the one in the bathroom and got into the O'Reilly's king-sized bed, which had been made up with fresh, peppermint-striped sheets. Bergdorf jumped in after her, licked her face, and finally settled down at her feet. From time to time, he made small whining sounds. He must feel the way she did, alone, confused, abandoned. They had that much in common but it was hardly a comforting thought, quite the contrary in fact. She would have wished that the O'Reillys had left behind a large, protective dog, a Great Dane or a German shepherd, instead of this pathetic, overbred animal.

From another apartment came sounds of a hi-fi or a radio playing rock music, somewhere a door slammed, water flushed, faint conversational voices could be dimly heard. None of it bothered Iris, actually she rather liked it, the knowledge that there were other people around, close by in case she needed them. Tomorrow she would make arrangements with the doorman to have Bergdorf walked twice a day, she would check out the neighborhood, locate the nearest market and liquor store, she might even buy some new clothes, Eastern clothes. Her bright, lemon yellow pants suit was okay for Southern California, but apparently it was not the sort of thing to wear in New York in October— women here seemed to dress in darker, more muted colors. As drunk as she had been earlier in the evening, she'd noticed that much. Feeling purposeful for the first time in a long time, Iris closed her eyes, and abandoned herself to the unfamiliar blackness.

Delicate, fragile, tender.

Ginger's description of her was the last thing she thought of before she drifted off to sleep. That, and the fact that her mother had named Elizabeth not after a flower, but after one of the most powerful queens who ever sat on the throne in England.

When she woke up it was after ten in the morning, and she remembered that she had had a strange dream. The only dreams she remembered were those she'd had just before awakening, so that was when it must have taken place, and she wished it had happened earlier in the night and that there was no recollection of it whatsoever. Unlike many people who seemed to be fascinated by theirs and other people's dreams, Iris couldn't bear talking or hearing about them. Dreams bored the shit out of her, simply because **they** were just that: dreams.

This one had been about her honeymoon, which she and Bob had spent in a motel directly opposite the main entrance to Disneyland. The dream was pretty true to life, as far as certain bare facts went. It had been Bob's idea to go to the Disneyland motel. He was from Wyoming ("Cody," he was fond of saying, "same town as Jackson Pollock"), and had never visited "The Magic Kingdom." He swore that that was the only way it was described in all the Anaheim literature he'd sent away for, long before he ever arrived in Los Angeles on a Greyhound bus, four dollars in his pocket, a blowtorch and a welding hose in an old suitcase.

Iris had made the traditional civic visit to Disneyland with Elizabeth and her parents soon after it opened, and had retained only blotchy, adolescent impressions of a sprawling world-within-a-world madhouse that she had no particular desire to see again. But Bob insisted. His enthusiasm and eagerness were touching. Let other people spend their honeymoon in Venice, Crete, Morocco, Yucatan, Hong Kong, Denpasar, St. Moritz, he was going to Disneyland, goddamn it, to see America.

At that point the dream and reality came to an unfortunate parting of the ways. In the dream they enjoyed four days and three nights (special motel rate) of uninterrupted pleasure-seeking, both in and out of bed. Happy, happy, happy, in the happiest publicized place on earth. In reality they spent four days and three nights (same special motel rate), restless, joyless, and only superficially communicative. She had known Bob less than a week when they decided to get married, and during that week they'd gone to bed exactly twice, the first time signaling the end of her much-hated virginity. Bob could hardly believe the virgin bit—he was dumbfounded, but afterward rather pleased as though he had tamed a rare, exotic bird.

"I don't believe it," he said when he saw the blood, despite the fact that she had warned him beforehand. "I just don't believe my own eyes."

"It's not ketchup."

He touched the stained sheet with his finger, as though to make sure. "It sure isn't. Hell, honey, you really are something."

It had been quick that first time, disappointing. They'd gone to the house he was staying at, a big rundown place off the Strip that he shared with what seemed to be an indefinable number of people of both sexes. When they were still in bed, a girl wandered in, stoned, mumbled something like, "Yeah, why not?" and wandered out again.

"It's rough when they all crash at the same time," was his only comment.

The second time they went to her place, but although there were no other people around to interrupt them, the love-making had been almost as quick and hurried as before. Iris blamed herself, her lack of experience. Perhaps she didn't excite him, didn't know how to please a man (what standards did she have to go by?), didn't know how to make him want it to last. But Bob was easily the most thrilling thing that had ever happened to her, the most magnetic man she'd ever met and she was determined to improve.

During their Disneyland honeymoon, her determination soon died. His sexual reactions were lazy, indifferent. He almost seemed amused by her passionate attempts to arouse him. That hurt worst of all, the possibility that he might be secretly laughing at her female ineptness, the probability that he did not find her desirable. Why had he married her, she wondered that first evening. Afterwards they'd taken a side trip to Knotts Berry Farm and Ghost Town, a ten-minute ride from their motel. It was one of the big local attractions, and besides, it was included in their special four-day, three-night package rate. Also included was a free drink at the Calico Saloon, where a line of cancan dancers kicked and ruffled their skirts up and down the length of an imitation wild-West bar. One dancer in particular seemed to catch Bob's eye, and it was then, feeling his excitement, that Iris questioned his reasons for marrying her.

"Because I love you, honey. Cross my heart."

That was his answer, the only answer she would ever get out of him until the last day in the hospital when he died of third-degree burns. *Sex says good-bye.* The words were like a puzzle she still could not figure out, just as for a long time she had not been able to figure out why her husband continued to make love to her in such a haphazard, careless way. It wasn't that Bob was impotent, no, not at all, and somehow Iris sensed it wasn't that he *couldn't* control his orgasm, but rather that he had no interest in doing so. Later, when she realized there was another woman, she knew her hunch about her husband was right. With this other woman, whoever she was, Bob would be another man, passionate, tender, concerned for her pleasure, more intent upon prolonging his own. He would be the man Iris wanted, the man she couldn't have. Which only made her love and want him all the more. Unlike her happy, honeymoon dream of last night, their true honeymoon at Disneyland had set the tone for one long year of married torture.

The telephone was ringing.

"Hello," Iris said.

There was a pause at the other end, then an English accent (masculine) said, "Sheila? Is that you?"

"No. She moved to Los Angeles. Did you call last night?"

"Last night? No, afraid not. When did she take off?"

"Yesterday. Would you like her new phone number?"

"Thanks all the same, but it wouldn't do me any good. Sorry to have bothered you."

Iris was about to say that it was no bother, but the line was dead. Why didn't any of these people leave their names? At least she could write Sheila and tell her who had called, it might be about an acting job, although in that case, why wouldn't they get in touch with her agent? Unless Sheila was between agents. That had happened to Elizabeth when she came to New York and switched from Ashley Famous to CMA. Iris remembered getting a letter from Elizabeth before she made the actual switch, and the anxiety her sister expressed during the period she was without someone to represent her professionally.

The phone rang again. This time it was Elizabeth. As soon as Iris heard her voice, last evening's events came rushing back to her with a sense of humiliation and shame. How could she have said all those dreadful, insulting things at the restaurant? Now, in the sober aftermath, it seemed that she must have been clear out of her mind, and for what felt like the millionth time she swore once again to stop drinking.

"Can I call you back?" she said. "I just woke up. I haven't even had coffee yet."

"You shouldn't drink coffee. Caffeine is almost as bad for your health as alcohol."

Elizabeth's tone of cool authority had an instant effect upon Iris, it made her want a drink that very second.

"Please, Liz, not first thing in the morning. Look, I'd really like to call you back. I'm still half asleep."

"You can't call me, I'm at the studio. We're about to do the blocking on the sets and I'm in two acts today, believe it or not. I don't say much, but I'm there. The only reason I phoned was to find out how you were feeling, and whether you needed anything. I realize that aside from Jamie and me, you don't know a soul in New York."

"You left out Mrs. Richmond."

"Who?"

"I told you about her. The lady next door."

"Oh, her. Neighbors are something else. Don't get too chummy, she'll want to know all your business."

"I don't have any business."

"Iris." Elizabeth's voice sounded strange. "You said something last night about Bob having an affair with another woman while you were married. I didn't want to talk about it in front of Jamie, but do you know for a fact that that's true? You never mentioned it before, and I never heard Ginger or Harvey mention it either."

"That's because they didn't know anything about it. I didn't tell them, I was too ashamed."

"But are you sure . . . ?"

"I can't prove it, if that's what you mean, but there were signs, little giveaways. They used to meet at the beach house in Malibu. Since Bob's studio was there, he had the perfect alibi."

"Darling, you know you've always had an overactive imagination. Isn't it possible that you might have imagined there was someone else, when in reality all Bob was doing was working on his impressionist sculptures?"

"I wish that that's all he was doing."

"And yet you never tried to find out who the woman was."

"What difference would it have made?" Iris was starting to lose her patience. "He didn't love me, he loved her. That was what mattered, not whether she was a blonde or a brunette."

"I suppose you're right," Elizabeth said, without much conviction.

In the background a man said, "Ready for No Fax, Liz."

"I have to go. We'll be blocking my uterus scene in a few minutes. I'll call you later, maybe during the lunch break if I have a chance. Think about getting a job. That's the most important part of all."

"What the hell is a uterus scene?"

"Bye, darling."

Elizabeth hung up the telephone in the control booth and went across the hall to Studio 19 where the rest of the cast was assembled to continue the rehearsal of that day's episode of "The Troubled Heart." The first rehearsal had started at eight-thirty in the morning and used simulated sets, with the director explaining each actor's moves, motivation, emphasis of speech, and not least of all, pace. Everything had to be timed down to the last split second. Most of the cast behaved like sleepwalkers during this first run-through, reading from scripts, sipping coffee, asking questions, stumbling over lines and cues, absorbing, assimilating, memorizing what amounted to a thirty-minute play in a few, concentrated hours. The only thing that surprised Elizabeth was not that mistakes were made during the actual taping of the show at three-thirty, but that more mistakes weren't made, worse ones.

The actors' schedule, typed on the bottom of each script, looked like Greek to Elizabeth the first time she saw it. Now it was as familiar to her as the show's makeup man, hairdresser, and wardrobe woman.

8:30–10:00	Dry for blocking
8:30–10:00	Makeup and Costume
10:30–11:00	No Fax
11:00–11:30	Camera conference
11:30–12:30	Fax 1
12:30–1:30	Break for lunch
1:30–2:00	Fax 2
2:00–2:30	Film check
2:30–3:00	Dress
3:00–3:30	Break, final notes
3:30–4:00	Tape for air

They were up to No Fax now, and in the studio the stage manager said, "Okay, kids, here we go for Act I. Craig Crawford's private office." Most of the act took place between Crawford and an underworld character who was supposed to be head of a narcotics ring. Elizabeth did not enter until the last few seconds.

"I'll cue you when to open the door," the stage manager told her.

He looked sleepy, too. Most of the cast and crew would

not seem to come to life for another hour, when the cameras and mikes were added, and Elizabeth often wondered what their ten million viewers would think if they could see these early, comatose rehearsals. Unlike the others, she had been wide awake for hours and felt wonderful, exhilarated, better than she had in a long time. There was nothing like making love to revitalize a tired person, and she certainly had been tired when she called Jamie after the theater last night, so tired in fact that if he hadn't wanted to see her, she almost might not have cared. She would have gone home and soaked in a hot bath, taken a sleeping pill, and gotten a decent night's rest before she had to get up at seven, do her yoga exercises, and grab a cab to the studio.

Jamie not only wanted to see her, as it turned out, he sounded eager, something he hadn't sounded like recently. Perhaps after all these months he was starting to fall in love with her, really in love. Elizabeth felt a glow of triumph when he apologetically said, "Do you mind coming over to my place? I'm still working and I'd like to get as much done tonight as . . ."

"No darling, of course I don't mind. I'll just stop by my apartment first and pick up tomorrow's script. That way I can go right to the studio in the morning."

It was quite a workload she carried these days, and if it weren't for her sensible health regime, she would never be able to maintain the frantic, pressured pace. Discipline. Without that, all the talent and hard work in the world would get you nowhere. She knew actresses far more gifted than she who'd dropped (or been thrown) out of the race mainly because they had never learned how to discipline themselves. And that was the crux of Iris' problem, if only she could learn to recognize it. Iris had never been taught the importance of discipline. Ever since she was a child she had lived in a world of the most permissive self-indulgence, doing just as she pleased, whenever she pleased. Her drinking was only one more symptom of her careless, disorderly approach to life. Disorderly people frightened Elizabeth. Having no regard for themselves, they had even less regard for the values of those around them. Nothing was sacred, nothing mattered, that was their unspoken attitude. Elizabeth knew they were to be pitied more than despised, that their pretense of freedom was the most restricting kind of strait jacket in the world, but try as she did, she could never really *feel* pity for them. Some mysterious part of her continued to envy their cool air of indifference.

"I think she needs professional help," Jamie said, when Elizabeth had gotten to the Des Artistes. "I know that your intentions are good, but in my opinion you're biting off more than you can chew."

"You're probably right, but you don't know the whole story. Iris has had professional help and it hasn't done a damn bit of good. Why do you think she's in New York? Our parents tried everything after Bob died, but Iris can be like a rock when it suits her. Immovable."

"Doesn't she want to be helped?"

"I no longer know what Iris wants and what she doesn't want. My sister is a mystery to me, she always has been. I do know that she's hysterically opposed to any form of psychotherapy. According to Ginger, Iris says that all the Beverly Hills analysts who tried to treat her were crazier than she was."

"That's the oldest cop-out in the world. Couldn't she be a little more original?"

"Wait. You haven't heard the rest. The reason she says they're so crazy is because whenever they used to ask her what she did with herself all day—this was after Bob had died—she told them that she watched soap operas, and their reaction invariably was that that was a pretty passive way to live."

"So?"

"So Iris contends they're a bunch of low-grade culture snobs who don't understand the artistic and social significance of soap operas, when anybody with half a head can plainly see that soaps are the only true, indigenous art form operating in the United States today."

"*Soap operas?!*"

Elizabeth had to laugh at his bewilderment. "Yes, darling. According to my sister, they're real American folk art, like jazz, which was also looked down upon at first. Iris says critics are automatically suspicious and afraid of anything that appeals to people on a gut level, anything that smacks of unpretentiousness, anything that grows out of the needs of the time. So they knock it."

Jamie shook his head. "That's remarkable. But when did she tell you all this?"

"She didn't. Ginger told me. My mother tried to get Iris

away from the TV set recently, and Iris asked whether she'd try to get her away if she were watching a classy production of Hamlet. Naturally my mother was confused and said she didn't understand what Hamlet had to do with it, which was when Iris screamed that soap writers are the Shakespeares of today, or Shakespeare was the soap writer of his day, or something to that effect. I can't remember. But that's when my parents realized she was in serious trouble."

"Shakespeare, eh?"

"Don't let it go to your head. My sister is crazy."

"So am I. About you."

"What brought this on?"

"Sheer, unadulterated lust."

But when they made love afterward, it was very tender, and they finally dropped off to sleep, their arms wrapped around each other. Jamie was still asleep when she left in the morning, his face very young and vulnerable in the early gray light. It appealed to Elizabeth that she was going off to work, while he would remain home. She felt surer of him, knowing that he would be at home, alone, and she wondered whether businessmen felt that way about their wives. It was an extremely pleasant feeling of possessiveness. Elizabeth enjoyed the mobility of her work, being part of a group activity, coming into contact with different people, and all the while having the security of knowing exactly where Jamie was: in his bubble. The fact that he could easily cheat on her during the day, if he chose to, was somehow not as threatening as would be his gallivanting around town, going to meetings, going to lunches, going to other offices, being personally in touch with the world. This way she could bring the world to him, she was his link with it, and she liked the sense of importance it gave her.

Unlike Sheila, who'd married another actor, Elizabeth could not conceive of ever doing such a thing. Actors were just about last on her list of potential husbands. Their narcissism alone was enough to rule them out, but that, coupled with the constant opportunities they had to meet other more attractive, more successful, more famous, more wealthy, more intriguing women, made them totally undesirable. Being married to an actor was Elizabeth's idea of choosing a life of perennial anxiety. She once asked Sheila whether it didn't bother her.

"Tom is too busy concentrating on his career to have

much interest in playing around," Sheila said. "That sort of thing usually happens to actors only after they become superstars, not while they're still in the struggling stage."

Sheila had been in the struggling stage herself when she said it, which didn't seem to stop her from playing around, but Elizabeth had not known about that at the time. And later, after she had accidentally found out, she still had no idea whether Tom knew, too. Probably not, was her hunch. The odd thing was that together Sheila and Tom O'Reilly appeared to be the happiest, most devoted couple Elizabeth had ever met. But Sheila was a far more complex person than Elizabeth had imagined at first. There were two images of Sheila that would haunt her forever. One was Sheila in her starched nurse's uniform on "The Troubled Heart," offering words of comfort to relatives of gravely ill patients. The other was Sheila naked, her red hair a tangle of curls, the afternoon she had seduced Elizabeth.

Chapter Eight

Sheila had not been on "The Troubled Heart" for quite a while before she and Tom took off for Los Angeles, and Elizabeth missed her. Sheila had a flippant sense of humor which seemed to prevent her from taking herself or anyone else too seriously. Ordinarily, Elizabeth would have resented such a capricious attitude, but from the beginning she found it hard to resent anything about Sheila O'Reilly.

Even after Sheila had slyly seduced her, Elizabeth could not summon up the sense of outrage she knew she should have felt, and perhaps that surprised her most of all. That she was not angry, that she accepted what had happened without any particular guilt or shame. Because although the incident came as an absolute shock to her, it did not remain an absolute mystery for very long ... her reasons for allowing it to take place. No, those reasons quickly became clear, and if nothing in Elizabeth's life had prepared her for a lesbian encounter, everything had certainly prepared her for the lure of flattery. Male flattery, female flattery, what did it matter when her taste for admiration was so insatiable?

"How's your new apartment?" Sheila asked Elizabeth on that fateful day. "Are you happy with it?"

It was a Wednesday afternoon in early March. They had just finished taping another traumatic episode of "The Troubled Heart," and were about to leave the studio. It had been raining since morning, a cold, grim rain that showed no signs of letting up.

"More than happy. Delighted. It reminds me of my house in Laurel Canyon, which had a kind of nutty, offbeat charm."

"For some reason, I don't see you as the nutty type. You're much too down-to-earth."

"My mother once told me a very interesting thing about the way people lived. She said that when it came to their homes, they tended to choose the opposite of what they were, because the contrast was soothing. I didn't understand what she meant at the time, but I do now. And she was right."

"You admire your mother, don't you?"

"Yes. A great deal."

"Why?"

No one had ever asked Elizabeth that question, and she had to think before answering. The emotion she felt about Ginger had always managed to escape definition.

"I guess more than anything else it's her energy." It sounded strange to put into words. "Ginger acts on her ambitions. She makes them come true."

"A realist."

"Harvey would laugh if he could hear you call her that. But you're right. She doesn't let her weaknesses get the better of her. She knows what they are, and she knows how to deal with them."

"I wish my mother had been that way. Realistic people impress me. No wonder you admire her."

"My younger sister doesn't. She and Ginger never got along, it was a clash of temperament right from the start. Iris is more like Harvey: a dreamer."

They stepped out into the cold rain.

"Why do you call your parents by their first names?"

"Ginger said she didn't want to be called 'mother'—it makes her feel old. I think she was trying to hang on to some kind of self-identity when I was born. She was afraid of getting trapped. Not that there was much chance of that. She never would have been happy confined to just a husband and children. She needed more of the world. Although it was Harvey's idea to start the gallery, it was Ginger who went ahead and did it."

Kerchiefs on their heads, boots hugging their legs, umbrellas opened, they were about to head in opposite directions when Sheila said, "If you're not busy right now, how about inviting me over for a cup of coffee? I'd love to see your new place."

"You're invited." Elizabeth stepped off the pavement into a puddle of water and looked down the avenue. "Come on, let's get this cab."

It was a well-kept, renovated brownstone in the East Seventies just off Fifth, with a polished-brass mail slot. They took the tiny elevator up one flight to what once was the parlor floor. Elizabeth fished in her purse for the keys.

"How wonderful," Sheila said, entering the high-ceilinged apartment. "You have a fireplace. And logs."

"And a refrigerator in the bedroom."

"Filled with vintage champagne, no doubt."

Actually, it was filled with Perrier water. "How'd you guess?"

"The question is, where can I hang my coat? I don't see any closets."

Elizabeth swung back one of the twin bookcases, revealing a large, walk-in closet. "That's what I meant about this place being offbeat. Would you like a cognac with your coffee? There's a bottle of Bisquit over there on the table."

"Love one. Why don't you get the coffee started, and I'll make a fire."

The kitchenette was wedged between the living room and bedroom, and was so small that Elizabeth could barely turn around in it. On the rare occasions that she drank coffee, she liked to make it herself, strong and black, with chunks of brown sugar. It tasted almost like a food that way. She handed Sheila two glasses for the cognac, feeling decidedly decadent. Ordinarily at this time, she would still be either in the studio reading through tomorrow's script with the rest of the cast, or here at home studying Italian from Berlitz cassettes that she played on her tape recorder. She was up to the restaurant part. *La mancia é inclusa?* But she was not in "The

Troubled Heart" tomorrow, and neither was Sheila, she suddenly realized.

"Won't your husband be wondering where you are?"

"On matinee days like this he stays at the theater between
performances. He likes to sleep in his dressing room and
have an early dinner sent in. It's the only thing that keeps
him sane, he says." Sheila poured herself another cognac.
"Skoal."

Elizabeth placed coffee cups on the round dining table. In
front of the table were bay windows that looked out on
water-logged gardens and still-barren trees. Rain slashing
across windowpanes and trees swaying in the heavy rain reminded Elizabeth of the opening-and-closing logo shots for
"The Troubled Heart." Dark, dismal, threatening. Nature had
chosen this day to imitate the mood picture that flashed
across television screens for millions of viewers each afternoon. Sheila had made a successful fire, and now sat down
for the coffee. Elizabeth finished her first cup, just as Sheila
finished her second glass of cognac and poured a third.

"You've barely touched yours," Sheila said.

"I'm not much of a drinker. I keep it mostly for guests."

"Hospitable you."

Elizabeth could not tell if she was being sarcastic, or if she
was high, or both. A feeling of uneasiness overcame her. She
barely knew anything about Sheila, they had never exchanged
more than a few words at the studio, impersonal words until
today. They were strangers really. Elizabeth wished her guest
would leave. She felt like taking off her pants suit, changing
into a robe and putting on the Italian records. *Mi porti, per
piacere, arrosto di manzo.* Most of all, she felt like soaking in
a hot bath and being alone. She poured some of the cognac
into her coffee and drank it down. The combined warmth felt
good, and she remembered that all she'd had at lunchtime
was an organic apple.

"Are you hungry?"

"Not particularly," Sheila said. "Why? Are you?"

"Sort of. I didn't eat lunch. I thought we might order
something. There's a Chinese restaurant nearby that delivers."

"Not for me, thanks. I'm fine."

Somehow Elizabeth could not imagine ordering Chinese
food for one person, it seemed indecent. There was some
Virginia ham in the refrigerator, and some lettuce. If there
was bread, she could make a sandwich.

"Would you mind terribly if I stretched out on your sofa? It's been a rough day."

"Of course not."

Taking her cognac with her, Sheila lay down on the black corduroy sofa that had come with the apartment. She pushed one of the throw pillows under her head, and her curly red hair spread out like a fan. Smiling, luxuriating, bootless now, she crossed her long, slim legs demurely at the ankles.

"This feels wonderful. I didn't realize how tired I was."

"I'm tired, too."

She said it almost apologetically, as though being the hostess should preclude such feelings. Elizabeth wished she weren't so polite. Iris wasn't polite. In a situation like this Iris would probably get drunk and pass out, leaving Sheila O'Reilly to her own devices. Although Elizabeth hated to admit it, there were times when she secretly admired her sister's brand of lunatic defiance, and this was definitely one of those times. There had been others. The evening of Iris' Sweet-Sixteen birthday party, she'd gotten a head start on all her guests and consumed so much of the fruit punch that she spent the major portion of the party in the swimming pool, floating on her back and singing, "You Are My Lucky Star" off key, at the top of her lungs, while Ginger and Harvey tried to prevail on her to come out and rejoin her guests.

"This goddamn party wasn't my idea," Iris replied. "I'm not rejoining anybody."

Ginger later confided to Elizabeth that she foresaw nothing but trouble for Iris, if she kept on in this vein. Which was when they started to send Iris to expensive Beverly Hills psychotherapists who couldn't seem to do much with her either. They told the Smalls that their daughter refused to cooperate on the most basic levels. Iris had gotten into one of her song-fixation periods, and whenever she objected to one of the doctor's questions she would launch into a fast chorus of "You Are My Lucky Star." After she got tired of that particular set of lyrics, she switched to "All I Do Is Dream of You," and it didn't take very long for the doctors to get tired of her.

"There is nothing we can do," Ginger and Harvey were repeatedly told, "unless your daughter wants to be helped. At the moment, she does not."

It was about then that Elizabeth had her nose fixed, and Iris, whose nose happened to be one of nature's more spectacular accomplishments, used to taunt her by humming "A Pretty Girl Is Like a Melody" whenever a bandaged Elizabeth was within earshot.

"Don't you have any compassion for your sister?" Harvey asked. "I'm surprised at you."

"You can't escape her, she's in your memory, morning, night, and noon ..."

Elizabeth would leave the room, not in tears but close to it. How could her own flesh and blood be so gratuitously cruel?

"She will leave you and then come back again ..." followed her upstairs to her room where she plunged into Stanislavski's *An Actor Prepares*.

"A pretty girl is just like a pretty tune ..." was Iris' last musical comment, the day of Elizabeth's nose-unveiling.

They had never spoken about it since then, yet Elizabeth still retained the emotional scars of her sister's ridicule, and she suspected that she would always be super-sensitive on the subject. One of her recurrent fears was that if she ever had a child, it would be born with her old nose, and Iris (assuming she had not drunk herself to death) would start singing hateful songs again. There had been times when Elizabeth was tempted to tell Jamie about the operation, but somehow she could never bring herself to do it. She had never been able to tell any man. She could not bear to admit that her elegant nose had been created by one of the best rhinoplastic surgeons money could buy, any more than Iris could admit that the reason she always wore her blonde hair in the same fluffy style was because her ears stuck out. Their parents' lofty aesthetic standards haunted them both.

Sheila seemed to have dozed off. Her emerald-green knit dress had ridden up to her thighs, and one hand fell languidly over the side of Elizabeth's sofa. Sheila's third glass of cognac, empty now, was still held in her other hand, the way a sleeping child might hold on to her favorite doll. For security. For the need simply to *hold* something.

Elizabeth understood that need only too well, since coming to New York six months ago. The loneliness, the uprootedness, the sense of being utterly cut off from all the warm and familiar things she had known all her life made each new day not merely something to be lived through but to be conquered by sheer, relentless will power. Getting a job on "The

Troubled Heart" was only a first step on the road to ultimate stardom, and as grateful as she was for the invaluable acting experience, she had no intention of ever falling into the cushy soap-opera life that appealed to so many other actresses.

The woman, for instance, who played the show's kindly matriarch had been on "The Troubled Heart" for twenty years and would probably be on until the day she died. Her acting ambitions, she once confided to Elizabeth, went no further than that, and she was not ashamed to admit it. Oh yes, many years ago, when she was first starting out, she'd had the typical Sarah Bernhardt fantasies, but they quickly faded after she landed the female lead in the series and realized that if she wanted it, this could become her permanent professional life, and a very comfortable one at that, with a great deal of time to spend with her family and friends. She would make good money, do a good job and have no anxiety about where her next part was coming (or not coming) from. Elizabeth had been amazed by the woman's serenity, her lack of ambition, her contentment with a secure, yet dull fate.

"But you see, I don't find it dull," the older actress said. "I find it pleasurable. Reassuring. It's like having a second family, working on daytime drama. It's as though Jeffersonville were my adopted home town. And after all, my dear, each show *is* different."

That the woman was an accomplished, seasoned performer Elizabeth could not deny—a first-rate television actress, but after twenty years of playing the same character, who, with half an ounce of talent, wouldn't be? Yes, there were actresses and there were actresses. Sheila was another example. Sheila had neither Elizabeth's ambitions, nor the other woman's quiet resignation.

After Elizabeth met Jamie and started to share his passion for old movies, Sheila would remind her of actresses she sometimes saw on those movies. Actresses who in one or two pictures might give a glimpse of something special, a sparkle that promised they would be heard from again in a much more spectacular way, and then nothing happened. They simply drifted out of the profession. Inertia? Disinterest? Other interests? Marriage? Disaster? Who knew? And Elizabeth felt that Sheila, for all of her spunky appeal, would drift the same way, and perhaps no one but Sheila would ever know why.

"Hey. Come here."

Sheila moved, stirred in her sleep, seemed to be talking in her sleep. But to whom?

"What is it?" Elizabeth asked.

"Come here." The languid arm now beckoned. "Must tell you something."

She was drunk, she was half passed out, and Elizabeth didn't know what to do with her. Reluctantly, she approached the sofa, thinking that maybe if she could get her to swallow some coffee, she'd even give her the Virginia ham sandwich she was going to make for herself—anything to get her on her feet and moving, coherent.

"It's really important."

Elizabeth sat down on the edge of the sofa and leaned over the prone figure. "What's important?"

Sheila wedged the empty cognac glass between two cushions and put her arms around Elizabeth. She hugged Elizabeth and smiled up at her through sleepy eyes.

"Being here with you. You're so nice. You're . . ."

Elizabeth extricated herself as gracefully as she could.

"Excuse me. I have to go to the bathroom."

After she was through urinating (quietly), she combed her hair, put on another coat of lipstick, blotted it, combed her hair again, sprayed herself with Joy, and squared her shoulders. She was wearing a cocoa-brown pants suit with a brown-and-white striped scarf at the neck. Her reflection in the mirror was that of a very beautiful, very self-confident young woman about to cope tactfully with an unpleasant situation.

"Would you like some coffee?" she asked, reentering the living room. "I think you could use some."

"No, thanks. No coffee."

"A sandwich then?"

"Hey. Come here."

Elizabeth felt the first stirrings of anger. Did Sheila have no consideration at all? Didn't it occur to her that Elizabeth might have things to do, people to telephone, letters to write, books to read, lines to study?

"Sheila, you've had too much to drink. Perhaps you should go home."

"No, no." Sheila shook her head definitely no. "I don't want to go home. Nobody's there except Bergdorf. Tom'll feed him when he gets back after the theater. Bergdorf's okay. Please come over here."

"Why?"

"Because I want you to."

"Why?"

"Because you're nice."

"In what way?" Elizabeth was feeling the tug between the need for flattery and the desire to get rid of her guest. "In what specific way am I so nice?"

"Come here and I'll tell you."

Why not? Elizabeth thought finally. Sheila couldn't rape her. She went over and sat down on the sofa. This time Sheila's hands drew Elizabeth's face down to her own, her lips to her lips, breasts to breasts, tongues touching. Elizabeth had never before been kissed on the mouth by a woman, she felt dazed, she could not describe the sensation; it was simply unreal, the meeting of two lipsticked mouths. Then she felt Sheila's hand glide over her breasts, stroking the nipples that hardened immediately, caressing, kissing, fondling, and so gently, so affectionately, that stunned as Elizabeth was, she could not seem to call up the degree of outrage that surely the situation warranted. She would never have dreamed that Sheila went for women, she would never have dreamed that she, herself, could permit another woman to go this far with her.

"Sheila, please, I . . ."

"Don't you like it?"

Elizabeth didn't know what to say. She didn't want to hurt Sheila's feelings. (She wouldn't worry about hurting a man's feelings, though.)

"It's not that, it's . . ."

"It's what?"

"I don't think we should."

Sheila smiled, and let her hand move down Elizabeth's pants' leg. "Press your legs together."

Elizabeth did, and felt Sheila's hand go in between and start to rub, slowly, up and down, around and around, back and forth, in and out.

"You're wet, you know."

To her embarrassment, Elizabeth realized it was true. But why should she be embarrassed? Sheila was exciting her in

the same way a man would, and she wouldn't be embarrassed
if a man were doing it. Men didn't wear lipstick, though.
Men were always telling her how quickly she became wet,
and they said it as a compliment, the way Sheila was saying
it now. Robert used to say it all the time when they made
love at the house at Malibu. Without really thinking, Elizabeth slipped out of Sheila's hold and took off the bottom part
of her pants suit. Then she took off her bikini panty hose.
She was standing up now as her clothes slipped to the floor,
Sheila watching every move, every nuance. She continued to
stand in front of Sheila until Sheila put her mouth to Elizabeth's wet, light-brown mound of hair, put her tongue inside,
quickly found what she was looking for, and hungrily began
to suck.

After a few seconds they went into the bedroom and completely undressed. Sheila, the taller and larger-boned of the
two, had smaller breasts, very pretty and firm, the nipples
very pink, as opposed to Elizabeth's, which were brown like
her hair. They lay down on the big double bed, Sheila on her
back, Elizabeth over her, kissing and gently biting one nipple
while her hand played with the other, then she held both
breasts as close together as possible and let her tongue go
back and forth between the two.

Sheila's eyes were closed and she was making soft sounds
in her throat, pleasurable sounds, ecstatic sounds. Elizabeth
didn't know if she would have the nerve to do it, but Sheila's
enthusiastic response spurred her on, and a moment later she
had slid down on the bed and was parting Sheila's legs, bury-
ing *her* head, using *her* tongue, unearthing *her* hunger, until
she could feel the throbbing come to a pitch of intensity as
Sheila moaned and shuddered and cried out in delight, and
shuddered still more with orgasmic vibration, rolling over at
last on her side and curling up, still shuddering, into a foetal
position, where she rocked back and forth, then collapsed
into languor and pulled a triumphant Elizabeth down beside
her.

They woke up hours later in the middle of the night, and
kissed again.

"I'm dying of thirst," Sheila said.

Turning on the lamp, Elizabeth got up and went to the refrigerator (which, for some reason, the previous tenant had
installed in the bedroom) and took out a couple of bottles of
Perrier. In the adjoining kitchen she put ice cubes in two

glasses and filled them with the bubbling water, came back and handed one glass to Sheila, who swallowed gratefully.

"Hey, wait a minute," she said a second later. "I thought you said before that that refrigerator was filled with champagne."

At three in the morning, with the world dark outside, and this strange, lovely, red-haired woman in her bed, Elizabeth said, "I'm a terrible liar."

"You certainly are. I suppose you'll tell me next that you've never made love to a woman before."

"Of course I have." She knew Sheila would not believe the truth. "A couple of times."

Sheila grinned at her in delight. "I'll bet you have. Hey, what's on TV? Would you like to see a movie?"

"Why not?"

Elizabeth reached over and switched on the set opposite the bed. The movie was a Western with Steve McQueen. She adjusted the contrast and volume, then lay back alongside her new lover, who gazed at her with affection, with desire, with the kind of approval that Elizabeth had thrived on all her life. Sipping Perrier and occasionally touching each other, the two women watched Steve McQueen make mincemeat out of the ubiquitous enemy.

Chapter Nine

Jamie had just finished writing another provocative episode of "The Troubled Heart" and was deciding what to do for lunch, when he thought about Iris. Having been in New York less than twenty-four hours, she was probably trying to decide the same thing. He remembered that when he'd gone to her refrigerator for ice cubes, all there had been inside were two lemons and a package of sliced cheese. Why not take her to a decent restaurant, someplace quiet and relaxed where they could talk? An idea had struck Jamie when he'd seen

Elizabeth getting out of bed that morning to go to the studio. It was an idea that could prove the solution to both Iris' problems and his, it was a brilliant idea if only she would go for it. Feeling hopeful, he dialed the number he'd copied down last night.

"How would you like to have lunch?" he said when she answered the phone.

"At Nature's Oasis?"

"No, I know a nice place not far from you. You can even have a drink or two if you promise not to overdo it. I want to talk to you about something."

"Like what?"

Like saving me a lot of money, anxiety, and very hard work, he thought. "I'll tell you when I see you. Wear something warm. The temperature's down to twenty-three."

He gave her the name of a restaurant and hung up before she could say another word. Jamie did not like to talk on the telephone, it made him edgy. Practically nobody talked on the telephone very long in "The Troubled Heart," they had their conversations in person, face-to-face. It was necessary for dramatic reasons, which was why characters on the show were forever dropping in on each other without having called in advance. At first it had driven him crazy, thinking up all the excuses and apologies for the dropper-inners, but after a while he got used to it.

I was just passing by . . .
I saw your car in the driveway . . .
Your line was busy, so I thought . . .
I hope this isn't a bad time for you . . .
Marc said you'd be home . . .
What I came to tell you just couldn't wait . . .

Yes, Jamie decided, as he put on his poplin coat with the Spanish lamb lining, that last one would do just fine, mainly because it wasn't far from the truth. But when he got to the restaurant, there was no sign of Iris and he realized that whether he liked it or not, he would have to wait. And pray that she didn't get drunk or lost somewhere along the way. He took a table, ordered a stein of dark beer and began his impatient vigil. . . .

Just as Iris was about to leave her apartment, punctual for

once in her life, Mrs. Richmond rang the bell and asked if she could borrow a can of Easy-Off for the maid.

"I'm not sure I have any." The only reason Iris knew about things like Easy-Off was because it was advertised on so many of the soap operas she watched. She had never cleaned an oven in her life. "I'll go look."

"I know that Sheila's maid used to have it all the time."

Iris finally located a can of the insidious-looking stuff in a cabinet beneath the sink and handed it to Mrs. Richmond, who thanked her and then admired her mole cape. "It must have been very expensive."

"Not really."

"Was it a gift?"

Iris remembered what Elizabeth had said about not getting too chummy with the neighbors. "Yes. From my husband."

The cape had come from one of the status furriers in Beverly Hills. Iris was surprised to find it there since mole was hardly a status fur, but the proprietor explained that style and cut were as important these days as the species of animal. The only thing Iris didn't like about the cape was its color, which reminded her of her childhood. Ginger had dressed her in blue from the time she was born, because of her violet-blue eyes. But Bob adored the cape, said it was very flattering and elegant, and she had to agree he was right. This was the first time she'd worn it since his death.

"I thought it might have come from an admirer," Mrs. Richmond said.

Iris did not like her tone, she did not like the smug expression in Mrs. Richmond's dark eyes, she did not like Mrs. Richmond, period. Yet in the past, she would have been stupidly polite.

"My husband *was* an admirer. Isn't yours?"

"The doctor is far too busy with his practice to pay much attention to women's appearances."

Some deepening resentment drove her on. "That's unfortunate, considering how much money you must have spent."

"Are you drunk again?" Mrs. Richmond stared at her, not smiling, not frowning, her features a smooth and pallid mask. "What do you mean? *I* must have spent?"

"On that face-lift of yours."

"You have a fresh mouth, young lady, widow or no widow. You'll never do as well as Sheila. Steak. That's your speed."

"What?"

But Mrs. Richmond was gone, taking the can of Easy-Off with her. Iris shrugged, and went to meet Jamie.

"I should have walked," she said when she got to the restaurant. "Taxis crawl in this city. At least mine did. Where am I?"

It was a huge, baronial, old-world place with a distinct flavor, different from anything she had ever seen in California; it looked as though it belonged in another country, in another century. In California every restaurant, no matter how unique or unusual the decor, looked like it belonged exactly where it was.

"You're in Vienna," Jamie said. "Welcome to the Schönbrunn Palace. This banquet will be in celebration of the Emperor Joseph II, and that beautiful cape you're wearing is perfect for the occasion. Would you like a drink?"

"I'd love one. It's a good thing Elizabeth isn't here. She'd have a double fit."

"Never mind about Elizabeth at the moment. What will you have?"

"Three guesses."

"One martini with Bombay gin," Jamie said to the German waiter, "and another stein of dark beer. We'll order in a few minutes." Then he turned to her. "What do you think of this place? Doesn't it remind you of something out of one of those Mittel-Europa movies starring Faye Emerson and Zachary Scott?"

"You're talking about old movie stars again. Not that I mind, but I'm sure that that's not the reason you wanted to have lunch with me."

The minute she said it, a wild thought flashed across her brain: what if his only reason was a sudden, uncontrollable desire for her? He might have been awake all night fantasizing about making love to her, making her respond to him (as Elizabeth had never responded?), making her forget there had ever been a husband who neglected her. She took out a pack of cigarettes and waited for him to offer her a light.

"How'd you like to help me write 'The Troubled Heart'?" Jamie said, striking a match. "For money, of course."

Iris was so surprised she couldn't speak.

"You did tell me you'd taken some TV writing courses at UCLA, didn't you?"

She nodded, still unbelieving, and inhaled deeply.

"Don't look so shocked. I'm not asking you to become an international drug smuggler. I'm offering you a very legitimate job. For very good money. What do you say?"

"But I've never had any practical experience. I mean, I'm not a writer. I wouldn't know where to begin."

"Aside from the UCLA courses, you've already begun in a sense. You're familiar with the show. You know who all the characters are, what their relationships with each other have been, what predicaments they're presently involved in, and so on. That's a tremendous time-saver for me, not having to explain it all to you."

But it was more than time that she would be saving him if she accepted. There was the matter of money. He could offer her much less than an established professional who would not only demand a much higher salary but would also expect to receive television credit as associate writer. By paying Iris right out of his pocket, nobody at the network or agency would know about the arrangement, and he would get exclusive writing credit. It was what he had wanted ever since his partner had died. Of course, when Iris became more experienced, he'd be glad to consider some other arrangement. But for now it would be a good and fair deal for both of them.

"Jamie, it's not that I don't appreciate what you're trying to do, but tell the truth. Elizabeth put you up to this, didn't she?"

He laughed, genuinely amused. "She not only didn't put me up to it, she doesn't even know about it. The idea hit me this morning. I would have told Liz, of course, but she was in a rush to get to the studio."

So he and Elizabeth had spent the night together after all. What a fool she was to have imagined, even for a moment, that Jamie could ever be sexually interested in her. Which only made her realize that he was truly serious about the writing job.

"I almost flunked the course at UCLA," she said, which wasn't true, but she didn't know what else to say.

"School's out, Iris. This is for real, and if you're worried about the technical details, don't be. I'll explain everything. In fact, I've brought some scripts with me." He reached over to the chair next to him and handed her a thick manila envelope. "There are a week's worth of old scripts inside. Read them when you get home, so you can see what the format is like. I've also enclosed some outlines for future scripts."

"Outlines?"

"Relax. I keep them very brief, only about a page for each half-hour show.

"The outline specifies the action, so that the second writer—that's you, angel—understands what's supposed to take place in each of the five acts. Then all you have to do is write the dialogue to fit the action."

The waiter arrived with their drinks.

"I like the way you say, *all* I have to do is write the dialogue, as though it were that easy. I know it looks easy when you watch it, but I'm sure that it's a very highly skilled talent." She took a cautious sip of her martini. "Frankly, I don't know if I'd be any good at it."

"There's only one way to find out." He glanced at the menu. "Try the venison with red cabbage. It's terrific here. Would you like me to order for you?"

Iris nodded. "Order a lot of everything. I think I'm going to need all the strength I can get."

The food was very hearty, rich and filling, and the portions were enormous. Iris had not eaten so much in a long time, and it felt good for a change to be full. She'd forgotten how enjoyable food could be, how pleasant it was to share it with someone you liked.

"Do you want dessert?" Jamie asked. "Or just coffee?"

"Just coffee, please."

He ordered the coffee, lit another cigarette for her and asked whether she'd made arrangements to have Bergdorf walked.

"I spoke to the doorman about it on the way out, and ..."

It was a half-truth; she had tried to speak to the doorman but he was busy with one of the other tenants whose dishwasher was broken.

"And what did he say?" Jamie persisted.

Torn between embellishing the lie or having Jamie think badly of her, she chose the former. "He said there's a high-school girl in the building who walks dogs to make extra money, and there'd be no problem."

"Good." Jamie regarded her approvingly. "Then that's settled. It seems to me you're off to a damned good start, considering that you've been in New York less than twenty-four hours."

"Is that all it's been? I can hardly believe it."

"Maybe this move East is the best thing that could have

happened to you. I gather you were pretty inactive in Los Angeles."

"You gather correctly."

"Look, I'm sorry." He put a hand on her shoulder; she liked the feel of it. "I knew that you'd had a rough time, but I didn't realize how rough until last night at the restaurant. When you talked about your husband's infidelity. It must have been very tough for you."

"It was, but I'd rather forget it."

"Sure. The only reason I'm bringing it up is because I imagine I seemed pretty insensitive last night. The truth is that when you mentioned the other woman, it reminded me of one of the situations on 'The Troubled Heart.' The Elizabeth situation. You see, if we have Liz go to bed with Crawford, she automatically becomes the other woman. Will the viewers buy it? That's what I was wondering."

"I don't think so."

Jamie's voice was eager. "Why not?"

"It'd be all out of character. You would have to do a complete character switch on her."

"They're done all the time." He was talking to himself. "A terrible tragedy could befall her. Like a death in the family, someone very close to her. We could write in a mother. Or else we could show her gradually responding more and more to Crawford's interest in her, until it gets to the point where sheer passion wins the day. That would take some building up."

"Maybe Crawford lies and tells her that he's going to get a divorce, and she believes him."

"Hey, that's a possibility and it never even occurred to me. You see? Now you understand why I need a second writer. That's what I meant before, about your being off to a good start. You've managed to get a job and a dog-walker, all in record time."

"Please, Jamie. No pats on the head."

"Why not? You deserve them."

"I don't think so. I don't really have a job yet, only a job offer. And as for the dog ..." Why had she lied about something so trivial? "We always had a dog when I was growing up, and even if someone had had to walk him—which nobody did, because it was California—it would have been a family enterprise. The dog belonged to all of us."

"What you mean is that it wasn't any one person's responsibility. And now it is, and you don't particularly like it."

"Yes, that's what I mean." Iris stared at her blunt fingernails, wondering why they never seemed to grow very much. It must be her diet. "Responsibility is not one of my major virtues. . . ."

"You don't care about anything!" Ginger used to shriek. "Not your appearance, not your grades, not the way your room looks, not the way *you* look. Nothing means anything to you. Nothing matters. That's what you're involved with—nothing. What's going to become of you?"

"Obviously, I'm destined to be a great success."

"As what? An irresponsible slob?"

Iris did not know how to talk to her mother; they existed on different, alien levels of communication. It was easier with her father only because he didn't berate her so much, not because he really understood. Ginger screamed, Harvey was silent, but each in his own way was disturbed about their younger daughter's defiant lack of responsibility, and Iris could see that according to their standards they were right. Unfortunately, they had standards that meant zero to her. The fact that they were supposed to add up to a great deal didn't matter. She had never learned how to go along with meaningless abstractions. It was one of the few things in her life she was proud of. That, and having married Bob. She was proud of two negative accomplishments. . . .

"You're too hard on yourself," Jamie said after the waiter had brought the coffee. "You don't love yourself enough."

He spoke to her as he would to a child, and she felt tears begin to threaten her careful composure. If only he'd look at her the way he looked at Elizabeth last evening when they left that dreadful restaurant, when he kissed Elizabeth outside on the sidewalk. No man had ever looked at her that way. Maybe no man ever would. If she didn't love herself enough, as Jamie claimed, was it any wonder? Nobody had ever found her particularly lovable. She succeeded in keeping back the tears.

"I'll try to improve."

"Good girl."

A child, a girl, but never a woman. Why? It couldn't be her age. Elizabeth had looked like a woman when she was in her teens; it was as though she'd been blessed with some secret female knowledge denied to Iris. Even Ginger, as eccentric and imperious as she was, conveyed a similar knowledge that men seemed to recognize at once. Were they born with it? And if not, how did they acquire it? Although this was not the first time Iris had considered the subject, it seemed acutely pertinent at the moment because of Jamie. His undeniable attractiveness. His kindness. His concern about her. She felt like laying her head on his shoulder, fondly, possessively, as though they were lovers who couldn't bear to be physically parted for more than a few seconds. His sandy eyes would look down on her with adoring attention . . .

"Hey," Jamie said, breaking her reverie. "Do you want more coffee or shall we go?"

"Let's go."

At the corner of Lexington Jamie hailed a cab and Iris decided to walk home. The sunlight in New York was so thin compared to California, so pale and cheerless. She missed her house with the eucalyptus tree outside, she missed seeing all those handsome, suntanned faces that she used to make fun of. She missed the sight of brightly colored convertibles zooming along freeways, the people inside looking so carefree and relaxed. People here looked tense, worried, and almost by reflex Iris hugged the manila envelope to her chest. A disheveled man coming in the opposite direction was talking to himself.

"You buy, you sell," he muttered, passing her.

When she got to her building the doorman was alone, and she explained her problem about finding someone to walk Bergdorf twice a day. He was very agreeable and said he was sure it could be arranged. It seemed there was a former Picasso Towers handyman who walked dogs for many of the tenants.

"He charges a dollar a walk." This was the same doorman who'd been on duty when she moved in yesterday, the one who looked like a Boston cop. His name was Mike. "Why don't I have him give you a ring?"

"That would be wonderful. Can he call me today? I'm anxious to get this settled."

"Sure thing. Now what apartment did you say you were in?"

"I didn't, but it's 22-G. I'm subletting from the O'Reillys." She felt sure that the Irish connection would appeal to him. "They've gone to Los Angeles for a while."

"The O'Reillys?" He looked suspiciously at her, all signs of friendliness gone. "Okay, Miss. I'll see what I can do."

"My name is Iris Barnes."

But he had picked up the house phone, and paid no further attention to her.

Chapter Ten

"Okay, Mrs. Malaprop," the director said to Elizabeth. "It's not introverted, it's not inverted, it's a *retroverted* uterus. Got it?"

She nodded. "I'm sorry, Al."

"Just stay cool. And don't forget, we need four seconds." He turned to the actress who played Craig Crawford's invalid wife. "In Act I, I want to change a shot, so when you come wheeling in, go *past* Elizabeth and then say your line. Got it?"

It was three o'clock, and the cast of "The Troubled Heart" had just finished dress rehearsal. During the half-hour break that followed, the director (trailed by his faithful production assistant) went around issuing final corrections and advice, while the hairdresser, makeup man, and wardrobe woman, dabbed at the actors, brushed, sprayed, combed, sewed, straightened. In the background, doors slammed, cameras moved, technicians talked among themselves.

"Twenty-five minutes to air," the stage manager said.

Elizabeth's energy level had started to wane sometime around Fax 2, which was when her uterus scene began to take on the comic proportions of an "I Love Lucy" misadventure. It was one of the things she still had not conquered, her high, early-morning vitality peak which tended to go slowly downward as the day progressed, so that at three-thirty when the show was taped, her feeling of vigor was dangerously low. She had tried everything: dexadrine, vitamin C, eating lunch, not eating lunch, a chocolate bar after dress, getting up later in the morning; she had even relented and drunk a couple of containers of coffee prior to air, but nothing did the trick. Her internal clock refused to cooperate with the rigid time schedule of the show, and it was only sheer professionalism that kept her from blowing her lines every afternoon.

Today had been worse than usual. It started with the first reading of Act V, which included her and Mrs. Crawford.

MRS. CRAWFORD: Tell me, Elizabeth, have you ever been married?

ELIZABETH (stiffening): Yes, once. My husband died.

MRS. CRAWFORD: I'm terribly sorry. Do you have children?

ELIZABETH: No, I . . .

MRS. CRAWFORD: You needn't talk about it, if you don't want to.

ELIZABETH (quickly, nervously): I had a miscarriage. My obstetrician warned me it might happen. It had something to do with an introverted uterus.

Everyone in the rehearsal room cracked up because the word "introverted" had actually been used in the script by mistake.

"I thought the writers were supposed to hire research people for this medical stuff," one of the actors said. "What's Jamie Mann doing? Pocketing the money and pulling our leg?"

"I prefer an extroverted uterus myself," the production assistant said. "They're more fun at parties."

"It's obviously a typo." The director was still smiling. "Change it to 'inverted.'"

Elizabeth made the notation on her script and presumably the matter was ended. But when they were doing Fax 2, the actress who played Mrs. Crawford said, "You know, 'inverted' doesn't sound right either. I'm almost certain there's another word for it."

They ended up calling Roosevelt Hospital and were informed by a nurse in Obstetrics that although "inverted" could be used, it was considered more appropriate medically to say "retroverted." Since they were working without scripts at that point, Elizabeth made a careful mental note of this second change. But during dress rehearsal, she said "inverted" before she could catch herself, which was when the director corrected her, and Derek finally arrived on the sound stage as he did every afternoon before taping.

"What's all this about an inverted uterus?" he asked.

The director wearily explained the situation, and said that it had been cleared up thanks to Roosevelt Hospital's friendly information service.

"I must say that I appreciate everyone's medical interest," Derek told them, "but if the writer used 'introverted,' then that must be the proper word."

"Are you kidding?" the director asked.

"Not in the least, Al. We pay our writers damn good money to research this sort of thing, and if Mr. Mann wrote 'introverted,' that's what Mr. Mann must mean."

The director rolled his eyes at Elizabeth after Derek had walked off. "Our leader says to go back to 'introverted,' so back to 'introverted' we must go."

"But it's ridiculous."

"So is this whole show. So what? So we do it his way. Who'll know the difference in Joplin?"

"I wasn't thinking about Joplin. I was thinking about the sponsor."

"Let Derek think about that."

"Fifteen minutes to air," the stage manager said.

The director and production assistant went back to the control booth. "Don't forget," the director's voice came over the p.a. system, "we still need four seconds."

Elizabeth retreated to a corner of the studio to mumble her lines to herself, to be sure to remember that it was an "introverted" uterus once more, and to speed up her delivery because they were running four seconds over.

"One minute to air," the stage manager said.

Talking stopped, actors cleared their throats, tension came over cast and crew as the red studio-light flashed on. Elizabeth sailed through her few lines of dialogue in the first act without anything going wrong. Acts II, III, and IV went smoothly except for a door sticking when it should have opened. In Act V it really happened.

MRS. CRAWFORD: You needn't talk about it, if you don't want to.

ELIZABETH (quickly, nervously): I had a miscarriage. My obstetrician warned me it might happen. It had something to do with an introspective uterus.

The actress playing Mrs. Crawford was so startled that if it hadn't been for the teleprompter, she would have missed her next line. Derek was infuriated. Al, the director, was torn between amusement and annoyance. The second cameraman yawned, and the stage manager turned green. But it was not until Elizabeth had taken off her makeup, changed clothes and gone home that she thought of the one person who would have truly appreciated the blunder: Sheila O'Reilly.

"I love it. An introspective uterus." She could almost hear Sheila's husky voice. "What do you suppose it's thinking about . . . ?"

Sheila and Tom were still in bed, still recovering from the previous day's jet lag, their suitcases on the floor, still unpacked. The early California sunlight fell across the handsome patchwork quilt that had been one of Iris's favorite wedding presents. They huddled together beneath the quilt, conspiring like schoolchildren.

"We probably should have had the telephone disconnected," Tom said.

"Probably, but it would have seemed so rude. As though we didn't trust her."

"It's not her, it's them."

"I know, but she didn't disconnect *her* phone."

"Idiot." Tom kissed his wife. "She doesn't have a *them*."

"According to Liz, she doesn't even have a *him*."

"Are you sure that Elizabeth never suspected?"

"Positive. What she did suspect, though, was that I was two-timing you, amateur style, and the dear girl was shocked."

"That's marvelous. But I still don't like the idea of Iris receiving your phone calls."

"Sweetheart, don't worry about it. All the schmucks will fade away as soon as they find out that little Sheila has left town."

"Unless . . ." Tom sat up in bed and lit a cigarette.

"Unless what?"

"Unless they figure that Iris is taking up where you left off. They just might, you know."

"Beautiful! That never even occurred to me."

Tom started to smile, then they were both laughing, kissing, hugging, planning the day ahead.

"Let's rent a white Rolls Royce," Sheila said.

"And have lunch at the Polo Lounge."

"And dinner at Perino's."

"Join the Daisy."

"Clothes at Jax and Dorsos."

"Fred Astaire's tailor."

"We must hire a pool man immediately. Did you see that gook?"

They leaped out of bed and began to dance nakedly around the bedroom that Iris had cried herself to sleep in so many times.

"WE'RE IN HOLLYWOOD!" they sang. . . .

MRS. CRAWFORD: You needn't talk about it, if you don't want to.

ELIZABETH (quickly, nervously): I had a miscarriage. My obstetrician warned me it might happen. It had something to do with an introspective uterus.

It was Wednesday afternoon, and Jamie Mann sat in front of his color television set, on his Eames chair, in his expensive duplex at the Des Artistes, and heard his own words being twisted into moronic imbecility. Poor Elizabeth. She told him what had happened with all that change of uterus dialogue, and about Derek stupidly interfering at the last moment. *Introverted* (the typist's mistake) was bad enough, but *introspective!* It was so damned ridiculous that Jamie had to laugh, and he gave credit to the director for letting it go rather than stopping the tape and doing the whole scene over.

But then Al was a loose sort of guy; he didn't get uptight easily, he wasn't like Jamie, who by now was convinced he had an ulcer. He never should have drunk that beer yesterday at lunch with Iris, bad mistake. No. Stick to milk and one oatmeal cookie in the morning. Somewhere he'd read that that was the right diet for anyone with ulcer problems. Then he remembered that he hadn't read it at all, he'd written it himself in some long-ago episode of the show, the dietary information having come from one of his own medical researchers. Funny. There were times, Jamie dreamily decided, when it was a toss-up where the real soap opera was being played, on stage or off.

As soon as he heard the familiar closing sound of organ music he turned off the set and analyzed what he had just seen. Jamie made it a point to watch the tragedies in Jeffersonville each day, and in the two years that he'd been writing the series, he'd missed only one episode. That was when he first became involved with Elizabeth last April (or was it March?) and his sexual eagerness for her had temporarily blotted out his professional responsibilities. He and Elizabeth were making love and he was so engrossed in exploring delicious avenues of sensuality that he forgot what time it was. Only afterward did he realize his oversight.

"Shit. I missed it."

"Missed what, darling?"

They were still in bed. "The show. *My* show."

"Don't make it sound like such a tragedy. There's tomorrow, and tomorrow, and tomorrow. . . ." She was laughing. "Fifty-two weeks a year of tomorrows, in fact."

"It may be just another acting job to you, but this show means a hell of a lot to me."

"What does it mean?"

He hesitated, hating her for making him reveal his own worst fears. "Money. Security. Professional recognition. 'The Troubled Heart' might not be Macbeth (secretly he suspected it was as good), but anything that consistently entertains millions of people each week must have some merit, wouldn't you say?"

"Of course it has merit. Look at all the cake mixes, toilet paper, and dishwashing liquid it sells."

She was still laughing at him, enjoying the power that came with having grown up financially secure. Her self-confidence irritated and fascinated him. *She's only an actress,* he reminded himself.

"You'd better start being a little more respectful or I'll write you out of the script."

But at the time they both knew it was an idle threat. He was too taken with her sexually to take it out on her professionally.

"And you, sir, had better start being a little slower in your love-making, or I'll write you out of my life."

Another idle threat. For she was taken with him, too. Satisfied that they each had thrown a sense of fear into the other one, they eagerly became locked in a tender, passionate embrace.

Unlike other soaps, "The Troubled Heart" was always taped one day in advance, for which Jamie was grateful; he found it easier that way to catch every nuance of personality, suggestion of plot possibility, an off-beat note, than if more time were to elapse between taping and airing. Sometimes just the way an actor said a certain line was enough to give Jamie an insight about how best to proceed with that actor's characterization. On the basis of first watching the actor who played Craig Crawford, Jamie decided to turn him from a mildly corrupt politician to an insidiously corrupt one, with a private life to match. Unfortunately the actor, who was enjoying the luxury of earning approximately one thousand dollars a week (he'd done only one "Ironside" and two "Mission Impossible" shots before that), knew when he was hired that he was going to be knocked off eventually. They couldn't tell him exactly when because nobody knew, Jamie included. Fan mail had been so heavy ("He's mean, he's cruel, he's sexy," declared millions of housewives, "he must be punished!"), that everyone at the network agreed to milk the situation for as long as they could before having Crawford murdered. It had not even been established who the murderer would be, not yet.

But that was not what was bothering Jamie at the moment. The murderer could be any one of a number of people presently involved with Crawford in any number of different areas of his life, or perhaps someone not yet written into the script. No. Crawford was hardly the problem. Elizabeth was the problem. She was just too damned blah. And it wasn't her fault, she could only work within the confines of the innocuous dialogue that had been written for her, that *he* had written.

Jamie remembered what Iris said yesterday at lunch, that turning Elizabeth into the other woman would be unbelievable to the viewers, that they wouldn't buy it unless . . . but why should he listen to an amateur tell him what to do with one of his own characters? Especially when in this case the amateur was the jealous, frustrated, screwed-up kid sister of that very character? Or, rather, of the character that actress played?

He was starting to do it himself, confuse the two identities. Before Jamie began writing the script he'd heard all the stories about how soap actors and actresses were forever being stopped at places like Gristede's and Bloomingdale's and given blunt advice by strangers who addressed them by their stage names. At the time he thought it was amusing; he also thought those strangers must be idiots, but now he wasn't so sure. Watching a character evolve in a story, day in and year out, watching him cope with deaths, birth, divorces, marriages, parents, children, wives, mistresses, relatives, friends, enemies, illnesses, fears, *problems* . . . it made you feel you really knew that person, cared about him, could approach him, show concern, pity, anger, contempt, whatever the particular situation on the show seemed to warrant emotionally, morally.

Was it possible, was it even vaguely possible that he had become bored by the real-life Elizabeth because he was bored by Elizabeth on "The Troubled Heart?" It was a crazy idea, but what if it were true? Feeling a sudden stomach spasm, Jamie went into the kitchen for a glass of milk. If he had an ulcer, it was his own fault for becoming too caught up in his work. He had only himself to blame, and that went for his relationship with Elizabeth as well. But which Elizabeth? He had written the lines for the TV Elizabeth, he had made her boring on the show, unexciting, uninteresting, passive. Yet the Elizabeth he'd made love to two nights ago was none of those things, she was tantalizing, sensuous, quite alive. Then why had he begged off yesterday evening, saying he didn't feel well, lying about having a temperature of one hundred and one when there wasn't a damn thing wrong with him except his ulcer, and the fear of getting romantically involved?

He had to laugh at his own miserable cowardice. No one was forcing him to become involved. If he wanted to break it off with Elizabeth, all he had to do was tell her so and that would be it. Lunch at Lutèce or Perigord Park. *Crêpes farcies.* A few tears (hers), a few kind words (his), and it would be over. Then the fun could really begin. *What* fun? He envisioned himself surrounded by hundreds of admiring, adoring, enchanting women, all competing for his attention, catering to his most frivolous whim, striving to satisfy his every need. There was only one sour note: how could anyone satisfy him when he didn't know what the hell it was he wanted?

The telephone rang. It was Elizabeth calling from Saks, where she'd been shopping for a change.

"I just saw the show," he said. "It's a miracle none of you broke up after that 'introspective uterus' remark. I don't know how you managed to keep a straight face."

"Never mind that now, darling. How're you feeling? Do you still have a fever? Have you called a doctor? Do you need anything?"

"Feeling better, fever down, have not called doctor, and need only love. From you."

"Would you like me to come over?"

"Actually, Elizabeth, I'm very tired. I'm still not quite up to par."

"Nonsense. I'll prepare a light supper for the two of us, and then I thought we could watch television. One of your favorite movies is on tonight. The old, spooky one with Claude Rains."

"The Invisible Man?"

"Yes, that's it. Remember the part you liked so much, when he takes off the bandages and he doesn't have a face, or a head, or anything? But I'm going to stop first and pick up some groceries. I should be there within an hour."

He was trying to remember her as she looked in bed, tousled and desirable, but all he could see was her television counterpart, prim and puritanical.

"I'm afraid I won't be very good company."

She laughed, purred. "You're always good company. And besides, I'm dying to make love to you. I missed you last night."

"I'm not sure I have the strength."

"I have enough for both of us. More than enough. See you in a little while."

Jamie replaced the receiver and cursed himself. He was a phony, a hypocrite, a liar and a fool. But this call from Elizabeth had settled it. There was only one way to find out how he really felt about her, build up her role in "The Troubled Heart," get her sexually involved with Crawford, turn her into a roaring bitch. Then if he still weren't interested, he'd call Lutèce for luncheon reservations and get the whole schizophrenic business over with, but fast . . .

When Elizabeth hung up the phone, she felt more insecure than ever about Jamie's love for her. She could tell that he was cooling off, becoming evasive, and she didn't like it one bit. More to the point she wasn't used to it, and it made her nervous to feel this unaccustomed loss of control. She stepped out on Fifth Avenue and decided to walk awhile before catching a cab to Jamie's place. It wasn't so much that she needed to think, but rather that she wanted thoughts to come to her, pleasant thoughts, reassuring ones to shore up her ego, thoughts about Robert.

"Everything about you is exquisite," he said once. "How many times have you been told that before?"

"Thousands."

It was a beautiful summer evening and they were at the Malibu house, having driven out separately only about an hour before from Beverly Hills.

"And you're just the bitch to say it," he said. "Have you had many lovers?"

"No."

"Would you tell me if you did?"

"No."

"Good, because I don't want to know."

The sound of the Pacific was close. They were in his studio, the one that six months later was destined to explode into fire as a result of his own negligence.

"Why did you marry my sister?"

"I found Iris' innocence appealing. Refreshing. At first, that is. But innocence can be very deceptive, it makes demands that people like me can't meet."

"What kind of demands?"

"Boring ones. Iris expects me to figure out her life for her. She doesn't have the vaguest idea what to do with herself. She wants me to be the focal point of her entire existence, and I don't want to be that, not for anybody. It's too tall an order."

"But didn't you know all that before you married her?"

"I didn't realize how deep it went. Her dependence, I mean. Hasn't there ever been anything she wanted to do?"

Elizabeth was sorry she had started talking about Iris; she resented another woman being the center of attention (particularly her brat sister), but if she refused to answer Robert's questions, or if she answered unsympathetically, it would lower her esteem in his eyes. Men were put off by women who were too nasty toward other women. Invariably they sided with the woman who was being attacked even if they didn't say so. But they secretly loved it if you knocked other men. Rivalry was the name of the game.

"When Iris was quite young, she used to paint watercolors. Of movie stars, of all things. It was odd. She'd copy their pictures from fan magazines. I remember she once did something like a dozen drawings of Elvis Presley before she got him right. She wasn't bad but she never wanted to be a professional painter. It was just a phase she went through."

"That's funny. She never mentioned it."

"She probably didn't think it was important enough. You see, the only thing my sister really wanted was to get married and have a baby."

They were dressed almost identically: white shirts and blue jeans. Elizabeth wore sandals; Robert, tennis shoes. They were both so good-looking, and they both knew it.

"If I asked Iris for a divorce, would you marry me?"

The question caught Elizabeth unawares. Robert was fun, she loved making love to him, she loved being in love with him, but marriage was not what she had in mind. Just as she didn't want to marry a sculptor or a painter, anyone artistically creative for that matter: *she* was going to be the star in the family.

"I could never marry you." She looked away. "It would destroy Iris. She's been jealous of me all her life. In fact, if she ever suspected there was anything between us I don't know what she'd do. I don't even like to think about it."

"But she'll have to find out sooner or later. We can't go on meeting like this. It's crazy, this sneaking off into the night. It's degrading to the three of us."

Ginger, Harvey, and Elizabeth. It had been just the three of them before Iris was born to interrupt the tight-knit trinity. After her birth, things had never been the same again.

"It's not degrading for Iris because she doesn't know. You come out here to work, that's what she thinks, and it's certainly not a complete lie. She has no reason to suspect that you're involved with anyone, least of all me."

"I could always tell her."

It was the first moment of fear she had known since the affair with Robert began. "If you did that, I would never come here again. Never. What's more I'd deny the whole thing and Iris would believe me, because she would want to. So you see, you wouldn't gain anything. And if you really do care about me, as you say, you'd have a lot to lose."

"*Care* for you? I love you. Don't you know that by now? What's this polite crap about *caring*? Since when have we become so damned polite?"

Matters had definitely gotten out of hand. She didn't want Robert to be in love with her, not the kind of love he had in mind, the kind that involved serious, reciprocal feelings. All she had counted on was a nice, deceitful, irresponsible, sexy affair, with no commitments.

"I'm not concerned about losing Iris." He had started to pace the patio. "I told you, I'm not in love with her. I'm in love with you. My marriage to Iris was a mistake."

Stanislavski hadn't prepared her for nothing. "I wasn't thinking about your marriage. I was thinking about your career."

He stopped, uncertainly. "What about it?"

"Ginger and Harvey would never forgive you if you walked out on Iris. Certainly not now, when you've been married such a short time. They might think you married my sister for opportunistic reasons."

"But that's ridiculous."

"They might not see it that way. They were very happy when you and Iris eloped to Disneyland, she's been a terrible worry to them right from the start. Your coming along when you did, well, you might almost call it a miracle. And if there's one thing I can honestly say about my parents, it's that they're appreciative. Generous. Think of all the shows they're arranging for you in Europe. They've got some very exciting exhibitions lined up. I've seen the agenda."

"I didn't have to marry Iris to get into your parents' gallery, if that's what you're implying. I would have gotten in sooner or later. Or one of the other good galleries on La Cienega. I'm a pretty talented sculptor, in case you hadn't noticed."

"So are a lot of hungry guys in L.A."

Her hunch was right. He was ambitious as she. The difference was, he didn't know how to hide it.

"What the hell is that supposed to mean?"

She stood up and stretched, knowing he could see the outline of her breasts beneath her thin white shirt.

"Weren't you working as a counterman at that chili place when you met Iris? And living in a broken down crash pad? And wondering when you'd get your first cheap commission? Look, Robert, I don't blame you for latching onto my sister, it was a great opportunity and you took it. Then we met, and this happened. I'm glad it happened because I like you, but I'll stop liking you very quickly if you ever admit a thing to Iris. Is that clear?"

She could see the struggle on his face, but it didn't bother

her for a second. She'd won and she knew it. He knew it, too. He grabbed her.

"If I didn't want to fuck you so badly, I'd either smack you speechless or throw you into the Pacific, clothes and all."

"I have a much better idea. Why don't we get undressed and go for a swim? I've just thought of a couple of interesting things we could do under water."

PART III

Chapter Eleven

A cab nearly hit Jamie as he ran across Third Avenue in the Fifties, against the light. If there ever was a story conference he didn't want to be late for, it was the one this morning at the agency, the one he'd been looking forward to for more than a week now.

"Idiot!" the cab driver shouted.

But Jamie was safely inside the revolving doors of the glass and chrome and modern-art skyscraper, walking quickly toward the robot elevator that would take him to the twenty-sixth floor, where the ad agency had its executive offices. In honor of the occasion, Jamie had chosen his Meladandri shirt, Dior tie, and Bernard Weatherill suit. His shoes were English. The overall effect was one of contrast and smooth contradiction, exactly the effect he tried to achieve at these strategic periodic meetings.

They never knew what he was going to come up with, none of them, not the network representatives, not the sponsor, not the agency VPs; he invariably surprised them with a few carefully thought out twists for future story lines. At times he doubly surprised them with his ingenious, last-minute plot improvisations. And as he stopped off the elevator and approached the slender, blonde receptionist, he decided once more that today was going to be no exception to his well-established pattern.

"Good morning, Mr. Mann." Her tone was precise, but not uninviting. "They're waiting for you in the green room."

He thanked her by name and walked down the expensively carpeted corridor, smiling to himself. Little did they know what they were waiting for, all those overpaid, anxious executives. In addition to a few other tricks Jamie had up his expensive sleeve, he intended to see to it that when he left the meeting that afternoon, not only would it be unanimously agreed that Elizabeth was finally going to have her affair with Craig Crawford, but she was going to have the bitchiest, most flamboyant, most provocative affair ever seen on staid daytime television.

And as he opened the door to the green room, he realized, not without pleasure, that he had started to fall in love with her already: the new Elizabeth he was about to create.

Elizabeth spent the morning doing her nails and studying her next script, then she dressed leisurely, carefully, and decided to walk to Iris' apartment. She needed the exercise. Between acting in "The Troubled Heart" and her off-Broadway play, she had given up going to the gym; there simply was not enough time, and even though she worked out regularly at home, it was not the same as being pulled and stretched and slimmed and strengthened on those marvelous machines five days a week.

On Madison Avenue, a delivery boy on a bicycle said something obscene to her. Big pumpkin displays seemed to be in the windows of all the luxury food shops, alongside cardboard witches and the usual exotic specialty items. And another art gallery had gone out of business, a sign announcing that the premises were for rent. The only discrepant note was that there wasn't a construction worker in sight. Elizabeth started to cross over to Park and see how the doormen looked, another sure barometer of the daily beat in this crazy but fascinating city.

Iris had invited her to lunch and she was not looking forward to it. But having spent a good part of her life doing things she didn't particularly relish, she was prepared to take this one in her stride because of what she hoped to accomplish today. Not that it would be easy, dealing with Iris had never been easy, her sister was too unpredictable, too ruled by every passing emotion, and lately, too drunk. Still, the attempt had to be made. A great deal was at stake, professionally.

"How could you, you bastard!" Elizabeth had screamed, when Jamie told her that he'd hired Iris to help him write "The Troubled Heart." "Iris doesn't know anything about writing for daytime television. In fact, I'm not sure she still knows how to write her own name. Since she's moved to New York, she's loaded half the time and asleep the other half. How could you do this to me?"

"To you? I thought you were anxious for Iris to find a job. I don't understand your attitude."

"I'm still in the series, remember? Which means that she'll be writing my dialogue as well as everyone else's, as often as you let her, and you know how much Iris resents me. I have few enough lines to say as it is, but with my sister's help I'll be lucky if I ever get to open my mouth again. Now do you understand?"

"Hey there, slow down. Iris has been hired to write only what I tell her to, and that's all. She has no say in the plot development, that's strictly my territory. So stop worrying. Iris can't change a damn thing. I doubt that she would try, but even if she did, I wouldn't let her get away with it. And I'm not just talking about your part, I mean all the others, too. Since my partner kicked off, I've become the sole head writer of the show and I intend to keep it that way. Iris will be paid to follow instructions. Period."

"I hope you get your money's worth."

"I will. Why the hell do you think I hired her to begin with? No cutthroat tactics like I might run into from a real pro. No competition. No interference. Okay, baby?"

"Okay."

But it wasn't. Jamie didn't know Iris the way she did; underneath that helpless, drunken facade, there was a mean streak in her sister, a vindictive streak. And it was possible that Jamie would get careless in time. At first he'd read every word Iris wrote, assuming she sobered up long enough actually to write anything, but after a while he might become a little too trusting, a little too complacent, lazy. . . it was an easy thing to happen; it had happened to her. Months ago she would have believed almost anything Jamie told her, but since that conversation with Derek last week, she was no longer so sure about Jamie's true intentions. As much as she and Derek disliked each other, it was possible he had inadvertently let the truth slip out when he said that Jamie did not want to build up her part, that he was the one standing in her way, opposing the affair with Crawford.

The doormen on Park looked alert, they seemed to be standing straighter than usual. And by the time she got to Lex, two hardhats had suspended their shoveling long enough to give her an enthusiastic once-over. The omens were good. Very good, Elizabeth thought, as she approached Iris' building and saw an attractive man emerging from the lobby. He was wearing sunglasses and an elegant maroon velvet suit, with a French cut. There was an air of arrogant vitality about him. Because of the dark glasses, she couldn't tell whether he had noticed her but she wondered where he was coming from and where he was going.

"Bonjour," he said, as he passed her.

She raised her chin a fraction of an inch. The omens were positively delicious.

Iris was still recovering from the events of the last half hour when the doorbell rang. To her relief, it wasn't Elizabeth, only the man from the Chinese restaurant delivering the lunch she had ordered for herself and her sister. He entered the O'Reillys' living room and looked cautiously around, as though expecting to see a second person.

"Five times I have been in this apartment," he said, in what struck Iris as a very insinuating tone. "Yes. Five times. I remember."

As she was writing the check, Ken P. emerged from the bedroom in his dark glasses and maroon velvet suit. The Chinese man's eyes gleamed.

"Yes, yes. This makes six."

He placed the delivery bag on the O'Reillys' round table in the dining alcove, and smiled at Iris when she gave him a one-dollar tip. He had a gold front tooth.

"Enjoy your lunch. Good-bye."

Ken P. had to be off, too. It turned out he was an interior decorator who worked exclusively for the beautiful people (or so he claimed) and was on his way that very moment to discuss changes in bathroom lighting in the twenty-room apartment of a famous French banker who had a thing about ostrich feathers. Ken P. himself had another thing, equally strange, which Iris was still trying to comprehend. It was difficult, though, because not only was her head spinning as a result of the last half hour, but Elizabeth was due any minute and she had to pull herself together and try to act normal. If that were possible.

"Will phone," Ken P. said, "as soon as they split for North Africa."

He lived with his wife and her lover, or was it Ken P.'s lover and the lover's wife? Iris couldn't remember, but it had not been a happy arrangement for a long time, which was why he had looked up Sheila O'Reilly. One of his clients had given him Sheila's name, he'd seen her only twice, found her charming, when, *voilá*, suddenly she was gone and a new voice was at the other end of the telephone—Iris' voice. He had called that morning, waking her up.

"No, it's not Sheila," she mumbled, wondering if these anonymous calls would ever stop. "She's moved to Los Angeles. Can I take a message?"

For some reason, he seemed to think that was very amusing.

"It's Ken P.," he said, after a couple of insidious chuckles. "Are you free this morning? I'd like to see you at eleven-thirty."

"What about?"

"Yellow Dragon."

"Excuse me?"

"You are taking Sheila's place, aren't you?"

"Of course I am." Subletting Sheila's apartment, was what he obviously meant. "Why else would I be answering this telephone?"

"Exactly. Then you must know about Yellow Dragon."

"But—"

"It'll be the same deal as with Sheila. Same service, same delivery. Does that answer the question?"

"Not quite."

"You don't get many lobsters in one day, now do you?"

Ken P. Yellow Dragon. Lobsters. It was some kind of code, it had to be. Suddenly it made sense, all these mysterious, monosyllabic, and non-syllabic calls she had been receiving since moving in here. *Sheila O'Reilly was a spy.* A secret agent. But for whom? Which country? How important a spy? She might even have been a double spy. Counter-espionage. It was the first thrilling thing that had happened to Iris since Bob Barnes had relieved her of her virginity in that crummy crash pad off the Strip, and she didn't intend to let this opportunity for adventure go by unexplored.

"I'll be expecting you at eleven-thirty," she said, hanging up before he could say another word, or surprise her with another incriminating question.

She jumped out of bed and chose a lavender dressing gown with long, fluted sleeves and a high, Mandarin collar, figuring it was a smart choice in case Ken P. was working for the other side. After that she combed her thick blonde hair, brushed her teeth, put on some lip gloss and a little mascara, and sprayed well with Norell. That was in case he was working for this side.

Then she closed the door to the bedroom, which was a mess, and went into the living room to draw the blinds. She had a dreadful hangover headache and the light that streamed in every morning was anathema to her sensitive eyes. It would be better with the shades drawn, just in case anyone in the building across the way could look in and observe the transaction that was about to take place. But what kind of transaction? Maybe Ken P. would give her something, microfilmed secrets of strategic missile bases off the coast of ... or maybe *she* was supposed to give him something. That could prove awkward, dangerous, too, if he were armed as he was bound to be. Iris poured herself a large Bombay gin on the rocks and drank it down for fast courage. Then she chose some records at random and put them on the stereo, poured herself a second gin and decided she was ready for anything. At precisely eleven-thirty, Mike, the Irish doorman, rang her on the intercom.

"You have a guest coming up."

"Thank you."

No names, no identification. No wonder he had looked at her so oddly the afternoon she told him she was subletting the O'Reillys' apartment. Perhaps he was onto Sheila's real occupation, perhaps Mrs. Richmond was, too. What was it she had said to Iris: "Steak. That's your speed." It hadn't made any sense at the time. How could it? It was another part of the code. God, if only she had thought to call Mrs. Richmond a few minutes ago, but it was too late now for illuminating explanations or explicit instructions. She was on her own.

"Well, well," Ken P. said, when she opened the door. "This is a pleasant surprise. Now that we've finally met, I'm glad Sheila has dropped out."

"She hasn't actually dropped out. She just decided to move to California for a while."

"Same operation there, I guess."

"Naturally."

He seemed pleased. "I'm glad to hear that. We don't like to lose any of you super chicks, not good for the old morale. Sheila should do well in L.A. She's a real pro."

"So am I," Iris said bravely.

"I can see, I can see. Well, shall we get started? I don't have much time."

"By all means."

Taking her by the hand, he began to guide her into the bedroom. She was about to protest that it was a bit on the messy side, but no doubt there was a very valid reason why the transaction had to take place in here. The heavy drapes. Of course. Nobody could possibly see through them, or maybe he knew that the living room was bugged, or maybe—it was too scary—maybe he knew that the information she had for him was always kept in the bedroom. But where? If there was a secret hiding place, she prayed to God that Ken P. knew its exact location, that Sheila had shown it to him in case she got caught, because otherwise, serious international trouble was about to descend in less than a minute.

"What are you doing?"

Ken P. had sat down on the edge of the bed and was starting to take off his shoes. He looked up at her, and removed his dark glasses, revealing small, dark, suspicious eyes.

"You don't want me to leave them on, do you?"

She remembered reading about spies using fake soles on their shoes, in which to conceal whatever it was they were concealing. That meant he had something to pass along to her, and not vice-versa. Iris was so relieved that she could have cried on the spot, but she sternly reminded herself it was vital that she maintain her composure until this whole business was finished. After he left the apartment she could indulge her emotions as much as she liked; she could also decide then what to do with the microfilm. All of that, later. The main point now was simply to get through the job ahead, and not blow it.

"If you want me to leave the shoes on," Ken P. said in a more conciliatory voice, "I will. It's up to you, honey."

"No, no. Please continue. I'll be right back. I have to get something."

She ran into the living room and gulped down some gin from the Bombay bottle, praying her courage would not desert her, but when she got back to Ken P., it seemed as though all the gin in the world would be of no use: he was stark naked. It was then that fear struck. Stories of mad rapists and escaped psychopaths flashed through her mind. What if he were one of those?

"Whre is it?" he asked.

"What?"

"The rope."

"Rope?"

"I thought that's what you went to get."

Iris' fears dissolved. Any rapist worth his name was bound to carry his own rope, which had to mean that *rope* was the code word for microfilm. She was learning fast, but it was all so damned confusing. If she had the secret information, why had he taken off his clothes?

"I have something terrible to confess. I don't know where the rope is."

To her surprise, he wasn't angry. "I understand. You haven't been in this place long. I guess Sheila forgot to fill you in on all the details."

"That's right, but I imagine you know where she kept it."

"Sure. In the broom closet, on the top shelf, next to the Handi Wipes."

"Wait here."

Iris had never seen a piece of microfilm before. Still, it shouldn't be hard to identify. Broom closet. Top shelf. Yes, there was the dustpan and brush, a can of Lemon Pledge, a package of HandiWipes, and a long, thick coil of rope. Real rope. Click. The film was concealed within the rope. Elated by this brilliant deduction, she grabbed the coil and took it back to the bedroom where she proudly presented it to Ken P.

"You do it," she said, girlishly."

"What? Are you nuts? I can't do it myself. What the hell do you think I am, a contortionist? Besides, even if I could, it wouldn't be any fun that way. Now you just start tying me up or I'm putting on my clothes, walking out of here, and you know what that means."

Insubordination. Incompetence. Duplicity. Defection. She'd be murdered, or worse yet, tortured and then murdered. She wished she knew which side they were working for, it might make it easier. If it were the United States, maybe she could sneak into the living room and call the C.I.A. for help.

"Come on," he said, sharply. "Tie me up, then stick me in the closet for fifteen minutes. No longer. You can set the clock on the oven. It rings when the time is up. Got it?"

She nodded dumbly, drunkenly.

He lay down on the floor, crossing his arms on his chest.

"WHAT ARE YOU WAITING FOR?"

Iris had never tied a man up before, it wasn't as easy as it looked, particularly with him lying there so passively, not helping at all, but she just kept winding the rope around and around as tightly as possible until she got to his erect penis. The only other penis that she had ever seen was Bob's, and she found it interesting that this one was thinner and considerably longer. She decided to bypass it. By the time she had gotten to Ken P.'s feet, there was just enough rope left to make a neat knot.

"Good work," he said. "Now push me into the closet."

She went to the open closet door, which was only a few feet away from his prone body, and with a couple of energetic shoves she had him safe inside and the door slammed shut again. As she began to leave the room, his muffled voice called out:

"Don't forget about the Yellow Dragon."

In the kitchen she set the oven clock for fifteen minutes, then collapsed on the sofa, exhausted. Elizabeth was not due for another half hour, thank God. She should have Ken P. dressed, out, and well on his way by then. But what did he mean about the Yellow Dragon? Iris had never felt so ridiculously confused, helpless, stupid, tired, frightened, bewildered, and fascinated in her life. She closed her eyes for a moment of tranquility, and the next thing she heard was the oven clock's sharp ring.

"I'm coming," she called out, staggering into the bedroom.

"So am I."

"Ready. Set. Go." She swung open the closet door, and in a burst of improvisation, cried: "Yaaaah! I am the Yellow Dragon!"

There on the floor was a roped and writhing Ken P., sexually assaulting her favorite, ankle-length Rudi Gernreich skirt. And there wasn't a piece of microfilm in sight.

"You didn't wear the mask," he pouted, when he had finished. "But I'll give you the hundred anyway. I'm not a lobster for nothing."

Chapter Twelve

If Iris thought she'd her fill of surprises for the day, she was mistaken, as she soon discovered. The luncheon proved to be more than a little jolting, in more ways than one. Elizabeth was difficult under the best of circumstances, always the perfectionist, the self-appointed disciplinarian, the stern moralist, but today she turned out to be unpredictable as well.

It took Iris a few minutes to realize that beneath Elizabeth's cool facade, she was uneasy about something, anxious. Usually it was Iris who felt that way whenever she came face-to-face with her beautiful sister, but she was still too caught up in the weird encounter with Ken P. to feel anything as lukewarm as uneasy, at this point.

Her emotional state was far more flamboyant: stunned, hysterical, incredulous. She simply could not get her mind off what had just happened. She couldn't believe that it had happened. Worse, she didn't know what she was going to do about it. For now that she understood the true nature of the telephone calls she'd been receiving (spies, indeed!), she realized that she had to make a decision as to how she would deal with them in the future. When Ken P. walked out the door all she felt was immense relief that it was over, but several minutes later something told her she was not off the hook so easily. Not that she couldn't get herself off if she wanted to, ah, but that was exactly it. She wasn't at all sure she wanted to. Shocking. . . . And then before she had time to arrive at any conclusions, Elizabeth was there, punctual as always.

"Where did you get that lovely dressing gown?" were Elizabeth's first words. "I don't believe I've ever seen it before, darling."

"There are a lot of things you've never seen." She was thinking of Ken P. in the closet, a memory she was not likely to forget as long as she lived. "I mean, it's new. I bought it at a boutique in Beverly Hills, just before I left."

Until today, Iris had been with her sister only one time since that first evening they'd had dinner with Jamie at Nature's Oasis. That was the time she had gone to the off-Broadway theater, also accompanied by Jamie, to watch Elizabeth turn in a moving performance as a prostitute who was down on her luck. Elizabeth's acting talent was undeniable; and observing her up there on the experimental stage, Iris experienced the same mixed feelings of jealousy/envy/frustration/admiration/hatred/pride that went as far back as she could remember.

"You were just great," she said to Elizabeth afterward, when the three of them were driving uptown. "So was the rest of the cast. It's hard to believe that none of you get paid for being that good."

"We're not in it for the money. Half the cast is on welfare, and the other half either do TV commercials or work as waitresses, cabdrivers, anything they can get."

"Admirable," Jamie said. "Except for you. It seems to me that you have a rather lucrative job on a certain television series."

"The question is, how long will I have it?"

"As you yourself said, there's always welfare."

"That's not very funny."

Iris was glad when they got to her apartment building, she did not enjoy being caught between the two of them in their own private warfare. They said goodnight to her and continued on in the taxi. Once upstairs, Iris couldn't get to sleep, and ended up watching movies on television until sheer exhaustion knocked her out sometime near morning. Since then she'd spoken to Elizabeth on the phone several times, but because of her sister's busy schedule they hadn't had a chance actually to get together until today.

"I'm going to have to take you shopping." Elizabeth kissed Iris on the cheek and gave her a fond hug. "I can see that."

"But why? You just said the gown was lovely." Ken P. had liked it, too. He was probably planning new assaults on it the next time. Assuming there was a next time. "Or are you trying to spare my delicate feelings?"

"I never pay false compliments, if that's what you mean."

It occurred to Iris for the first time that her sister was one of the biggest liars she had ever met. Why hadn't she realized it before?

"The gown is fine for flopping around the apartment," Elizabeth went on, "but I suspect that your other clothes are all wrong for New York. It happened to me when I first moved here. I looked like a hillbilly the first few days, wearing all those California pastels. So I spent an afternoon at Saks and changed the image, and that's what you're going to do, darling. I'll help you. Today after lunch, if you're not busy."

"I can't imagine you looking like a hillbilly." She wondered what Elizabeth wanted; something definitely was on her sister's mind, and it wasn't clothes shopping. "As for Saks, thanks but no thanks. I'm not in the mood."

"Don't be stubborn. I know why you haven't been going out. You can't fool me. You don't have anything suitable to wear."

"Maybe I don't have anywhere to go." Besides, the most exciting things seemed to happen right at home. "I'm not exactly being deluged by dinner invitations. And as for the daytime, being a writer—if that's what I am—has certain advantages. Nobody cares what you wear when you're working. I can write naked, if I feel like it."

Elizabeth's eyes went to the empty typewriter on the O'Reillys' teak desk. "That's one of the things I wanted to talk to you about. Your writing. Have you been doing much of it?"

"I wrote two scripts. Didn't Jamie tell you?"

"No." Elizabeth had started to take off her suede coat, but stopped, seemingly stunned. "He never said a word." She proceeded to hang the coat in the hall closet, then came back and sat down on one of the tubular chrome chairs. "But that's wonderful, Iris. Marvelous. You must feel very proud of yourself."

"Not at all. I feel very frustrated."

What she wanted to say was that the work had proven to be as difficult as it was emotionally unrewarding. A little more than a week had passed since Jamie suggested she try helping him write "The Troubled Heart," and she was still very discouraged. Not just about her ability to succeed as a television writer, but discouraged about everything concerning her life in New York. She remembered all her old fears of moving East, how apprehensive she'd been that evening at the Polo Lounge when her parents first mentioned it. And those fears turned out to be more than justified.

New York was a nuthouse.

Nothing about it made any sense, and Iris would wake up each morning with the same sinking sensation of horror that, yes, she was here, yes, another day had to be gotten through, no, unfortunately she wasn't dreaming. Before opening her eyes she would sometimes think she was back home in her own bed with the patchwork quilt, in her own quiet house in the Hollywood Hills, and then Bergdorf would start to whine, or the ghastly police, fire, and ambulance sirens would start somewhere outside (she had never heard so many sirens in her life), and the whole nightmare of her present situation would hit her with renewed force.

What was she doing here, cooped up in an alien apartment, in an unpleasant city, with an unhappy dog, trying to fill in bits and pieces of dialogue for a soap opera, when it had quickly become apparent that she was not suited for the job? She knew she wasn't suited because even though Jamie did his best to be diplomatic, he firmly rejected the few, minor contributions she tried to make to the story line. He knew exactly what he wanted in each episode, and all he asked of her was to knock out his ideas as fast as possible and keep her advice to herself.

"Now, now," he said to her, only yesterday. "Let me worry about the situation between Elizabeth and Craig Crawford. That's not your concern."

"But when you hired me that day at lunch, you seemed interested in my suggestions."

"I am interested. I just happen to think it's a bit presumptuous of you to try to influence the plot so early in the game. You have to learn your craft first. Relax. In time, I'm sure that ..."

Of course he was right, it undoubtedly was presumptuous of her, yet who wouldn't feel frustrated under the circumstances? The fact that he paid her one hundred dollars a script hardly seemed to matter. To feel valuable, important, needed was what mattered. Money *per se* was not the point. Like Elizabeth, she had plenty of it, their parents had seen to that, but unlike Elizabeth, she had no talent. She'd never had any and she probably never would, and in a way she no longer gave a damn. To fall in love and have that love returned was what she wanted. All the corny, old-fashioned things that women didn't seem to care about any more. A home, a husband, children.

Plus a bed-life of intense sensuality. She'd been having so many fantasies on that score that she had sent away for one of those plastic vibrators that were supposed to be so sensational. It arrived yesterday, very white and virginal-looking, complete with extra batteries, but she hadn't yet worked up the nerve to try it out. The prospect seemed so obscene, a mechanical penis, when what she longed for was the real thing. Ken P. had the real thing, as her Rudi Gernreich skirt could well testify to. It hadn't done her any good, though. Not directly at any rate. Yet on some strange, indirect level, the encounter with Ken P. struck her now as being far from oppressive. She wasn't quite sure why. Perhaps because for once in her life she felt a measure of control; she was the one in command, he needed her. Or perhaps because there was an insanity about it that seemed to reflect the mass insanity in New York. At least the Ken P. variety had an element of grotesque humor, which was more than could be said about "The Troubled Heart," with its doleful emphasis upon tragedy and tears.

Instead she said, "I'm frustrated because I'm not sure that my scripts were any good."

"What was Jamie's reaction? He's the final judge."

"He seemed satisfied. He's going to have to fix them up in places, is what he said, but on the whole he thinks he can use them."

"Then why the long face? If I were you, I'd be thrilled. Encouraged."

"It depends on how things work out in the future." What if all the anonymous telephone calls suddenly ceased, now that her curiosity had been aroused? "It's much too soon to tell."

"Everything is going to work out just fine. Stop sounding so pessimistic."

"Realistic."

"That's a new word, coming from you. And I'm delighted to hear it. You see? I was right. This move to New York was just what you needed to snap you out of your lethargy. I can hardly wait to write Ginger and Harvey, they'll be so delighted."

"Please, Elizabeth. Don't do anything rash. Let's give it a little while longer."

"Whatever for?"

"To see whether I really have the knack."

"But that's where you're so lucky, Iris. Even if you find yourself floundering at first, you've got Jamie to help you, and he's the best there is."

"All the help in the world won't help, unless . . ." She was thinking again of the incident with Ken P., and how she had played it by ear. "It takes a certain kind of talent. It might look easy, but even with my limited experience I can see that it's an extremely tricky business."

"Which is why it's extremely lucrative."

And tax-free, too. "I suppose. But I'd still prefer it if you didn't say anything to Ginger and Harvey for a while. There's no point in getting their hopes up."

"Then you're going to stick with it?"

"Definitely."

They sat down at the O'Reillys' round dining table and began to spoon out the contents of the Chinese lunch that Iris had ordered. In between bird's nest soup, butterfly shrimp, and Moo Goo Gai Pan, Elizabeth continued to talk in the same optimistic, supportive vein that somehow reminded Iris of exactly the way she sounded on the show whenever she tried to reassure Craig Crawford that his invalid wife was bound to get well soon. Duplicitous.

"*Do you realize*—" Elizabeth paused for theatrical emphasis, "that this is the first time in your life you've ever taken anything seriously? Other than Bob, of course."

Bob seemed so long ago. In fact everything that had happened to her in her entire life, prior to the last week, seemed to belong to some remote sphere of hazy, ancient times.

"No," Iris said, half truthfully. "I had realized it."

Realized what, though? What was it that she was suddenly taking so seriously? Her ability to write "The Troubled Heart," or her ability to fill Sheila O'Reilly's shoes?

"It's true just the same," Elizabeth droned on. "I know it's taken you a long time, but there's no doubt in my mind that you've finally started to learn the value of hard work."

Was that what bothered her? The possibility that, as hard as she tried, it might not be the kind of thing one could learn? "Maybe you have to be born with it."

"Nonsense. Any reasonably intelligent person who wanted to apply herself could master it, I'm sure."

Iris wondered where Sheila O'Reilly kept the Yellow Dragon mask. Perhaps she'd taken it with her when she moved. After Elizabeth left, she would search the apartment.

"You're not eating, Iris. Is something wrong?"

"I have a terrible hangover." Just the smell of food made her ill, but she knew she had to try to eat. At least this was an improvement over canned ravioli, and all that other crap she used to force down her throat in Los Angeles. "I drank a fifth of Bombay yesterday." Not to mention the few belts she'd had that morning. "I found the most wonderful liquor store just around the corner. They deliver until midnight. Everybody in New York delivers. It's a whole new way of life." She cut a piece of butterfly shrimp in two, and bravely put half of it into her mouth. Then she chewed and swallowed, a major accomplishment considering how lousy she felt. "Mrs. Richmond gave me a list of all the places in the neighborhood that can't wait to come running over with your order. I figured it out, Elizabeth. If I wanted to, I wouldn't ever have to leave the apartment except to take the garbage to the incinerator and pick up the mail." She was rattling and she knew it. The manic phase had begun. "Although, if I paid Pepe a few extra dollars, he'd probably be glad to take care of that, too."

"Who is Pepe?"

"He walks Bergdorf. In fact, he's at the park with him right now, thank God. I got Pepe through the doorman. He used to be a handyman in the building, but they fired him for incompetence. He's a good dog-walker, though. He seems genuinely fond of animals."

"And you still seem to be genuinely fond of gin. I can't believe it, Iris, that you drank a whole fifth yesterday."

"Well, it's true. And I'm going to drink another fifth today. I ordered a case. They give you a discount if you do that. In fact, I think I'll have a quickie right now. I'd ask you to join me, but I know what your answer would be. Excuse me a moment."

When she returned to the table with a huge glass of Bombay on the rocks, Elizabeth seemed paler beneath her carefully applied makeup.

"I don't understand you, Iris. How can you write if you've been drinking? Doesn't it make your mind fuzzy?"

"No, it makes it crystal clear. The only time my mind is fuzzy is when I'm not drinking. Did you ever notice a funny thing about soap operas? They don't start drinking until "The Troubled Heart." And the good women only have a small sherry, if that. Although if something terrible has happened to a beloved member of their family, like murder or overnight blindness, they might be persuaded to choke down a fast brandy. For medicinal reasons, of course. Otherwise, forget it. I've made a study of drinking habits on soaps. They're very amusing. You can tell immediately who the heavies are, they all drink and smoke a lot. Like your boss, Mr. Crawford. As soon as I saw him with those awful cigars, I knew he was unscrupulous. And that bottle of Scotch he keeps in his office." Iris rolled her eyes. "No good will come of him, that's for damned sure."

"You sound like quite an expert."

"I'm trying, but there's an awful lot to learn." Such as, what the hell was a lobster? "Jamie pointed out something interesting the other day, something I'd never realized before. In spite of the fact that practically all the action in soap operas takes place inside people's homes, you never see a television set in any of them. What do you think of that?"

"Fascinating."

"It sure is, but you didn't ask why. Aren't you curious?"

"Very well." Elizabeth seemed to be getting more annoyed by the minute. "Why?"

"Because if the viewer sees a television set, she's liable to remember she's watching television, not real life, and apparently they're afraid—the sponsor, or the network, or both—that that would kill the whole, phony illusion. Jamie figured it out. He's quite smart, you know."

"It sounds like the two of you have been spending some time together."

Iris giggled. Drunk again. "It sounds like you're jealous."

"Just trying to protect my investment, that's all. Not that I don't trust you or Jamie, but a woman can never be too sure. Jamie is a very attractive man, and you're very impressionable. That could make for a dangerous combination."

"Elizabeth, do you realize that what you just said could be a speech right out of 'The Troubled Heart'? Here's a spooky thought: maybe if you play in a soap opera long enough, you begin to speak like one. Think like one. Did that ever occur to you?"

"No."

"Why not?"

"Because it sounds stupid."

"Not to me, it doesn't. It sounds very logical."

"I find it quite amazing, this sudden passion you seem to have developed for realism and logic. It's so unlike you."

"Perhaps I'm changing. That's what you wanted, isn't it?"

Iris wished the telephone would ring. This time she would be prepared. Surely not all of Sheila's clients were closet freaks. There were bound to be others, perhaps even weirder weirdos, and she couldn't wait to find out what variety of men would be willing to pay for her costly services, nor what she would have to do to earn the money. It did not seem likely that they all would be as easy to please as Ken P., and she supposed she should be glad that he was the first one. After tying him up, she never touched him again except to untie him, and he never touched her; and within half an hour she was one hundred dollars richer and a stranger was apparently a great deal happier. It seemed like a fair enough exchange. She wished she could tell someone about this interesting experience of hers, but it was out of the question. Who would believe her? Certainly not Elizabeth, and probably not Jamie. They would think she had lost her mind. Then she remembered her next-door neighbor, Mrs. Richmond. She would ring her bell as soon as Elizabeth left. Something told Iris that while Mrs. Richmond was no more of a spy than Ken P., she knew a few things that might prove very illuminating. The only problem was that Elizabeth seemed to have no intention of budging. Her annoyance of the past few minutes had shifted, a new mood was taking over, a different style, a more conciliatory tone; the actress was about to switch roles. If Iris had not seen this metamorphosis take place many times in the past, she would have been intrigued. As it was, she felt only vaguely curious about what Elizabeth had on her mind.

"We've had our differences in the past," Elizabeth began, choosing her words carefully, "but we are sisters, and surely that counts for something."

"I suppose so."

"Oh, Iris, you know so. All the things we've been through together over the years. Like when I had my nose fixed, and you used to go around singing that dreadful song. What was it called?"

" 'A Pretty Girl Is Like a Melody.' "

"That's the one. Or the time we stole Harvey's car and I taught you how to drive. Or when we were kids and we man-

aged to get that terrible German housekeeper fired because
she wouldn't let us eat Twinkies between meals. Remember?"

What Iris remembered most was how much she and Elizabeth used to fight, how Elizabeth invariably won, how furious
Iris had been at having to share Elizabeth with their parents,
particularly since Elizabeth had had them all to herself to begin with. Was that why Ginger and Harvey used to take the
side of their older daughter? Because Elizabeth had been
their first-born love? Pillow fights would turn into hair-pulling
fights. No matter what Iris did, her sister was always older,
stronger, bigger. Elizabeth once cut up one of her favorite
dolls and then denied it, saying that Iris had done it herself in
a moment of jealous rage. *How could you,* Ginger asked Iris,
you bad girl?

"In our own way, we've always been very close," Elizabeth
was saying. "And that's why I know you won't let me down,
now that I need your help."

Help! was what Iris had screamed, when Elizabeth pushed
her into the swimming pool before she knew how to swim.
Fortunately, it was the shallow end, and their nursemaid,
who was sunbathing a few feet away, opened her eyes just in
time to safely fish out the five-year-old girl. Ginger was never
around then, except to tuck them into bed at night and make
sure they said their prayers. Iris had always been convinced,
in later years, that if they hadn't had separate rooms, Elizabeth probably would have killed her in her sleep.

"It's about 'The Troubled Heart,' and that bastard, Jamie
Mann." To Iris' amazement, Elizabeth had begun to sob.
"He's trying to get me fired, and you're the only person in
the world I can turn to." Her mascara had started to streak.
"I WANT TO KILL HIM!"

Better him than me, Iris thought.

"Of course, I'll try to help you," she said, holding back a
triumphant smile. "Just tell me what I can do."

Chapter Thirteen

"I'm decidedly against it," Derek said to the men gathered at the conference table. "As I've indicated before, I don't believe the change would be believable."

"I agree," the sponsor's representative said. "And even if it could be made believable, in terms of some trumped-up character motivation, I think our viewers would seriously resent it. They'd clobber us. Up until now she's been presented as a nice girl, decent, respectable." He hesitated, searching for a more convincing word. "Reserved. On the demure side."

The agency supervisor jumped in. "Virginal."

"Precisely," Derek said. "Despite the fact that she's a divorcee. She's one of those virginal-looking divorcees, as opposed to the other type."

The agency man continued. "We can't go around turning decent, respectable women into tramps overnight, and that's just how she would appear if we suddenly have her hopping into bed with Crawford. Not only is he too old for her, but he's married, and he's involved with the syndicate. My God, we're trying to sell wholesome food products to a supposedly wholesome group of eighteen- to forty-nine-year-old housewives. You just can't get away with that kind of role switching and still expect the viewer to march into her local supermarket and pick up our sponsor's products. At least that's how it looks to me from where I sit."

"Virginal is exactly the point." At these meetings, Jamie always bore in mind that his contract could be canceled every thirteen weeks, no security there; on the other hand, he could cancel too, simply by pleading insanity. "Remember *The Moon Is Blue?* 1953. And the censorship crap that Preminger had to contend with, because the word *virgin* was actually used on an American screen for the first time? That's where we're stuck, gentlemen, in 1953, and we're going to continue to be stuck there in terms of ratings unless we wake up and realize that this is twenty years later and the world has changed."

"I've always wondered whatever happened to that little actress who played the lead in the movie," the sponsor said, drawing concentric circles on an initialed memo pad. "She disappeared overnight, as far as I can recall."

"That's what will happen to us, unless we wise up." Jamie glanced at the Piaget watch that Elizabeth had given him for his birthday last month. It was twelve-thirty, and he was just really beginning to attack. "Look at our opposition. You've got a dumb game show on one network, so dumb that it's consistently beaten us in ratings for the past season. And the new soap on the other network is rapidly gaining ground. Do you know why? Because they're dealing with more volatile themes than we are. Drug addiction, abortion, women's lib, racial problems, teen-age sex. They're stealing our viewers by exploring more timely subjects, or at least making a stab at it."

"Our ratings did jump a couple of points," the sponsor admitted, "when we dramatized that marijuana situation last year. But of course we had the guy clearly shown as an unscrupulous hippie type. It was obvious from the start that he had an antisocial mentality. Whereas with Elizabeth, I repeat, we have a decent, respectable girl from a supposedly decent, respectable family. How do we turn her into a bitch and not expect to lose substantial sales?"

"I'll tell you how," Jamie said. "She's not going to be a bitch. She's going to be a victim of circumstances. A very sympathetic victim."

The slender, blonde receptionist came in to announce that luncheon would be served momentarily. The agency supervisor thanked her and turned his attention back to Jamie, as did the others.

"What we do first of all is give her a mother. Make the mother materialize, that is. We could sign up some aging character actress who's down on her luck, but used to be pretty hot in the old movie days. The mother's been living in Seattle or someplace like that for the last seven hundred years, but now she decides to come to Jeffersonville to visit her only child."

"Seattle is a lousy market," Derek said. "Besides, why does she choose this particular time to put in a motherly appearance?"

"Because she's dying."

"Of what?" the sponsor asked. "You've got to be careful about death. It's anxiety-making."

"Sickle-cell anemia. It's hereditary, you know."

"But that's a notorious Black disease," Derek protested. "Don't tell me that you're planning to give our nice, respectable Elizabeth a Black mother, in addition to an immoral affair with a married politician old enough to be her father. We'd end up with a 'one' rating. That's if we were fortunate. More likely, we'd all be chopped into small pieces and fed to the contestants on our opposition game show."

"The mother will be quite white, WASP, and widowed. The stoic type who doesn't want her daughter to know how ill she is, but does want to spend her last days with her. As for the sickle-cell anemia business, don't forget we have a sizeable Black audience, and our point will be—never overtly stated, but undeniably implied—that Blacks aren't the only ones afflicted with this unfortunate disease. True, they're in the majority, but whites aren't completely immune to it either. A very democratic touch, don't you see? Elizabeth's mother's condition will stand up as valid after I substantiate it medically, so don't worry about that part."

"Okay," the sponsor said. "So now she's got a mother with a creepy minority disease. Now what?"

"We milk this unfortunate situation for as long as we can, it will be very touching, very sad, lots of pathos possibilities. Elizabeth is all the family this poor woman has in the world. Her husband died years ago."

"Not of the same thing, I trust," Derek said.

Everyone laughed, including Jamie, who knew Derek was trying to trap him, intimidate him, humiliate him, and keep Elizabeth's part at its present minimal status. Whatever it was that Derek had against Elizabeth, at least it wasn't the knowledge of her relationship with Jamie. Thank God for that. Jamie shuddered just at the thought of Derek ever finding out. The Englishman's arrogance would be even more unbearable than it already was.

"We do a flashback on the father," Jamie went on. "We make him a strong, gutsy, outdoor type, very appealing. Masculine, but gentle. Let's see. Seattle. He was drowned in a boating accident, something tragic like that. Cut down at the height of his manhood. His widow has had to raise Elizabeth by herself; more sympathy builds for both mother *and* daughter. Okay. Now for weeks or months, depending on how long we can effectively interweave this with our other plot lines, Elizabeth remains in the dark about her mother's condition until the symptoms start to become too obvious."

"What are the symptoms?" Derek asked.

"Abdominal pain, leg ulcers, general feeling of debilitation. This disease is often mis-diagnosed, which is what makes it so tricky; the symptoms could be applicable to many other illnesses. That's why it's so perfect for our purpose, because it's not immediately apparent to Elizabeth what's wrong with her mother. It could be any one of a number of things. They have to do tests at Jeffersonville General Hospital. We could go on with this one for an entire year, if we wanted to. Maybe work in a hospital romance on the side. But in the upshot we have our brilliant resident doctor make the correct diagnosis, and he breaks the news to Elizabeth, who by now is in pretty bad emotional shape as a result of all the suspenseful waiting. The mother dies. Elizabeth cracks up. You name it, she's got it: sorrow, misery, guilt, loneliness, and *fear*. Remember, the disease is hereditary. We play this up for all it's worth. She's scared stiff. She needs comfort, tenderness, a kindly shoulder to cry on."

"Craig Crawford's shoulder, I assume," Derek said, looking trapped at last.

"Right. And we go a few steps further. Don't forget that Crawford's wife is an invalid herself, paralyzed, confined to a wheelchair. When Crawford realizes the extent of Elizabeth's vulnerability, he tells her that an operation is being planned for his wife, one that hopefully will make her able to walk again. As soon as his wife is cured, he says, he can divorce her and they can be married. That's the clincher. Crawford's promise of marriage." The fact that he had stolen this last idea from Iris didn't bother Jamie in the least. Wasn't that what subwriters were for? "Elizabeth believes him precisely because she is decent and respectable, and therefore assumes he is. Besides, she's been hung up on the guy for a long time now. She wants to believe him. So, on a Friday show we finally have her succumb to his conniving charms. Does that make her a bitch? Does that seem out of character with the Elizabeth we've known all along? No, it shows her in a new and different light, a woman who suddenly needs to be loved, a woman caught with all of her defenses down."

"Not to mention her tights," Derek said.

"I still don't know about the sickle-cell stuff." The sponsor looked worried, but Jamie could tell that he had capitulated, as had the others. They knew a grabby situation when they heard one. "It might sound too patronizing. Know what I mean? As though we were trying to cut in on the Blacks' medical territory."

A low cholesterol, low calorie luncheon was wheeled into the room by a young Black woman in a starched uniform. She gazed impassively at the men seated at the conference table, served the meal, asked if anything else was needed, was told no, that it was all fine. Then she left.

"What we have to do," Jamie said, when the door had closed behind her, "is get back our ten million wholesome viewers. When you stop and think that daytime programming is the major profit area in network television, what's one lousy case of sickle-cell anemia if it's going to result in the hottest bit of adultery ever seen on a half-hour soap? Patronizing? Not at all. I say it's humanizing. Equalizing.

"And I'll tell you something else. There's an audience out there we haven't even tapped yet. Not the traditional peanut-butter-buying housewife, although God knows I'm not putting her down, but soaps are starting to become an underground status symbol among better educated people in urban areas more than any of our surveys have shown to date. And these people are sick of the typical one-dimensional characterization, like the good women versus the bad. They understand the appeal of ambivalence, the appeal Elizabeth will have after she makes it with Crawford. Numbers, gentlemen. We're in the numbers game. We're selling thirty minutes of advertising a week at eleven thousand dollars a minute. How many people do you want to be looking at those thirty commercial minutes? Elizabeth and Crawford will pull in the numbers, I guarantee it."

"Bette Davis, P.G. Wodehouse, and Van Cliburn admit to being soap addicts," the sponsor said. "So was Tallulah Bankhead before her unfortunate death. But they're celebrities. It's a different bag."

"How do we know that Bette Davis doesn't like peanut butter?" the agency man said. "Or Wodehouse, for that matter? Who's to say?"

"Sometimes I wish I were back producing prime evening

TV." Derek looked wistful. "One variety or crime show a week, and the guidelines were a damn sight more clear cut."

"So were the financial losses," Jamie pointed out.

Then they began to eat.

Chapter Fourteen

Even now, seconds after Elizabeth's hysterical outburst, Iris could not believe that her sister's fears of being fired from "The Troubled Heart" were justified.

"Of course, I'll try to help if I can," she said, feeling important and needed for the second time that day. "But it doesn't make any sense. Jamie loves you. Why would he want to do such a terrible thing?"

Elizabeth wiped her eyes, which were blurry with tears. "Maybe it's not Jamie, maybe it's Derek Christopher. Maybe it's both of them, I don't know. All I do know is that something funny is going on, and I don't mean amusing. There's a story conference being held right this very minute and one of the decisions that's going to be reached will involve the part I play in the series. And frankly, Iris, I'm afraid of what that decision will be."

They were still seated at the luncheon table, bravely trying to make the best of the Chinese food before them, neither succeeding too well, Iris, because of her hangover, and Elizabeth, because of her tearful distress.

"Why does that name sound so familiar?"

"What name?"

"Derek Christopher."

"Because you've seen it on the credits. He's the show's producer, the rotten English bastard. On the other hand, maybe it's the sponsor who wants me out. Or the agency guy. They once canned an actress on another soap because there was a shakeup in agency personnel, and the new man decided that the actress was too young-looking for the part. She wasn't. He was just trying to throw his weight around."

The way Elizabeth had thrown hers around when they were children. "I still don't see what I can do. You yourself just said that your fate was being decided right now."

"True, and there wouldn't be a damn thing you or anyone else could do if I'm going to be written out altogether. But they might compromise and agree to leave me in, strictly as a foil for Craig Crawford. 'Would you like another cup of coffee, Mr. Crawford?' Even Geraldine Page wouldn't get far with lines like that, not unless she took off her clothes and did a double somersault at the same time. That's where you enter the picture, Iris."

"Where?"

"With Jamie, of course."

This had been one of the most confusing days Iris had ever spent. "I don't get it." She hadn't gotten the microfilm either, because it didn't exist. Maybe this conversation with Elizabeth didn't exist, maybe she was dreaming it. Or maybe she had dreamed up Ken P. and the Yellow Dragon.

"You're helping Jamie write the show, aren't you? You said you've done two scripts already and that he liked them, which means you'll be doing more in the future."

"So?"

"So you're not exactly uninfluential. It wouldn't have to happen all at once; you could be subtle about it, lead up to it gradually. As time goes on and you continue improving in your work, and I'm sure you will, Jamie will become more and more dependent upon you. Just as he was on his late partner, even though he hates to admit it. And at that point, if you told him you thought it would definitely strengthen the show for me to have the affair with Crawford, he very well might be persuaded to listen to you. Now do you understand?"

So this was why Elizabeth wanted to have lunch today. She might have suspected that her sister's motive would not be a social one. Manipulation. Elizabeth was good at that. Iris knew she should be angry, yet in a backhanded way she admired Elizabeth's deviousness, her single-mindedness, her sheer determination to triumph no matter what the odds. She admired all these traits because she possessed none of them herself.

"Jamie can't be expected to listen to me on the subject," Elizabeth said. "He would think I was using him sexually to get my part built up. That's why my hands are tied, because of my personal involvement with him, but yours aren't. They're absolutely free."

"How can you say that? I'm your sister. Wouldn't that make it awkward for me, as well? To show favoritism toward you?"

"No, because Jamie thinks you hate me. Which means that he'd be very apt to take you seriously."

"I'll do the best I can." She wondered if she meant it. She wondered where Jamie had gotten the idea that she hated Elizabeth. From Elizabeth? "But I think it's only fair to warn you. Don't start counting your chickens. It might take a while, and even then I'm not sure I could do anything for you."

Elizabeth's mouth tightened. "Why not?"

"Jamie doesn't want my suggestions. I tried to give him a few ideas the other day, they were only minor things, but he became very cold. He told me not to be presumptuous, said that I should learn my craft first. And I suppose he's right. What do I know about this business, anyway?"

"Well of course you have to learn your craft, that goes without saying." Elizabeth's suspicions had relaxed; she was back to seduction. "But it doesn't mean you might not have a worthwhile contribution to make right now, in terms of the story line."

"How do I know it was worthwhile? Jamie didn't think so."

"That's typical of you, Iris. You always take the negative approach. Downbeat. As your sister, I find it very depressing. And I'm not just talking about this particular situation. I mean your lack of self-confidence in general."

Unfortunately, Elizabeth was right. She'd never had the strength of a single conviction in her life, not unless another person seconded the motion. It was as though, by herself, none of her beliefs seemed to count for anything.

"You're lucky," she said. "You have enough self-confidence for the two of us."

"Napoleon said that luck was a matter of intelligence. It's an interesting remark, don't you think?"

"I have the feeling you're trying to tell me that I'm not very bright."

"There you go again. Please don't be silly, Iris."

"It's not silly, though, is it? The fact is that I'm not very bright, I'm not very attractive, and I'm not at all talented."

Except when it came to Yellow Dragons. "I suppose it's no wonder that aside from Bob, no man has ever been interested in me. And Bob's interest sure didn't last long."

"You never gave anyone a chance to be interested. Don't you realize that you've secluded yourself all your life? Before your marriage nobody could get you to go anywhere, and during your marriage you'd be hiding in some corner whenever and wherever I saw you. At parties, the tennis club, the beach, even openings at the gallery, where you should have felt most at home. Of course Bob's death must have come as a terrible shock, but it was no reason to lock yourself in your house and live like a hermit for a whole year. Ginger told me that you practically never went out."

"It was better than having to face people. I was always afraid they'd be laughing at me."

"Laughing? Why?"

"Because of the other woman. I never knew who she was. I still don't. Maybe nobody does, but how could I be sure? It was easier to be alone, less humiliating." She did not expect Elizabeth to understand what it was like, the fear of being ridiculed behind one's back. Ridicule was something Elizabeth had never had to live with. "Even though it's all over now, I still wonder who she was. I'll probably never find out, yet I can't help wondering."

"Just last week you said you didn't care, that her identity didn't make any difference to you."

Iris remembered the conversation. "I know I said it, but it's not true. I've tried to convince myself I didn't care; it was easier that way. That's the other thing I don't have, guts. If I did, I would have made it my business to find out who she was and put a stop to it. However—no brains, no looks, no talent, no guts. If it weren't so pathetic, I'd laugh."

"I'm going to tell you something, and you had better listen." Elizabeth's voice had changed into hard certainty. "It's disgraceful, the opinion you have of yourself, the way you're constantly demeaning yourself, running yourself into the ground. Good God, Iris, don't you have any pride either?"

"Pride stems from accomplishment. I haven't accomplished anything to be proud of."

"Is that why you're slowly drinking yourself to death?"

"Probably. No self-esteem. All those therapists I went to knew that was the problem, but they couldn't help me do anything about it. We never got to first base. That's why I finally gave up. I decided I was beyond help, it was just a waste of everyone's time. I went to five of them, you know. All with different approaches, different tactics, different theories. Directive, nondirective, Reichian, Jungian, existential, I even got into Scientology at one point. That's where you become a 'clear.' "

She laughed in bitter memory of those endless grapplings with herself. "I was too muddy to become a clear, it would have taken the rest of my life. I didn't think it was worth it. I didn't think enough of myself to bother. And obviously, I still don't."

Then Elizabeth said something that stopped Iris cold.

"But you're brilliant."

"What?"

"I said you're brilliant. I've always thought so. I admit it's a strange kind of brilliance, it doesn't focus on anything except self-destruction, it takes no positive shape. And that's what makes it so sad. You've never figured out what to do with it, except pour another drink and pity yourself, you damned fool. Don't you understand anything?"

"In addition to all my other deficiencies, I think I've lost my marbles, too. Either that, or my hearing. You can't possibly be serious."

"I'm serious, all right. You just can't stand an honest compliment. You never could."

"Is that why you've never paid me one before?"

"I have, but you wouldn't listen. You want to believe the worst about yourself, because that way you needn't try to accomplish anything. You can sit around, wallowing in your misery. Ever since we were kids I've known you were basically smarter than me. That's why I always worked harder, all those dancing and singing and acting lessons, all that ambition, determination to be successful. What you don't realize is how hard I have to work, how much effort I put into everything I do."

"Whereas I put no effort in at all."

There were tears in Elizabeth's eyes again. But who was she crying for? Herself, and the thought of all that effort? Or Iris' unfortunate lack of it?

"Why didn't you ever tell me this before?"

"It's not an easy thing to admit. It hurts too much."

The concept of Elizabeth being hurt was a concept foreign to Iris. Outside, another police siren (or was it an ambulance?) started its hysterical, piercing, shrieking scream for the millionth time since she had moved into the O'Reillys' crazy apartment, and Iris felt as though she were an integral part of that siren, one unending scream that would not, could not make up its mind how, or when, or where to finish.

"If it hurts so much to admit," she said, "why did you decide to do it now?"

What she meant was: "Why now, since you've successfully managed to ruin my life for twenty-three years?"

But even that was a lie. Elizabeth hadn't ruined her life. Ginger and Harvey hadn't ruined her life. Bob hadn't ruined her life. She had ruined her own life through cowardice and self-indulgence; still she couldn't swallow the responsibility for it. No. She had to find someone to blame, although (asked the muse) how could she be sure it actually was ruined? Terribly melodramatic. She'd been watching "The Troubled Heart" for so long that she had become like Elizabeth; they both were emulating its maudlin tone of endless catastrophe. And yet, wasn't that what the last twenty-three years had been for her? Endless, unremitting catastrophe. Yes, it was imperative that she find someone other than herself to blame for it. Anyone. Ruined! It was much easier that way, delicious, sweet. But by telling her that she was brilliant, Elizabeth had refused to accept the burden of blame. How neatly her sister managed to wiggle out of the hot seat, how cleverly.

"Why *now*, you ask?" Elizabeth was looking out the window, something having caught her eye. "I'm not quite sure. Maybe because you seem so down, when you have all the reason in the world to feel encouraged, a career to look forward to, a fantastic city to explore, people to meet, the beginning of a new life. Or maybe it's because it's about time someone tried to get through to you. I could never bring myself to do it before this. It's not an easy thing to admit, that you've been jealous of your own sister for as far back as you can remember."

"That's very funny." Iris could feel the butterfly shrimp turn over in her stomach. "Hilarious, in fact. You've been jealous of *me*."

"Yes, in a way. In the way I just described. Did you know there's a whole pigeon colony on that rooftop over there? They're all lined up in perfect formation."

"I'm not interested in pigeons. I'm interested in jealousy, since you raised the subject. What about *my* jealousy?"

"What jealousy?"

"You must be kidding, Elizabeth."

"I don't know what you mean."

"You were always the beautiful one, the glamorous one, the talented one, the sexy one, the favored one. Do you suppose it was such a breeze growing up in your shadow? Even if now you suddenly decide to announce that during all those years you spent ruining my life, you secretly believed I was brilliant? Brilliant, my ass. Do you think that that changes anything? Do you think you can buy me off so easily?"

Elizabeth had stopped looking at pigeons; now she looked down at her plate. "Why would I want to buy you off?"

"Guilt."

"I have nothing to feel guilty about."

"Don't you?"

"No. And what's more, I don't like ambiguous conversations. If you have something on your mind, please tell me what it is."

Iris watched her sister, marveling at how quickly her uneasy expression of a moment ago had changed to one of calm, regal composure, how miraculously Elizabeth seemed forever dressed for whatever role she was about to assume. It was a knack she'd had since childhood, that uncanny ability to be wardrobe-prepared for the upcoming scene. Today her outfit was ingenious, as usual (and yet, how could she have known in advance what to wear, unless somehow. . . ?). A cashmere sweater set; a short-sleeved pullover and a long-sleeved cardigan. Iris remembered the set well, it was lovely, cocoa-colored like Elizabeth's hair, so simple, so unassuming, so innocent. But Iris refused to be fooled. There were two of them, that was the point. Maybe she was brilliant after all. Something that Bob once said to her came to mind:

"You have no guile. You wouldn't understand."

"Understand what?"

He merely shook his head. "Don't try."

At the time, she thought he was talking about his work, the frustration of all those years of repeated attempt for acclaim, and repeated failure, and perhaps wanting to tell her (but ashamed to) that one of the reasons he'd married her was because of the break he hoped to get with her parents' prestigious gallery. She had longed to say, "Please don't feel guilty. I know you love me. I know that one of the reasons you married me was because of the gallery. I don't blame you for it. Just as long as you love me."

But she couldn't say it. She didn't want to embarrass him by verbalizing his motives, exposing them. It was only a year later, when he died, that she knew it wasn't one of the reasons he'd married her; it was the only reason. In light of everything that had happened during that year, what other reason could there have been? She had to stop thinking about Bob. A fifth of Bombay a day. Another wave of hangover nausea came over her. She had to stop drinking, too. She had to stop hiding. The typewritten list she had found that first evening. Suddenly she remembered hiding it in the top bureau drawer.

"What do I have to feel guilty about?" Elizabeth persisted.

Iris was wardrobe-prepared too, in her Mandarin gown and Norell cologne. The victimized widow, television writer, and Yellow Dragon expert. The words *Yellow Dragon* were on that list.

"I have a hunch you knew all along who Bob was having the affair with, and that you've just been trying to spare me. Well, I don't want to be spared. If you know who she was, there's no need to go on feeling guilty about keeping it a secret. Just tell me and get it over with. I won't drop dead."

"Iris, you're incredible." Elizabeth was laughing now, a fond, sisterly laugh of relief. "Nobody could make you up in a million years."

"What's incredible about me?"

"Your memory for one thing. It's so erratic. Don't you remember that I didn't even know there *was* another woman, until you yourself told me so last week? It was the first time I ever heard of the whole sordid business."

Elizabeth was right. She had forgotten. The alcohol was starting to affect her brain. "I'm sorry, Liz. Forgive me for accusing you. I guess I'm grasping at straws."

"There's nothing to forgive. I'm just sorry you were subjected to such a dreadful experience, but you have to forget it. It's over and done with. You must keep telling yourself that. If you don't, you'll go crazy."

"I can't forget it. There was a song Bob used to sing whenever he'd come home after seeing whoever he was seeing. In fact, that's what it's called. 'When I Get Home.' The Beatles recorded it way back.

> I've got a whole lot of things to tell her
> When I get home.
> Come on, if you please,
> I have no time for trivialities
> When I get home.

But he never told me anything, and when we were together, about all he did have time for were trivialities. So his choice of song was pretty damned ironic, but then so was our marriage. Farcical, really."

"I refuse to listen to another word." Elizabeth pushed back her chair from the table. "I've been meaning to ask you. How much is Jamie paying you?"

"One hundred per script."

"That's very good for starters."

And Ken P. had paid one hundred for an orgasm. She wondered if she would ever hear from him again. It seemed odd that he would want to hand over that much money for the privilege of coming on a stranger's closet floor, but who was she to quibble about a person's erotic preferences? She was so inexperienced in that area; it was ridiculous, almost unbelievable, considering the degree of sexual freedom that existed in the world today. Ken P. would probably faint if he knew that she had gone to bed with only one man in her life, her husband, and not very often at that. In all likelihood he would feel cheated.

Iris had never thought much about call girls before; they'd existed in the back of her mind as a dim and shadowy group of people who led unnatural lives, definitely not people she was bound to meet or have much in common with. True, she hadn't met Sheila O'Reilly, but Elizabeth had; they used to be friends, they worked together on "The Troubled Heart." Still, Iris felt certain that Elizabeth had no knowledge of Sheila's weird double life. Elizabeth would be shocked, outraged. And yet in terms of experience, Elizabeth was far more worldly and experienced than she, and *she* wasn't shocked. She was something else. Intrigued as all hell.

"By the way," Iris said, "I received a postcard from Sheila. She sends you her regards."

"Oh, really? I was thinking about her just the other day. I wondered how she and Tom liked living in California."

"Apparently they love it. She says they're both crazy about my house, and then she asked after Bergdorf. And that was about it."

"It sounds like Sheila: direct, and to the point. If you write to her, please say hello for me. And now I have to be going, I have an appointment at the trichologist's." Elizabeth stood up. "Thank you for the terrible lunch. Cantonese is out. Fukienese is in. And remember, darling, that I'm counting on your help with Jamie."

"Perhaps you won't need it."

"We'll see. I must say I'd give anything to know what's going on at that meeting this very minute. Anything."

At which point, Iris' telephone rang.

A man with a pronounced British accent said, "We've never met, but I rang you up once before. Last week, I believe."

"Who is this?"

"Derek Christopher. And I'm going to have to make this rather brief. I've stepped out of a meeting, you see."

Chapter Fifteen

Across the room Elizabeth was getting her suede coat out of the closet, putting it on, adjusting her lip gloss in the hall mirror.

"I'd like to see you at three-thirty," Derek said. "If you're free, that is."

"Yes." Iris spoke quietly into the telephone, all too conscious of Elizabeth's presence. "That will be fine."

"Super. Until three-thirty, then."

"Who was that?" Elizabeth asked, after Iris had hung up.

"Mrs. Richmond."

"What did she want?"

It occurred to Iris that if she weren't lying, she might have told Elizabeth it was none of her damned business.

"She invited me to dinner tonight."

"Well, I'm glad you've at least made one friend. Although as I said before, it's not such a smart idea to become too chummy with your neighbors. Privacy is a valuable commodity in New York."

"It's just going to be the two of us." Iris' mind was still befuddled from the telephone call. "It seems the doctor will be working late, and I guess she's lonely."

"You didn't tell me she was married to a doctor."

"I've never seen him, but that's what she says. He's a bone surgeon."

"Doctors are always working late, whenever they want to play around. It's one of their occupational advantages. Emergencies."

"Sometimes I don't even think he exists. For all I know, Mrs. Richmond invented him."

"Or maybe he's dead, but she just can't accept it. Like a Tennessee Williams play, with those batty women clinging to a lost dream."

"That would be amusing."

"If it weren't tragic."

Why was it, Iris wondered, most things that struck her as funny, struck Elizabeth the opposite way? Did it mean Elizabeth had no sense of humor, or that she had no sense of compassion? Because it would be sad if Dr. Richmond were actually dead and Mrs. Richmond refused to acknowledge that harsh but inescapable fact. Still, she couldn't help it. The thought made her want to laugh.

"Bye-bye," Elizabeth said. "We'll get together again very soon."

They brushed each other's cheeks with airy, make-believe kisses; then Elizabeth was gone, and Iris looked at her Mickey Mouse watch. It was a few minutes past two. She had an hour and a half to get ready. But for *what?* The coincidence of Derek Christopher calling her when he did—seconds after Elizabeth had voiced her curiosity about what was going on at the meeting—was almost too incredible. Yet she probably shouldn't be surprised; it had been an incredible day and it seemed as though it would continue in that vein. Maybe in years to come, she would look back upon it as her own, private, longest D-Day in history.

But first things first. She started to clear the table, put the china in the dishwasher, freeze the remaining food in Baggies, and take the garbage out to the incinerator. The incinerator room was directly opposite her apartment, which made it very convenient. Iris felt sorry for those tenants who lived at the far ends of the floor and had to carry their garbage yards and yards to get rid of it. They always looked stupidly embarrassed, clutching a plastic trash-can liner in their hands as though they were afraid a stranger might grab it from them and run off with it as his own. People were peculiar about garbage. It probably went back to their toilet training, a subject she had no desire to think about right now.

As soon as she had double-locked her door and was about to go into the bedroom and dig up that typewritten list, the bell rang. For a second, Iris panicked. It couldn't be—not unless he were Superman; he had just telephoned. To her relief it was only Pepe, returning from the park with Bergdorf. Pepe held the Yorkshire terrier in his arms, the leash sticking out of his back pocket. The minute he put the dog down on the floor, Bergdorf ran into the kitchen and started to lap up water as though he had been lost on the Sahara Desert for a week.

"He's a good little fellow."

Pepe always said pretty much the same thing whenever he returned from an outing with Bergdorf. And so did Iris.

"Yes, he's very sweet."

"I come again at nine o'clock tonight."

They went through this ritual every day, but Iris was so delighted to have found someone to take the damned dog off her hands that she wouldn't have cared if Pepe had stood there and read the Bible to her in Puerto Rican. He was a godsend; and apparently he thought the same of her because instead of the customary two daily walks, she had suggested that he take Bergdorf out three times a day. She told him she would give him twenty-five dollars a week for his services, and was that all right? Pepe seemed to think that was marvelous, which made everyone very happy. Including Bergdorf, who was so tired from all his outings that instead of racing hysterically around the apartment, as he had the first couple of days, unable to calm down, he went right to sleep almost as soon as he came home. Iris couldn't stand hysterical dogs; she felt too much that way herself.

And nervous.

The list was exactly where she remembered putting it, in the top bureau drawer under a pile of cashmere sweaters.

Tutti Frutti	Harold
Yellow Dragon	Ken P.
Strawberry Flip	Derek

And on, and on, ending with:

Bubble Bath	Charles

Her hunch had been right. Derek's name was indeed on the list (how many Dereks could there be in New York?), but the fact that he once was a client of Sheila's didn't necessarily mean that that was why he was coming over to see her at three-thirty. It could be for other reasons, Iris mused. Like what? "The Troubled Heart." After all, she was now a bona fide writer for the show, and perhaps Jamie had told Derek what a competent job she was doing, and he was simply paying her a visit to discuss future plot developments, character motivation, things like that. Or, perhaps it was to be a plain courtesy call that a plain courteous businessman might make to a new member of his staff. She could imagine the conversation that was about to take place.

"Miss Barnes, it certainly is a pleasure to meet you at last. Our head writer, Mr. Mann, has told me what a good job you've done on your first two scripts. I want you to know that all of us at the network appreciate your efforts on behalf of 'The Troubled Heart.' Welcome aboard."

She would be charming, but businesslike too. "Thank you, Mr. Christopher. It was very kind of you to take the trouble personally to pay me this visit."

"No trouble at all, Miss Barnes."

"Mrs. Barnes," she would say, gently, "I'm a widow."

He would look properly sympathetic, then they would have tea, exchange a few more pleasant formalities, shake hands, and he would leave. It was possible that that was how things would go. But was it probable? Yesterday Iris would have unhesitatingly said yes, but after the events of today she was no longer sure of anything. What was even worse (terrible, in fact) was a ghastly indecision on her part. Which Derek Christopher did she look forward to meeting: a polite and kindly television producer, or a lustful and kinky nut who wanted to get laid? If he fell into the second category, a very important question had to be answered, and *now*. Iris looked at Bergdorf, who had just padded into the bedroom and hopped up on the chaise for his afternoon nap.

"What the fuck is a Strawberry Flip?"

An hour later the scene in the O'Reillys' living room had changed considerably. It was a little after three and Iris, now wearing a cream-colored suit that buttoned to the neck, was seated on the sofa looking discreet and slightly schoolgirlish. At least that was how she hoped she looked. She was sipping a very indiscreet Bombay on the rocks, but trying to offset the gin's pungent aroma with intermittent squirts of Binaca into her mouth.

Concentrated golden breath spray, it said on the label. All she knew was that it tasted lousy, her headache had gotten worse, and yet when she studied herself in the mirror a moment ago, she might have been an advertisement for clean, healthy living. It was a miracle. Gone was the haggardness from her face, the droop of her chin, the lines under her eyes. She looked as sparkling and wholesome as those young housewives on television commercials, who were forever stuffing themselves with creamy cottage cheese or yummy yogurt, while smiling complacently into the camera for being such good girls.

In fact, one of those commercials was on right now, blaring away on the TV set facing her. In another few seconds the soap opera that preceded "The Troubled Heart" would go into its second lugubrious act. It was counting on a tricky tubal pregnancy situation to hold its audience, but the latest Nielsens showed that it still trailed "The Troubled Heart" in ratings. Iris had been so busy during the past hour that it hadn't occurred to her before: if Derek were on time, he would arrive precisely at the start of his own series.

Like the possibility of Dr. Richmond being dead and buried, this, too, made her want to laugh. Everything about the timing of today's events had been as perfect as the movement of her Mickey Mouse watch which she still wore. She had considered changing to her Corum with the dials made of violet bird feathers, but the Mickey Mouse seemed more appropriate somehow. Maybe because she had bought it from a junkie on the Strip for two and a half dollars the same day she met Bob.

"You've got to tell me," an actor was saying to an actress on the television set. "If anyone has a right to know, I do. Darling, I'm your *husband*. I love you."

"I love you, too."

"You're both reading from the teleprompter," Iris said aloud. "You can't fool me. I'm a pro."

Across the room, the round dining table that only a short while ago had held the disarray of a Chinese paper-carton luncheon was now set with a silver tea service for two, a Limoges dish with croissants and Dutch biscuits, another, smaller dish of strawberry jam, a still smaller dish of whipped-butter swirls. On the kitchen counter was a tin of Twining's Earl Grey tea; on the electric range, a kettle filled with cold water. Besides changing her clothes, that was what she had been so busy doing since the telephone call from Derek—obtaining the ingredients for their afternoon refreshment.

Luckily the gourmet shop on Madison Avenue sold everything she needed, so she'd had to make only one stop, although if she had had the time, she could have prepared delicate cucumber and/or watercress sandwiches, with the crusts neatly trimmed away. That was all she remembered from her Evelyn Waugh course at Marymount. What an English tea supposedly consisted of. Then at the last minute she recalled somebody telling her that while the French took lemon with their tea, the English preferred milk. Deciding to be prepared for any and all emergencies, Iris had placed both a creamer of milk and a dish of paper-thin lemon slices on the lovely crushed-velvet tablecloth that she'd found hanging in the O'Reillys' linen closet.

The only reason she found it was because she had a sudden brainstorm after returning from the gourmet shop that maybe the Yellow Dragon mask was in there, beneath the fitted flowered sheets and extra-thick terry-towel stuff. But no such luck. In all probability, Sheila had taken the mask with her in case she ran into any potential Ken P. victims out in California. If they existed on the East Coast, why not the West? Maybe there were hundreds, thousands of them all over the goddamn country, being passively tied up that very minute and shoved into strangers' dark closets. It was a thrilling thought, somehow, a whole secret syndrome of crackpots that only a select few (like herself) knew about. They probably even advertised in papers like the *Free Press*, and whatever its equivalents were in other United States cities.

It sounded like an angry bulldog: five loud barks of the apartment's intercom. Iris ran into the kitchen and put her mouth next to the obscene metal slits.

"Yes?"

Dead silence.

"Yes? Yes?"

Nothing.

Five more barks. She was starting to panic. What if her end of the system were out of order, and Derek would leave, thinking she had stood him up? Then she realized she had forgotten to push the "talk" button.

"You have a guest coming up," Mike said. "A Mr. Christopher."

"Thank you."

She gulped down the remainder of her drink, squirted with Binaca a few more times, then rinsed out the glass, smoothed her hair, and thanked the fates that she was on the twenty-second floor so she had time for such necessities before any arrival could get to her. Bergdorf, apparently awakened by the sound of the intercom, had emerged from the bedroom and was dancing around at her feet when the doorbell finally rang.

"Hello," Iris said nervously.

"I'm Derek Christopher. How very nice to meet you." He spotted the Yorkshire terrier immediately. "Well, well, I see that Bergdorf is still with us. May I come in?"

"Oh yes, of course." She opened the door wider, and followed him into the living room. "Won't you sit down?"

He chose one of the tubular chairs and took a cigar out of his inside blazer pocket. The band on the cigar said "Upmann."

"Do you mind? Can't buy these here, you know. Have to smuggle them in from London."

"Why is that?"

It was barely a flicker of the eyelid. "Because they're Cuban, my dear."

She had wondered what he would look like; now she knew. Tall, narrow frame, sort of washed-out blondish, flabby. In addition to the navy blazer, he was wearing a gray and white striped shirt, crimson tie, gray flannels, and what looked suspiciously to Iris like Gucci moccasins. They were a familiar status symbol in Beverly Hills, but she was surprised to find them on the feet of this self-composed Englishman here in the O'Reillys' apartment in New York.

"And now, for the next thirty minutes, 'The Troubled Heart,' brought to you today by . . ."

On the television set was the opening shot of the show's logo: trees swaying in a heavy rain, rain slashing across windowpanes, the visual mood as dark and threatening with potential disaster as the sound of the announcer's voice, the ominous crescendo of background organ music.

"That's an X-66 Hammond." Derek lit his cigar. "The man who plays it claims that only one percent of his selections are happy ones. But I'm sure that that doesn't surprise you, since apparently you're one of our faithful viewers. Or have I caught you on an off day?"

"No. I'm a faithful viewer."

Derek smiled, really smiled for the first time. He had bad teeth. "This is rather awkward. Do you realize that I don't know your name? I was in such a rush when I rang you up this afternoon that I forgot to ask."

"Iris."

He seemed satisfied. "That's a very pretty name. Very fitting."

No Miss Barnes? No Mrs. Barnes? "Thank you. My mother is a great lover of flowers."

This time it couldn't be called a smile, it was a smirk really. "Anything you say, love."

"What?"

"I said if you wish to be called Iris, it's fine with me."

Iris knew she had had too much to drink, but something was screwy here. "I don't understand, Mr. Christopher. What do you mean, *if* I wish to be called? I didn't have much of a choice when I was born."

The smirk faded and something else took its place, a shifting of perception. "I must say your approach is a bit different. Refreshing, in fact. Most of the girls, you know, well, they use made-up names, it's a kind of protective device which I quite empathize with. One must watch out for oneself."

"Oh, I do." So he fell into the second category. "But in other ways."

"I'm glad to hear that."

He was probably thinking in terms of contraceptive methods, guarding against VD, paying off the doorman, etc. When she was married to Bob, she had taken the pill. But she hadn't taken it for a long time now, she didn't even own a diaphragm. It was something to consider, what she would do in the future to avoid becoming pregnant. That is, if she decided to go on with this insane masquerade.

"Let's not be too revolutionary in our approaches." He blew cigar smoke at her. "No Mr. Christophers, please. Derek, if you will."

"Derek."

On "The Troubled Heart," one of the actresses was saying: "You rejected me after I lost the baby, and you know it."

Derck's back was to the set. "I produce that show, in case you're interested."

"Really?" Iris was seated on the sofa, facing him and the set. "That's fascinating. What a coincidence, meeting you like this. I like to meet men who do things I admire."

"Then I gather you weren't joking before. You're truly fond of the show."

"Oh, more than fond. You might say I'm hooked on it. I watch it every day. If I'm not busy, that is. If I am busy, Mrs. Richmond next door fills me in on what happened."

"Extraordinary."

"You've played me for a fool," the actress cried, "but you won't get away with it. I warn you. For once, you've gone too far!"

"She's good, isn't she?"

"She's my current favorite," Iris said. "But getting back to that business of using real names. You know, your approach is pretty off-beat, too."

"How's that?"

"Not only do most men give you a phony name, but they lie about where they work as well."

"Perhaps I should be more careful, but I was spoiled by Sheila. I couldn't very well lie to her, since she knew me from the show. She played a nurse for a while on 'The Troubled Heart.' Were you aware of that?"

"She mentioned it once in passing."

"Dear, dear Sheila." He turned and glanced around the room, spotting the tea service for the first time. "What a charming idea. I am impressed. Very thoughtful of you, Iris. Although, to be brutally frank, at the moment I would like a drink. Gin and Schweppes, if it's not too much bother."

When Iris returned with his drink, he said, "Everything in

the apartment seems to be the same. Exactly as Sheila left it. You haven't made any changes at all, not even to take down those dreadful animal paintings."

A cat, zebra, kangaroo, pelican, turtle. In the kitchen, an elephant. In the bedroom, an antelope.

"They are dreadful, aren't they? I wonder why she put them up."

"You mean, you don't know?"

"I can only assume that she has lousy taste in art."

Derek relit his cigar. "Undoubtedly."

"What other reason could there be?"

"None, I'm sure."

Iris didn't like it. She didn't like not knowing things she was supposed to know. Maybe Mrs. Richmond could tell her about the paintings, since it was now obvious that their existence had less to do with aesthetics than she had previously imagined. Or if Mrs. Richmond were in the dark, perhaps she would telephone Sheila long distance and ask her. There were a few other questions she would like to ask Sheila, providing she didn't lose her nerve.

"Fool your husband?" an announcer was saying on the TV set. "You can, with our instant coffee. And he'll love you for it."

Derek stood up and moved over beside Iris. Putting his hands firmly on her breasts, he kissed her mouth, then backed away, an expression of dissatisfaction on his face.

"You're wearing a bra."

"Shouldn't I be?"

"Of course not, love. And a pants suit, to boot . . ."

It was an extremely expensive and elegant Galanos. "Don't you like it?"

"Under different circumstances, I would positively adore it. But I was expecting something, shall we say, a bit more seductive?"

She smiled the most demure smile she could dredge up. "I'm sorry if I've disappointed you."

"You haven't been in this business very long, have you? Come on now, confess. Tell Derek the truth."

Some instinct made her say it. "The men in Bel Air prefer bras and pants suits. They're so bored with the nudity scene out there."

"Bel Air?" His watery blue eyes seemed to dilate. "What do you know about Bel Air?"

"Just about everything. That's where I was living up until a few weeks ago."

"How extraordinary."

She had hit the nail on the head, all right, he was impressed. "So you see," she went on, more self-confidently now, "it's not that I'm a novice, as you might have assumed, but sexual preferences do vary depending upon locale. What's popular in one part of the country doesn't always make it somewhere else. But I'm glad you told me. I'll remember next time."

"Bel Air." He still couldn't get over it. "That's one of the wealthiest, most prestigious communities in the United States."

"And one of the kinkiest. There was a certain movie magnate who had the most unusual tastes you could conceive of. I can't tell you his name, of course, but he sure was imaginative. His films are world-famous. His home life is a model of domestic bliss. No scandals ever reach the press. But when he used to visit me . . . well . . . he was an amazing man."

"What did he like to do?"

"I'd rather not say."

"See here, I'm not asking you for his identity, just what it was that turned him on so. Curiosity, that's all."

Iris moistened her lips with her tongue. "If you're a good boy, perhaps I'll tell you. Later. Unless you're in a big rush."

"No, no, I have plenty of time. Do you?"

"Time is money."

"I understand. Prefer it that way myself. You Americans have a quaint expression: wham, bam, etcetera. I believe you know what I'm referring to."

"Of course."

He shook his head negatively. "Not for this chappie."

"You're becoming more unusual by the moment."

"And you're becoming more devastating. As for recompense, don't give it another thought. I'll make the afternoon well worth your while."

"I should hope so."

"So they prefer bras and pants suits in Bel Air, do they?"

The last act of "The Troubled Heart" was just winding up. Elizabeth and Craig Crawford were in a two-shot, and Elizabeth was speaking:

"I like working for you, Mr. Crawford. It's—"

There was a moment's hesitation, and Crawford said, "Very pleasant? Yes, it is."

The camera came in for a closeup of Crawford's scheming face, and the organ music, which had been steadily underscoring their words, now hit a single, discordant note, and the show was over for the day.

"She blew it again." Derek's voice had turned to granite. "And that fool man is going to build up her part."

"Excuse me?"

"Nothing. Sorry, love. Business talk is a bore. Be an angel and turn off that damned telly. Sheila used to have a few Ray Charles records that I liked. Would you mind putting them on the stereo?"

While Iris was looking through the record stacks, she realized that what he had said was: "And that fool, Mann, is going to build up her part." So Elizabeth was not to be written out, after all. Iris smiled. Her sister had wasted her time coming over for lunch today, and that pep talk about Iris being brilliant, she might have saved herself the trouble. Apparently, Jamie was not Elizabeth's enemy. Derek was. He had begun to pace back and forth across the room, stopping finally at the round dining table, which he examined with renewed interest.

"Biscuits, croissants, butter, milk, lemon. You've thought of everything, haven't you?"

"Even the tea. It's Earl Grey."

"Perfection."

"You left out the strawberry jam."

Ray Charles began to sing: "I had the craziest dream last night, yeah, I did, I never dreamt it could be, but there you were . . ."

Derek held out his arms. "Come here, you clever little girl."

Iris walked slowly into his embrace. "Shall we have tea now?"

"No, my dear. Tea can wait. Suddenly, I cannot. Now we shall have the strawberry jam."

Chapter Sixteen

"Do you mean, let's just have biscuits and strawberry jam?" Iris said. "Wouldn't you want something to wash it down with?"

"I wasn't thinking of eating it."

Things were getting screwier by the minute, but she was determined not to show her mounting confusion. After all, she was supposed to be a highly paid West Coast call girl, sophisticated and self-confident.

"Well, if you weren't thinking of eating it, what were you thinking of?"

"Your eating it."

"Alone?"

"Not exactly." He took off his blazer and loosened his tie. "You see, I was sent to a perfectly dreadful boarding school when I was only six years old. It was living hell. The older boys bullied the younger boys, and the masters bullied everyone." Derek unzipped his fly. He had on red-and-white checked shorts. "They were sadistic bastards, the whole lot of them, with their canes and rulers. One error in Latin declension, and your hand was sore for a week. But it was the afternoon teas that I dreaded the most." His penis was very erect now, and very small. "I had always disliked strawberry preserves, they make me sick to my stomach, and at that particular school it was the only kind they served. One ate it, or else. Tiptree was the brand. You don't see it much over here, except in certain rare specialty shops. Sheila used to buy any old brand. She was casual about such things, indifferent to the subtle distinctions of life. Why the hell are you staring at me like that?"

"Because the jam in that dish on the table happens to be Tiptree."

The expression on Derek's face went from amazement to unconcealed delight. "But that's remarkable! I can hardly believe the coincidence. I'm stunned. Would you mind fetching the jar and bringing it to me." He was massaging his penis, as though warming it up for some special treat. "I want to look at the filthy label. It's been years since I've laid eyes on my old nemesis."

"I thought that putting it in a dish would be a little more gracious."

"No, no, my dear. The jar. You haven't——" He stopped, afraid to finish the question.

"Thrown it out? No. I'll get it."

When Iris returned, Derek's blue eyes glistened, even his voice sounded different, higher, as he recited the wording on the jar. " 'Wilkin & Sons, Ltd. Tiptree Little Scarlett Strawberry Preserve. Net weight 12 ounces. Tiptree, England.' " His erection looked as though it were about to detach itself from his body at any moment, and begin circling the room in wild giddiness. "A perfectly despicable boy, at least twice my size, once rubbed it all over my bed clothes. The headmaster thought I had done it myself out of sheer perversity. I not only received the caning of my life, but I was forced to eat double helpings of Tiptree preserves every day for the next two weeks. I used to upchuck immediately afterward. I'm sure you can imagine the effect that that experience had, and continues to have upon me, even after all these many years."

"I'm the same way about oatmeal, because my mother used to make me eat it every morning except weekends. She sprinkled wheat germ on top."

He seemed not to have heard her. "I loathe strawberry preserves, and I doubly loathe the Tiptree variety. Although, to be perfectly fair to the manufacturer, I have been assured by a great many people that it's a very superior product."

Iris started to giggle out of sheer nervousness. "I don't understand what it has to do with me, but if it bothers you that much, why don't I put the jar back in the refrigerator and take the dish off the table?"

"Oh, no." He seemed horrified by her suggestion. "That isn't the point at all. Not at all. I'm delighted to see that the jar is only two-thirds full."

"That's because the other third is in the dish." What were they talking about? She thought of her ambiguous conversation earlier in the day with Ken P. "I'm sorry you have such bad associations with something so delicious. I took a little taste of it when I was spooning it out."

Derek smiled again, revealing his bad teeth. He really should have them capped, Iris decided; he would be a disgrace in Beverly Hills (not to mention super-exclusive Bel Air), where everyone had capped teeth, even the servants. She and Elizabeth had had theirs done several years ago.

"A little taste." Derek seemed amused. "Now wouldn't you like a bigger one?"

"Frankly, I've never enjoyed eating alone."

"Your approach is charming, but let's not be too coy about this. Remember, my dear, I am the customer. Now you put your hand in that jar and take out a good sized scoop of the terrible red stuff, and then you very neatly coat my penis with it. But first I must remove the rest of my clothes."

Sunlight hit the dining table, and the venetian blinds were wide open.

"Maybe we should go into the bedroom," she said. "It's darker there."

"I don't care to go into a darkened room. Right here will do just fine."

At least Ken P. had had the modesty to want to be tied up where nobody could see him in his terrible abasement.

"What about the neighbors across the way?"

"What about them?" He stood up, removed his tie, shirt, trousers, checked shorts, then sat down again on the sofa. "I suggest you take off the top of that charming pants suit, and the bra, of course. You're not in Bel Air now, love."

Having just decided that she must be insane, Iris started to do as she was asked, wondering what he would think of her breasts, which were rather attractive, although not as large as Elizabeth's. If Elizabeth could see her now, she probably wouldn't be able to open her mouth for the next ten years.

"That's a great improvement," Derek said, once she was standing naked from the waist up. "Very pretty, indeed." He cupped both breasts in his manicured hands and gently lowered her to the carpeted floor, placing her at his feet. For some reason, he had not removed his socks (which were too short) or his shoes. Then he put the Tiptree jar in her hand and said, "Very well. You may begin."

All Iris could think of at first was the possibility of getting the gooey stuff on the O'Reillys' sofa, but if worst came to worst she would just have to have it recovered. Maybe she would do it in crushed velvet, like the tablecloth. As she applied the preserves to Derek Christopher's small, throbbing penis, she could feel his eyes on her, watching every move-ment of her hand. In a funny way, it was like frosting a cake. Her mother's cook sometimes used to let her help with the chocolate frosting on one of her double-layer specialties. In this case, however, there was an underside that was tricky, because if she put too much on, it was bound to slip off; but finally, after diligent and delicate application, she had com-pleted the peculiar task.

"Now go and wash your hands," he said, "but leave the jar here. Then when you return, you will have the lovely oppor-tunity very slowly to start sucking every last bit of Tiptree preserve off my prick. But not to completion. So please don't be too efficient, because I have no intention of ejaculating in that pretty mouth of yours."

Iris was about to ask where he did intend to deposit his sperm, but something told her that she already knew and it was best not to think about it. While washing her hands in the bathroom, she decided it was also best not to think about the fact that Derek Christopher couldn't have picked a less experienced girl for this particular endeavor (he should have gotten Elizabeth). In her one year of marriage, she had gone down on Bob exactly twice; he told her that she had no tal-ent for it, which meant she was going to have to develop some very fast, or Derek would conclude that she was the inexperienced person he had first taken her for. She dried her hands and reassured herself that if she put her heart in it, she couldn't fail. Technique undoubtedly counted for a great deal in cases like this, but surely enthusiasm and the desire to please couldn't be dismissed as meaningless virtues.

"Are we ready?" Derek sounded as though they were about to begin a tennis match. "I'd prefer it if you sat on the floor. This sofa is low enough for both of us to be comfort-able, wouldn't you say?"

Iris nodded. Then, doing as he asked, she began the job at hand; and as she studiously licked away the preserves, he caressed her nipples, which made her so excited that she be-came wet almost immediately. In a few seconds she was trembling; her entire body felt hot. The only other times she had experienced such strong sexual sensations were when Bob used to make infrequent love to her. But that, certainly, was understandable. Her reaction here was as surprising to Iris as was the strangeness of this stranger's request. And just as she had removed the last particle of preserve with her tongue, she started to come in her Peter Pan bikini panties. Letting go of Derek, she crossed her legs tight in order to prolong the intensity of orgasm.

"I'm coming," she cried. "I'm coming, goddamn it."

"So am I."

And so he was, filling the hated boyhood jar of preserves with spasmodic thrusts of that grayish-white substance that Iris had seen too little of in her deprived, almost virginal life. Then, when it was over for both of them, she started to laugh as she hadn't laughed in a very long time (if ever).

"Now I get it. Oh, it's hilarious. Whoever would have guessed? Nobody. Not in a million years. Nobody, I tell you."

Derek had placed the Tiptree jar on the floor, and some of its contents spilled over onto the O'Reillys' tan shag rug.

"What the hell is so bloody funny?"

"It's you."

"Yes? What about me?"

"You." She was laughing and pointing at him. *"You're* the Strawberry Flip!"

When Jamie left the agency meeting, he did not go directly home as he had intended to. Just before the cab reached the Des Artistes, he told the driver to continue on to Columbus Avenue where there was a certain crummy bar he suddenly felt like stopping at.

"Right here will do."

Overtipping, he got out and entered the semideserted saloon. It was one of those places with grimy windows and an atmosphere of no hope, not much talk, and very little action. Most of the people who frequented it had long since given up whatever dim illusions they'd once had, and were resigned to playing out the remainder of their lives against this backdrop of boozy noninterference.

Maybe that was why, at the moment, the bar appealed to Jamie so much: it was quite the opposite from where he had just come. He loved the craziness in contrast. Jamie prided himself upon being able to navigate in any kind of social circle and still feel at home. Although it had occurred to him at times that the reason he felt that way was because he didn't really feel at home anywhere. He could just imagine Derek Christopher walking into this bar, it would be instant disgust, fear, confusion. But then Derek had gone to one of those su-per-fashionable boarding schools (probably Heatherdown at

Ascot), continuing on to Eton, of course, and higher snob achievements.

While Derek was undoubtedly playing soccer on those green, green English fields, Jamie, having dropped out of M.I.T., took off for Miami with something like forty-five dollars in his pocket. Until this day he still had no idea why he'd chosen Miami, except that he'd never been there and it was supposed to be warm. Then a strange period in his life unfolded. He won a mambo contest in a state of drunken frenzy, and was later reduced to giving mambo and cha-cha lessons to aging divorcees who couldn't afford expensive face-lifts. It was not one of Miami's better hotels. They'd paid him fifty cents for a half-hour lesson; and, as if that weren't humiliation enough, he'd had to bribe one of the beach boys to let him sleep in a cabana at night. In order to keep warm he used to turn on the shower because it was a pretty chilly Miami season, one of the coolest they'd had in years.

"Bourbon on the rocks," he said to the bartender. "Make it a double. Water on the side."

The bartender looked like his customers, but had a slight edge over them by way of a girlfriend who read palms at an East-side cocktail lounge, and had put up the money for the bar license. The bartender liked his job because it kept him away from the palmist as much as possible (she was obsessed with the length of his lifeline), and close to the supply of alcohol he had come to depend upon more and more in recent years.

"How's that soapy show of yours doing?" the bartender asked. "Any good murders recently?"

"No, but I'm working on it." Maybe he would eventually have Elizabeth knock off Craig Crawford. Or maybe one of the syndicate would do it. "There's nothing like a good, juicy murder to hike up the ratings."

The bartender shook his head, as though it were all beyond him. "That's some hell of a business you're in. But to each his own."

The color television set in the bar was tuned to the World Series, for which Jamie felt grateful. In another few minutes "The Troubled Heart" would be on the air, on another channel, and if there was one thing he didn't feel like watching just then, it was his own dramatic creation. He didn't want to hear the words he had written, and he didn't want to see the actors going through all the stereotyped gestures that accompanied the words. Now that he had had his triumph at the agency meeting, he was starting to go into a fast emotional decline. That was the trouble with success, it was so anticlimatic somehow, perhaps because of the compulsive need to go on to greater and still greater successes.

"You're right," he said to the bartender, who was watching a double play. "It is a hell of a business."

If anyone had told Jamie ten years ago, when he was giving cha-cha lessons in Miami, that this was the way he would end up making a living, he would have laughed in the person's face. And rightfully so. He never had had any writing inclinations at all; it was one of those fluke things he'd fallen into. And since the life-expectancy of a soap writer amounted to about a year, he might very soon fall out; he'd been at it for more than three years now. The memory of how it had all started tickled Jamie.

At a party in New York he met the daughter of the head writer of "The Troubled Heart," the guy who had kicked off recently after completing episode #1102. Jamie and the daughter went to bed the same night they met, and a few days later she invited him home for dinner. Home was where she lived with her parents, a voluptuous co-op in the East Sixties. Jamie and her father hit it off right away, and after dinner they spoke about work, ambitions, occupations. In a spurt of desperation, Jamie professed to being a hung-up writer.

"What have you done?" the father asked.

"A few short stories."

"I'd like to see them."

"I'm afraid they're not very good, sir. Fiction isn't my thing."

"I'd like to see them, anyway."

The next day Jamie got in touch with an old friend, a guy who had studied creative writing at the New School, and asked if he could borrow some of his stories, explaining the reason for the request. Fortunately, the friend had a weird sense of humor and said okay. The stories were very heavy on dialogue. Daddy was impressed and offered Jamie the same setup that he'd recently offered Iris. In time he became so good at writing the series that they had to give him screen credit. He then joined the Writers' Guild of America, not because it was mandatory but because it gave him a sense of professional authority. As for the daughter, she ran off shortly afterward with a cinematographer who had a washer-dryer in his bathroom. Jamie still saw them from time to time.

Thinking about his unlikely beginnings in the business made him think of Iris. Something told him that despite her hangups, she was going to turn into a very good little helpmate. The two scripts she'd done had been good, damned good, she had a flair for the shmaltzy note. He wondered what she would think when she found out that Elizabeth's part was going to be considerably built up. Which reminded him. He had to call Elizabeth and tell her the good news.

"Could I have some change for the telephone?" He handed the bartender a quarter. "I have to make a very strategic call."

Someone had just hit a home run, and the bartender's eyes were glazed with ecstasy as he slid two dimes and a nickel across the old wooden bar. "I used to be a pitcher in the minor leagues."

"I'd hate to tell you what I used to be."

Jamie walked to the rear of the room where the phone booth was, but when he dialed Elizabeth's number, all he got was her snotty answering service.

"Miss Small's residence."

Jamie felt like saying that Miss Small's residence was very small indeed, but experience had taught him not to fool around with answering service operators. With rare exceptions, none of them had any sense of humor, not that he could blame them. He'd rather still be giving cha-cha lessons, or selling shoes at Kitty Kelly (another one of his wonderful jobs), than taking other people's messages.

"Please tell her that Mr. Mann called———"

"Thank you."

"That's not the end of my story. Also, please tell her that she's home free. She'll know what I mean."

There was an abrupt click at the other end.

"Fucking cunt," Jamie said to himself.

He sat down on the same barstool he'd been sitting on before. "I guess I'll have another double and then call it quits." The man next to him was new; he had on a cap, and for some reason Jamie decided he was a plumber. "Only this time, make it a Jack Daniels."

"I once pitched a no-hit, no-run game," the bartender said.

"But you've got to be young for that stuff. Me? I'm forty-seven."

"I'm thirty," Jamie said.

"I'm thirty-eight," the plumber said. He looked ten years older. "This business is aging."

"Which business is that?" Jamie asked.

"I repair TV sets. Those crazy housewives, either want to fuck you, or they think you're fucking them. Moneywise, that is. Sometimes both. I mean, some of them get this notion that if they jump into the sack with you, you're not going to charge them for your work. It's very aging."

"I might have been able to make the majors," the bartender said, "but then I met this palm reader, and I got lazy."

All Jamie could think of was Marlon Brando in the rear seat of the car in *On the Waterfront*, saying to Rod Steiger, "I could've been a contender." Oh Christ, he was back to old movies again. He finished the Jack Daniels in two fast gulps, paid the bartender, tipped him, and decided it was time to go home. The first thing he would do when he got there was rip off his Bernard Weatherill suit, Dior tie, Meladandri shirt, and take a long, hot bath. His muscles ached. The next thing he was going to do was sit down at the typewriter and begin a plot synopsis for the Elizabeth-Crawford romance situation.

As he walked out of the bar, he thought of Iris again. He would call her tomorrow and set up a lunch date. She was obviously the kind of person who needed constant encouragement and approval, or else she was liable to cop out on him professionally. It was important to be careful with drinkers; they had weak egos.

Then he thought of making love to Elizabeth tonight.

Then he thought of Iris again. Naked.

Then he thought of what it would be like to be in bed with the two of them at the same time. For some reason that he didn't fully understand, the fact that they were sisters made it seem more exciting than if they had just been any two attractive girls.

"The hell with Derek Christopher," Jamie mumbled, as he went down the street toward the Des Artistes. "Any schmuck can play soccer, but how many people can live in a cabana with only a shower to keep warm?"

Chapter Seventeen

As Elizabeth entered her pied-à-terre (she preferred to think of it that way, rather than as a midget-sized flat), the telephone was ringing.

"I tried to call you before," Jamie said, "but you were out."

"I had an appointment at the trichologist's. A new one. He did the most fantastic things for my hair. First he massaged a thick almond-cream into my scalp, then he put me under a steamer, then he wrapped my head in an ice-cold towel."

She was rattling on for fear of what Jamie had to say to her about the outcome of the story conference. "It was quite a sensation, wonderful, really, and after that, all the cream was washed off. But here is the most interesting part: he took sections of my hair and twisted it into ringlets. *Ringlets*. You know how straight my hair is, I couldn't figure out what the hell he was doing—"

"Shut up, Elizabeth. I gather you haven't called your service yet."

"No, I just this minute walked in."

"We've won."

For a second, it didn't register. It was the "we" part that threw her, because for months now she had been only half convinced that Jamie was on her side, and sometimes she felt less than half sure. Just last night she'd had terrible, monster dreams of him, in which he was trying to push her off a cliff onto the jagged rocks below.

"We?" she said.

"You're going to have the affair with Crawford. I outmaneuvered every bastard at that meeting. It's definite, Elizabeth. Your part will be built up. In fact, I'm going to start work on the synopsis immediately."

"Then he trimmed off the wispy ends. That was the reason for the ringlets." She sank down into the black corduroy sofa.

"Oh, Jamie, I can't believe it. I thought that . . ." *You were against me,* was what she was about to say. "I thought that I'd really had it on 'The Troubled Heart,' that I was finished."

"Hardly." At home now, he was wrapped in an oversized bath towel, smiling with the beneficence of a kindly old billionaire who has just given away half his fortune to a starving stranger. "You're just beginning."

Elizabeth touched her smooth, glossy, shiny, new hair.

"But what happens? Between me and Crawford, I mean? How does the affair begin? When? Will his wife die? Will I marry him?"

"Hey, take it easy. I realize that you're excited, but give a guy a chance. I haven't yet figured out the details. No point in doing that until I knew for sure that we were home free."

There was that "we" again. If only she could believe in it, really believe, but it was too slick. She remembered something that Sheila had once told her about the way actors were treated on soaps:

"They like to keep you in the dark about the specifics of what's going to happen. They're afraid that if they tell you everything, you'll start playing the end too soon. Like, if they know that you're going to marry someone in six months, but that right now the affair is very turbulent, they won't tell you about the marriage. They want you to *play* the turbulence, not knowing how it will resolve itself. Maybe they're right, but I think it's a stinking put-down method, treating us like schoolchildren. I mean, if you were in a Broadway show, you'd know how it was going to end and you'd still do a good job, so what's the big difference?"

"I'm sorry, darling," Elizabeth said to Jamie. "I didn't mean to push you, it's just that I'm so overwhelmed by today's decision, I still can't believe it."

"Believe it."

She hesitated before asking her next question, trying to make it sound as casual as possible. "Did Derek try to give you much static?"

"You and he have never gotten along, have you?"

"Does anybody get along with Derek Christopher?"

"That wasn't what I was asking."

Jamie was shrewd, but he could only surmise, never know about her hideous encounter with Derek in his fashionably off-beat little house on Patchin Place in the Village. The reason he had rented it, he told Elizabeth at the time, was because it reminded him so much of the mews houses in London, and besides, e.e. cummings had once lived next door. Then he became smashed on gin and tonic and began to quote from "love is more thicker than forget (more thinner than recall)," after which he admitted to having a rather unusual penchant for strawberry preserves, and would she mind getting a jar of it from his fridge.

When Elizabeth asked what on earth he wanted it for—she couldn't imagine the impeccable Derek suddenly start to gobble it up by the spoonful—he began to explain his nasty secret, but she wouldn't let him finish. She wanted to tell him that he was sick as hell, but had to keep reminding herself that he was the producer of "The Troubled Heart," and it wouldn't be the most diplomatic thing for her to do, considering their professional relationship. Using her most tactful wiles (without vomiting at the same time), she finally let him make love to her; something told her that if she didn't, she just might be out of a job the next day. And besides, concurrent with her feelings of disgust, she actually felt sorry for the poor, pathetic bastard. Then, in the middle of the night, a strange thing happened.

He woke up suddenly, saying, "Oh, my God. I've got to leave."

"What is it?"

He was staring across the room at something, which finally in the dim light Elizabeth managed to distinguish. It was one of those wooden automatic valets, on which he had hung his clothes before getting into bed.

"What is it?" she repeated.

Whereupon he ran across the room and began dressing in the biggest hurry Elizabeth had ever seen a man get dressed.

"Where are you going?"

"I've got to get home. On the double." He stuffed his tie in his pocket and nearly ran out of the room without his shoes. "My wife will never forgive me."

"What?!"

"My wife, I tell you," he said, coming back and putting on his shoes. "You don't know her."

"Listen, you idiot." Elizabeth was laughing at last, aware of the fact that his wife had stayed behind in London. "You *are* home."

It was only then that Derek Christopher fully awakened

and realized the folly of his behavior. Slowly, he started to remove his clothes, an expression of relief on his haggard face. His only words were: "Thank God. You don't know what a bitch Wicki is."

Lying awake in the darkness, Elizabeth realized that he would never forgive her for having seen him in such a ludicrous situation, not to mention her sketchy knowledge of the strawberry business, and she was right. Whenever he had a chance after that, he always managed to give her as hard a time as possible on "The Troubled Heart." She had long since decided that the day she quit the show (or was fired), she would ask him whose apartment he thought he was in that night, and how well he knew the woman's husband. Or how slightly. She amused herself at the prospect of seeing his discomfort as he remembered that memorable near-exit from his own home at three in the morning.

"It's true," Elizabeth said now to Jamie. "Derek and I have never gotten along. Call it bad chemistry, I don't know. I just know that he never liked me, and that's why I was wondering whether he tried to override you at the meeting today."

"Let's just say that he put up as many roadblocks as he could possibly conceive of. Fortunately, I was able to outthink him. Anyhow, it's all over, and unless I miss my guess, you're good for at least another year on the show, if not more. Would you like to go somewhere tonight, after your play, and celebrate?"

"I'd love to."

"And no Nature's Oasis."

"Since you're the hero of the day, I'll let you decide."

"Fine. Why don't I pick you up at the theater? And that reminds me, I want to talk to you about that play you've been knocking yourself out in."

He would want her to leave the play, she knew it.

"I'll see you tonight. And thank you again, darling. You've made me the happiest hysteric in this crazy business."

He laughed. "With the most beautiful hair."

"Wait until you see it."

"I'll wait, but it won't be easy."

"You'll manage, Jamie. You always do."

"What you mean is that I always have."

"Have what?"

"Been a good little boy."

"I've never thought of you that way," she lied. "Ciao."

She put her hands to her eyes, shutting them tight. The question was: did she want to leave the play? Did she really have to? Plenty of other soap actresses moonlighted and were able to carry it off. But in her case it was slightly different, she didn't want to antagonize Jamie. No. She couldn't *afford* to antagonize him, it would be like slitting her own throat. And yet the play was important to her; it gave her a sense of what it would be like to be in the real theater, in a Broadway production someday, it gave her hope that as much as she was presently dependent upon "The Troubled Heart," she wouldn't always continue to be so. Maybe if she explained it that way, Jamie could be made to understand how she felt. He had always been so sympathetic to her professional aspirations. Elizabeth picked up the telephone and dialed her answering service.

"Mr. Mann called," the operator said. "He said to tell you that you're home free."

"Is that the only message?"

"That's it."

Elizabeth laid down the receiver and stretched out on the sofa. Home free. But she wasn't free at all, not really, not after today; she was indisputedly in Jamie's debt and she wasn't so sure she liked it; she didn't like the idea of being indebted to anyone. But then it occurred to her that if it weren't Jamie, it would have been Iris, and there was no question in Elizabeth's mind that if forced to, she would choose Jamie over her kid sister any day of the week.

When she told Iris at lunch that she'd always thought Iris was brilliant, she'd meant it. There was a scary undercurrent about Iris' brain; yet she'd meant it, too, when she said that her sister's brilliance didn't focus on anything except self-destruction. After all, what had Iris ever done except recently manage to turn out two scripts? Not that that was anything to be sneered at, but Elizabeth wondered (now that she happily no longer needed her sister's professional help) how long Iris' nascent writing career would last. Endurance. That was the key to success, that and persistent hard work. Iris had never worked at anything in her life, not even the one thing that meant the most to her: her own marriage.

And hadn't Iris (as though guessing Elizabeth's true thoughts) bitterly, drunkenly retaliated by saying that she, Elizabeth, had always been considered the beautiful one, the glamorous one, the talented one, the sexy one, the favored one? And wasn't it all true? Favored. Not only by their parents, but by Iris' own coward of a husband. For as much as she had been sexually drawn to Robert and their sub rosa relationship, she never respected him for two-timing Iris with his own sister-in-law. The fact that she hadn't particularly respected herself either was something Elizabeth did her best not to dwell upon. But it had been a rough moment there at lunch today, when Iris accused her of being guilty. For one terrible instant she was certain that Iris had somehow discovered the whole rotten truth, had known all along, was trying to trick her into a delayed confession. Elizabeth smiled to herself because she had tricked Iris instead. So who was *really* the brilliant one?

Her thoughts went back to Jamie. Okay, she was indebted to him, no point in denying that, but only temporarily. Only until she established herself in the strong role that he was about to write for her, the role that could bring the theatrical exposure she needed to further her more-ambitious-than-ever career. Getting up from the sofa, Elizabeth went to her desk and took out the Italian-language cassettes and put the next lesson on her tape recorder.

Voglio un lavaggio di capelli e anche un manicure.

She had never forgotten Sheila's telling her about the actress who was originally supposed to have played the part of Elizabeth on "The Troubled Heart," and how she had been signed by Preminger at the last minute to do a movie in Spain. For some reason, Elizabeth saw herself in Rome. Pasolini, DiSica, Antonioni, maybe even the great Fellini himself would direct her someday. It never hurt to learn a foreign language. Bilingual actresses saved production dubbing expenses.

Voglio un lavaggio di capelli e anche un manicure, Elizabeth began to chant in her best Roman accent.

And later that evening, while Elizabeth and Jamie were celebrating with champagne and eels in green sauce at Quo Vadis, Iris was sitting in Mrs. Richmond's spacious kitchen, sobbing into her cup of Lipton's tea.

"Are you sure you don't want any sugar or lemon?" Mrs. Richmond asked for the second time.

Iris shook her head negatively. "No. Really. This is fine."

"How about a nice piece of sponge cake?"

Again, Iris shook her head. "No, thank you."

Ironically, her lie to Elizabeth that afternoon about having dinner with Mrs. Richmond had turned out to be true. Or perhaps it wasn't so ironic after all, because ever since her encounter with Ken P. that morning (could all these things have possibly happened in one day?), she felt convinced that Mrs. Richmond was the only person she could turn to in hope of getting some pressing questions cleared up. Like the meaning of Ken P.'s remark: "I'll give you the hundred anyway. I'm not a lobster for nothing."

Before Derek left, he had handed her fifty dollars without saying a word, and Iris couldn't help wondering whether being tied up and shoved into someone's closet was automatically worth twice as much as coming in a jar of Tiptree Preserves. Maybe Sheila had decided that it was. Or maybe there was a general call-girl rule about such matters, a sliding scale of payment for various disgusting acts. Because as amused as Iris had been when she realized that Derek himself was the Strawberry Flip, her sense of humor went into a sharp and very unfunny decline not long after his departure. Disgusting was how *she* felt, depressed and depraved by her own participation in such low-life behavior. *How could I have*, she kept wondering, once Derek was gone.

"You're positively smashing," were his last words to her as he went out the door, headed for God-only-knew-where.

Probably to his girlfriend of the moment, to whom he would make normal and nonsensical love, a girl who would never have any idea of his strange inclinations. Even cuckoo Ken P. undoubtedly did not ask the couple he was living with to tie him up and stick him in a closet for fifteen minutes. They were his friends; he would be too ashamed to make the obscene request.

And it was at that moment, sitting on the O'Reillys' sofa, still naked from the waist up, drinking her tenth (?) Bombay of the day, that the entire call-girl message came home to Iris with thundering clarity: friends, wives, girlfriends, fiancees, all of them had to be sheltered, no, absolutely *must* be sheltered from the shame of whatever it was that the men they were involved with secretly, sexually craved. Which was why these men had to pay a professional stranger for it. Because the stranger didn't count, wasn't a real person, was not supposed to have real feelings, was simply supposed to do their bidding, ask no questions, take whatever amount of money the act was worth (by whichever method was devised), and pass no judgment. For how could a whore dare to judge morally the behavior of others? By her own choice of profession, she had forfeited that simple but basic human privilege.

"So that's why you're crying," Mrs. Richmond said, seated across from Iris, drinking her own tea (with sugar and lemon). "Okay, now that you've told me your story, I'm going to tell you something. You think Sheila O'Reilly cried? She did not. She was a smiler. If you can't smile afterwards, you shouldn't do these things. Think of the memory of your poor, dead husband."

"He might be dead," Iris sobbed, "but he wasn't poor. I mean, he wasn't Mr. Nice Guy. He was a rotten, cheating rat, and I'm glad he's dead. He deserved to die after what he did to me."

"Okay, go ahead, tell me what the rat did. Not that I can't guess. I wasn't born yesterday. I'm old enough to be your mother. You think *you* have problems? When you've lived as long as I have, you'll know what problems are. Why do you think it's eleven o'clock at night and the doctor still isn't home?"

Iris blew her nose with a Kleenex from the box that Mrs. Richmond had put on the table hours ago. "I don't know. Why?" So there really was a doctor.

"Because he's having an affair with that divorced *shiksa* nurse of his. And I'm having my menopause. Hot flashes, cold flashes, all from the chest up. And it doesn't come and go overnight, that you can be sure of. Years. That's what goes by with these flashes. Sure, he tells me he's got an emergency operation on a patient who just broke her leg. He's operating, but it's on no patient, and it's got nothing to do with broken legs. Eat a piece of sponge cake and you'll feel better. There are people in this world with problems worse than yours, much worse, and one of them is sitting opposite you this very minute. Do you see me crying? What's the use? I used to cry. Then I thought, what good does it do? So now I cook and bake a lot, I work with alcoholics at Bellevue, I'm taking a speed-reading course. I talk to the doorman, Mike, the one who's on in the morning, I watch that soap opera your friend told me he writes. I keep busy."

"I wish I had never moved into Picasso Towers."

"It's not a bad building." Mrs. Richmond looked reflective. "There are some nice people living here, you should meet them. A lot of widows, divorcées, women with one breast, women who've had hysterectomies and they're not even my age, women with paralytic children, women with husbands who are impotent. I meet them, I talk to them. It makes you feel better to know that you're not alone in the world. Drink your tea before it gets cold."

Iris dried her eyes and took a sip of tea, but it only reminded her of the elaborate tea service she had prepared that afternoon for Derek Christopher before finding out the true purpose of his visit. They never did get around to drinking the Earl Grey, or eating the croissants and Dutch biscuits she had so naively purchased. They were still sitting on the dining table, growing staler by the minute. She would freeze them in Baggies, as she had done with the remains of the Chinese lunch. You never knew when you might want a croissant in the middle of the night. Besides, Ginger had drummed it into her and Elizabeth never to waste food.

"And it's not because of the starving children in India," Ginger used to say. "It's because if you can freeze something, why throw it away? The cook will use it eventually. It's the people without freezers, those are the ones who are out of luck. Not us."

"You're not drinking your tea," Mrs. Richmond said. "Is it too strong? I can add some boiling water."

At this point Iris would have agreed to almost anything Mrs. Richmond suggested, just so long as she stopped talking about hot flashes and women with one breast.

"Yes, maybe a little hot water, if it's not too much trouble. And the goulash was delicious, it really was. My mother never made a meal as far back as I can remember; we always had a cook. On her night off, we'd order chili from Chasen's. That was fun. Or else we'd go to La Scala, the Polo Lounge, the Luau. The Hot Dog was fun, too. You know, inverse chic, with all those Rolls Royces pulled up in front of it."

"No wonder you're degrading yourself with lunatics like the two you just described. What was your mother doing that she was too busy to cook for her own family?"

"She and my father own an art gallery in Los Angeles. It keeps them very occupied. It's a very successful, demanding business. But I don't care to talk about my parents, at least not now. The reason I really rang your doorbell earlier was because I wanted to ask you a few questions. I don't know if you know the answers, but I thought it was worth a try."

Mrs. Richmond, wearing a green monklike gown, her auburn hair perfectly chignoned, poured some of the tea out of Iris' cup and poured some boiling water into it.

"If it's about Sheila O'Reilly and that wonderful sex service she was running in apartment 22-G, I know all the answers. Or at least most of them. Sheila used to like to confide in me. Go ahead. Ask."

"What's a lobster?"

"A hundred-dollar schmuck."

Iris blinked. "Excuse me?"

"It's a dope who pays one hundred dollars to get whatever he came for. That's what he's known in the trade as—a lobster. Now if he pays seventy-five dollars, he's a roast beef. And if he pays fifty, he's a steak."

So Derek was a steak. "What if he pays more than one hundred?"

"It's not too often that that happens, believe me. But if it does, he's a bottle of champagne."

"And if he pays less than fifty?"

"Direct him to West Forty-fourth Street."

"Mrs. Richmond, are you trying to tell me that—?"

Iris was so dumbfounded by this new barrage of information that she could barely summon up the words to finish her sentence, but she needn't have worried. Mrs. Richmond was ready to step in.

"I'm trying to tell you that those are the code words the girls in the business use when they talk to each other. You see they recommend customers to each other all the time, there are a lot of referrals going on in this business, and the girls are afraid that the telephones might be tapped. So they make up these lobster and steak names, instead of coming right out with the actual amount of money the schmuck is willing to pay. Or the amount they can squeeze out of him."

"But if it's something that the girls only use among themselves, how come Ken P. knew that he was a lobster?"

"A masochist like that, maybe it amused Sheila to tell him, I wouldn't put it past her. A real Ph.D. cloud case, that's what she was. I'll bet you didn't know she had a Ph.D. in Sociology. And look what she decides to do with it, become a hooker. I'll give her credit for one thing, though, she handled herself beautifully. No hysterical scenes in apartment 22-G, none that you could hear, anyway, and you know what these walls are like. No payoffs to the cops, and no handouts to the doormen. She tipped them well whenever they did anything special for her, but otherwise not a cent. She must have been pulling in a thousand a week, that's what I figure, and she never worked weekends. I could hear the schmucks coming and going, doors slamming, and that's all I could hear. Except for one person. But you'll find out about him, if you keep it up."

"Who was he?" Iris tried desperately to think of the names on Sheila's typewritten list. "What did he like to do?"

But Mrs. Richmond was adamant. "I just told you. Keep up the good work, and you'll find out for yourself. And when you do, ring my bell afterward. If it's on a Friday, I usually make roast duck with orange sauce. The doctor got tired of stuffed chicken years ago."

Several hours later when Iris was back in her own apartment getting ready for bed, the telephone rang. She hesitated. It was after midnight and it had been a long day, an incredible day; she was exhausted. But then she remembered the agency story conference that had taken place that afternoon. What if it were Elizabeth calling to tell her the outcome? With a feeling of trepidation, she picked up the receiver.

"We've won, we've won, we've won!" It was indeed Elizabeth, more jubilant than Iris had ever heard her. "I've never been so happy in my life. Jamie really did it, the angel, he outsmarted every bastard at that meeting, Derek Christopher in particular, and the result is—"

Iris was jealous, angry, ashamed of herself, unable to help it. "You're not going to be written out of the series. Your part is going to be expanded, you're going to have the affair with Crawford."

"Yes, and it's going to be a beautiful part. Jamie and I just had dinner and he told me a couple of his ideas. It's going to be a part that, it's going to be a *showcase* for my acting ability. Iris, do you realize what I'm saying?"

Iris realized. That her sister no longer needed her help now that she was on her way to potential stardom. And Iris didn't doubt for a moment that Elizabeth would make it; Elizabeth had always achieved whatever she set out after. Elizabeth was the achiever in the family.

"Congratulations, Liz. I think it's simply wonderful. I told you that you had nothing to worry about."

"I'm so happy I could die."

Iris felt like dying, too, but not exactly for the same reason. Then she remembered Derek, the Derek she had seen that afternoon (and would undoubtedly see again), the Derek who had been Elizabeth's adversary (and would undoubtedly not get over his setback too quickly), and a tremor of hope went through her.

"Congratulations." she repeated. "It's going to be very exciting for me, too. Helping Jamie write your new part."

"I know. I couldn't have a better team on my side. I'm really lucky."

Elizabeth's own words about Napoleon came back to her—that luck was a matter of intelligence.

"Let's talk about it some more tomorrow, okay?" Iris said. "I'm bushed, and you must be, too."

"You can say that again. Good night, darling."

Iris put the receiver back on the hook. Suddenly, she felt wide awake, enthusiastic, alive. Whoever said there wasn't room in one family for two achievers?

PART IV

Chapter Eighteen

"You can't fool me, you scheming bastard." Elizabeth seemed unaware of her own shrill voice; what had happened to all that careful modulation she was ordinarily so proud of? "I just read through the next batch of scripts, two weeks' worth, and I see what you're trying to do to me. Do you understand? I see what your fiendish mind is leading up to."

Jamie went over to the harvest table, picked up a bottle of Chivas Regal, poured a generous shot, drank it down in a couple of gulps, and silently congratulated himself for having moved into a building with soundproof walls. He had never seen her like this before, uncharacteristically out of control, rage contorting her lovely features into an ugly mask of hysteria. Although he had not thought of Elizabeth's predecessor, Gina, for several months, she now came into sharp, unrelieved focus. It was the day he told her that they had had it and she tried to hit him over the head with his own castiron skillet, and had then refused to leave the apartment. Only many weeks later did he discover that she had gone through his library of books, and written the same good-bye message on the flyleaf of each one: *Albert was a better lover than you.* Since he had no desire to communicate with her again, he never did find out who the hell Albert was, but as a result of Gina's vengeance he now owned something like three hundred books with torn-out flyleaves. You could never tell what particular form their lunacy was going to take, until disaster actually struck.

"What is it that you think I'm trying to do to you?" He kept his voice as calm and emotionless as possible. "Go ahead. Tell me."

"It's not what I think. It's what I know." She had begun to pace up and down his long, wood-paneled living room, reminding him of Bette Davis as the evil twin sister in *A Stolen Life.* "You're slowly starting to turn me into a drunk on the show. You've begun to build up to a very distinct alcoholic personality. It's all right there."

She pointed toward the manila envelope of scripts that lay on the harvest table, next to the Scotch. "First, I get smashed at lunch, seemingly innocent enough: it could happen to anyone. But the seed is planted, because when I go home for dinner that evening, I order a bottle of wine. There's no occasion for it, either, although I pretend I'm doing it for my mother's sake, to cheer her up a little. My mother takes one sip of the wine, I drink the whole bottle and become giddy."

"You're worried about her health. Your mother's medical symptoms are becoming more distressing to you every day."

"Who are you trying to kid, Jamie? You know that only so-called bad women drink on soaps."

"But you wanted this part. Of course you're a bad woman. You're about to have an affair with a corrupt politician, who just happens to be a married man with an invalid wife. How bad can you get on daytime television, short of being a murderer or dope pusher?"

"There are different ways of being bad. Misguided bad. Bitchy bad. Ruthlessly bad. Even tricked into badness. But alcoholic bad? Me? I mean, the me on 'The Troubled Heart'? That sweet, innocent girl, who's had probably three champagne cocktails in her life is about to start downing martinis for breakfast. I can see it coming. And to think I believed you after that last story conference, when you told me what a fabulous part you were going to write for me. How stupid I was, how naive. I thought you meant a *strong* part. I even let you talk me into quitting the off-off Broadway play, in order to concentrate on Elizabeth. What a trusting jerk I've been."

"But it is a strong part."

"No. You can't portray an alcoholic as strong. They're weak, ineffectual people and you know it. They're pathetic. Losers. The makeup man will have a field day, turning me into a cosmetic wreck. I can see the bags under my eyes already, the stringy, unwashed, unset hair, that terrible, unhealthy pallor. Jamie, how could you?"

He had been dreading this inevitable moment. "Elizabeth, please listen to me. It wasn't my idea. I swear it."

She stopped in the middle of the room, her elegant Galanos chiffon stilled at last. "Really?"

"There's no point in being sarcastic."

"Is that all you have to say?"

"It was Derek's idea."

"You're a liar."

"It's the truth, Elizabeth. You have to believe me."

"I've believed you for too long. That's been my mistake."

"He was determined, I tell you. I couldn't talk him out of it. You know he's never liked you. You admitted it yourself."

"How convenient of you to have a ready-made scapegoat. Naturally, Derek is the perfect person to pin this on. Given all the circumstances, he's the most plausible villain, isn't he?"

When Jamie told a lie, it sounded like the truth. When he told the truth, it sounded like a lie. Why was that? he wondered. "I couldn't talk him out of it." He was repeating himself, something he rarely did. "Nothing I said worked. Nothing. He was adamant."

They were standing only inches apart now, facing each other. In a second, her mask of anger had begun to dissolve, as fear set in. "Then you admit it. You really are going to turn me into the town drunk, aren't you?"

"Yes."

"I was hoping . . ."

"That you'd misconstrued the clues in those new scripts?"

"Yes."

"No, you didn't, I regret to say. Alcohol is the way you cope with your guilt for wanting to go to bed with Crawford. You despise your own immoral desires. We have you pictured up until now as a very moral type girl, remember?"

"And then when my mother dies, and I actually start the affair with Crawford . . ."

He spoke almost mechanically. "In about a month from now."

"Then I really hit the bottle. Right?"

"Right."

She confronted him with an attempt at calm detachment.

"Do you expect me to believe that Derek dreamed up this nasty little twist all by himself?"

"He not only dreamed it up, he managed to get the sponsor and the agency guys on his side. They thought it was a terrific idea, very grabby. As Derek pointed out—quite accurately, I'm afraid—there are a hell of a lot of secret housewife-lushes all over this country. These women will be able to identify with, empathize with Elizabeth's predicament. And furthermore, don't forget that Derek is married to the sponsor's niece. Derek Christopher pulls a lot of weight in policymaking decisions, he's not just another producer of daytime TV."

"Pass the buck. That's the story of your life, isn't it?" Fear and detachment had given way to her earlier stance of bitter, frustrated anger. "You once told me something I've never forgotten, Jamie. It's something very appropriate to this situation, although I'm sure you don't want to hear it. Why should you want to? You're a coward. And like most cowards, you don't even have the guts to take the blame for your own shameful actions. Disgusting."

He debated making himself another drink, decided against it. Yet this impasse with Elizabeth was becoming more unpleasant by the minute.

"Iris is going to be here soon. Don't you think you should try to pull yourself together before she arrives? You wouldn't want your sister to see you in this condition, now would you?"

"That's exactly what I mean. Pass the buck, this time to Iris. You're the one who doesn't want to see me in this condition. You can't stand the sight of any display of emotion, you never could. It figures. Who else but someone who was terrified of emotion would end up writing soaps? If it weren't so damned ironic, I'd laugh. But what's the point? The joke is on me. I have no intention of laughing."

She's going to start crying, Jamie thought. He could feel the barrage of tears coming on. Christ. Why did they all cry? Because it was their most effective weapon and they knew it, the bitches; they knew that only a man with a concentration-camp mentality would not be affected by a woman's quiet (or unquiet) sobbing. His mother used to cry whenever she became frustrated about something, and his father invariably gave in. *I won't be like him.* But the resolution was thirty years too late. He was like his father in many ways, even though most of the time he managed to dispel the notion of there being any parallels between them.

"We have a Christmas party to go to, as soon as Iris gets here," he reminded Elizabeth, trying to ward off her tears. "If you don't care about your sister seeing you like this, think of the cast. Think of the crew. Better yet, think of Derek. Do you want to give him that pleasure, after what he's done to you?"

"Very clever, but you didn't let me finish what I was going to say. Regarding your masterful ability to pass the buck.

The story you once told me about Stanley. *Ricorda?* That's Italian for *'Remember?'* "

"Okay. Get it out of your system."

"How when you were very young, if you ever did something that displeased your parents, you'd say that you hadn't done it at all, that Stanley, who lived next door, had done it. Well, Derek has become your grown-up Stanley. That's my modest conclusion."

"Ask him yourself if you don't believe me."

"You know I'd never sink to that, which is the only reason you're suggesting it. Again, very clever, Jamie. Because I have too much pride to give Derek the satisfaction of thinking he might have hurt me, and you're damned well aware of it."

"In that case, you'll just have to take my word on the matter. You have no other choice."

Elizabeth opened her mouth to say something in rebuttal, realized the futility of it, walked over to the six-foot wicker Mickey Mouse statue that Jamie had recently purchased, and angrily pulled off some of the silver tinsel.

"Who ever heard of trimming a Mickey Mouse monstrosity like a Christmas tree?" she said, instead. "Only someone as unpredictable as you."

"I think it's kind of original, myself." The doorbell rang. "Here she is, Miss America."

Iris was wearing her blue mole cape, no makeup, and a pair of slinky satin culottes that could only be partially seen since she made no attempt to remove the cape. She took two gift-wrapped packages out of a shopping bag, and handed one to each of them.

"I'm not going to be able to make it to the party, but Merry Christmas anyhow." She walked unsteadily to the sofa and collapsed on it. "Could I please have a drink? I've got the most horrendous hangover."

"What do you mean?" Elizabeth sat down at the foot of the sofa. "I thought you were looking forward to going to the studio and meeting everyone. At least that's what you said last week. Good God, isn't there anybody I can believe any more?"

Iris looked questioningly at Jamie.

"She doesn't believe the alcoholic switch was Derek's idea," he said.

"Why not?"

"Because she thinks it was my idea."

"You're damned right I do," Elizabeth said.

"While you two are slugging it out, can I have a drink?"

"You've had enough, more than enough," Elizabeth reproached her sister. "You know, they only throw these studio parties once a year, every Christmas Eve. I should think you'd be anxious to meet the actors you've been writing for. Don't you have any curiosity? Not to mention the director, and our devious, but all-powerful producer. You've never laid eyes on any of them."

"Maybe another time."

"If she doesn't want to go, she doesn't want to go," Jamie said. "Besides, in her condition, she's better off getting some rest. I assume that when we leave here, you'll be returning to your apartment, Iris."

"Where else? Just give me one drink and my presents, and I'll be on my way."

"It's going to have to be Scotch," Jamie said. "I'm out of gin."

"Just so long as it's at least eighty proof."

Jamie handed her a drink, ignoring Elizabeth's frown of disapproval; then he went upstairs to the room he had converted into an office. Both his and Elizabeth's gifts for Iris lay on the leather studio-couch where he sometimes took catnaps in between writing segments of "The Troubled Heart." The gifts were in Saks boxes, festively adorned with Christmas wrapping paper and crimson ribbons. At Elizabeth's suggestion he had bought Norell perfume for Iris, while Elizabeth decided upon a mauve wool pants suit with a Swedish designer's label.

"She's been in New York for more than two months now," Elizabeth said to him last week, when they'd gone shopping, "and the poor kid hasn't bought a stitch of clothing for herself. She owns a few cashmere sweaters, one Rudi Gernreich skirt, one cream-colored pants suit, and that's it. For winter in New York, I mean. When I asked her why she didn't buy something to wear, she said she had no place to go, and that she virtually lives in all those trailing, at-home outfits she's so fond of. I can't imagine what she does with herself all day. Aside from that woman who has the apartment next door, I don't believe she's made one friend—male or female—since she got here. And you know how hard I've tried to introduce her to people in the last couple of months."

It was true, he had to concede that much about Elizabeth. Rivalry or no, she had done her best to broaden the incredibly narrow scope of Iris' life, but Iris remained adamant in her pursuit of solitary confinement. With the exception of Elizabeth and himself, she had shown no interest at all in meeting other people.

"She writes 'The Troubled Heart,' and she watches soaps," Jamie had said in response to Elizabeth's conjecturing. "That's what she does all day."

"You left out her preoccupation with Bombay gin."

"True. Drinking the way she does must consume a great deal of time and energy. She told me that she generally passes out in the evening after 'Eyewitness News.' The early edition. I think she's hung up on Geraldo Rivera."

But even though he had flippantly tried to explain the extent of Iris' activities, he himself was somewhat baffled. Explanations were one thing, comprehension was something else again. She was strange, almost eerie; he'd thought so right from the start, from the very first moment he picked her up at JFK when her opening comment to him was: "Harzt Mountain Bird Seed." Still, she was no fool; she had caught onto the knack of soap writing much faster than he would have believed possible, the girl had an undeniable talent for it. Her arrival in New York could not have worked out better for him, professionally, if he had arranged it himself. And he was still only paying her one hundred per script, which was peanuts compared to what he would have had to pay an experienced professional. The odd part was that she didn't seem to evince any desire for more money, didn't seem to realize that if she asked for twice that much he would have given it to her. Between two hundred and two hundred and fifty dollars was about the going rate for sub-contracting writers, although he knew of one guy on a rival network who was getting away with paying one hundred and fifty to some eager young woman, anxious to break into the field. But one hundred a script! It was ridiculously low, unheard of, ingenious of him. Whenever he felt guilty about shortchanging Iris, he reminded himself of her Bel Air background of luxury, compared to his own growing-up years when he was forced to use the living-room sofa as his bed; there was only one bedroom, and it belonged to his parents. No wonder he had chosen this sprawling barn of an apartment. Even the renting agent was mildly impressed when he heard that it was going to be a single occupancy.

Jamie picked up the gifts for Iris and started toward the stairs, hoping that Elizabeth would have calmed down by now, realizing that no matter how much money he made the rest of his life, no matter how successful he became, no matter how large an apartment he leased (or purchased), he would never fully recover from the deprivation of those early formative years. To this day, he could not look at a convertible sofa without feeling sick to his stomach.

"That's what he's trying to convince me of," Elizabeth was saying to Iris, as Jamie came into the living room. "That it was all Derek's doing. You've never met Derek Christopher or you would see why I find it an extremely farfetched story."

Iris looked at her sister with such innocence that Jamie could have kissed her. "I don't understand."

"Derek hasn't had an original idea in his life. Why should he start now? It doesn't make sense."

"Well, as you said, I've never met the man but I don't think Jamie would lie to you about something as important as this. Besides, he told me the same thing."

"And you believed him, of course."

"What reason would I have had not to?"

"Call it gullnerability."

Both sisters were seated on the sofa, huddled together like schoolgirls, their voices clear and distinct because Elizabeth had not yet lowered hers to its naturally moderate tone, and because Iris always spoke louder when she was drinking. On the few occasions that Jamie had seen her sober, or relatively so, he was always surprised at how low-pitched her normal voice was, how almost inaudible. She needed to drink for courage, but there was an audacity, an insanity about her drinking that in some peculiar way impressed him. Of course if she kept it up she'd have cirrhosis by the time she was thirty. It was plain that she didn't care whether she lived or died, was unremorsefully killing herself while numbing the pain of consciousness. Any form of extremism had always presented an inexplicable fascination for Jamie, perhaps because he denied himself the privilege of self-indulgence. He'd mentioned it to his agent last week.

"Only those who grew up financially secure seem to be able to permit themselves hedonistic luxuries, without feeling guilty in the process."

THE THREE OF US

It was a good line, a bit heavy to stick into "The Troubled Heart," although maybe not. Every once in a while it wasn't a bad idea to slip in a pretentious piece of dialogue, thereby reminding the viewer that she was watching the handiwork of people more intelligent than she. The actors, of course. That was what a small percentage of soap addicts believed, that the actors made up their own lines as they went along. A still larger percentage believed that the actors weren't actors at all, but were really the characters they portrayed, living in the very real town of Jeffersonville. There was the famous story of a leading soap actress who went home to the Midwest to visit her family and was warmly greeted by her grandmother, who addressed her by her television name. As crazy a phenomenon as it might appear to the non-soap viewer, Jamie could understand the confusion in identities that took place when someone played a provocative role over a period of time. It was a fortunate coincidence, he thought, that Elizabeth was Elizabeth, on TV and off.

"Merry merry merry Christmas." He kissed Iris on the cheek, and handed her the two gifts. "The small one is from me. I hope your sister gave me the right steer. But you can't open them now. You have to wait until tomorrow."

Iris had started to attack the crimson ribbons. "Don't be silly. I have no intention of waiting. I've never been able to wait for anything in my life."

"Why did you give her that drink?" Elizabeth demanded of him. "Can't you see the shape she's in? Or don't you care?"

"I'm not her keeper."

He felt like saying, "But I wouldn't mind being her lover." In the two months since he and Iris had been working together, he'd begun to develop a nagging curiosity about what she would be like in bed. Whether she would be much different from Elizabeth. Of course she would, she was different from Elizabeth in every other respect; why shouldn't the dissimilarity extend to the erotic? There was an undeniable appeal about the fact that she had made it with only one man in her life, that conniving sculptor she married. Jamie wanted to teach her the sexual ropes, because something told him that she would be a more-than-avid learner. Even now, half-bombed, without makeup, her hair a mass of disheveled blonde Priscilla Lane curls, there was a quality of the sensuous about her. He had become more and more aware of it within ... he tried to think back to the first time it hit him, but he couldn't remember the exact moment of recognition. Neither could he imagine what had caused the change in her. For he felt certain that it was a fairly new quality; she hadn't had it when they'd first met, of that he was certain. But what could possibly account for it? According to Iris herself, she was leading "a completely sexless life, goddamn it." Even Elizabeth confirmed that fact, saying her sister wasn't really interested in lovemaking, never had been, and was jealous of Elizabeth's own strongly defined eroticism. Maybe. Jamie wondered.

"Thank you. Norell." Iris opened the bottle and dabbed some of the perfume on both wrists, then touched her finger to her nose. "That's so I can smell it, too."

"I assume you're going to open mine now," Elizabeth said, in resignation.

Iris smiled as she took the mauve pants suit out of its mounds of tissue paper. "It's lovely, Liz. Exactly what I needed. Jamie, did I ever tell you how my darling sister used to try to give me her cast-off clothes when we were growing up? She said that if she didn't give them to me, they'd only go to one of the help. Don't you think that's a riot?"

"If we're going to that party, we'd better get a move on." Jamie spoke quickly, hoping to avert an argument between the two women. "Iris, are you sure you don't want to change your mind and join us?"

She was putting the Norell in her purse, putting the pants suit back in its box, tying the box with the crimson ribbon, using it like string.

"I'm not up to a party. I would appreciate it, though, if you got me a taxi when we go downstairs. I don't like this neighborhood. It gives me the creeps."

"I'm going to have to get three taxis. Elizabeth and I don't want to arrive together. Nobody connected with 'The Troubled Heart' has the vaguest idea that we're—" He was about to say "in love," but changed it to "romantically involved." "And we'd like to keep it that way. As for the neighborhood, you probably went toward Amsterdam the last time, instead of Central Park."

"What last time?" Elizabeth asked.

"The last time Jamie and I worked together," Iris said.

"I didn't realize that you'd been here when I wasn't."

"You were at the studio, taping the next day's show." Iris buttoned her cape. "I guess you're going to be there a lot, now that your part is becoming so large."

"Drunkenly large."

Elizabeth would nail a point into the ground, Jamie thought; she did not give up easily, not when she was this upset. He had been pretty upset himself when Derek first suggested the character switch from nice, quiet, ladylike Elizabeth to a burgeoning, then a full-fledged drunk. He knew that the real-life Elizabeth would hate the prospect of playing an alcoholic; she would have to be made up to look haggard, sloppy, out of control, an addict. She would have to become on the TV screen what she felt her sister had become offscreen: a pathetic and unpalatable mess.

He bravely put his arms around Elizabeth. "It's going to be a good, juicy part. Something to really sink your teeth into. This is what you've been waiting for, the chance to show what a fine actress you are. Well, your chance is about to arrive, sweetheart."

Elizabeth rewarded him with a chilling glance of helpless, hopeless anger. *"Grazie."*

"Prego."

"I didn't know you knew one word of Italian."

"There are a lot of things about me that you don't know."

"Such as?"

They were in the elevator now, he and the two witches.

"Such as the time Gina and I had an argument, and she threw all my clothes down her incinerator while I was sleeping."

"What did you do?" Iris asked. "How did you get home?"

"I wrapped myself from head to toe with two rolls of her aluminum foil, and walked out into a raging snowstorm. When people stopped to stare at me on the street, I told them that I'd been foiled."

Even Elizabeth couldn't help smiling. "You just made that up, Jamie."

"No, it's the truth. I swear it."

"Just like you still swear that it was Derek's idea to do me in on the show."

"Corretto."

Iris was enjoying a private, drunken giggle, and when

Jamie got her into the first empty taxi that came along, she
rolled down the window.

"Now you're the one who's been foiled, Elizabeth."

Then the light changed and her taxi was off.

Chapter Nineteen

But the minute the taxi pulled away from the Des Artistes,
Iris' facade of levity dissolved, and guilt set in. She was
guilty about two things, and had been for some time:

1. The continuation of her call-girl activities, starting with
   Ken P. (two months ago).
2. The fact that she had convinced Derek Christopher to
   turn Elizabeth into a drunk on "The Troubled Heart"
   (about six weeks ago).

Not that Derek needed all that much convincing; he lit up
like Jamie's Mickey Mouse Christmas-tree substitute as soon
as she made the suggestion. It happened during his fourth
visit to her apartment for another sensational Tiptree orgasm. They were almost like old friends by then, and, as she
had discovered with many of the men she'd been seeing,
Derek enjoyed sitting in the living room and talking awhile
before getting down to business. Iris had the feeling that, like
the others, he found social conversation an effective way to
relax and unwind before the kinky stuff began.

Iris didn't mind. In fact, she rather enjoyed these talk ses-
sions; they were cozy, pleasant, comfortable. Her visitors
(she still could not think of them as crass customers) would
lead off with whatever happened to be on their minds that
particular day, and since for the most part they were married
businessmen, the subject invariably turned to either their
marital or professional interests. Men had told her the most
intimate things about their wives and, without naming com-
panies or personnel, about their business problems, all of

which she found quite illuminating. People had never confided in her before, although she quickly learned that three subjects were taboo in her new profession: politics, religion, and modern art. They were too controversial, too emotionally loaded. Steer clear of them. It was Derek who tipped her off on that score just before they had started talking about "The Troubled Heart," by far their favorite topic of conversation.

"Why do you imagine Sheila has all these idiotic animal paintings on the walls?" He indicated the cat, zebra, kangaroo, pelican, and turtle. "Because she assumes they're great art?"

"But, honey, that's what I asked you the first time we met. And all you did was clam up."

"The reason is because no man in his right mind could possibly object to those innocuously painted creatures. No arguments could ensue. Sheila was very clever about little things like that, I must say. She knew how to avoid controversy during business hours."

Iris was about to reply that that certainly was perceptive of her predecessor when she remembered that she was supposed to be an experienced, knowledgeable call girl, aware of such occupational hazards. She cursed herself for having forgotten to ask Mrs. Richmond about the paintings.

"Perhaps that's how it's done in New York, but in Bel Air it's considered quite the thing to have as much interesting and provocative artwork around as a girl can afford. It raises her cultural standing in the eyes of the client—her appreciation of the aesthetic—and I never heard of an argument arise as a result of it. In fact, it invariably makes a girl's price go up. But as we've discussed before, these matters do vary from city to city, and I appreciate your clueing me in."

She suspected that Derek would faint if he knew of her parents' art gallery and her own longtime, firsthand familiarity with the world of painting and sculpture. There was no question in Iris' mind that Derek would absolutely faint if he knew that she had anything to do with "The Troubled Heart" (other than watch it), by way of being Elizabeth's sister and Jamie's second writer. It was amazing how easy it had been to keep her association with Derek a secret from Elizabeth and Jamie, and her association with them a secret from Derek. Having a last name different from Elizabeth's certainly helped, as did her not yet being entitled to a screen credit of her own. Still she felt it was more than both those pieces of good luck that had saved the day.

It was something else.

Iris wasn't quite sure what, except that since she'd moved to New York, everything that had happened to her seemed to have been almost fatalistically designed to ensure her success in playing the last role on earth she could have imagined for herself: a conniving and ingenious double-dealer. She wondered how long it would be before she was found out. She wondered *how* she would be found out. By whom. And perhaps most tantalizing (masochistic?) of all, what would happen to her as a result of the disclosure. Every quivering, delicious, outrageous, lunatic, self-destructive possibility had come to mind; but what amazed her most of all was that mixed in with her feelings of guilt were equally strong feelings of defiance. Half the time she didn't give a damn what ultimately happened, and the other half she cared very much, was afraid. It was like being on a precarious seesaw, not knowing how to get off.

"It feels like it's going to snow," the cabdriver said.

"Good."

"What's good about it?"

"I've never seen snow in my life."

"You're kidding. Where're you from?"

"Los Angeles."

"You've never seen snow?" They had stopped for a light. "You haven't missed much. Snow in the country, maybe that's okay, but snow in New York . . ." He let out a disparaging whistle. "Terrible. A mess."

"Weather doesn't mean much to me. I'm a call girl. I work at home."

The driver turned around and looked at her, laughed. "Sure. And I'm J. Paul Getty."

There was one way of getting off the seesaw and she'd been thinking about that, too. Go back to L.A., back to the solitary, virtuous, innocent life she had led there, the life she'd known only through her television set. But even when she considered the possibility of such a move, she realized that it was impossible. She could never go back to that cocoon, that dream world, that hypocritical world of soap operas where the family unit represented everything good, decent, worth saving in society. What a laugh. Iris now understood the immense popularity of a soap like "The Trou-

bled Heart"—why it attracted ten million viewers a week,
why it had attracted her: because it appealed to all the neglected, frustrated women all over the country—women left
alone, women with unfulfilled dreams, women getting older,
women losing their looks, women who never had looks to
lose, women on the verge of losing their men, women who
had already lost their men, women whose men had other
things on their minds besides them.

But on soaps the only thing men *did* have on their minds
was women. That was the clue. Even bitches were constantly
being paid attention by the various men in their lives,
whether they were husbands, lovers, sons, nephews, uncles,
fathers, grandfathers, grandsons, fathers-in-law, sons-in-law,
employers, doctors, lawyers, politicians, friends of the family.
In a town like Jeffersonville, no business appointment was too
important for a man to cancel on the spur of the moment in
order to rush to the aid and comfort of a distressed woman.
And it didn't matter if that woman was sixteen or sixty,
wealthy or poor, beautiful or plain, neurotic, psychotic, alcoholic, homicidal, suicidal—there was always a man too ready
to help her. No. *Eager.*

Whereas the men Iris had been encountering lately were
rushing to her for help, men who needed her to aid and comfort them before they were able to go back to their offices,
or home to their neglected wives, broken washing machines,
demanding children. And yet these were not men about to
get divorced, or even thinking of divorce; in their own way
they liked their jobs, loved their families, and would probably
be lost without both, but Iris had come to realize they would
be equally lost without girls like her who provided the flattery
and stimulation they could not find at home or at the office.
It made her wonder whether her father had ever gone to call
girls, whether Ginger knew about it and didn't care; or
maybe her father was one of the lucky few who were satisfied with what they had.

Of course there were men who, if not entirely satisfied,
went to amateurs for gratification, the way Bob had done.
But now that Iris knew what she knew, she would have
preferred it if he'd sought the services of a professional;
she would have felt less jealous, less unloved, less rejected.
She still felt unloved because men did not pay her for love
and gypsy violins, they paid for their itch of the moment. She
temporarily cured that itch and they were grateful; at times,

affectionate. Attentive, certainly, which was more than could be said for Bob. She almost had to laugh. The men she saw now made her feel more important and needed than she had ever felt in her life. Perhaps they were her oddball way of getting back at Bob. In that case, writing "The Troubled Heart" also could be a way of getting back at Elizabeth. It was possible.

And as the taxi pulled into the circular driveway of Picasso Towers, Iris wondered if perhaps she hadn't found her life's work at last, her double work of revenge. If that were true, she had her own well-meaning parents and sister to thank for it; her parents because they talked her into moving to New York against her will, and Elizabeth because she had so conveniently (if naively) arranged for the O'Reillys' sublet. Perhaps she had Bob to thank most of all, for having married her without caring for her, for cheating on her throughout their marriage, and finally for dying on her and leaving no explanation with which she could console herself for his cruel and mysterious behavior.

It serves them right that I've become a whore, Iris thought, as she fished in her purse for the cab fare. *A double whore.*

"You're really a secretary, aren't you?" the driver asked.

"How did you guess?"

"Call it feminine intuition."

"No, really," Derek said, his surprise genuine enough, that afternoon six weeks ago. "What made you suspect that Elizabeth would end up having an affair with her boss?"

"You mean, she *definitely* is going to?"

"Definitely."

"Oh, I think that's terrific." Iris clapped her hands, trying to feign girlish enthusiasm, excitement. "I can hardly wait for it to begin. That's just what the show needs, in my opinion: a good, hot, sexy romance."

"We think so, too, but what intrigues me is why you felt that the story line would go that way."

"It just seemed obvious. It's seemed obvious to me right from the start, from the time she first began working for Craig Crawford, that that was the direction things would take. They've always been attracted to each other, anybody could see that."

Derek honored her with a patronizing smile. "Because, my

dear, that's the way we've been playing it. Writing it. Directing it. Slanting it. The attraction part. But very often, on soaps, a potential romance will be indicated and then for various reasons too complicated to go into, we'll decide to scrap the entire idea. That could have happened in this case. We might have decided that the Elizabeth-Crawford combination just wasn't smashing enough, and that would have been the end of that. Finis. But you're not in the business, so naturally you wouldn't be aware of all the inherent possibilities."

Iris was enjoying herself immensely; he was such a smug fool. "When you say 'we,' who do you mean?"

"It's usually a collective decision. The sponsor and the agency people have their say, the writer, of course, and as producer I'm not exactly uninfluential. We have periodic meetings to resolve matters like this. And at the last meeting we did precisely that—the resolution being that our Cinderella girl was finally going to turn to S-E-X."

"Extramarital S-E-X," Iris pointed out.

"Don't you think it would be believable in Elizabeth's case?" he asked quickly. "You must, or you wouldn't have reached the same conclusion yourself."

"I think it's beautifully believable; people really enjoy seeing anyone who's as virtuous as Elizabeth has been until now give in to temptation. The innocent sinner. It makes people feel less guilty about their own sins, if you know what I mean."

Derek planted his hands on Iris' breasts, which were tantalizingly visible through the filmy gown she wore. "You're a very clever little girl, did anyone ever tell you that?"

"And very sinful."

"Very," he agreed, laughing. "I can see where I might be tempted to ask your advice in the future. How would you like to become 'The Troubled Heart's' unofficial consultant?"

"You're teasing me. That's not kind."

"I'm not teasing at all. I'm perfectly serious."

"In that case, I'm flattered."

"Good. Good."

"There's only one thing," Iris said hesitantly.

"What's that?"

"If my advice means that much to you, I think I should be paid for it. Strictly off the record, of course."

"But I pay you fifty dollars every time I come back."

"Ideas are extra."

"How much extra?"

"Shall we say another fifty? If they're acceptable, of course. Otherwise we'll go on as we are, with the original fifty."

"Clever *and* enterprising." Derek regarded her admiringly. "Very well. I'm game."

"That's wonderful, because I have an idea right now."

He looked at his watch. "Can you make it brief? I'm going to have to dash in about twenty minutes."

"You're always running out on me, you foolish man." Since his Tiptree orgasm only took about four minutes, Iris figured she had more than enough time. "My idea is that Elizabeth must be made to pay for her immoral behavior. And pay dearly."

"That gocs without saying. All immoral behavior is ultimately punishable on 'The Troubled Heart.' Otherwise we'd never sell another jar of our delicious peanut butter, cake mixes, and the rest of that bilge. Sorry, Iris, but that is not a fifty-dollar idea."

"You haven't heard what I had in mind."

"Don't tell me. Let me guess." His arrogance had returned. "She becomes pregnant by Crawford and goes to a neighboring city where abortions are legal."

"Wrong. She turns into an alcoholic, because of her guilty conscience."

Derek, who had just been about to take a sip of his gin and tonic, stopped in mid-movement, his eyes significantly blank. In the next apartment Mrs. Richmond slammed a door so hard that the zebra on the O'Reilly's wall shook in its frame. Derek finished his drink in one swallow, and a slow smile of satisfaction spread over his pale features.

"It's a brilliant idea. Inspired. And what's more, I think the sponsor will go for it. He's a confirmed teetotaler; he would consider it the most appropriate punishment for Elizabeth's sexual digressions."

"What about the others? What do you think their reaction will be?"

Derek was beaming. "That's for me to worry about. An alcoholic. Very fitting indeed. The illegal abortion thing has been done to death on soaps and, frankly, I can't remember a female alcoholic situation in one hell of a long time. Speaking of time . . ."

As Iris went into the kitchen to get the Tiptree preserves,

she could not help wondering what the supercilious Derek Christopher would think if he knew that he had just elevated himself from a lowly steak to a gorgeous, classy, fresh Maine lobster.

Chapter Twenty

Elizabeth was in her cab, heading south to the Christmas Eve studio party and wondering whether perhaps she hadn't been too hard on Jamie after all, too unfair. Perhaps it *was* Derek's fault, turning her into a drunk on the show. She wanted to believe that Derek was to blame; Iris certainly seemed to believe it, not that that proved much. Iris was so naive she probably would have believed whatever Jamie told her. He had such a sincere manner. Besides, what difference did it make to Iris *who* had dreamed up the nasty character switch? None at all. What interested and undoubtedly amused Iris was the fact that her sister should be made to suffer on television from the same affliction that she herself was stuck with in real life.

Now you're the one who's been foiled, Elizabeth.

But foiled by whom?

Elizabeth leaned back against the cold taxi seat and shivered in her lavish de la Renta red-fox coat, in her Galanos chiffon, in her unsteady (and "troubled") heart. However, after a few minutes, she began to examine the situation in a more objective, constructive light. If Jamie were lying, it could only mean that he had started to fall out of love with her; why else would he want to play such a dirty trick? If he were telling the truth, it could only mean that Derek had gotten the upper hand at last; how else could he play such a dirty trick? Either way it didn't look good, but she had long ago learned to probe beneath the surface for hidden, built-in opportunities; and as the taxi pulled up in front of the studio door Elizabeth Small decided that it was about time she changed her name to Elizabeth Mann. In fact, it was the perfect time.

Behind her, another taxi discharged its passenger, a furtive and apprehensive Jamie. At first he pretended not to see her. Then he smiled. Weakly. Guiltily. Sincerely.

"Hello there," she said, in case anyone from the show overheard them. "Don't you write 'The Troubled Heart'?"

I used to, Jamie thought, still recovering from the unpleasantness of Elizabeth's earlier attack. He had known she would be angry when she read the new scripts and found out how they planned to change her part; he'd been prepared for her outrage, but not for her vitriolic disbelief in his integrity. That was what hurt the most, that she thought he was lying to her about whose idea it had been. In effect she was calling him a double-crosser. That, combined with a sense of loss over his own material, made Jamie wish that he were anywhere tonight but here. He wished it weren't Christmas Eve. He wished Elizabeth didn't look so lovely, so betrayed. He wished that he didn't have to face that prick, Derek Christopher, and try to be polite to the man responsible for the entire mess.

"Yes, I'm the writer," Jamie said, feeling like an idiot. "And you play the part of Elizabeth. Very competently, I might add."

Elizabeth was about to say something equally innocuous when another taxi came to a stop and let out four of the cast, including the actor who played Craig Crawford. He had brought his wife along, a beautiful woman much younger than himself; she bore no resemblance to his ailing, invalid wife on the show. Elizabeth and Jamie waited until the new arrivals had settled the taxi fare, and amidst ebullient holiday greetings and theatrical kisses allowed themselves to be caught up with the others, as they made their camouflaged entrance into the huge complex of network studios to celebrate the eve of Christ's birth and the continued success of "The Troubled Heart."

Uptown. East.

A tall, light-skinned, straight-haired, expensively tailored Puerto Rican walked casually past the doorman of Picasso Towers, through the ornate lobby and to the side elevators, where a door opened at a touch of the "Up" button. Inside, the man tapped number 22 with an Italian capeskin glove.

In the other hand he carried a red TWA tennis bag, attached to which was his racquet in a matching TWA tennis cover. Neat. Practical. Economical. And very American. Frederico Perez whistled a few bars of "Silent Night" as the elevator sped upward to apartment 22-G, where Iris was expecting him. As usual, he could hardly wait to get there.

She opened the door immediately, her clinging, hot-pink cashmere gown worn off the shoulders (as he told her he preferred it), and not a stitch underneath. "Freddie! Merry Christmas. Come in, come in."

"How've you been, honey?" He moved into the O'Reillys' living room with the same casual ease that marked his recent appearance on all the top TV talk shows. "I rushed like hell to get here, even stopped right in the middle of a hot chapter. Glad you could make it, but I'm afraid I don't have much time."

They never had much time, none of them except for Bubble Bath Charles, who had been there earlier in the day, soaking in pine-oil-scented water for close to two hours while telling Iris the most insipid jokes she had heard in years. Example:

"A man meets two of his friends at a bar. He turns to the guy on his right and starts to talk politics, whereupon the bartender says, 'Sorry, no political conversations allowed in here.' Okay. So the man turns to the guy on his left and starts to talk religion. The bartender says, 'Sorry, no religious conversations either.' 'How about sex?' the frustrated man asks. 'That's okay,' replies the bartender. 'In that case,' says the frustrated man, 'go fuck yourself.'"

Since Charles was willing to shell out one hundred dollars for this erotic hydrotherapy treatment, Iris couldn't very well not laugh. In fact, she felt sorry for him, the poor dear. It seemed that when he was a child his mother used to pretty much ignore him while he took his evening bath, and always hurried him out of it and off to bed before he was ready to go. That was the beginning of his hangup, he had told Iris: bubble baths equaled sexual attention times the speed of orgasm squared (he was a nuclear physicist). He never asked Iris to undress, and he never touched her. All she had to do was sit at the edge of the tub, let out the water, at which strategic time he would ejaculate into the last of the pine-oil-scented bath bubbles. Upon leaving, he would kiss her on the cheek and quote Einstein. "When does Zurich stop at this train?" She was not supposed to answer.

"I'd like a fast drink." Freddie tossed his English camel's-hair coat on the shag rug. "J&B on the rocks. Then let's get started, okay? My in-laws are coming over for dinner. In fact, why don't I change while you make the drinks?"

"Anything you say."

Perez' movements were swift, smooth. In the time it had taken Iris to step out of her gown and mix two drinks, he had divested himself of his street clothes and now sat on the sofa, wearing only a white sports shirt with the famous Lacoste Alligator emblem, and on his feet a pair of Adidas tennis shoes. Iris knew that he had bought both at Feron's, just as she knew that he used a Head fiberglas racquet and played at the River Club.

Freddie Six-Love was a real gold mine of information regarding his personal tennis habits, as well as a compulsive, self-styled historian on the game in general. Iris didn't give a damn about tennis (which she'd played occasionally on her parents' own court in Bel Air), but she liked Freddie, and it seemed to mean so much to him—his knowledge of the sport, his apaprent expertise, his pride in it all—that her brain absorbed whatever he had to say on the subject as eagerly as her body absorbed his gusty lovemaking. As a result they had hit it off very well right from the start. The fact that he kept on the Lacoste shirt and Adidas shoes throughout everything, didn't bother her in the least. She was just grateful that unlike Bubble Bath Charles and many of the others on Sheila's list, he offered no explanation and no excuses for this peculiarity of his. That was the way he was. Period. Besides, she'd had her first major orgasm with Freddie Perez, so she was willing to make all kinds of concessions.

"And a Happy New Year." He raised his glass to hers, just as his penis raised itself. "Iris, darling, you look more ravishing than ever. Come here. Sit down on me. I want to touch you."

Her hair and her ass were what interested Freddie; he was no breast man—again, unlike so many of the others who seemed to be strictly tit-happy. Freddie's preferences undoubtedly had to do with his Puerto Rican heritage, even though he was born in this country and educated at Princeton, home of Fitzgerald, his favorite writer. His father, he once told her, had come to the United States from Ponce when he was sixteen years old and worked first as a waiter and then as maître d' for an elegant East-side restaurant that was recently torn down to make way for a high-rise apartment building. Now the old man was retired and lived with his second wife in a semi-fashionable Queens suburb, where he basked vicariously in his son's literary importance.

"Ah, that feels good. But don't squash my balls. Move over a little."

Iris obligingly moved to Freddie's right, her naked back toward him, her drink still in her hand. Freddie didn't mind if she drank while he began his preliminary play, in fact he was less uptight than most of the men she saw Monday through Friday (she was like her sister in that regard: neither call girls nor soap actresses worked on weekends). Freddie's hands were now exploring the smooth skin of her buttocks, gliding over them like butterfly wings, gently drawing them apart. The first time he had done that she felt certain he was going to stick it in, and she panicked. That had never happened to her before and something told her she wouldn't like it. But she needn't have worried. The only person he did that to, he wearily explained, was his wife, because, being a rigid Catholic, she refused to use any contraceptive device. The ass-touching thing with Iris was just a little warm-up serve.

"Up to net. The first volley." Freddie was engrossed in a world of his own. "Crosscourt. Down the line. Down the middle. Second set six to three. Maybe I'll win a love game at the start of the third."

"Your backhand is beautiful."

"Arthur Ashe has a fantastic backhand. So does that crazy Rumanian. He's got one of the best topspin forehands as well. But let's not digress."

"From what?" As though she didn't know.

"The befuddled origins of tennis."

Iris was pretty well acquainted with the script by now, having heard it several times before, although Freddie didn't always tell it in its entirety. He was whimsical about what he chose to emphasize on any given day, quixotic when it came to selective details. Loose. Which reminded her that Pepe was still out with Bergdorf and she was somewhat concerned; only last week he had let Bergdorf off the leash and the dog was nearly run over by a panel truck. Mike, the daytime doorman, related the incident and told her to warn Pepe about letting the dog loose. Pepe promised it would never happen again.

"The origin of tennis." Freddie sighed fondly, expectantly. "It was invented in France in the eleventh or twelfth century; even the historians aren't sure. The French adopted it from the Irish game of handball; they took it outdoors and played it with the palm of their hand, using an embankment to hit the ball over. They called it *Le Paume*."

Whereupon Freddie lifted his right palm and smacked Iris across the ass with a pleasantly stinging blow, for which she was ready. Ginger and Harvey should see her now. Not to mention Elizabeth and Jamie.

"I didn't hurt you, did I?" he asked with genuine concern.

"No, but take it easy. I nearly spilled my drink."

"If I only had Stan Smith's serve." Freddie went on dreamily. "In time, the French began to dislike the stinging sensation when their palms hit the ball, so they began to use gloves. Go get my gloves, honey."

The capeskin gloves were in his coat's righthand pocket. Iris took them out and handed them to Freddie, who slipped them on.

"This time sit down facing me, but don't sit altogether down, hold yourself up a little. There. That's perfect. So what happened was that the gloves softened, but didn't completely deaden the stinging sensation. Like this."

A very gentle blow, almost a whisper. She continued to straddle him as he put his glass of Scotch down on an end table and caressed her gleaming blonde hair with his gloves.

"But the French, you know, they are resourceful. They substituted a paddle to replace their poor, stinging palms, and the paddle of course is the grandfather of the modern racquet."

Iris was attuned to his timing. "Should I get the racquet now?"

"Please."

She could have gotten the racquet when she'd gotten the gloves, but she knew Freddie didn't like that, he liked to watch her ass move around as much as possible; he teased himself that way. Iris unzipped the TWA tennis cover and playfully held the racquet in front of her face, peering through it with crazily widened eyes, an expression of mock horror on her face.

"What now, Your Royal Highness?"

"Hand me the racquet, lie down across my knees, and cut the comedy."

Iris did as she was told. The only reason she disliked this position was because it made it almost impossible to drink her drink without choking, but she knew she wouldn't have to maintain it for long. Freddie then laid the racquet across her ass, and proceeded to rub it back and forth, slowly, as he went on with his tale of tennis lore.

"Eventually the game was moved indoors because that way it could be played in all seasons, whatever the weather; but it required so much space that they could only play in castles. And since castles belonged mostly to kings, the game became known as Royal Tennis and finally as Court Tennis. But then in the thirteenth century, King Louis the Ninth made the game illegal for priests; he said playing tennis was unbecoming to religious dignity and he outlawed it for the clergy. Oddly, he was later canonized as a saint. Who can understand these things?"

Freddie put his long, slender fingers through the side strings of the racquet and began to knead the pale flesh on Iris's buttocks. "The English discovered the sport in the fourteenth century and called it tennis by mistake. While watching the French play, they kept hearing the constant drone of *ten-ez* which they thought was the name of the game, but actually it only meant *play ball* in French. Fascinating, isn't it?"

Iris nodded her head vigorously. This part of the story was taking longer than usual, and she wished he would get on with it, which he did after a few more flesh-kneads.

"King Edward the Third, who had originally imported tennis for his subjects, became an overnight enthusiast himself. And pretty soon the popularity of Court Tennis in England was almost as great as in France (except with the poor clergy). We now skip a couple of centuries which I don't have time to go into because of my in-laws coming to dinner, and you can get up, sweetheart; I want to go down on you. You finish the rest of the story, okay?"

He removed the racquet and they both went into the bedroom, which was softly lit by a yellow candle enclosed in a hurricane shade. Some men preferred the stark whiteness of the overhead ceiling fixture, but Freddie was not one of them. A tennis romantic, right to the end. Going down on her seemed to excite him very much, yet he rarely asked her to return the favor. Again, another departure from the norm, but definitely.

"In 1873 a British major introduced the sport to his friends at a lawn party at his home," Iris said. "His friends loved it but couldn't reconcile themselves to the major's name for it. *Sphairistike*, which is Greek for *ten-ez*. Anyhow, that was the beginning of Lawn Tennis as we know it today."

Freddie looked up from his endeavors, ever the strict professor. "How did it get to this country?"

"By way of Bermuda in 1874. One of the major's party guests was on furlough from his station in Bermuda, and when he returned, he took along tennis equipment and introduced the game to his fellow officers. Then about a year later an American girl visiting the British colony tried the new game and was enchanted with it. Just like Edward the Third. I think I'm going to come, Freddie. She was responsible for bringing tennis to the United States, her name was—"

But the name got caught in Iris' throat, only to emerge in a far different although certainly related form, when Freddie Perez, who was now inside Iris, began to reach his own frenzied climax seconds later.

"PANCHO GONZALES!"

Then he rolled over on his side and burst into loud sobs for reasons that Iris had never figured out. She didn't worry about it too much, though, because Freddie's crying invariably subsided as quickly as it had begun, and with as little embarrassment or explanation. In a few minutes he was impeccably dressed once more, his TWA bag and racquet case in hand, seventy-five dollars on the end table next to his watery glass of scotch. Iris had put on a long, zippered robe and was combing her hair in the hall mirror.

"I'll call you soon," Freddie said.

"Have a nice holiday."

"You, too, honey."

He reached for the knob just as the doorbell rang. For a moment Iris froze, then she remembered Pepe.

"It's only the guy who walks my dog."

As she opened the door, an exhilarated Bergdorf came running into the apartment, barking with excitement, while Pepe remained patiently on the threshold and handed Iris the leash. "He's a good little boy, I don't let anything happen to him."

The two men looked at, through, and beyond each other

with only the skimpiest, split-second flicker of acknowledgment. Then Pepe turned and walked down the long corridor toward the service elevator, which was tucked away next to the emergency staircase. Frederico Perez pushed the button for the passenger elevator opposite Iris' apartment and with a quick wave of his expensively gloved hand was gone.

Iris locked the door behind him and went into the bathroom to douche with Cupid's Quiver, and to wonder what the learned population of Manhattan would think if they knew that she had just been sucked, fucked, and tennis-slapped by the first Puerto Rican in history ever to win the Pulitzer Prize for literature.

"Probably not much," she said to Bergdorf, who had followed her in and watched while she squirted the premeasured cleansing liquid up her vagina. This was the champagne-flavored one. Wedding Ring Alan, who was due in about fifteen minutes, told her he was crazy about it.

Chapter Twenty-One

Alan was typical of most of the men Iris saw, except for his insistence upon taking off his wedding ring before she went down on him. Most married men either didn't wear rings or didn't give a damn, but Alan said it would be sacrilegious to his wife to come in a stranger's mouth with the ring still on.

Iris thought that was pretty funny and had to control herself from laughing, unlike Alan, who found absolutely no humor in the situation at all, no, not a trace of amusement, even though one of the big glamor stocks had just moved up ten points, finishing at 375, its highest price since the end of the year. Yes, Alan was a stockbroker, by far the most popular occupation among the men who visited apartment 22-G.

"But why is that?" Iris had asked Mrs. Richmond over the Christmas holidays, when business was slow.

"Why not? Those Wall Street wheeler-dealers know a simple financial transaction when they see one; they appreciate it. You render a service; they pay for it. It's straightforward, uninvolved. Look at it this way: what's their other alternative, the poor schmucks? Getting a girlfriend on the side, right? But that can become complicated, and besides, it's unpredictable, time-consuming, and in the long run it costs them more money. Not to mention all the mental anguish."

Mrs. Richmond was right at home in soap-land with expressions like "mental anguish," but Iris had recently been forced to learn diplomacy and discretion and therefore didn't say anything. Just as she hadn't said anything when Wedding Ring Alan told her he liked the champagne-flavored Cupid's Quiver better than the other fragrances (jasmine, raspberry, and orange blossom), she merely thought it odd that he would know the difference since he never went down on her; but since he did stick his finger in from time to time she decided he probably smelled his pinky all the way home to Chappaqua and dreamed of Moët and Chandon.

"You know what happens with a married man who wants to play around," Mrs. Richmond said. "First he has to wine and dine the lady in question. That's before the big seduction act. Taxis, restaurants, tips to maître d's, martinis, dinner, liqueurs. Even if the girl does go to bed with him, chances are that between the martinis and his anxiety he's liable to be either impotent or too fast. A sexual failure. Does anybody care if he's impotent or too fast with you? A man who goes to you doesn't have to prove his virility one way or the other. He can lie there like King Farouk while you work him over, or he can come in one second and feel marvelous, not a guilt in the world. Okay, never mind that, let's say that with the girlfriend he's neither of those things, he's superman, now he's got her where he wants her but there's still a very important consideration. Sheila explained all this to me. Otherwise, how would I know?"

"What's the consideration?"

"There's no guarantee that the future girlfriend is going to do what he wants, that is, if he gets up the nerve to ask for it. Half the time they're afraid to ask, embarrassed, ashamed of their peculiarities. You should understand. Take The Screamer. What nice girl in her right mind is going to put up with a nut like that, opening all your windows so that not just me, but the whole neighborhood can hear him shouting at the top of his lungs: LOOK AT ME, MYRON MEISELMAN,

THE EX-YESHIVA BOY, GETTING BLOWN BY AN EAST-SIDE HOOKER! Those Hasidic Jews, they're all in the Forty-sixth Street jewelry business; it runs in the family."

Many of Mrs. Richmond's allusions escaped Iris, who had been trying like hell since Ken P. to catch up with the New York idiom, a lot of which seemed to have strong Jewish implications, even more so than the Beverly Hills variety. She was working on it, though, and considering the fact that her first meeting with Yellow Dragon had taken place in October, and The Screamer conversation with Mrs. Richmond last month, snowy December, Iris figured she was making progress.

"I'll tell you something," Mrs. Richmond went on. "Personally, I'd rather that the doctor paid for it and came home to dinner at a reasonable time instead of spending all those after-work hours with his nurse. Believe me, I'd *prefer* it. He gave her a sable coat for Christmas; I saw the bill from Revillon. You know what I got? A fun fur. Besides, I'm afraid that at any minute she's going to call me in the middle of the night, insisting I give him a divorce. She'll be hysterical. Crying. Or threatening. She'll tell me he doesn't love me any more, that he hasn't loved me for a long time. I don't even want to think about that phone call I'm going to get some morning at two o'clock when I'm sound asleep. It makes me nervous."

Which immediately made Iris wonder whether Dr. Richmond took off his wedding ring when the nurse went down on him. Maybe she didn't do that. Maybe Mrs. Richmond had never gone down on him either (it wasn't Kosher). It had nothing to do with being Jewish; in all fairness to her next-door neighbor Iris had to admit that much. In her own one year of married life she'd gone down on Bob exactly twice, not that she didn't want to please him, she wanted that more than everything, but he'd been so disparaging about her ability that she never tried again. The fact was that she didn't really know what to do, her technique, apparently, was lousy. She should have asked her sister, the cocksucking authority of Beverly Hills High, what to do. But then, how had she known with Derek? Instinct. Desperation. Pride. She *had* to know; it was as simple as that, he thought she was a red-hot Hollywood hooker, whereas Bob Barnes had known her for exactly what she was when they met: a twenty-one-year-old virgin, with no sexual expertise. Bob was undoubtedly rolling over in Forest Lawn this very minute, disturbing all the other corpses. Hideous thought. Then why did it strike her so funny?

Iris knew why. It was one question she didn't need Mrs. Richmond to answer; she could answer it herself. Because who the hell ever heard of a call girl moonlighting as a writer of soap operas, or vice versa? Nobody. Not Mrs. Richmond (who still had not been filled in on Iris' double life), probably not even Harold Greenwald who was supposed to be one of the leading authorities on the subject of prostitution. Maybe she would write him a letter and tell him the interesting news, except that she didn't have time these days for idle correspondence. She was far too busy shuttling between her two disparate worlds, the only tangible connection between them being Derek Christopher, who didn't need glamor stocks to move up ten points in order to feel euphoric. By having succeeded in turning Elizabeth into an incipient drunk on "The Troubled Heart," he'd fixed both Elizabeth's and Jamie's wagon, but good. Elizabeth was miserable, Jamie was infuriated, Iris was delighted, since the whole scheme had been hers to begin with and nobody knew it except Derek, who had no way of knowing her motive.

"I've got control!" Iris said to the four living-room walls.

Although mixed in with her feelings of bitchy accomplishment were equally strong feelings of guilt, and she vacillated between the two extremes to a painful degree. Being a secretive, behind-the-scenes manipulator wasn't a one-hundred-percent bed of roses, but it was the first real sense of power that Iris had ever experienced in her life and when she was not busy despising herself, she could not stop priding herself on how neatly, how ingeniously she'd maneuvered it all. Beautiful. There was nothing like revenge. Except shame.

"I'm disgusting!"

"I'm clever!"

"I'm horrible!"

"I'm brilliant!"

"I'm despicable!"

"I'm inventive, resourceful, talented!"

"I'm cruel, dishonest, depraved!"

"I like myself in spite of everything!"

"I hate myself because of it!"

"I've got a great future ahead of me!"

"I'm going to jump out the window immediately!"

Instead, she switched on the O'Reillys' Sony TV to follow Elizabeth's continuing descent to the depths of alcoholism and disaster. She had written today's script herself, using Jamie's authoritative plot outline as a guide. Poor Jamie. He had begun to hate the Elizabeth he now saw on the television screen, with her stringy hair and dark shadows under her eyes, her growing lack of coordination. It was too bad that Elizabeth happened to be such a competent actress, so convincing in the role—too bad for Elizabeth but perfect for Iris, who had recently started to realize that her sister was losing Jamie's love.

"And now," said the lugubrious announcer, "for the next thirty minutes, 'The Troubled Heart,' brought to you today by . . ."

Iris raised her glass of Bombay in anticipation of her own handiwork (at the same time feeling her duplicity more poignantly than ever), and wished that Derek would hurry up and get there. Ordinarily he would be at the studio at three-thirty, watching the taping of tomorrow's show, but he had promised to dash over to Picasso Towers this afternoon and join her in what he said would be "the next juicy episode *re* Elizabeth's growing dependency upon alcohol."

Iris had somehow managed to keep a flattering smile on her straight face. "I still can't believe that you talked them into making her a lush."

"Oh, I talked them into it all right. Your own fifty-dollar idea, love. But naturally, that's off the record. That it was your idea, and not mine."

"Who could I possibly tell?"

"Not a damn soul." He laughed, pleased with his coup. "You don't know anybody."

"Nobody connected with the show, you mean."

"Nobody who would believe you for a minute, is what I mean."

Derek's insistence upon always having the last word reminded her of Ginger, who was the same way, although since she left California Iris had started to see her parents in a new and different light. Her quiet, resigned father, her very unquiet mother; but when it came down to it, which one of them *really* had the last word? Iris no longer felt so certain that it was Ginger; something told her that beneath her father's public facade of acquiescence lurked a more steely will than she had imagined, and that her mother privately respected and obeyed it.

The doorbell rang.

"Hello, love." Derek invariably looked as though he were about to go sailing for the weekend. "Got caught in a nasty traffic jam; thought I'd never make it in time. How about a drink?"

"My pleasure."

She moved obligingly toward the bar she had set up in one corner of the O'Reillys' living room. Since becoming a call girl, even her walk had changed. It was slower, more provocative; she was more conscious of her body than she had ever been before, in fact she was starting to appreciate her body as a result of all the compliments that were constantly being showered upon it. Men thought she was wildly sexy, "a super bod," as Tutti Frutti Harold said, after completing the first heterosexual fuck of his fucked-up life. It seemed that even though he had tried repeatedly with Sheila and other women, he was never able to maintain an erection long enough to put it in, move it around for three seconds and come.

"It was always back to the same old boring sixty-nine bit for me," he told Iris, kissing her toes in appreciation for saving him from an unwanted homosexual future. "I'm forever in your debt."

Then he asked her what she did about working when she had her period, to which she replied that she took a vacation on those days. It was an utter lie. Thanks (again) to Mrs. Richmond, Iris had discovered what was known in the trade as sanitary sponges. They resembled little baby sponges, and were readily obtainable at any drugstore, although the druggist gave her an immediate wiseguy glance which led Iris to conclude that the only babies who used them were the good-looking, grown-up, professional variety like herself.

Actually, the sponge surprised the hell out of her. If she inserted it deeply enough before getting into bed with someone, the sponge stopped the flow of blood to the extent that so far no man had ever suspected she was menstruating (Freddie Six-Love had even gone down on her on the first day of her period, without suspecting a thing). After the man left, Iris would take out the sponge, wash it, put it away, and replace it with a Playtex deodorant tampon. She never bothered with Feminique or any of those boring vaginal sprays; they were too heavily perfumed, and men didn't like them.

Besides, she practically had a medicine chest full of the four different fragrances of Cupid's Quiver.

Even her favorite contraceptive, Delfen Foam, was delicately scented, according to the ad in *Vogue*. Iris decided upon Delfen shortly after the initial meeting with Nebraska Tailspin Rudolph. He was a crop duster from Hastings and zeroed in on her with the hardest, longest, and (she feared) the most fertile penis in captivity, nearly scaring her out of her wits that she would wake up the next morning pregnant with triplets. Rudolph's only quirk, aside from wearing airplane goggles in bed, was that he had no quirk. He just liked to fuck, in every possible position, and for a seemingly inhuman amount of time before coming. After two hours with him, Iris felt so fatigued that she was through for the day, and bowlegged.

Rudolph told her that he was one of the best crop dusters in the business, which Iris didn't doubt for a second. She merely prayed to God that she never had the misfortune to eat an ear of corn that had been dusted by the relentless, superenergized Rudolph; every niblet was bound to be in a state of sheer, vegetable exhaustion.

"Here we go," Derek said. "I saw the taping yesterday. You should get a kick out of this first act."

Iris sat down beside him on the corduroy-covered sofa. She knew the script almost by heart, having rewritten it four times until she got it exactly right. The scene took place in Jefferson General Hospital, where Elizabeth's mother had been admitted for a series of tests that would hopefully determine the nature of her illness. It was noon, and Elizabeth had come to the hospital to join her mother for lunch and find out how she was feeling. The dutiful, loving daughter. Except for one jarring fact: she was more than slightly smashed when she got there.

NURSE: (*Glancing uneasily at Elizabeth*) Well, now you two have a nice lunch, and I'll be back in a few minutes to see if everything is all right.

MOTHER: (*Thin smile*) Thank you, Nurse. (*Nurse leaves*)

ELIZABETH: (*Moving toward bed*) Mother, darling, how are you? (*They kiss, Elizabeth sits down on chair next to bed*)

MOTHER: I'm a little tired, dear. That's all.

ELIZABETH: (*Making obvious effort to sound cheerful, gay*)

What did they do—wake you up last night to give you the perennial sleeping pill?

MOTHER: (*Forced laugh, exhaustion is apparent*) No, Liz, they were kind enough to give it to me *before* I dozed off.

ELIZABETH (*Looks with distaste at the two luncheon trays*) Well, I see that our menus are quite different—(*Smiles brightly*) Too bad that we can't switch. I don't have much of an appetite today

MOTHER: I'm sorry to hear that—(*Glances wanly at her own meager tray, compared to Elizabeth's full one*) Unfortunately, I have to remain on a restricted diet while they're taking these tests. Doctor's orders, you know.

ELIZABETH: Of course ... (*Mind seems to wander for a second*) How about the abdominal pains? Have they subsided at all?

MOTHER: They're giving me something for it. I'm quite comfortable, dear, if that's what you mean.

ELIZABETH: I'm glad. . . . (*Unfolds paper napkin on lap, picks up fork with unsteady hand*) Shall we eat?

MOTHER: Your grandmother, my mother, once told me that only animals *eat.* . . . (*Swallows a spoonful of soup*) People *dine.* This consommé is delicious. I wonder why they didn't give you any.

ELIZABETH: ESP. They know that I've never cared much for consommé. . . . (*Distasteful expression on face as she forces herself to go on eating*) Remember you used to say that I was the only child in our neighborhood who couldn't be lured by alphabet soup?

MOTHER: (*Dreamily*) It's such a shame that you never got to know her better. She was a wonderful woman.

ELIZABETH: Who? (*Confused, slurring words*) Who was a wonderful woman?

MOTHER: Your grandmother. She died when you were so young. (*Conscious for the first time that something is wrong with Elizabeth*) Are you all right, Liz? You seem a bit ... jittery. You're not worried about me, are you? (*Bravado*) I'm going to be just fine.

ELIZABETH: (*Quickly*) Of course you are. I know that. Just fine. . . . (*Slowing down*) Yes, I was very young when she ... passed away. (*Their eyes meet, mutely acknowledging death*) I barely remember her—(*Forcibly brightening*) My, we sound gloomy! I don't like that, no, not one bit! (*Looks around room at vases of flowers*) Those yellow roses are lovely. I don't believe they were here yesterday, or am I wrong?

MOTHER: Now isn't that just like me? I'm becoming more and more forgetful by the minute. Mr. Crawford sent them to me. They arrived this morning.

ELIZABETH: (*Surprised*) You mean, *my* Mr.—?"

MOTHER: (*Innocently*) Yes, dear, *your* Mr. Craig Crawford. I thought that was very considerate of him.

ELIZABETH: (*Tightening, defensive*) He's a very considerate man, Mother. A very *thoughtful* man.

MOTHER: (*Surprised by Elizabeth's tone*) I'm sure he is. You will remember to thank him for me, for sending the roses, won't you? I would call him myself, but I imagine he's also a very busy——

ELIZABETH: (*Cutting in without realizing it*) You see, his wife is an invalid. She's confined to a wheelchair. He's had many years to learn how to be considerate. . . . (*Caught up in her own conflicted world*) Many, *many* years.

MOTHER: I'm sorry to hear that about Mrs. Crawford. . . . (*Truly concerned now*) Liz, I know that *I'm* supposed to be the patient, but you seem so strange today, so tense, moody. Don't you feel well? Didn't you get enough sleep last night?

ELIZABETH: (*Nervously running hand through limp hair*) Well, not really, Mother. You see, I was up rather late. . . .

MOTHER: (*Very curious now*) Did you go out, dear?

ELIZABETH: No, no, I didn't go anywhere. I was—— (*Abruptly reaches for coffee cup, spills some coffee on her skirt, tries to laugh it off*) I'm just as clumsy as ever—— (*Wipes skirt with paper napkin*)

MOTHER: Dear, I don't mean to pry, but if you didn't go out, then why were you——?

ELIZABETH: (*Cutting in again*) Why was I up so late? (*Mother nods, eyes intensely upon Elizabeth*) I was reading, Mother. I took a very interesting book out of the lending library, and I became so caught up in it that (*shrugs*) I guess I lost all track of time.

MOTHER: (*Quietly, but with disbelief*) I see. What *kind* of book?

ELIZABETH: (*Caught off guard, lights a cigarette*) Does the smoke bother you, Mother? If it does, I can put this out.

MOTHER: (*Negatively shaking head*) No, no, dear.

ELIZABETH: Actually, it was a book about cooking. *French*

cooking. I've always been interested in foreign cuisines, particularly the French.

MOTHER: (*As nurse enters the room*) Really? That's odd. You never mentioned it before, at least not that I can remember——

NURSE: Is your luncheon all right, Mrs. Smythe? Miss Smythe? Is there anything I can bring either of you ladies?

MOTHER: (*Disturbed, her eyes still on Elizabeth*) No, Nurse, thank you . . . everything is . . . fine. . . .

(*And fade out*)

MUSIC: BRIDGE TO:

2ND COMMERCIAL

Derek switched off the television set, just as the peanut butter pitch came on. "Sorry, love, but I don't have much time today. I've got to get back to the office. What do you think of the new, bombed-out Elizabeth? Pretty effective, I'd say."

"Extremely effective, her acting. And the change in appearance. That stringy hair, the lines under her eyes. How do they do that? The makeup part, I mean."

Derek stretched his long frame. "I repeat, not enough time to discuss all of that at the moment. Now why don't you be a good girl and go get your Uncle Derek that fantastic little jar of you-know-what?" He smacked her playfully on the ass. "On the double!"

As Iris went into the kitchen for the ever-present Tiptree preserves, she could not help feeling that even though she had just seen a good actress at work, another part of her willfully resisted that simple fact; it saw something else: a pathetic, real-life lush. Iris felt a sharp sense of sorrow for Elizabeth. But *which* Elizabeth? The drunk on the television screen, or her own teetotaling sister? Strangely, she wasn't at all certain. Maybe both. Maybe neither. Maybe it was herself she felt sorry for.

Derek's voice reached her from the other room. "I said, on the double."

"Coming."

His eyes glistened when she returned with the jar of English preserves. "Ah, there we are."

"I couldn't find it for a second." She smiled her new, seductive call-girl smile at Derek, who was half undressed.

"My but you're an attractive man. You have very nice shoulders."

"I appreciate the compliment, but what I'd appreciate even more would be for you to take off that damn gown so we can get going."

As Iris started to slip out of the gown, she wondered what kind of shoulders The Storm would have, and what he would want of her. He was due in less than an hour and, never having met him before, she was quite curious, although at this point she doubted if anything about the male sex could surprise her. Yet, at times, it all seemed distinctly unreal. The men. Their desires. Her role in fulfilling those desires. Jamie swam into view: unknown, unexplored, mysterious. He had started to look at her strangely lately. Perhaps she was becoming a mystery to him, as well. A tantalizing one. She hoped so.

"Shall we turn our attention to this fellow over here?" Derek indicated his semi-erect penis. "He's becoming rather impatient for a taste of those filthy preserves."

Chapter Twenty-Two

"God, but I look rotten," Elizabeth said.

"No, you don't."

They were lying in bed, Jamie's bed, a sea of black satin sheets.

"How can you say that?" she demanded. "Look at me."

He smiled indulgently, and looked at her. "You look great." Then he added, "As usual."

But her eyes were on the television set, watching the reflection of her own haggard face. "Christ, but that makeup guy knows what he's doing. He put some kind of grease on my hair yesterday. See how stringy it seems. Dark pencil under my bottom lashes. I'm afraid to imagine what cosmetic horrors are next on the agenda." Then she realized that Jamie had been looking at *her,* not the set, and she laughed;

in her ears, it sounded like a cry, a plea. "You fool. I mean on 'The Troubled Heart.' Don't I look simply terrible?"

He lit a cigarette, stalling, just as Elizabeth had lit a cigarette in the previous act when visiting her mother at the hospital. "You look exactly as you're supposed to for someone who's been hitting the bottle for days."

"Ugly."

"You're an actress. A professional. At least I always thought you were. You're doing a fine job."

That was the only way he could get to her since the alcoholic transformation had set in, by gently, repeatedly reminding her of her pride in her craft. Somehow his approach was becoming less and less effective, as her TV image of dissipation became more and more convincing. Or was he simply running out of patience?

"A fine job of looking unattractive, you mean."

"Elizabeth, you cannot afford this ridiculous vanity and you know it. Half the actors in New York are out of work, and you're making, how much, three hundred dollars a day? And you're complaining."

"Three-ten." Petulance did not suit her. "Besides, it isn't *half* the actors, it's more like *most* of the actors. And as for the money being good, so what? I have money."

"Then quit the damn job, and give it to somebody who needs it!"

He threw off the covers and got out of bed. The woman was impossible, spoiled, unreasonable, selfish; she wanted everything exactly her way. He couldn't help it; the phrase came to mind: lap of luxury. Well, it was true, that was how she'd been brought up, she and her mysterious sister, the at-home queen of the Upper East Side. Lately he'd been thinking about Iris a great deal; the attraction was growing, flourishing, in spite of the meager soil. Jamie realized he must look ridiculous, nakedly pacing up and down the dimly lit bedroom, exasperated, fuming, avoiding what he knew would be a hurt and bewildered expression in Elizabeth's eyes. They no longer agreed on anything, maybe they never had, maybe he'd just been deluding himself for almost a year that they had anything in common. His mind was crawling with clichés. Who gave a damn about what people had *in common?* Screw that middle-class concept. What did he have in common with Iris, for that matter, except "The Troubled Heart"? But then he had that with Elizabeth as well; at least they used to have it to share and enjoy before Derek Christopher stepped into the plot picture and ruined everything. Scheming English bastard. Jamie felt like killing him. He felt like kissing and caressing the inaccessible Iris.

"There's no need to raise your voice," Elizabeth said, in her own carefully modulated one, not realizing how hard it was to look and sound dignified when you were undressed.

"I'm sorry." He wasn't. "It's just that I don't understand you any more. If you don't give a damn about the money, what about the experience you're chalking up? Surely, that must count for something."

"Oh, absolutely. All I have to do now is wait for some theatrical genius to rewrite *The Lost Weekend* with a female lead, and I'll have it made. Right, Jamie?"

An hour ago they had been sensuously happy, engrossed in each other's bodies; now it seemed like a distant dream, unreal, almost shameful. Perhaps the only place they'd ever gotten along was in bed, and perhaps, finally, that was all they had together. It wasn't enough. How could he make such tender love to a woman he basically disapproved of? But men did it all the time; even worse, they bragged about it, the idiots. No. Jamie wanted more, he wanted . . . Iris.

"Come back to bed," Elizabeth urged him. "I won't say another word about my appearance. I promise."

She held out her arms; she was smiling, supplicating him. She looked quite lovely in the dim, late-afternoon light, her brown velvet eyes flecked with gold, bare shoulders gleaming.

"Come on, Jamie."

On "The Troubled Heart," Elizabeth was speaking to her mother's physician in his office at the Jeffersonville General Hospital.

ELIZABETH: But surely you can tell me *something*, Doctor.

DOCTOR: I'm afraid not, Miss Smythe. We haven't completed the hemological workout.

ELIZABETH: What's that?

DOCTOR (*smiling*): Blood tests.

ELIZABETH (*agitated*): I don't understand. My mother has been here for three days!

DOCTOR: Yes, I know—(*hesitates*) Are you feeling all right, Miss Smythe? If you'll pardon my saying so, you don't look too well."

ELIZABETH: Never mind how *I* look. (*Openly hostile now*)

It's my mother's condition we're talking about, and I'd like to know what's wrong with her.

DOCTOR: So would we, so would we. But I'm afraid that the tests we've taken so far aren't sufficient to determine the nature of her illness. However, in a few days we should have—

ELIZABETH: Yes, I know. *(Deprecatingly) Conclusive* results.

DOCTOR: I certainly hope so—

ELIZABETH: Thank you, Doctor. And good-bye. *(Elizabeth leaves office in flurry of drunken defiance. Startled doctor watches her go)*

(And fade out)

MUSIC: BRIDGE TO:

3RD COMMERCIAL

The minute Jamie got into bed, Elizabeth said, "They used a red pencil on the bottom rim of my eyes. That's why they appear so bloodshot."

"I thought you weren't going to talk about your appearance."

She bit her lip. "I can't help it."

"Very well. In that case, you might be interested to know that they'll be putting glycerin on your face pretty soon."

"Glycerin? What's that for?"

"It's used to simulate perspiration. Drinkers tend to perspire heavily."

"Sweat is what you mean." She shuddered. "I despise sweaty people. They're revolting. Clammy. Sticky. I can't stand looking at them, let alone touching them." She ran her fingers over her face as though to reassure herself that her skin was cool, that nothing had changed, that she was still the impeccable person she'd always been. "Glycerin!"

Jamie sighed softly. It was hopeless, he decided, she was a hopelessly narcissistic case, as were most actors he had met, they couldn't seem to forget their faces for longer than a few minutes at a time. Yet, how could you blame them? Their faces were (or weren't) their fortunes, every new line a threat to their existence, the discovery of a wrinkle a major disaster. What a dismal way to live, how they must tremble at the thought of old age. Was that why he felt so drawn to Iris? Because in spite of her faults, her drinking, her eccentricities, her childishness, she did not share Elizabeth's obsession with appearance? If anything, she seemed almost oblivious to her outward being, as though she had long ago resigned herself to not being a spectacular beauty, and by doing so had freed herself from the very insecurities that plagued her beautiful sister. Vanity, thy name is Elizabeth.

Not that Iris didn't have her own grab-bag of insecurities. Jamie was all too well aware of them, particularly that sordid business about her late husband's prolonged unfaithfulness. *Sex says good-bye.* The dying man's final words tantalized Jamie, as much as they confused and horrified Iris. Like her, he wondered what they meant. Perhaps nothing, if Bob Barnes had been delirious when he spoke them. Still, it was a strange farewell message to an unloved wife, sadistic if consciously intended. No wonder Iris felt hurt and betrayed, cheated by Bob right up to the very end. Her ostrich reaction afterward was understandable; it was human. But to feel equally hurt and betrayed by a little glycerin and red eyeliner was pathetic in its sheer egocentricity. At least Iris cared enough about another person to be vulnerable to wounds. Recently, Jamie found himself wondering whether Elizabeth had ever cared for anyone in her life, including himself, or whether her gestures of love and affection were merely another piece of effective play-acting.

"Are you still angry at me?" she asked, laying her head on his shoulder.

"No."

"Then why are you so quiet?"

"I don't have anything to say."

"Jamie, when is my mother going to die?"

"I don't know."

"But you're the writer of the show. You must know."

"Soon," he conceded. "Very soon."

"What does she die of?"

"She'll get an infection. People with sickle-cell anemia don't fight off infections very readily; often they prove fatal."

"When will this infection set in?"

He moved out of her reach. "It hasn't yet been determined."

"You mean, you haven't outlined that part of the story?"

"Correct."

"Why is it that I don't believe you?"

"Beats me."

"Because you're lying, Jamie.

"Okay."

"Okay *what*, for God's sake?"

"Okay, I'm lying."

"Are you?"

"Sure." Elizabeth's mother was scheduled to die in four weeks; pneumonia complications. "I'm a chronic liar."

She was starting to get nervous, she had never before seen him like this: totally cold and withdrawn. "You don't have to be so difficult. It's not as though I were asking for some top government secret. I think it's disgusting, patronizing, this habit of never telling the actors what's going to happen when. We're treated like idiot children."

"Only because that's the way you behave."

"I beg your pardon."

He sat up straighter, his eyes fixed on the last act of "The Troubled Heart." It did not include Elizabeth, which was why she was no longer watching it, she was watching him now, waiting for his apology. Jamie suddenly felt very tired.

"Look, Elizabeth, your mother will die shortly; in your state of grief you will jump into the sack with Craig Crawford and become the dangerous other woman in his life, your drinking will become progressively worse. That's all I know at the moment."

"The dangerous other woman," she said, contemptuously. "How can a poor falling-down drunk be dangerous, except to herself? Tell me that."

"You're not exactly going to be falling down, it won't reach those Skid Row proportions. We'll make your behavior relatively discreet, ladylike, sympathetic despite the fact that you're having an affair with a married man."

"Sympathetic? I'll bet Iris won't see me that way."

It was the first remark of hers that interested Jamie. "Why not?"

"Do you think Iris could possibly have any personal sympathy for a woman who tries to steal another woman's husband? After what she went through with Robert?"

"Robert?"

Elizabeth looked at him as though he were a ghost; then she calmly said, "Bob. Robert Barnes. Iris' husband."

"I hadn't thought about that. Yes, I can see your point. There is a certain kind of weird poetic justice in Iris' putting words into the mouth of the other woman, making her come to life, making her suffer the way she's suffered."

"She'll have a wonderful time!" Elizabeth's laughter was

harsh. "It will be a real catharsis for her. Getting back at a
hated, unknown rival via the auspices of television. Symbolic
revenge. Self-vindication. I'll bet she turns Mrs. Crawford
into a saint. I'm afraid to think what she'll do with me, if you
let her. She'll make mincemeat out of me before our ten million viewers."

To his surprise, she began to cry. More to his surprise, for
once in his life he did not feel moved by a woman's tears; he
felt bored. He wished she would get dressed and go home.
One of Jamie's favorite movies, *Elizabeth The Queen*, starring Bette Davis, was on in half an hour and he wanted to
watch it. Alone. Without interruptions. Then he remembered
that she had a rehearsal at the studio this afternoon, it was a
runthrough of the script that would be taped tomorrow. Had
she forgotten?

"Shouldn't you be getting ready to leave?" he asked.

She wiped her eyes with the back of her hand. "I don't
know what's gotten into you today, Jamie. You're not yourself. If I've done anything—"

"No, no." Now that she was going, he could afford to be
generous.

"Then what is it?"

"I'm just in a lousy mood." He hated himself for ducking
the issue, but at the same time he didn't have the energy to
confront her with his accusations. "I'm tired."

"You weren't too tired to make love to me, I noticed.
Somehow you never seem too tired for that."

"Neither do you," he replied, realizing that his answer
made no sense. "It's a two-way street, after all."

"Jamie, please look at me."

He looked at her and saw her grim television image.

"Jamie, don't you love me any longer?"

Had he ever said that he did? Perhaps in an off-guard moment of passion, but certainly not otherwise; he was careful
about things like that, very careful, afraid of being trapped at
some future date by his own rash words. Women remembered.

"Elizabeth, can't we talk about this some other time?"

She methodically began to peel off her dark-red polish.
"I know what it is."

"What *what* is?"

"Why you're starting to fall out of love with me."

"Why?"

Bad. Tacit admission that he had once been in love with her. But if he denied her charge, that would be even worse. Then he would have to admit that he had never loved her, never.

"You don't consider me attractive any more," she said. "You watch me on 'The Troubled Heart,' and you're turned off by what you see. That's the truth, isn't it?"

"It's more complicated than that."

"How? Why? In what way?"

How could he explain? He found it difficult to explain to himself, painful. The sloppy, hostile, boozed-up Elizabeth on the show bore no resemblance to the real-life Elizabeth he knew, certainly not in those outward specifics. But on another, deeper level, Jamie did perceive a resemblance between the two that troubled him, had troubled him for some time now. Both Elizabeths shared a similar relentlessness, an underlying quality of deceit and shallow disregard for anyone who got in their way or tampered with their opportunism. It was ironic, he thought, that Elizabeth should imagine he objected to her video self for surface physical reasons, when the true objection went beyond that to the depths of her non-video character.

"Aren't you going to say anything?" she asked.

He shook his head. "You'd better be going."

She did not move.

"Tune in tomorrow for the continuing story of 'The Troubled Heart,' " said the announcer, as organ music played the show's theme, and credits rolled rapidly down the television screen.

Written by Jamie Mann.

He had to start thinking about getting a credit for Iris; she deserved one, she was more than carrying her weight, and it wasn't fair that she remain anonymous much longer. Today's script had been good, so good in fact that he hardly had to change a word of what she had written. A tremor of jealousy pulled at Jamie, a tug of resentment. She was so damned talented. *Admit it, you competitive bastard,* he said to himself, *admit you're afraid that she's more talented than you.* He admitted it and felt better; he felt more honest, he felt more like Iris. But there was still the sticky problem of Elizabeth. What to do with her? He couldn't just callously toss her aside. He had cared for her once, still cared with the remnants of an old, washed-out emotion. The hard, sad fact was that she no longer excited him outside of bed, and he suspected that pretty soon she would not excite him there either. To his amazement, he heard her say:

"Jamie, let's get married."

Chapter Twenty-Three

She left his apartment about twenty minutes later (just as The Storm was arriving at Iris') and caught a cab to the studio. She would be late for rehearsal and she didn't care. Let them wait for her, or let them go ahead without her; either way it didn't seem to matter. Elizabeth had just experienced the first major setback of her life. Jamie wasn't the least bit interested in, didn't have the vaguest intention of, would not even consider the possibility of marrying her! She was dumbfounded by his negative attitude, incredulous at first, and now, depressed.

"I have no plans to get married," he said flatly. "Not to you, not to anyone. I like living alone."

She never realized how much she hated living alone until he said that. Neither had she realized how involved she'd become with Jamie, how much she took him for granted and expected that he would always be there whenever she needed him. In the past he seemed so susceptible to her needs, so acquiescent in his own undemonstrative way. Something must have happened, he was different now, changed, she no longer wielded the upper hand. What had she done wrong? Her survival theory of love—she had abandoned it on meeting Jamie; that was her initial and most consequential mistake. She should have immediately found another man to distract her, to keep her emotions dispersed.

But she hadn't, like a fool she'd played it straight, and Jamie knew it, capitalized upon it, could afford to feel superior and independent because of it. Maybe there was another woman. It wasn't a new thought, but neither was the logical comeback: when would he have had time to find someone else? She saw him practically every day, and on those days when they did not get together they spoke on the telephone. Jamie always seemed to be home, alone, writing; he was just too damned busy to go running around New York chasing women.

Somehow that made Elizabeth's sense of rejection even worse, more humiliating. If he preferred another woman to her, she might be able to understand it, certainly she would want to meet the competition and see what it had to offer that she did not. But to be rejected in a vacuum! It was the most insulting rejection of all, inexcusable. It gave her nowhere to hide, there were no rationalizations to explain his blunt dismissal of her. Inadequate. Unworthy of him. Not fascinating enough to be taken seriously. In effect, that was what he had told her.

I have no plans to get married. Not to you, not to anyone. I like living alone.

Elizabeth put on her tortoise-rimmed glasses and tried to study the script that would be taped tomorrow, but it was no use, she couldn't concentrate on the meaning of the words. All she could think of was that the words had been written by Jamie and/or Iris. For the barest of seconds, a wild notion spinned across her brain. Jamie and Iris. Not and/or. Just *and*. But that was impossible, unfeasible, unthinkable that there existed any romantic attachment between the two of them. Men were never attracted to Iris, how could they be? She was an instant turnoff with her persistent drinking, her infantile outbursts, her refusal to face reality. New York, unfortunately, had done nothing to change Iris. Ginger and Harvey would be so disappointed to find out that their plans for their younger daughter had failed, they were counting so much upon the move East to have a beneficial, energizing effect on her.

Elizabeth had counted on it, too, had felt optimistic when Iris first began writing "The Troubled Heart," but after a while that premature optimism faded. Elizabeth still could not understand how Iris blithely managed to turn out competent, professional scripts while at the same time remaining her old, careless, alcoholic self. In fact it was nothing short of a miracle, and Elizabeth did not believe in miracles; she believed in hard work, order, reason, the very virtues that Iris seemed most to disdain. It was as though her sister's ability to function as a television writer existed on a separate, isolated plane, removed from every other facet of her fragmented personality. When Elizabeth questioned her about it, Iris' reply was typical:

"What's one thing got to do with another?"

"I would have imagined that an exciting new career like this would have given you self-confidence, made you want to expand your style of living."

"I like the way I live. It suits me."

"But how can it? You don't go anywhere, you don't do anything interesting, you refuse to meet new people. You're still the same stubborn shut-in you were in California."

Iris smiled through narrowed, violet eyes. "Not exactly the same."

"I meant except for your work, which is certainly an encouraging breakthrough. But don't you want to meet men? Aren't you lonely, cooped up here by yourself most of the time?"

"I'm used to loneliness."

"That's my point. You can't go on pining away for Bob the rest of your ilfe. It's not healthy, it's not natural. Don't you want to fall in love again?"

"I was in love once, thank you."

Iris' bitterness chilled Elizabeth, she felt it as a personal attack upon the disruptive part she had played in her sister's unhappy marriage, even though Iris could not have intended it as such. There were so many things Iris was ridiculously unaware of, and at moments Elizabeth longed to tell her that she missed Robert too, probably more than Iris did, more than Iris *could*, considering how slightly Iris had ever known her own husband. The circumstances under which he died, for instance. Burned to death by a 6,300-degree oxygen-acetylene flame, the amount of intense heat needed to turn metal to liquid and produce the sculptures for which Robert Barnes had become posthumously famous. The Malibu police chalked his death up to one of those typically unfortunate accidents, with which they were all too familiar.

"These guys get careless after awhile," the officer in charge had said. "They're in the middle of welding something, they've been at it for hours and they stop for a break. Maybe they have to go to the john. Or they want a glass of beer. Or they need a breather and decide to take a fast swim. You see, in their minds they're not through working for the day; that's how come they tend to overlook the safety shut-down measures. So what happens? They forget to turn off one of the tanks' gauges, or maybe they forget the torch valves. Result: instant combustion, good-bye sculptor."

What the police and Iris did not know was that Elizabeth had persuaded Robert to join her for a walk on the beach that last evening. It wasn't until they had descended the rocky steps leading to the moonlit sand that he suddenly remembered he hadn't released the pressure from both regulators. Breaking loose from her grasp, he began to race back to the house to head off the explosion and save his work. Her cries were lost on him against the pounding of the ocean. And it was only seconds later, when she saw the house explode in flames, that Elizabeth frantically managed to climb up to her car, drive to a public telephone and make an anonymous call to the police.

She had thought about that night many times since. If it weren't for her insistence that Robert walk with her on the beach he would be alive today, alive to protect her from Jamie's callousness. No, that was putting the cart before the horse. If Robert were alive, Jamie would never dare affect a callous attitude toward her, Robert's very presence would preclude such a possibility, Robert's obvious infatuation would make Jamie sit up and take notice. Jamie would be jealous, wondering what it was that Robert saw in her that he failed to perceive, what specific quality of appeal. Men were kept in line by the threat of other men, that was all there was to it, and the hell with women's liberation.

Elizabeth's eyes went once more to the script on her lap, to the xeroxed words of dialogue that she would shortly be reading with the rest of the cast, and resentment flared. If it weren't for Jamie, she would have quit the series as soon as they decided to turn her into an alcoholic. It was definitely not her kind of role; she found it obnoxious, revolting, and there was no law that said she had to play it. But if she didn't, she might never see Jamie again. "The Troubled Heart" was the one sure bond between them; she couldn't take the chance of severing it. As long as she continued to act in the show that Jamie continued to write, there was still hope of saving their relationship; but should she walk out now ... Elizabeth was afraid to think of the possible consequences.

And yet by playing such a dismal part, day after day, she was surely undermining whatever glamorous appeal she once held for him. Whichever way she turned, a hideous trap lay in wait. If only he had wanted to marry her, if he had been enthusiastic, overjoyed at the prospect, everything would be solved. Again the thought of another woman hit her, and again she pushed it out of her mind. This time it returned, nagging in its quiet persistence. She was starting to understand how Iris must have felt discovering that Robert was unfaithful. Destroyed. Devastated. Well, at least Iris could put those emotions to good use in writing "The Troubled Heart." Iris would have the vicarious satisfaction of taking out her past misery on a television character named Elizabeth.

But what would she, Elizabeth, have from here on in? Only the daily nightmare of being forced to learn lines that would condemn her for making love to another woman's husband. As though the upcoming affair with Craig Crawford were entirely her doing, her fault alone. It wasn't right that the burden of responsibility be placed on her shoulders when he was equally to blame; it wasn't fair, goddamn it. Robert's tanned face came into focus, his eyes dark with reproach.

Essex says good-bye.

But she had tried to stop him from going back to the house that night at Malibu, she had called after him, she hadn't wanted him to die. She was innocent! There was only one problem: who could she tell it to?

Jamie was drinking a can of beer, eating a ham sandwich on white bread with a lot of mayonnaise, and watching the final scenes of *Elizabeth The Queen* (made in 1939). Bette Davis was just about to sentence Errol Flynn to death, after which the six o'clock news would come on with its usual array of strikes, murders, international intrigues, and Vietnam peace talks. If Jamie played his cards right, he could put off all writing obligations until at least seven-thirty by remaining where he was, in bed, and merely flicking the TV remote control switch from channel to channel.

He had told Elizabeth that he would not be seeing her later on in the evening because he had so much work to catch up on. It was only a half-lie, the work part being all too true. The fact was that after what had taken place earlier, he didn't feel like seeing her again until next Christmas, but he didn't have the balls to tell her so. In the past, when things were going smoothly between them, he would have eagerly used this time for writing so that he would be free and clear later on to have dinner with Elizabeth, to make love to Elizabeth, simply for the pleasure of being in Elizabeth's company. He would not be sitting here like an idiot, glued to maximum TV.

The impression of her head on the pillow beside him had begun to fade, but it was still there, faint, unmistakable. Even her perfume lingered in the air. She was gone, but the memory stayed . . . her distress about her appearance on "The Troubled Heart," her aggressive proposal of marriage. The latter had made him realize at what different extremes the two of them were in their feelings for each other. Where were her sensitivities? Hiding, no doubt, for her not to see the emotional distance that separated them. She should have taken it slow, she should have withdrawn, given him time to come around. She should have let him alone. Instead, anxiety had pushed her to the totally unexpected, totally absurd suggestion of marriage. Jamie bit into his sandwich, relishing its soft, gummy texture. Yes, Elizabeth had made the mistake of advancing when the wise tactical move would have been to retreat. But people in love did not understand the meaning of retreat; even its concept was too threatening. Jamie knew. He had had to hold himself back in recent weeks to keep from advancing toward Iris. He would not do that until he felt sure of success.

The Earl of Essex knelt before his queen, stoically accepting his doomed fate, murmuring regretful good-byes to the woman he loved. It was the late sixteenth century on Warner's back lot: Spain and England were at war, Errol Flynn had screwed up at Cadiz, Bette Davis very rightly suspected that he wanted to rule her empire, and she wasn't having any. Then, in a poignant farewell, Elizabeth the Queen called Lord Essex by his given name, Robert, and he said something equally poignant in return.

Jamie sat up very straight, beer, sandwich, movie forgotten.

Essex says good-bye.

After that, it wasn't hard to figure out the rest.

It was clear and mild in New York when The Storm arrived at Iris' apartment, fifteen minutes early. Derek had left only seconds before when the doorbell rang, much to Iris' surprise. It was the first time that any man had been early since she began getting paid for her call-girl services. A few minutes late was not unusual, but apparently nobody wanted to get there ahead of schedule and take the chance of running into another man. Ken P., who had turned into a steady, satisfied customer (he gave Iris a homemade Yellow Dragon mask on his second visit), summed it up rather neatly, she thought:

"The guy coming in is like a guy on a long movie line, waiting to see the big attraction. He feels sort of dumb just standing there, waiting, trying to hide his eagerness. Then out of the theater comes the guy who's already seen the show. He's relaxed, kind of flippant. The suspense is over for him, he knows the score. Did you ever see the look that passes between these two guys? The one on line is always slightly embarrassed, the other one is always slightly condescending even though he might have just had the worst time in his life. That's why nobody likes to get here early: they don't want to be caught waiting by another guy who's sampled the merchandise. Too ego-deflating."

But such considerations did not seem to bother Larry (The Storm), who breezed in humming "The Impossible Dream," looked Iris up and down, professed to preferring tall redheads like Sheila, then qualified his remark by saying, "No offense, honey. You're a cute chick. A little on the flat-chested side, but what the hell. If I were a tit-man, I'd have lined up a 36-C for sure, right?"

"I should think so."

"Bet your ass I would have," he said, jovially.

"Would you care for a drink?"

Behind steel-rimmed glasses, his eyes glittered. "What did you have in mind?"

"Anything that appeals to you. Scotch, bourbon, vodka, cognac, you name it."

"Not to my taste. Hard liquor insensitizes the palate. But that's okay." He indicated Iris' glass of Bombay. "You go right ahead. Only hurry up. I have to be out of here in twenty minutes, that's how come I took the chance of arriving a little early. Tell me something. Did I just miss bumping into another guy?"

Iris hesitated, remembering Ken P.'s insight into the subject; still she had the distinct feeling that Larry was asking for a positive response. "Yes, as a matter of fact you did. A few seconds earlier and the two of you would have collided head on."

"No kidding." His face confirmed her hunch, he was brimming over with excitement. "What kind of guy was he? I mean, what was his kick?"

Derek and his Tiptree preserves were too unattractive a story, she could not imagine any man getting turned on by hearing about it, and that was what Larry obviously wanted for openers: vicarious gratification. Instead, she told him about Black Butterfly Pete, who had been there the day before.

"This man insists that I be dressed all in black. Black garter belt, black stockings, black heels, black gown, no bra, of course. The first thing he does when he gets here is to smoke a couple of joints to put him in the right mood, then we go into the bedroom, which has to be lit by candlelight."

Larry began to run his hands over her body, he was breathing more rapidly now. "Go on."

"Well, once in the bedroom I take out all my chain belts and the vibrator, then I have to lie down on the bed and he places the chains across my back. He doesn't wrap them around me, just places them over me. Then, it depends. Some days he wants certain things, other days are different."

"What did he want today?"

"Oh, he wanted me to screw myself with the vibrator."

"Did you do it?" Larry had removed his clothes and now wore only his watch and steel-rimmed glasses. "Did you come?"

"Yes," Iris lied. "I had a sensational orgasm."

He had his hand up under her gown, stimulating her. "Then what happened?"

"He fucked me until he was satisfied, then he went to sleep."

"Sleep? For how long? Who's got time to sleep in the middle of the day?"

"He ended up sleeping about an hour. But he always wakes up a couple of minutes right after he's dozed off, and he always has the same request."

"Yeah? What's that?"

"He wants a cookie."

"You've got to be kidding."

She laughed. "No, I swear it. That's what he craves. A cookie. So I give him one—"

"Which brand?"

"Toll House."

Larry shook his head. "No, I don't handle that account."

"Anyhow, he eats the cookie, goes back to sleep, and then when he wakes up, he pays me and leaves."

"Wow. You really get all kinds of nuts in this business, don't you?"

"I wouldn't call them nuts, exactly. Everybody has a little quirk or two, and so long as they're harmless, I don't mind."

"You've got nothing to worry about with me, honey. I'm as harmless as they come. But as you say, we all do have our little quirks."

"What are yours?"

"That's right." He glanced at his watch. "I'd better get started. Keep that gown on, I prefer it that way. I can look up the tunnel."

"With what? A telescope?"

Larry laughed appreciatively. "You're okay. You've got a sense of humor. I like that."

Whereupon he leaped up, ran to the living-room windows, and began to shake and rattle the venetian blinds. "Hear that? That's thunder." Then he made a wild dash to the wall light switch which he flicked on and off, on and off, on and off, click click click. "That's lightning, honey. Got it?"

Before Iris could reply, he jumped up on the O'Reillys' tan corduroy sofa and lay down flat on his back. "Okay, now pee on me."

"What?"

"I said, pee on me. And keep your skirt down."

Iris stood over him, thinking it was fortunate that she had to go to the bathroom as a result of all that Bombay. Still it was difficult to pee in that position, a problem she had never been confronted with before.

"I'm waiting," he said.

The sound of flushing water in another apartment did the trick, and a minute later she was able to let go with a minor torrent. She heard him rapturously mumble something about "the golden shower," then she shut her ears and eyes until it was over and he had dried himself off with Viva paper towels from the kitchen dispenser. Larry did not handle the Viva account either.

"That was real good," he said now, wiping his glasses on one of the sofa's dry spots. "Tasty."

Iris managed to keep from throwing up by wondering what to do about the O'Reillys' poor, abused sofa. Between urine and Tiptree preserves, there was little doubt that she would have to get it recovered. The only question was, in what kind of material? Ordinarily her first choice would be crushed velvet, she had a passion for its texture, but practicality ruled that out. Vinyl seemed to be the only logical solution. Maybe she would do it in fire-engine red, supposedly a sexy color.

"Are you finished?" she asked The Storm. "I mean, don't you want to—?"

"Christ, honey, have a heart. Thunder, lightning, rain. Who the hell can make love in this lousy weather?"

PART V

Chapter Twenty-Four

The weeks began to slide into months for Iris as she settled into her schizophrenic routine of kinky call-girl dates and mushy soap writing. A number of interesting things had happened recently:

1. Elizabeth and Jamie had broken up, each refusing to talk about the reasons why;
2. Elizabeth's mother had died of sickle-cell anemia on "The Troubled Heart," and Elizabeth was now established as a girl with a heavy drinking problem;
3. In spite of the problem, she and Craig Crawford were having their long-awaited love affair;
4. Craig Crawford's wife was starting to get wise to them, as a result of which the show's ratings had gone up three points;
5. Mrs. Crawford's suspicions about her husband were set off by his absent-minded humming of the Beatles' song, "When I Get Home," upon several occasions;
6. It had been shown earlier that Crawford's secretary, Elizabeth, was very partial to the Beatles (being of the same generation), so it wasn't very hard for Mrs. Crawford to put two and two together;
7. The song-humming bit had earned Iris another fifty dollars from Derek, who thought it was a splendid idea because one of the show's goals was to capture a younger housewife audience by use of contemporary themes, and (as Derek said), "What could be more contemporary than narrowing the generation gap by means of an erotic involvement?"
8. Iris earned another fifty dollars when she suggested that Elizabeth end up killing Craig Crawford because he had lied about leaving his wife to marry her (Derek simply loved that one, since it meant an early

demise for Elizabeth, who would have to be punished
for her crime—i.e. written out of the show);

9. Elizabeth had lost ten pounds since the New Year and
seemed to be visibly suffering in the guilt-ridden role
of the other woman;

10. Iris could not decide whether her sister was an even
more brilliant actress than she had always thought her
to be, or whether the role of villainess was made to
order for someone of Elizabeth's devious personality.

It was raining outside, a dark, dismal, March rain, not unlike the opening and closing spots on "The Troubled Heart."
Iris lay in bed contemplating point #10 on her list of interesting things, and waiting for the sound of the doorbell to announce that Pepe had arrived to take Bergdorf for his morning outing. She had to be sure to tell Pepe not to come for
the dog this afternoon, as he usually did. She would make up
some excuse, since she could hardly divulge the real reason:
On-The-Rocks was due at one-thirty, and he liked to have
Bergdorf around while he was there; he claimed it was more
homey that way.

"He wear his sweater, no?" Pepe said, when he arrived
with her copy of the *New York Times*.

"Oh yes, of course. I nearly forgot."

The terrier, who had recently gotten a trim at one of the
most expensive dog parlors in Manhattan, looked like a sausage when Iris finally managed to get the yellow wool sweater
on his skinny, squirming body. The poor thing weighed no
more than three pounds, despite the fact that he ate enough
for a dog twice his size.

"Nervous little fellow," Pepe said, with genuine affection,
taking the leash from Iris, who was delighted to see them
both go.

"Overbred."

She wouldn't be caught dead walking an overbred dog that
resembled a yellow sausage, but apparently it didn't bother
the unflappable Pepe in the least. There was no accounting
for taste, Iris decided, as she went into the kitchen to boil
water for her morning coffee. She was sipping a glass of stale
champagne and glancing through the *Times*, when an ad at
the bottom of the Fashion/Furnishings page caught her eye.
The caption read:

Meet Ken Peterson
at Bloomingdale's
Tomorrow at 3:00

The advertisement went on to say that Mr. Peterson, "a giant among American decorators," would meet the public the following afternoon in Bloomingdale's bookshop to autograph copies of his new, informative guide to interior design. The book was priced at twenty dollars, and there was a small, smiling photo of the distinguished author.

Iris nearly choked on the champagne. Ken Peterson was none other than her very own Yellow Dragon Ken P. She had no idea that he was so successful, and she wondered what his public would think if they could see him on the closet floor, violating her Rudi Gernreich skirt. Maybe they wouldn't find anything odd about it; maybe she was the only one who continued to cling to some stubborn, idealized norm of sexuality despite a mountain of personal proof to the contrary. Maybe every man in the world was basically a weirdo at heart, and she was just finding it out. Or maybe she was finding it out because only the weirdos went to call girls. The last argument seemed infinitely more logical, which made it infinitely more suspect. If there was one thing she had learned since moving to New York it was that logic seemed to be about the last trustworthy guide to masculine behavior.

Which made her think immediately of Jamie, and what he would be like in bed. She had never asked Elizabeth about him, and Elizabeth had never volunteered any intimate information, and that was probably just as well because Iris didn't think she could have stood it at this point to be told that Jamie was as cuckoo as all the other men she met. In her mind, he occupied a special sanctified place far above the rest of his sex, and that was the way she wanted to keep it.

A moment later, the water in the kettle came to a boil, and the telephone rang. Maybe it was The Storm, telling her he had the media report she had asked him for last time. She hoped so, if it contained what she was convinced it would, she just might be in business.

"Hello," Jamie said, tentatively. "I didn't wake you, did I?"

"No, I was just about to have coffee."

"If you'd rather, I can call you back in a few minutes."

"Really, it's okay. You sound strange. What's happening?"

"Derek phoned me a little while ago. It seems the sponsors

have started to receive carloads of mail complaining about Elizabeth's antisocial behavior on the show. They're upset as hell."

"Who? The sponsors or the viewers?"

"Both."

"What are they upset about?"

"Well, apparently, we've overdone it with Elizabeth. Her drinking is too heavy, too unladylike, her extramarital affair with Crawford is too morally unacceptable. Probably because of its coming on the heels of her mother's death, and also because Crawford's wife is a helpless cripple. I'm quoting *them* now. Anyhow, the upshot is that our dear viewers are offended, indignant, their pious mentalities are outraged. In short, they're screaming bloody murder."

"I had no idea that fan mail was taken so seriously."

"You'd better believe it is."

"Okay, but if the viewers are as upset as you say, how come our ratings are higher than they've been in over a year?"

"I'll get to that in a minute. Right now the main point is that the sponsor has put Derek on the spot, and that's exactly where he's putting us—or rather, me. I tried to tell him it wasn't my idea to turn Elizabeth into a lush, that I fought against it, that it was his brainstorm, but he doesn't care about that now. All he wants to know is, what are we going to do to remedy the situation?"

"You're the expert." Derek was bound to be infuriated with her because of this turn of events. He was so cheap, he would probably want his fifty dollars back. "What *are* we going to do, Jamie?"

"The only thing I can think of offhand is that we have Elizabeth kill Crawford as soon as possible. Then we get a fast murder conviction on her, and wind up the whole damn affair in a hurry. Meanwhile, I'll start working on future plot lines which we can begin writing into the script while the murder trial is going on. Sidetrack the damn viewers. Maybe we could use a complicated pregnancy situation with the older son and that cute little nurse he just married. It turns out there's something wrong with the combination of their blood types. The RH-negative factor. What do you think?"

Elizabeth was about to become jobless, and Derek was about to descend wrathfully upon her, that was what she thought. "I'm not sure. I'm still trying to absorb all this. I mean, how seriously can we take these letters if more people than ever are watching the show? Maybe we're only hearing from a handful of Baptist nuts."

"The sponsor seems to think not, judging from the number of letters that have been pouring in. And I'm afraid he's right." Jamie sighed. "He thinks that the higher ratings simply mean the viewers are anxious for the ax to fall on Elizabeth's head. They want her punished, and *soon*. Otherwise they're going to start switching channels. I knew we never should have made her a drunk; I knew it was a mistake. Goddamn that idiot Derek; I tried to reason with him."

"Does Elizabeth know about this yet? That she's going to be written out so soon?"

"No, you're the first person I've called. I haven't spoken to Elizabeth in more than a month. Under the circumstances, I thought that maybe you could . . ."

"Tell her?"

"Yes."

"I will, if you want me to."

"I'd appreciate it, Iris. I know I'm passing the buck, but I really believe it would be more acceptable coming from you. Less painful for her. She hates my guts enough as it is."

"I'm sure that's not true." Iris hoped it was. "She might be unhappy over the breakup, but I doubt if she hates you."

"Oh, she hates me all right," Jamie said, with an almost miserable glee. "First, I wouldn't marry her. And now she's going to think that she's being written out of the show because it was my idea to make her a lush to begin with. She never believed Derek was responsible for that little twist."

So that was what the big parting was all about: marriage. For once, Elizabeth hadn't gotten her own demanding way. Iris felt a flood of satisfaction at the thought of what this setback must mean to Elizabeth, how unprepared she must have been for it, how difficult it must be for someone who was accustomed to success to be suddenly confronted with blank failure. How sweet.

"I'm supposed to have dinner with my sister this evening. If you'd like, I'll break the news to her then. Or is it too soon?"

"No, no. The sooner, the better. Get it over with. That's terrific, Iris. I mean, it will be a great load off my mind."

And conscience. "Consider it done."

"That's wonderful." Then as a polite afterthought, he said: "You're sure it's not asking too much of you?"

"Of course not. After all, she is my sister. Isn't that what families are for? To help each other out when the going gets rough?" She started to laugh at her own words. "I think I used that speech in the last episode I wrote of 'The Troubled Heart.'"

"I know what you mean. It gets you after a while, doesn't it?"

"What?"

"The whole morality bit on soaps. Which reminds me, Iris. There's something I've been wanting to talk to you about for some time now."

"Yes?" His voice sounded so strange. "I'm listening."

"Not on the telephone. I was wondering whether we could have lunch or a drink, or something, one of these days."

"Now who sounds like 'The Troubled Heart'?"

"Oh, you mean the eyeball-to-eyeball confrontation thing, as opposed to telephone talk?"

"Of course. The characters have got to be dealing with each other in person for it to be truly dramatic. Isn't that one of the first rules you taught me? I know what, Jamie. You could drop in on me unexpectedly, and then apologize for not calling first. Or you could say that you were passing by and saw my car in the driveway, so you knew I was home."

"Except that you don't have a car. And if you did, it wouldn't be sitting in the driveway of that monster apartment building of yours."

"We'd never make it in a soap. We don't live in our own little homes, in small towns like Jeffersonville, with our very own devoted families hovering around, ready to come to our aid at the first sign of trouble. We're too sophisticated for that stuff."

"Are we?" Jamie asked.

It was only after they said good-bye that Iris realized they had not made a date for lunch (or a drink, or something), and she was sorry now that she had sidetracked him in soap opera conversation. Or was she? The tone of his voice—so serious, so compelling—had frightened her a little, no, more than a little, frightened her to the point where she didn't want to hear what he had to say. What if it were something like, "I love you, Iris. I've loved you for a long time." For a moment she contemplated calling him back, knowing she wouldn't, didn't dare. She was too much of a coward although the real question lingered. What was she afraid of? Jamie's confession of love? Or Elizabeth's fury when she found out about it?

Iris spent the rest of the morning avoiding that last question by working on a script she had started the day before. It was the last act that had caused all the problems, and she was determined not to let it happen again. The act involved two characters, Craig Crawford and his betrayed wife; and every time Iris had gotten to the part where the wife accused the husband of being involved with another woman, she felt like crying and could not continue.

If only she had accused Bob, dug deeper into the mystery of his sub rosa relationship, been brave, he might be alive today. He might eventually have stopped seeing whoever he was seeing, and not gone out to the house in Malibu on that fateful night. But instead she'd done nothing, said nothing, dug her head into the sand, and pretended nothing was wrong.

Iris began to type:

MRS. CRAWFORD: Since my accident I know I haven't been much of a wife to you. Certainly not the wife I wanted to be, used to be——

CRAIG CRAWFORD (*Pained, trying to hide guilt*): Please, Jeanette, don't blame yourself. It isn't *your* fault.

MRS. CRAWFORD (*Emphatically moving wheelchair closer to husband*): I didn't say it was.

CRAIG CRAWFORD: But I thought you meant——

MRS. CRAWFORD:—that I had failed you?

CRAIG CRAWFORD (*Avoiding her gaze*): Yes. Well, something like that.

MRS. CRAWFORD: No, my dear. I don't blame myself as much as you might like to think. And I don't hate myself. The person I hold responsible for what's become of our marriage is——

CRAIG CRAWFORD: Me, of course.

MRS. CRAWFORD (*Wry smile*): For a brilliant politician, Craig, you can be an emotional fool at times.

CRAIG CRAWFORD: And exactly what is that supposed to mean?

MRS. CRAWFORD (*Looking away*): I blame *her*. (*A star-*

tled Crawford stares at her wordlessly) Yes, I blame *her* for taking you away from me. I blame *her* for coming between us. I blame *her* for capitalizing upon both of our weaknesses. . . . *(On the verge of hysteria)* I blame *her* for everything!

CRAIG CRAWFORD: Jeanette, please, dear. Don't do this to yourself. You've been under a terrible strain these last months. Don't start imagining——

MRS. CRAWFORD *(Controlling herself)*: It won't work, Craig. I *know*.

CRAIG CRAWFORD: Know what? *(Really frightened now)* Jeanette, what on earth are you talking about?

MRS. CRAWFORD: I believe it's called adultery. Or do you prefer unfaithfulness? Yes, Craig, I do know. And I know who she is. . . . *(Hysteria starts to build up again)* And *she's* the one I blame! Your precious, wonderful, conniving little *Elizabeth! (Collapses into tears as shattered Crawford stares at her mutely, guiltily)*

Iris laid her head down on the typewriter and cried until the sounds of a barking dog reached her ears. Only then did she realize that the doorbell must have been ringing for seconds. She looked at her watch. It was one o'clock on the dot. Punctual as always, Pepe had returned with Bergdorf.

"Something is wrong?" Pepe asked, seeing her tear-stained face. Ever since he had run into the only famous Puerto Rican novelist right there in Iris' apartment, Pepe had regarded her with a mixture of admiration and deep, peasant suspicion.

"No, I'm all right. Thank you. Did Bergdorf have a nice walk?"

"He's a good little fellow," Pepe said, true to form.

After he left, Iris washed her face, dabbed on her call-girl makeup, and changed into a jersey halter-gown designed in dramatic, diagonal shades of gray. Then she put "The Troubled Heart" script into the desk drawer, and covered the typewriter with a bolt of silver metallic material she had picked up in the fabric department of Gimbel's East. She had gone there shortly after her first encounter with The Storm, to have the O'Reillys' sofa reupholstered. Gimbel's East had done a spectacular job, and the sofa now gleamed in all its shiny, fire-engine red, urine-and-Tiptree-resistant-vinyl glory, defying anyone to abuse or stain it again.

After she had filled the new Lucite ice bucket to the brim,

Iris mixed herself a weak Bombay and tonic, and decided to play a few Ray Charles records in anticipation of Ernie, who was due any minute. He would be gone within an hour despite the ice-cube treatment he insisted upon, which meant that she would still have time to squeeze in two soaps before "The Troubled Heart" came on the air. And hopefully, before the day was over, she would hear from The Storm with the good news she was counting on. In fact, she couldn't imagine why she hadn't heard from him by now, unless the report was taking longer to compile than he'd anticipated.

"Hello, honey," Ernie said, minutes later. "How've you been?"

"Just wonderful." She put her arms around him. Brut. "And you?"

"Can't complain." He was a tall, distinguished, graying man in his late forties, who operated a very successful chain of apparel shops in the South and Midwest. "Business is up. I feel terrific. And now I'm here. I'm a lucky guy."

He had three children and a photogenic wife who was a great asset to him in promotion. Her picture appeared from time to time in *Women's Wear*, launching a new line of products or publicizing the opening of their latest branch store.

"Let's go inside and relax," Ernie said, picking up the Lucite ice bucket in one hand, and holding Iris fondly around the waist with the other. "I'm a little wound up. Just got back from Dallas this morning."

"Well, in that case we'll have to unwind you. Won't we?"

"If anybody can, you can, honey."

Bergdorf was sitting on the bed when they entered the darkened room, and he barked with delight at the familiar sight of Ernie.

"There's a good boy," Ernie said, patting the dog on the head. "There's a good little fellow."

Usually, Iris did not permit Bergdorf to remain in the bedroom if she was with someone, but Ernie insisted upon having the dog present. It was as though he needed an audience (even if only a three-pound Yorkshire terrier) to witness his exhibition of great staying power. Iris thought it was sort of sad that any man should place so much importance on how long he could make love before ejaculating, but that was Ernie's hangup. Sheila had not nicknamed him On-The-Rocks for nothing. Without getting a fistful of ice cubes jammed right in his balls at strategic intervals the poor bastard would have come in the usual two minutes flat.

Chapter Twenty-Five

"Would you ladies like a cocktail before dinner?" the waiter asked.

"Yes," Elizabeth said. "A Manhattan. Iris?"

"I'll have Perrier water."

"What's the matter with you?" Elizabeth said, after the waiter had walked away. "Are you sick?"

"I'm thirsty."

"Well, well. This is a switch."

"It certainly is."

Both women were dressed in black. Elizabeth in a black wool jumpsuit with maribou at the neck and cuffs, Iris in a shimmering brocaded black satin caftan. In Iris' case, the black seemed to highlight her radiant features and shiny blonde hair, but with Elizabeth it merely seemed monotonous.

"You're looking wonderful," Elizabeth conceded. "Is that because you're no longer drinking?"

She wanted to tell Elizabeth that she looked wonderful, too, but it was such an outrageous lie that she didn't have the nerve. "I didn't say I wasn't drinking. I'm just not in the mood right now."

She was in too good a mood, was what she meant. The Storm had called before she left the apartment, informing her that the demographic report on soap operas was completed, and that as far as he could see, it bore out her main assumption: for the majority of soaps, ratings were lower on the West Coast than any other part of the country.

"You look like the cat who's just swallowed the you-know-what," Elizabeth said. "Is there something you're not telling me?"

When they were eighty-three and eighty-five years old, re-

spectively, Elizabeth would still play the part of big sister. "It
seems I'm the widow of a very famous man," Iris said.
"When I picked up my mail on the way out, there was a catalog of Bob's work, with glowing quotes from some very distinguished art critics. Plus a copy of the gallery invitation
that Ginger and Harvey sent me."

"Yes, I know. They're having a retrospective of his sculptures. The champagne opening is tonight. In fact, it's probably taking place this very minute. Don't you wish you were
there?"

"Not particularly."

"I do. I think it would be fun. New York has started to
bore me."

"This is a double switch."

"Don't you miss California at all?" Elizabeth asked, with a
touching poignancy.

"I hadn't thought much about it lately." Except as the
place where "The Troubled Heart" drew only a three-percent
rating.

"*I* miss it. I'm considering moving back."

Iris felt jolted. "What about 'The Troubled Heart'?"

"I meant, when my job comes to an end."

The possibility of being in New York alone, without Elizabeth, had never occurred to Iris. Even though she didn't see
her sister very often, it was important to know that she was
close by, and the thought of a three-thousand-mile separation
struck a chilly note.

"Is something wrong, Elizabeth? You seem dejected."

"I'm worse than dejected. I'm depressed as hell."

"I'm sorry to hear that."

"Are you?" Elizabeth raised her chin. "I should have
imagined you'd be very pleased."

"You're impossible. I was just thinking how much I would
miss you if you moved back to California, and then you go
ahead and make a bitchy remark like that."

"Maybe my television personality is starting to rub off.
Jamie once said that that happened to Ronald Colman in *A
Double Life*. I didn't see the movie, did you?"

"Not that I can remember." The subject of Jamie was an
awkward one, and at the moment Iris had no wish to pursue
it. "I've never been to this restaurant before. It's rather nice."

They were at the Stanhope. "Jack Kennedy used to stay at
this hotel. And that's George Feyer at the piano."

"Who's he?"

"Oh, he recorded all those tinkly albums years ago. Echoes of Paris, Echoes of Rome, Echoes of Vienna. Actually, he's Hungarian. Where the hell is our waiter? Do you see him?"

"He's about to descend with the drinks. I just realized why I ordered Perrier. I was reading a book by François Sagan, and somebody in it drinks Perrier a lot."

"Jamie said that after *Arch of Triumph* came out, everyone switched to Calvados. For some reason, Jamie knows the most incredible amount of junky facts. He can tell you the oddest things."

Apparently, there was no avoiding the subject. "Just the other day he and I were talking about *Gone With The Wind* and he said that Jennifer Jones's real name was Phyllis Isley."

The waiter placed their drinks on the table, and asked if they wished to see menus.

"Not just yet, thank you," Elizabeth said, before Iris could say anything. "Then you've seen him?"

"Jamie? No, we were talking on the telephone. I mean, when we had the Jennifer Jones conversation. I can't remember the last time I saw him. Ages ago."

She remembered perfectly: it was the day he had asked her to come over to his apartment to discuss the plot synopsis he had completed for the next six-week segment of "The Troubled Heart." He was wearing a red turtleneck sweater, and his hair was still wet from the shower. It was the day Iris realized she was in love with him.

"Jamie and I talk on the telephone a great deal," Iris rattled on. "You can get a lot done that way."

"I suppose it depends on what you want to get done. Cheers." Elizabeth demolished the Manhattan in no time flat, and ordered another. "I haven't spoken to Jamie in more than a month."

"Yes, that's what he said."

Elizabeth glanced at her sharply. "That's what he said *when*?"

"Today. He called me this morning."

Iris took a deep breath, undecided whether this was the right moment to break the bad news to Elizabeth. Maybe it wasn't such bad news, though. If Elizabeth were as dissatisfied with New York as she claimed to be, getting written out of "The Troubled Heart" could be a blessing in disguise.

"What did he call about?"

"The script," Iris said. "I've been having a rough time with certain parts of it. Like the scene I wrote this morning. It's between Craig Crawford and his wife. She becomes hysterical and accuses him of being unfaithful to her. She even knows who he's been unfaithful with. You."

Elizabeth's laughter was tinged with mild contempt. "She'd have to be damned-near blind not to know it."

"I suppose."

"Frankly, I'm surprised that you're having trouble with the writing. So far, the scripts have struck me as being very smooth, very professional. Of course I can't tell which scene you were responsible for, and which are Jamie's, but overall, I haven't been aware of any rough edges. Maybe that's the crucial test, the fact that I can't tell where you begin and Jamie leaves off."

"That's a nice compliment. Thank you."

Elizabeth brushed it away. *"Prego."*

"Liz, what's wrong?"

"Nothing. Everything. Does it matter? Anyhow, I don't know. My whole life seems to have collapsed. Did that ever happen to you?".

Iris looked at the pink tablecloth, at the crystal and china and silver, and saw the gallery invitation she had received a short while ago. The photo on front was of Bob's ten-foot bagel sculpture. In the catalog was a photo of Bob himself, tanned, smiling, a lock of black hair in his eyes.

"How stupid of me," Elizabeth said. "But you have gotten over Bob by now, haven't you?"

"Some days I think so, other days I'm not so sure. He cheated me by dying. If he were alive, I could have gotten over him much more easily."

"I should imagine it would be just the opposite."

"No," Iris said emphatically. "Because now he'll never change. I'll always remember him as he was when I was in love with him. But if he had lived, he would have changed, I would have changed, something would have happened to change our relationship one way or the other. I'm stuck with a ghost."

"That's the way I feel. Only he's alive."

Iris could not believe the degree of physical deterioration that had affected her sister, it was as though some uncanny makeup man had applied all his skills to age her ten years. The last time they had been together was . . . when? Iris tried to remember. Before Elizabeth's mother had died, which meant before the affair with Craig Crawford had gotten under way, before Elizabeth and Jamie had broken up. At that meeting Elizabeth looked only slightly less fabulous than usual, and had done a great deal of complaining about the cosmetic assault she had to undergo every time she appeared on "The Troubled Heart." All that shading of cheeks and toning down of lipstick, that hollow, gaunt, debilitated image she was supposed to reflect. Now it had come true.

"You must miss Jamie very much," Iris said. "I'm sure he misses you."

"He'll get over it."

"You will, too. These things take time."

"Thanks for the penetrating advice. What makes you think I haven't gotten over him already?"

"Maybe because you've been talking about him ever since we got here."

Elizabeth stiffened. "I wasn't aware of it."

"That's okay. I understand how you feel."

"You do? Then perhaps you'd like to explain it to me."

Iris ignored her sister's sarcasm. "You miss him and you're miserable, right?"

"Wrong, my darling sister, but I'm beginning to follow the workings of your romantic brain. You think I'm in this state because of Jamie. Because we broke up."

"Aren't you?"

"Certainly not! Don't be ridiculous." Elizabeth let out a short, shrill laugh. "I don't know how you arrive at these strange conclusions, Iris."

"I don't see anything strange about assuming that, as far as Jamie is concerned, you feel rather . . ." Iris tried to choose a strategic word. "Shall we say, regretful?"

"What I regret is the *necessity* for the breakup." Elizabeth was being strategic too, speaking slowly, thoughtfully. "But necessary it was. You see, I was perfectly content to go on the way we were, but Jamie wanted to get married. I didn't. What's the matter? You look surprised."

"I am."

"I can't imagine why. He's not the first man who's proposed marriage to me, you know."

If Elizabeth were telling the truth, then Jamie had been lying earlier. "I guess I'm surprised because you never told me this before."

"There are a lot of things I don't tell you," Elizabeth said, with a sly smile reminiscent of her former self. "Just as I'm sure there are a lot of things you don't tell me."

"But my life is so uneventful, what could I possibly have to tell?"

"Oh, we all have our little secrets." Elizabeth looked around for the waiter, spotted him, and beckoned. "Let's order, shall we? I'm starving."

During the meal, which Iris started off with stuffed artichokes, and Elizabeth with oysters on the half shell, George Feyer played "Mimi," and by the time they had both gotten to the Chateaubriand he was on "The Last Time I Saw Paris," and Iris was saying, "If Jamie isn't the cause of your blues, then what is? Or do you want to keep that a secret too?"

"No, not at all. It's work."

"Problems with other actors?"

"Problems with my part."

"Oh?"

"I despise playing that stupid, sloppy drunk. It's all I can do to drag myself to the studio every day. In fact, if I weren't so professionally conscientious I would have walked out as soon as Derek decided to turn me into a lush."

"Then you no longer blame Jamie for that?"

"The only thing I blame Jamie for, aside from our breakup, is letting Derek and the sponsor talk him into making me an alcoholic. He should have stood his ground. After all, he *is* the writer of the series. The head writer, I mean. And he was opposed to it right from the start."

"Elizabeth, I've never asked you this before, but why do you and Derek dislike each other so much?"

"How do you know that *he* dislikes *me*? You haven't even met the man. Or has that changed since the last time we spoke?"

"No, I've never laid eyes on Derek Christopher in my life. It's just that whenever you talk about him I get the impression the two of you have a mutual hate thing going on. And I was merely wondering why."

"Conflicting temperaments," Elizabeth said, attacking her steak. "Bad biochemistry. We never did hit it off. Sheila used to like Derek, or at least she pretended to. Sheila had a way, though, of getting along with the most unlikely people. Have you heard from her lately?"

"Not a word since that one postcard I received shortly after I moved here. I wonder how she's doing."

"Knowing Sheila, I'd say she was doing just fine. She doesn't take life too seriously. Playing an alcoholic wouldn't bother her in the least, she'd probably think it was great type-casting. Not that Sheila could be accurately described as a drunk, but it wouldn't be accurate to call her a teetotaler, either."

"Nor you, for that matter."

"Don't try to be sarcastic. It doesn't become you. And as far as liquor goes, I don't care for the filthy stuff any more than I ever did. This is what's known in the trade as researching a role."

"I thought it was a role you hated."

"I do. But for the time being I'm stuck with it, and I want to give as good a performance as possible."

"I watch the show every day, and I'd say that so far you've been very effective, very convincing."

"That's what my agent says, too."

"Well, then cheer up. It's not as though you're going to be in 'The Troubled Heart' forever."

"Thank God."

Iris smiled. "As a matter of fact, you're not going to be in it much longer."

Elizabeth laid down her knife and fork, and reached involuntarily for the empty Manhattan glass. "What the hell is that supposed to mean?"

The gallery on La Cienega was jammed with the usual preview crowd of actors, hippies, freeloaders, art lovers, art haters, and those special mailing-list names that regularly received printed announcements of a new show. Sheila and Tom O'Reilly had recently been added to this privileged list, but this was the first opening they had attended. As they entered the gallery, they were confronted by Bob Barnes's ten-foot steel bagel sculpture which occupied the focal place of honor in this retrospective of his work. There was a red star on the wall next to the sculpture, alongside the title and year of execution: *Bagel With One Bite Taken Out, 1971.* The bite mark was emphasized by a real lipstick smear.

"Quaint," Sheila said, stoned.

"I'll bet he got the idea from a remark Dorothy Parker

was supposed to have made. It was when she was working for one of the movie studios as a screenwriter."

"What did she say?"

"Something to the effect that when she thought of Hollywood, she saw a Rolls Royce with a woman's elegant, jeweled arm dangling out the back window. The woman is wearing furs and evening clothes, and in her hand there's a bagel with one bite taken out of it."

"Sometimes you amaze me. How did you know that?"

Tom O'Reilly, medium height, blondish, chiseled features, smiled at his statuesque wife. "I read, darling. Try it sometime. There aren't any commercial interruptions."

They had both just been signed to play a husband-and-wife team on a new TV comedy series that would be a summer replacement for an established variety show. Should the O'Reillys' debut be successful, there was an excellent chance they would be signed to an even juicier contract for the big Fall television season. It was the kind of opportunity that many actors would kill for. But in a recent interview in *TV Guide*, the O'Reillys nonchalantly passed it off as "a lovely fluke," and were described by the reporter as being, "iconoclastically, almost suspiciously unassuming."

"Shall we mingle with the masses?" Sheila asked.

"Let's."

Wearing matching pairs of jeans, they started to circulate among the talking, laughing, dissenting, smoking, wine-sipping crowd that had come to pay homage to the late Bob Barnes. Two waiters weaved in and out of the clusters of guests, one bearing a tray of champagne-filled glasses, the other a variety of colorful canapés. Sheila selected anchovy paste and olive on a Melba round, and Tom, a sesame seed triangle topped with pimento cheese. Fortified with glasses of champagne, they made their way into the second room where Ginger and Harvey were surrounded by an assortment of well wishers.

"Harvey, look who I see," Ginger said, loud enough for the O'Reillys to hear. "Television's answer to Nichols and May."

Pleased with their new status, Sheila and Tom approached, smiling, and shook hands all around. The others, sensing their time was up, discreetly withdrew, leaving the two couples together.

"It's so good to see you both again," Ginger said. "How have you been?"

"Happy," Sheila replied. "And thank you for putting us on your mailing list. You've collected quite a crowd here tonight. Are these openings always so festive?"

Harvey cleared his throat. "Well, this is a special occasion. Our late son-in-law, you know. How do you like the show?"

"Dear, you're not supposed to go around asking that question," Ginger said. "It puts people on the spot."

"That's exactly what it's intended to do. I'm interested in people's reactions. What's so terrible about that?"

"Nothing at all," Tom O'Reilly said. "Sheila and I were just saying how much we like Barnes's work. It's strong, direct, but with humor. In certain ways the bagel piece reminds me of a bronze by Degas, of a ballet dancer. What he did was put a real satin ribbon in her hair, the way Barnes has used real lipstick instead of paint to get his point across."

"We have an art historian in our midst." Ginger seemed very pleased. "Most of the pieces have been sold, I'm delighted to report. And the critical reception has been excellent. It's such a shame that Iris couldn't be here tonight."

"Have you heard from her recently?" Sheila asked.

"Not a word."

"She's probably having too good a time to bother writing letters."

"I don't know about that." Harvey was frowning. "We do hear from Elizabeth from time to time and she claims that Iris has become as much of a shut-in in New York as she was out here. Apparently, she just isn't interested in meeting men. She must have taken poor Bob's death even harder than we imagined."

"Maybe she's busy concentrating on her job," Sheila suggested.

"That's not enough for an attractive girl of Iris' age," Ginger said. "You think she'd be anxious to get out and meet new people, wouldn't you?"

"I suspect that in her line of work, she meets quite a few new people all the time."

Ginger and Harvey seemed to ponder this remark. Then Ginger said, "That's a thought. You mean, by writing 'The Troubled Heart,' she would get to know the actors and director and other people connected with the show? Through daily business association?"

Sheila O'Reilly drained her glass. "It certainly seems logical."

After Iris and Elizabeth parted at the Stanhope, Iris took a taxi back to Picasso Towers. She had a ten o'clock date with Bubble Bath, who had called earlier in the day saying he had a batch of new jokes to try out on her while he soaked in the tub. According to him, one of them explained the origins of the phrase, "You've got to be kidding," and was quite a lulu. Iris couldn't wait not to hear it.

"You see, during the Second World War, there was this American sergeant who had to find a place to sleep for twenty-five of his men," Bubble Bath said, almost immediately upon settling into Iris's fragrant, sudsy tub. "This was in a small town in Italy right after the U.S. Army had marched in, and housing facilities were pretty grim. Anyhow, the sergeant's got this one guy named Cox, who immediately shacks up with a local girl, so he's taken care of. Then one of the townspeople suggests that they try the local whorehouse because it has so many rooms. This seems reasonable and the sergeant goes over to talk to the madam, one of those Anna Magnani types.

" 'Signora,' he says. 'I wonder if you could help me out. I need to find places for my men to sleep overnight. Can you accommodate us?'

" 'How many men do you have?' she asks.

" 'Twenty-four. Without Cox.'

" 'You've got to be kidding!' "

Bubble Bath clutched his rubber duck and nearly drowned laughing.

Chapter Twenty-Six

It was April in New York.

Elizabeth had knocked off Craig Crawford by slipping an ounce of chloral hydrate in his martini glass (Jamie's idea), and Elizabeth's lawyer was now trying to suggest the possibility that it was Mrs. Crawford who had committed the murder (Iris' idea, for which Derek Christopher had paid another fifty dollars). Hate mail against Elizabeth was pouring into the network, with outraged viewers demanding a fast conviction of first-degree murder. Some of the letters were unusually vitriolic.

You are a sick and disgusting person to have done the evil thing you did to Mr. Crawford.

You will burn in hell for this taking of a human life.

You lost whatever judgment you had when you started drinking the devil's poison. Liquor has affected your brain and soul.

It was bad enough what you did to Craig Crawford, but to try to implicate his poor, helpless, cripple of a wife in your own murderous schemes is the most unforgivable thing I have ever heard of.

You have one death on your conscience. Now you are trying to make it two. Have you no shame at all?

I hope they give you the electric chair.

You are sin incarnate.

Drunken whore!

Iris and Jamie figured that they could wrap up the court trial by the end of the month, Elizabeth would be found guilty of first-degree murder, and that would be that. Elizabeth was becoming more and more engrossed in her role, while at the same time saying how much she despised it. The evening at Stanhope when Iris told her that she would be written out by the end of April, Elizabeth's response was typically ambivalent:

"Thanks for the big favor. I knew I could count on you."

"From what you've been saying, I should think you'd be pleased. You just said you hate the part."

"That isn't the point."

"Then what is?"

Elizabeth hesitated, finding it difficult to express her sentiments. "Nobody likes to be dispensed with, and I'm no exception. You're all trying to get rid of me, that's what I object to."

"Not *you*," Iris tried to explain. "The character you play."

"That's what Derek said, but I don't believe him. I don't

believe you, either. I think you're all in this together. Derek, Jamie, and you. None of you likes me."

"I like you." Iris felt like a terrible hypocrite because it had originally been her idea to turn Elizabeth into a drunk. "You're my sister."

Elizabeth regarded her with suspicion. "Sometimes I wonder about you. I don't think I know you at all."

Iris was contemplating this exchange as she got into her pale-green gown in anticipation of Derek's arrival at three-thirty that afternoon. She hadn't seen much of him recently, and this was supposed to be a reconciliation meeting. He had been infuriated with himself, and finally with Iris, for listening to her suggestion about making Elizabeth a drunk on "The Troubled Heart." The sponsor was still talking about what a grave error in judgment it was, conveniently forgetting that he had okayed it at the time. But now with Craig Crawford murdered and a conviction in the offing, tensions had eased among the network's decision-makers, and Derek wanted to forgive and forget what he referred to as "the whole bloody mess." Iris had just finished putting on green eyeshadow when the doorbell rang. It was only three o'clock, it would be unusual if it were Derek arriving half an hour early.

"Who is it?" she called out.

"Jamie."

"Just a second." Jamie had never seen her dressed and made up for one of her appointments, and there was no time to do anything about it. "I'm coming." She undid the double lock. "What a nice surprise."

For a moment he seemed dumbstruck by her appearance; then he said, "I saw your car in the driveway, so I knew you'd be home. I hope I didn't get you at a bad time."

It was, word for word, the same exact dialogue that Iris had written for Elizabeth in a recent episode of "The Troubled Heart."

"Very funny," she said.

"Are you going somewhere?"

She had to get rid of him before Derek arrived or it would be a catastrophe, probably the worst of her life.

"I'm expecting someone. An old friend of the family. He just got into town and will only be here a few days. I was feeling unattractive, so I thought I'd change my clothes. How do I look?"

The pale-green gown clung in all the right places and Jamie gave her an appreciative, if suspicious, once-over.

"You look very pretty. I never realized what a pretty girl you are. You've changed a lot since you first moved here. New York seems to agree with you."

"You're very sweet."

"Not really." He seemed uncomfortable. "Would it be too much of an imposition if I asked you for a drink? I promise I won't stay more than a few minutes. But I did want to talk to you."

If he drank fast, he'd be out of her apartment in plenty of time. He *had* to be out. The thought of him and Derek colliding head on, terrified her. "What would you like?"

"A light Scotch on the rocks." He noticed that she was not holding the usual glass of Bombay. "You've been cutting down lately, haven't you?"

"Yes, I don't seem to have as much need for the stuff as I used to." Now that Elizabeth had taken over as resident drunk on "The Troubled Heart."

"I'm glad to hear that. What caused the big change? A man?"

Was he jealous? It seemed too good to be true. "Not exactly. In fact, I really don't know. I just found myself drinking less and less each day. It was one of those gradual things."

He walked to the window that overlooked the rooftops of New York. His hands were in his pockets, his back to her.

"I apologize for dropping in without calling first, but I was in the neighborhood and——"

"You thought you'd take a chance."

He didn't laugh, he didn't move. Iris had never seen him so tense before. She longed to kiss the deep frown lines on his face, she wanted him to take her in his arms and not let go. She wanted to smother him with kisses, as she was sure Elizabeth had never done. Instead, she went into the kitchen for ice cubes. When she returned with Jamie's drink, he was still standing in front of the window in the same exact pose.

"It can't be as terrible as all that," she said. "Whatever you wanted to talk to me about. What is it? More trouble at the network?"

"No, this has nothing to do with the show." He turned around, accepted the drink she gave him, took a long swallow and said, "It's something that involves you personally, Iris."

She began to get a sick, sinking feeling. What if he had found out about her call-girl operation? But how? Through whom?"

"I'm listening," she said.

"Let's sit down."

She glanced quickly at her watch. It was ten past three. Her anxiety about getting rid of Jamie was surpassed by her curiosity about what he had to say. She led him to the red vinyl sofa, and they sat down, one at each end, Iris curling her legs under her, Jamie with his feet planted solidly on the floor.

"It's about your marriage," he began. "Perhaps I should keep my mouth shut, but I'm afraid I can't. The more I've thought about it, the more I realized that I had to tell you. No matter what the consequences are."

"My marriage? But what could you——? I don't see how——" She was stunned, bewildered. Nothing he might have said could have frightened her more than this unexpected reference to her marital disaster, not even the call-girl thing. "What about my marriage?"

"The first evening you were in New York you said that your husband had been unfaithful to you. Remember? We were all having dinner at that organic restaurant. Nature's Oasis. You and me and Elizabeth. And you blurted out the whole sordid story."

"I remember. So what?"

"At the time you claimed that you never had any idea who the other woman was."

"That's right. I didn't then, and I don't now. What are you trying to say?"

"What if I told you that I'm pretty sure *I* know who she was?"

Iris's throat felt very dry. She swallowed and tried to keep her voice steady. "I don't understand. You didn't live in California. How could you know?"

"Call it writer's intuition, but I'm certain I'm right. You see, I was watching an old movie on television one afternoon not too long ago. *Elizabeth The Queen,* with Bette Davis and Errol Flynn. That's when it hit me."

Perhaps he had gone mad. Or was playing some cruel joke on her. Yet he seemed perfectly serious, solemn, sane.

"Go on."

"Elizabeth had been at my place earlier that day. She made a reference to your late husband, but she called him Robert, not Bob."

"Nobody ever called him Robert. At least not that I know of."

"I didn't think so. That's why it stuck in my mind."

"I still don't see what that has to do with——"

"In the movie, Queen Elizabeth is in love with Lord Essex, whom she finally condemns to death. It's only at the end, when he's about to die, that she calls him by his first name: Robert."

Iris's heart was beating so loudly that for a minute she didn't hear the doorbell ring.

"I suddenly thought of your husband's last words," Jamie said. *"Sex says good-bye.* At least that was how they sounded to you at the time. But what if he really had been saying: *Essex says good-bye?* Who do you think he would be speaking to?"

This time Iris heard the doorbell, heard her heart collapse within her. "To Elizabeth."

"That's right. Your sister was the other woman."

Iris stood up and moved toward the door. Her legs were shaking so badly that she was amazed they were able to support her. She opened the door and stared dumbly at Derek Christopher, who was carrying a gift-wrapped bottle under his arm.

"You look like you've just seen a ghost," he said. "May I come in?"

She opened the door wider. He entered quickly, then stopped dead at the sight of Jamie on the sofa. "What the hell?!"

Jamie seemed equally, if not more dumbfounded. *"Derek."* He looked at Iris for an explanation. "I thought you said you were expecting a friend of the family. What's going on around here?"

"Precisely what I would like to know," Derek said.

"It's rather complicated." Iris was surprised she was still standing up, let alone talking, when by all rights she should have fainted seconds ago. "I'm not sure that I can explain it properly."

"How do you two know each other?" Jamie demanded.

"The very question I was going to ask," Derek said. "I

suppose the answer is obvious, but I must say it is an odd co-incidence in a city of this size."

"I don't see anything obvious about it at all," Jamie said. "You can't possibly be a friend of the family, and since you aren't, why did Iris tell me that you were?"

"Of course I'm not a friend of the family, you stupid bugger. I'm here for the same reason you are. I simply find it a bit awkward that we should have run into each other this way, but I suppose these unfortunate accidents do happen from time to time, eh, Iris?"

She nodded weakly.

Jamie got to his feet. "Everyone seems to understand what's happening, except me."

"What's happening," Derek said, "is that your time is up, so why don't you run along like a good chap, and let the next fellow have his fun?"

"Fun? What the hell are you talking about? Iris, what is he talking about? I didn't come here for fun!"

"I always thought you were a bit cuckoo," Derek said, "but now I'm convinced of it. If you don't come here for the proverbial good time, may I ask why you are here?"

"You may not, because it's none of your goddamn business. It happens to be a very personal matter, concerning Elizabeth, Iris and me. Period."

"Elizabeth? Surely you don't mean Elizabeth Small? You couldn't mean her. That wouldn't be just an odd coincidence. It would be absolutely uncanny."

Jamie gulped down his Scotch. "I don't know what you mean by that remark, but I see nothing uncanny about it. Why shouldn't I be referring to Elizabeth Small? She's Iris' sister."

"And your ex-girlfriend," Iris added in a faraway, dreamy voice.

"I believe I'm going quite mad." Derek put the gift-wrapped bottle on the round dining table, and sat down on one of the tubular chairs, still wearing his coat. "That's impossible." He looked from one to the other. "Your sister. Your ex-girlfriend. Elizabeth? No. I don't accept it. This is some sort of monstrous joke. It has to be."

"It's not a joke," Iris said. "It's all true. In fact, you haven't heard the half of it."

"Do you mean to say there's more to this incredible farce than I've already been told?"

"Fun, good times, a farce." Jamie pointed an accusing finger at the producer of "The Troubled Heart." "The only farcical aspect to this situation is that you happened to come blundering in on the middle of an extremely serious conversation that Iris and I were having. And I still would like an explanation as to what the hell you're doing in this apartment. It can't have anything to do with 'The Troubled Heart,' or am I wrong?"

Iris opened her mouth to say something, but Derek cut her off. "Very well, Jamie, since you pretend to be so damned dense, I am here to get laid."

"Not laid, exactly." Iris was thinking of Derek's continuing love affair with the jar of Tiptree preserves. "It's more bizarre than that."

"Laid?!" Jamie was beside himself. "Do you mean that you two have been having an affair all this time? Why you rotten, miserable, English bastard. Don't you know that Iris is practically a virgin?"

"I'm glad you said *practically*." Derek laughed and removed his coat. "Although I must admit it's a rather strange way to describe one of the most remarkable call girls I've ever met."

"CALL GIRLS!" Jamie shouted.

Before Iris could stop him he had punched Derek to the floor, chair and all, and now stood over him, daring him to get to his feet. Derek touched his nose, which had begun to bleed, as Iris went into the bedroom for a box of Kleenex. When she returned, the chair was upright once more and Derek was sitting on it, holding his head back to keep the blood from running down his shirt. Iris pulled out three Kleenexes and gave them to Derek, who pressed them to his nose, at the same time nodding his dazed thanks.

"This has turned into a most unusual afternoon," he mumbled. "Most unusual."

"Something tells me the worst isn't over yet." Jamie looked at Iris, who tried to avoid his accusing eyes. "Not by a long shot."

Chapter Twenty-Seven

After Derek's nose had stopped bleeding and Jamie had calmed down somewhat, Iris said: "It's all my fault, this whole, terrible mixup. I've lied to both of you, and I apologize. I really feel awful."

"*You* feel awful!" Derek touched his nose lightly. "Think of how I feel, coming over here in perfectly good faith with a vintage bottle of champagne. And then this."

"Iris," Jamie said, "what is this call-girl nonsense he's been raving about? Would you please explain?"

"I have not been raving."

"I'm asking her, not you, buster. Well, Iris?"

"It's true. I've been working as a call girl for almost as long as I've been in New York. I found Sheila's list of customers in a bureau drawer the very night I moved in."

"Sheila O'Reilly? You mean, she was a call girl, too? What am I saying? You can't be a call girl. It's impossible. You've been helping me write 'The Troubled Heart.'"

"What's that?" Alarm spread over Derek's pale face. "Iris, a writer? You must be insane."

"No, he's not," she said.

"Of course, I'm not. She's been my second writer for months now. And a very competent one at that."

"She can't have been," Derek said. "I've been paying her fifty dollars a visit. She's a famous Bel Air hooker."

"I just pretended to be."

"*Pretended?* Are you trying to tell me that I've been giving away my money to a rank amateur?"

"I wasn't exactly an amateur by the time you came along. I had the Yellow Dragon first. Actually, he's a famous interior decorator, even if he did ruin my Rudi Gernreich skirt. I'm too ashamed to send it to the cleaner's any more."

"I want my money back," Derek said. "I also want the money I gave you for all those hotshot ideas of yours. Such as turning Elizabeth into an alcoholic. That went over like a lead balloon. And to think I paid you an extra fifty for it."

"A lobster is a lobster is a lobster."

"Hold on." Jamie was staring at Iris. "Do you mean that it was your idea, and not Derek's?"

"That's right."

"And when you suggested it to him, he had no notion that you were connected with 'The Troubled Heart'? In any way?"

"Of course I had no notion," Derek said. "I merely assumed she was an enterprising little call girl who liked our show. That's what she told me. How could I ever have imagined she was one of its writers? No screen credit, no giveaways. God, what an ass I've been."

"I'm the ass," Jamie said. "First for believing in your innocence, Iris. And secondly, for believing that this English idiot could think up any plot idea, lousy or not." He and Iris had resumed their seats on the red vinyl sofa, across from Derek. "It's too incredible."

"I figured out what soap operas and call girls have in common." Iris laughed. "Neither of them work on weekends."

The two men did not laugh. They looked at each other, then they looked at Iris, then they looked at each other again, the same stunned expression on both their faces. Finally, Jamie spoke.

"I just realized something. If the alcoholic switch was Iris's idea, then she's the one responsible for getting her own sister written out of 'The Troubled Heart.'"

"That's correct," Derek said. "And all this time, Elizabeth has been blaming me."

"Why shouldn't she blame you?" Jamie asked. "You took credit for it, schmuck. Before you realized it was going to backfire on you. I always said that that alcoholic twist was for the birds. But what I'm curious about now, is whether you thought so too, Iris."

"Certainly."

"And yet you did it to your own sister." Jamie's voice trailed off as he recalled the original reason for this visit of his. "You did it purposely. Vindictively. Even though you didn't know about Elizabeth and your late husband until just a few minutes ago. Unless you've been lying about that, as well."

"I didn't know," Iris said flatly.

"What late husband?" Derek demanded.

"His name was Bob Barnes," she said. "We were married for a year."

"What happened to the poor chap?"

"He burned to death."

"I see." Derek was still in a state of shock. "Then that's why you and Elizabeth have different surnames. It's all starting to make some sort of weird sense. What a masquerade! And to think that I was utterly taken in by it."

"I was taken in, too," Jamie said. "So innocent, so sweet, so shy with men. That was my opinion of you, Iris. It made me feel very protective toward you. AND ALL THE TIME YOU WERE FUCKING FOR MONEY!"

"There's no need to raise your voice," Derek said. "And I resent your calling me an idiot and a schmuck. I don't even know what a schmuck is, but I resent it very much."

"Shut up."

"See here!"

"Just shut up a minute. Iris, since we've gone this far in truth-telling, I think you should call Elizabeth and ask her to come over here right away. We might as well have all the principal players present."

Derek glanced at his watch. "She's at rehearsals."

"I don't give a damn if she's at the world disarmament meeting. Tell her that the writer and producer of 'The Troubled Heart' require her presence immediately. Never mind. I'll do it myself." He walked to the telephone, just as the doorbell rang. "Who the hell is that? Another customer, Iris?"

"I'm not expecting anyone. Maybe it's Mrs. Richmond. She lives in the next apartment."

Iris went to the door.

"I hope I'm not interrupting anything." Mrs. Richmond, holding Bettina on a leash, stood on the threshold. "But I heard loud voices. I wanted to make sure you weren't in any kind of trouble."

"That's very thoughtful of you. Won't you come in?"

"I can only stay a moment." Mrs. Richmond stepped into the apartment. "Bettina hasn't been out yet, and it looks like it's going to rain. Incidentally, I just got through watching 'The Troubled Heart.' Did you see it today? It was very exciting." She glanced curiously at the two men. "I hope I'm not interrupting an orgy. I wouldn't want to interfere."

Bergdorf came running out of the bedroom, barking, and tried to attack Bettina. Iris picked up the Yorkshire terrier, who was still growling. Then she introduced Mrs. Richmond to Derek Christopher.

"This is the producer of your favorite soap opera."

" 'The Troubled Heart'? I'm thrilled. And isn't that gentleman on the telephone the writer of the show? I met him the first day you moved into Picasso Towers. Remember? When he had to throw water on the dogs in order to separate them?"

"I remember."

It had been six months ago, but to Iris it might just as well have been six years. So much had happened to her that she could not believe all the changes. Becoming a writer, becoming a call girl, falling in love with Jamie, learning about Elizabeth and Bob. In fact, more had happened to her in these past six months than in her entire life. She was still trying to digest Jamie's statement that Elizabeth had been the other woman in her marriage (as well as in Craig Crawford's marriage). Part of her said that his proof was not based on solid fact, it was intuitive, circumstantial; yet she knew he was right. Perhaps, on some level, she had known it all along. How could Elizabeth have done such a base thing to her, to her own sister? How could Bob have betrayed her that way? How could she have been so stupidly naive? All of her old feelings of rivalry with Elizabeth loomed larger than ever before, but there was one big difference now: she no longer felt so helpless about competing. Then something struck her. Had Jamie confronted Liz with his accusations? Obviously not, or he would have said so. Which meant that when Elizabeth arrived in a few minutes, she would be put on the witness stand for the first time. Iris could hardly wait.

"Jamie, you remember my next-door neighbor, Mrs. Richmond," she said, after he had gotten off the telephone.

"It's nice to see you again." Jamie's face was drawn, his voice lifeless. "Elizabeth will be here shortly."

"Today's episode was very exciting," Mrs. Richmond said. "When is that terrible girl, Elizabeth, going to be convicted?"

"Soon."

"And she'll be here soon," Iris added.

"Do you mean in this apartment? That drunken murderer?"

"She's not a murderer." Iris wondered what a crime against one's own sister could be called. "She's an actress."

" 'The Troubled Heart' is so convincing that half the time I forget I'm watching professional actors at work. I think they're really the people they pretend to be on the television screen. Silly, isn't it?"

"It's very complimentary. It shows what an effective job we do," Iris said. "Isn't that true, Jamie?"

"Very effective." He looked impassively at Mrs. Richmond. "Iris wrote today's script, in case you're interested."

"I still don't believe it," Derek said.

"I don't follow you," Mrs. Richmond said.

"I'm the associate writer on the show," Iris said.

"But that's impossible. You're a call girl, and if anybody should know it, it's me. My God, you've confided in me often enough. So what's this business about being a writer?"

"I'm a writer *and* a call girl."

"That doesn't make sense." Mrs. Richmond's voice had turned belligerent. "That's the most illogical thing I've heard in a long time."

"Why?" Iris asked.

"Because writers aren't call girls, and vice versa. I mean, if you were a writer, why would you want to lower yourself to being a call girl? And if you were a call girl, you wouldn't be smart enough to be a writer. That's why."

"But apparently I am smart enough. Anyhow, I don't see why you consider a call girl to be on a lower plane, particularly since her work requires as much ingenuity and imagination as a soap opera writer's, if not more."

"I resent that," Jamie said.

"She might have a point," Derek said.

"Absurd!" Mrs. Richmond said.

"Why are you getting so angry?" Iris asked her. "I thought you liked me."

"I did like you, before today."

"You mean, before you found out that you couldn't pigeonhole me so neatly."

"I don't like hypocrites," Mrs. Richmond said. "Or liars, or fast talkers. And you're all three."

"No, I'm not. I never said I didn't write 'The Troubled Heart.' You just never asked me."

"I suppose you think you're pretty cute, don't you? Taking advantage of the kindness of strangers?"

"How did I take advantage of you?"

"I trusted you," Mrs. Richmond said. "I felt sorry for you because of the terrible, sordid life you were leading. And now you tell me that you weren't leading it at all."

"She was leading it," Derek said. "And I should know. I was paying her plenty to get my jollies."

"You?! You mean, the producer of 'The Troubled Heart,' you've been using the services of a call girl? That's disgraceful. When I first dropped in this afternoon, I thought I might be interrupting a friendly little orgy, but this is worse, much worse. I'll never be able to watch 'The Troubled Heart' again, not after what I've learned today. As for you, Iris, I don't know what to say. Words fail me."

"Why don't you congratulate me?"

"For what?"

"Look at all the people I've rescued from the routine boredom of their lives. Think of the men who come here for a little amusement, at the very time their wives are home watching 'The Troubled Heart,' for a little escape. I'm saving a hell of a lot of marriages one way or the other. Doesn't that call for congratulations?"

"I'm going to make myself a drink," Derek said. "I can't take any more of this sober. Can I get anybody anything?"

"Not for me, thank you. I have to be going." Mrs. Richmond moved toward the door. "It's simply shocking. To think that a prostitute has been writing my favorite soap opera. It's more than shocking. It's immoral."

"Oh, well." Iris smiled. "Once a whore, always a whore."

But she stopped smiling a second later, after Mrs. Richmond left and Jamie slapped her across the face. "You're not a whore, and I don't want you say it."

"Take it easy, old boy," Derek said. "You're stronger than you look."

Iris had begun to cry, Jamie was trying to comfort her, and Derek was drunkenly smoking one of his Upmann cigars when Elizabeth arrived.

"What's going on around here?" she demanded. "Why did you send for me?"

"It wasn't my idea." Derek's words were only slightly blurred, his dignity was intact. "I can assure you that."

"What happened to your nose?"

"Your *friend*, Jamie, punched me."

Elizabeth looked at Jamie. "What does he mean?"

"It means that he knows we used to be more than just friends."

"Who told him?"

"I did." Iris wiped her eyes with the back of her hand. "But that wasn't what started it. Jamie became angry because Derek referred to me as a call girl."

Elizabeth sank into the tubular chair alongside Derek. "A call girl? Why would you say a thing like that about Iris?"

"Because that's what I've been doing for the last few months," Iris said. "I mean, in addition to writing 'The Troubled Heart.' I've been working as a call girl."

Elizabeth stared at her much as Jamie and Mrs. Richmond had upon hearing the announcement, except that instead of becoming angry, she burst into laughter.

"You? A call girl? That's the funniest thing I've ever heard. Why, you're practically a virgin. Except for Robert, you've never been to bed with a man in your life. I don't think you'd know what to do in bed."

"You'd be surprised."

"I want my money back," Derek said.

"What money?" Elizabeth asked him.

"The money I paid her for catering to my sexual needs, as well as the money I paid on three occasions for various plot ideas concerning 'The Troubled Heart.' Such as turning you into an alcoholic, my dear Elizabeth."

Elizabeth became pale. "I thought that was your filthy idea."

"So did I," Jamie added. "Until this afternoon."

"It was Iris' filthy idea," Derek said. "I merely took credit, and discredit, for it. It was also your sister's idea to have you kill off Craig Crawford, which I eagerly accepted, because it meant getting you written out of the show sooner than originally planned."

"I can see that this has been a very busy afternoon," Elizabeth said. "I won't bother asking how you found out that Iris and I are sisters, Derek. It seems fairly obvious by now. But how did you and Iris meet? When? I didn't think the two of you knew each other."

"Oh, we're old friends," Derek said. "I've been to this flat many times before today. Isn't that true, Iris?"

Iris nodded. "Derek was my second customer."

"Customer of what?" Elizabeth asked.

"Prostitution," Derek said. "It seems that only the professional ladies are willing to indulge my somewhat odd sexual fancies. You should know that, Elizabeth. If you use yourself as an example of the uptight amateur."

Now it was Iris and Jamie's turn to be startled, much to Derek's amusement. "Yes, I once made the mistake of trying to seduce Elizabeth, and she objected. Rather violently, as I recall."

"What you wanted to do was disgusting."

"Oh, I don't think it's so terrible," Iris said. "It just depends on your outlook."

"You mean, you did it?" Elizabeth seemed more dumbfounded by this piece of information than anything else she had heard so far. "With the strawberry preserves? How could you?"

"It was easy. He paid me fifty dollars."

"Whore!"

"I've got worse names for you."

"I doubt that."

"Don't."

"You're sick, Iris. I've always known it."

"You're not exactly Miss Mental Health yourself. The trouble is, I *haven't* always known it."

"Oh dear, oh dear." Derek shook his head sadly. "I cannot stand family squabbles. Nothing is ever resolved. Such a waste of time, so messy."

"You're a fine one to be talking about who's messy," Iris said. "I had to have this whole damned sofa recovered because of you and your Tiptree preserves. Because of you and The Storm, I should say. Between the two of you nuts, you stained it beyond belief."

"What's The Storm?" Jamie wanted to know.

"It's not a *what,* it's a *who.* As for his real name, I have no intention of telling. Clients' identities are strictly confidential."

"My own sister," Elizabeth said. "A common prostitute."

"I was a very exclusive prostitute. My starting price was fifty dollars. And in case you're interested as to how I fell into a life of sin, ask your old friend, Sheila O'Reilly."

"If you're trying to imply that Sheila had anything to do with it, all I can say is that that's typical of you, Iris. Always put the blame on the next person. You've never learned how to accept responsibility for your own actions. Never."

"I hope you have."

"And what do you mean by that?"

"Bob Barnes. That's what I mean."

"What about Bob?"

"Why don't you call him Robert, the way you used to when you were alone with him? Out at the beach house in Malibu?"

"I don't know what you're talking about."

"Tell her, Jamie."

Elizabeth turned toward Jamie, her eyes dark and frightened. "What's going on around here? What do you know about it?"

"Everything."

"He figured it out," Iris said. "I was too close to the truth to see it. How you both must have laughed at me. You and Bob. Poor, simple, naive, unsuspecting Iris. Did you have a good time making fun of me? Was it amusing? I'll bet it was. And you call *me* a whore. That's a laugh."

"Stop it!" To Iris' amazement, Elizabeth had begun to sob. "It wasn't my fault. I never wanted to get involved with Bob. I was never in love with him. You have to believe that, Iris."

"What are you saying? That Bob was in love with you? Is that it?"

"Yes."

"But you didn't return his feelings?"

"No."

"Then what the hell were you doing with him for an entire year? Can you explain that?"

"It was just one of those things I drifted into." Elizabeth's mascara was running, her voice was unsteady. "And after it had begun, I didn't know how to get out. Bob kept threatening to tell you everything if I left him."

"Oh, I see. You stayed with him to protect me."

"That's right."

"You're a disgusting liar, Elizabeth."

"It's true." She had begun sobbing again. "I swear it!"

"Liar!"

"This beats anything I've ever seen on 'The Troubled Heart.'" Derek stood up to make himself another drink. "You Americans certainly are an emotional lot."

Chapter Twenty-Eight

"We have feelings," Elizabeth said to Derek. "Which is more than can be said for a cold fish like you. That's why I could never quite believe that turning me into an alcoholic was your idea. There was too much pathos involved in the concept. Definitely not your cup of tea."

She regarded Iris bitterly. "I should have known that you were the one behind it. And I should have known why."

"I could say the same about you and Bob. *I* should have known."

"You've always hated me, Iris, haven't you?"

"You've hated me, too. The only difference is that you could never admit it to yourself. At least I recognized the rivalry between us. You refused to. When I decided to turn you into an alcoholic, I did it on purpose. But when you stole my husband, you deluded yourself. God knows what you were thinking, what crazy rationalizations you came up with, but I doubt that you ever admitted it was because of competition."

"It wasn't."

"If you weren't in love with Bob, as you claim, then what other reason could there be?"

"He pursued me. It was very flattering. Every woman likes to be pursued by a handsome man, it makes her feel desirable."

"Even when that handsome man is her own brother-in-law?"

"It's not as though we flaunted it in front of you. We were discreet. We didn't want to hurt you."

"I wanted to hurt you," Iris said. "And I've succeeded. You're being written out of 'The Troubled Heart,' thanks to me. Just as you wrote me out of my own marriage. Don't you see what our parents have done to us? They've turned us against each other."

"That's a terrible thing to say about Ginger and Harvey."

"No. It was a terrible thing for them to *do*, even if it wasn't intentional. They didn't mean it to happen, but they couldn't prevent it. They never loved us. They made us compete for their love."

"They loved me," Elizabeth said.

"Did they? If they had, you wouldn't be so damned insecure about everything. You wouldn't have tried to take Bob away from me. We're both insecure. We even try to hide it in similar ways."

"Like what?"

"Like lying and cheating."

"I only lied about Bob to protect you from being completely shattered." She almost believed it herself. "Think of what your reaction would have been had you known at the time that I was having an affair with him. You would have gone to pieces."

"Probably. But that's not really the issue."

"Then, what is?"

"Think of *why* you were having an affair with him."

"I've already explained."

"No, you haven't."

"Very well. You explain it, since you suddenly seem so knowledgeable about everything. Go ahead."

"It was a way of getting closer to Ginger and Harvey."

Elizabeth stared blankly at her sister. "What?"

"Don't you know where our parents' love went? To people like Bob. To the artists they handled. They didn't have enough left over for us. That's the real reason you became involved with Bob. It was the reason I married him. Bob was the closest we could get to what we couldn't have: Ginger and Harvey's love."

"I can't accept that."

"Maybe it's too painful."

"If what you say is true, then how do you account for the feeling I have that Ginger and Harvey did love me?"

"Because compared to me, you certainly were more favored, more indulged. But when you think about it, it's a pretty bleak comparison. Maybe that's why I can see it more clearly. I was more deprived."

"They gave us everything," Elizabeth insisted.

"Except the one thing that meant most of all. So what happens? Look at our behavior. You have a sneaky affair with my husband. I manipulate you into a television role you despise, and out of a job that could have benefited you professionally. What kind of behavior is that?"

"Pretty crummy."

"You're damn right. That's why I'm glad this has come out in the open at last. All the lies, intrigues, plotting, all the petty schemes we've indulged in. I don't want to live that way any more. It's self-defeating. No matter how many victories we may think we win, in the end we lose."

"It's as though we've been pawns of our parents all our lives."

"Exactly. They've directed our every move. Our every deception."

"But they didn't mean to," Elizabeth said, weakening.

"I know. That's why it's taken us so long to catch onto what's happening. To realize what fools we've been."

"I resent being called a fool."

"Then why did you lie to me about the reason you and Jamie broke up? It was a stupid, foolish lie, unworthy of you. Why couldn't you have told the truth?"

During this exchange between the two women, Derek had been quietly drinking himself into a stupor, while Jamie paced the living-room floor, Bergdorf at his heels. Now he stopped and confronted Elizabeth.

"What's this about our breaking up?"

"Nothing."

"Elizabeth claimed that you were madly in love with her," Iris said, "and that you gave her an ultimatum: marriage or good-bye. According to Elizabeth, she chose the latter. Isn't that true, Elizabeth?"

"You have no right to put me on the witness stand this way. No right at all. I haven't committed a crime, and I won't be cross-examined."

"Very well. In that case, I'll take your word for it. Since you don't want to marry Jamie, I can only assume that you aren't interested in him any longer. Right?"

Elizabeth looked trapped, and nodded her head.

"That's wonderful," Iris said. "Because *I'm* interested. In fact, I'm in love with him."

"What?!" Elizabeth said.

"Oh, dear," Derek said.

"This is even better than *Cobra Woman*, with Maria Montez," Jamie said.

Then for a while nobody said anything, each lost in private thought, each trying to pull together the shreds of the day into one cohesive pattern, each waiting for something to happen. Iris waited for Jamie to say that he felt the same toward her. Elizabeth waited for him to say that he did not. Jamie waited for a sign from Elizabeth that she was not going to fly into a murderous rage because of Iris' confession (I'm still afraid of her, he thought). And Derek simply waited, hoping somehow for a miraculous, last-minute sexual reprieve. It was Elizabeth, finally, who broke the heavy silence.

"You tricked me!" she shouted at Iris. "You miserable little cheat. You stole him away from me behind my back, that's what you did."

"You can only steal something if it belongs to someone else. Jamie doesn't belong to you. You yourself just said that you weren't interested in him."

"Only because you tricked me into saying it. And after all your noble talk about truth and honesty, all that junk you've been handing me about competing for our parents' love. I nearly believed you, too."

"I meant what I said."

"Sure you did."

"I didn't trick you into anything, Elizabeth. You tricked yourself by your own lies. Don't you see that?"

"I'll tell you what I see. That I'm a goddamn fool. You were right about that much. A fool to have listened to you, have believed you were on the level. You've always wanted what I had ever since we were kids. Now you want Jamie."

"Yes, I do."

"I'll tell you what *I* want," Derek said. "My money back. I've been taken in."

"Shut up," Jamie said.

"I will not. I was deceived."

"Would you like another bloody nose?"

"Not actually. But how about a Bloody Mary?"

"That's a great idea," Iris said, getting up before another fight started. "And I shall do the honors. Bloody Marys for everyone."

As soon as she disappeared into the kitchen, Derek walked over to the double window and planted himself in front of it. The light was starting to change, it was getting dark outside, and heavy clouds moved across the sky, signaling the possibility of imminent showers. Seconds later the sky opened up, and it began to rain. Trees swaying in the rain. Rain slashing across windowpanes. Dark. Dismal. Brooding. The opening and closing shots of "The Troubled Heart," Derek thought, wondering if any of the others had noticed the similarity, his eye meanwhile tracing a flurry of pigeons on a rooftop across the way.

"How did you find out about Bob and me?" Elizabeth whispered to Jamie, who had crouched down beside her chair so that they would not be overheard by Derek.

"You referred to him as *Robert*."

She seemed disappointed. "Is that all? That one little slip?"

"Not exactly. Call it writer's intuition."

"I call it something else: tricky."

"Yes, but I was right, wasn't I?"

"You couldn't have proven it. I could have denied the charge."

"But you didn't."

Her streaked mascara looked like soot beneath her eyes. "No."

"Why not? I thought for a minute that you might."

"Perhaps because I'm tired of pretending. Tired of lying."

"Then Iris was right. The game isn't worth it."

"I suppose." She seemed exhausted. "It's a relief to get it off my chest at last."

"I can imagine. It must have been a pretty heavy burden to carry around all this time."

"The odd part is that I don't feel as guilty as I thought I would. About Iris knowing, I mean. I feel much more guilty about saying that you wanted to marry me. Much more ashamed."

"Why?"

"Because I loved you." Elizabeth stood up, and smiled in theatrical regret. "And I lost you. I was too ashamed to admit that you didn't love me, so I turned it around and made it seem that you did. To the point of desperation. And that it was I who had pulled out. Foolish, wasn't it?"

Jamie had stood up, too. "It's very flattering."

"Yes, from your standpoint. But from mine . . . well, we all have so much damned pride."

They were only inches apart. "False pride."

"That's what I meant."

"Iris doesn't," he pointed out. "She's just admitted she's in love with me. That took guts."

"Either that, or sheer stupidity."

"Why stupidity?"

"First, she announces she's been working as a call girl. Then she says she's in love with you. After the first statement, does she seriously expect you to be interested in the second?"

"It would seem so."

"And are you interested?" she said, more sharply than she had intended.

"I don't know. I find it hard to think of Iris as a call girl." But the idea excited him. "It's too incredible."

Elizabeth touched his sweater with her clear red fingernails. "Maybe she was lying. To get attention. I wouldn't put it past her."

"Somehow I don't think so."

"Jamie?"

"What?"

The closeness of her had aroused him; brought back memories of the two of them locked in each other's arms, enjoying the delicious warmth of intimacy. He had a sudden urge to kiss her, to refresh his memory even more. She was starting to slip away in time, to join the procession of women who had come before her, and he didn't want that to happen. Ordinarily he would not have cared, might even have been glad to get rid of every vestige of her as he had with the others, but something in him resisted that complete obliteration which in the past he'd found so comforting. Of course. Elizabeth was the chain, the link. To Iris. She could not be destroyed. Without her, Iris was incomplete, just as without Iris, Elizabeth was partially lacking. He needed the two of them in order to make one.

"What is it?" he said to Elizabeth's upturned face, her streaked eyes, her tense mouth.

"I've missed you very much."

"I've missed you, too." He wasn't sure whether he wasn't telling the truth. "It's been rather lonely."

"What about Iris?"

"What about her?"

"She must have taken off the edge."

He questioned her silently.

"The edge of loneliness," Elizabeth said. "As opposed to 'The Edge of Night.'"

"Iris and I have never gone to bed."

"You haven't?" Elizabeth's eyes seemed to lighten. "How interesting. I thought that surely . . ."

"No. Never."

"Why not?" She was becoming coquettish now. "Don't you find her attractive?"

"Very." He looked toward the kitchen, where the sound of clicking ice cubes could be heard. "And apparently, so do a lot of men."

"You didn't think she was attractive at first," Elizabeth persisted. "When you first met."

"Not particularly."

"What made you change your mind?"

"It was a gradual thing. She began to change. It probably started when she started to go to bed with . . ." He gestured toward Derek. "Other men."

"But you didn't know that she was."

"I must have sensed it." He felt sure now that he had. "There was something different about her. Something sensual."

"And yet you never tried to make love to her?"

"I was involved with you."

"I mean, after we broke up."

"I thought about it, but she seemed so innocent."

"You just said she seemed sensual."

"Both. It was confusing." Jamie realized now how truly confusing it had been, how he had tried to push Iris out of his thoughts except as a writing associate, how dismally he had failed. "She was a mystery. That's one of the reasons I came here today."

"To solve the mystery?"

"Yes. At least to try. I didn't count on Derek showing up. Nor that woman next door. Nor you, for that matter." He took a breath. "I'm glad you did."

Elizabeth stepped back a foot or two, as though to appraise him more clearly. "Are you in love with her, Jamie?"

"I don't know," he said, just as Iris came into the room carrying a tray of Bloody Marys. "I'm not sure."

"Are you in love with me?"

"I don't know that, either."

"He's not sure which one of us he's in love with," Elizabeth informed her sister. "Just in case you were wondering. How do you like that for being on the fence?"

"I suppose it's his prerogative."

"Personally, I consider it one of the most arrogant, insolent, insulting remarks I've ever heard."

"At least he's honest."

"I'm sick to death of this emphasis on being honest. The hell with that! I want devotion, not honesty."

"Buy a dog."

"If you two are going to start that dreadful bickering, I'm going to leave," Derek said. "I should be leaving anyway. It's become painfully obvious that I'll never see my money again."

"Is that all you can talk about?" Jamie asked. "Money?"

"I feel that I've been taken advantage of. Rather badly, as a matter of fact. And I think some retribution should be made. That is, if Iris has a bone of decency left in her body."

"I've got something even better," Iris said, handing out the drinks. "I've got an idea for a new soap opera. Want to hear it?"

Chapter Twenty-Nine

They sat down without another word, all of them except Iris, who remained standing as she prepared to outline the thoughts she had been working on for the past few weeks. She was triumphantly aware of their eyes upon her, felt she could gauge the curiosity of their minds, anticipate the amazement that would strike them when they heard what she had to say. For surely, it was a stroke of professional inspiration on her part. And surely, they would consider her the last person in the world to have thought of it. Iris stifled a smile. It was as though being a call girl, cheat, liar, drunk, and triple-crosser, was about to pay miraculous dividends, judging by the expressions that were hovering in the wings, getting ready to flicker across their three receptive faces.

"I've been studying research reports that analyze demographic breakdowns of soaps like 'The Troubled Heart,'" she began, "and it turns out that less people watch us on the

West Coast than in any other part of the United States. So, keeping that in mind, I have an idea for a soap that instead of being set in some mythical town in the East or Midwest, as most of them are, would take place in Los Angeles (as you all know, 'The Troubled Heart' draws only a three-per-cent rating in Los Angeles, as compared to, say, a ten-per-cent in Kansas City, or an eighteen-percent in Pittsburgh).

"For visual identification we could use a shot of International Airport and the freeways, but the show itself would originate from New York, since the sets are all interiors anyway. My point is that I think we'd stand a good chance of attracting a lot of those nonviewers out on the West Coast, because of the show's locale. In addition to which, I think we'd be able to hold on to the hard-core mass of regular soap viewers who've probably become bored by now with the same old undefined, small-town setting. Result: high ratings *all* over the country."

"But small-town settings are what make soaps so appealing," Elizabeth said. "It's a case of Middle America watching Middle America."

"Middle America is a state of mind, not a state in the Union. The problems on the L.A. soap would be similar to the problems on other soaps, the same kind of anxieties, conflicts, aspirations, the same emphasis on the nuclear family. The only difference would be that the action takes place in a large city that has a highly publicized glamor appeal. And I think we could cash in on that appeal, without harming ourselves, by having a slightly more sophisticated cast of characters, wearing slightly more sophisticated clothes, living in slightly more sophisticated homes. But still trying to cope with emotional crises that are familiar to everyone everywhere.

"In other words, we give the non-L.A. housewife a vicarious sense of what it's like to live in L.A., at the same time that she's watching the daily unfolding of typical small-town problems she can personally identify with. And we give the West Coast housewife, who normally doesn't watch daytime TV, an incentive to do so because of the show's local appeal. Los Angeles happens to be perfect for our purposes, since it's really a very large city made up of a bunch of very small towns scattered all over the place. So we're not even begging the issue.

"Now as for the main characters. At the nucleus of our

story we have two attractive sisters with very different and conflicting personalities, goals, emotional makeups. They're portrayed right from the start as being inevitable lifelong rivals. What happens to these sisters and their respective families, children, parents, friends, etc., will be the continuing focal point of the series."

There was dead silence.

Then Elizabeth said, "Somebody must have thought of using Los Angeles as a soap background. Still, it's never been done before. I wonder why."

"I believe the official network thinking is that people in the West spend more time outdoors than people in other parts of the country," Derek said, "and that's why daytime TV does so badly out there. Meaning that a Los Angeles background would just be a waste of time."

"That sounds like network thinking," Jamie said. "Negative as hell. But, instead of saying all the people are outdoors and that's that, why not figure out a way, as Iris has, to bring them indoors? At least for half an hour a day. Particularly if that half hour falls just before or just after twelve noon, when all the Mommies are home anyway, giving their kids lunch."

"Uh-uh," Elizabeth said. "Distances are too great out there for children to come home at lunchtime. They're more likely to eat in the school cafeteria."

"Then why not program it later in the afternoon? Say, around four o'clock? Wouldn't most of our potential audience be home by then, maybe starting to get dinner ready? Also, the later it is in the day, the more sophisticated you can make it, which I think is the way soaps are going anyhow. It seems to be the trend."

"Besides," Derek added, "our current four o'clock game series is a disaster. This could be a logical replacement, and in my opinion, a highly successful one. Frankly, I wouldn't mind producing it."

"It's the first exciting idea I've heard in a long time," Jamie agreed. "I wouldn't mind writing it."

"And I wouldn't mind playing the lead." Elizabeth directed a sarcastic glance at her sister. "Now that I'm going to be out of a job."

"I'm delighted that you're all so enthusiastic," Iris said. "But as creator of the show, where does that leave me?"

"Making a pile of M-O-N-E-Y," Derek said. "Which

means that you won't have to continue your illicit sexual activities much longer."

"Oh, I didn't do it for financial reasons. My family is very wealthy. I did it for the experience."

"What are you saying? That you took my money under false pretenses, and you didn't even *need* it?"

"That's right."

"Contemptible! Shocking! Corrupt!"

"I don't see why you're getting so excited. You had a good time with me. What difference does it make whether I was practically a virgin, or not?"

"Disgraceful! Absurd! Revolting!"

"If it makes you feel any better, I resign from that profession as of this minute. In the future, you'll have to find another girl to pay fifty dollars a visit to. I've decided to go straight."

"And about time, too. If there's anything more duplicitous than a virgin masquerading as a hooker, I'm sure I don't know what it is, and I don't want to know." He stood up, weaving slightly. "I must be shoving off, or there'll be no Strawberry Flips for this chap tonight."

"What was that about Strawberry Flips?" Jamie asked, after the door had closed behind Derek.

"It's his little specialty," Iris said. "Would you like to try it?"

"I might, if I knew what it was."

"I know what it is," Elizabeth said, "and it's absolutely disgusting."

"Did it ever occur to you that what you consider disgusting might appeal to me? It's just possible that you've never tapped all levels of my sensuality." Jamie languidly put an arm around Iris's shoulder. "Maybe you'd like to pick up where your sister left off."

"Maybe. Although I think she was right about the Strawberry Flip."

"I'm open to any and all suggestions."

Iris thought a moment of Sheila's memorable list of clients and their preferences. "How about the Black Butterfly?"

"It sounds intriguing. What is it?"

"Come into the bedroom, and I'll show you."

"Have you lost your mind?" Elizabeth said. "You're about to jump into the sack with him, and he won't even say which one of us he's in love with."

"Who cares? I'm willing to take my chances. Are you?"

"You're depraved."

"Call it what you like. All I know is that I've wanted to go to bed with Jamie for a long time now, and I'm not going to miss this opportunity. As for you, Elizabeth, you can do whatever the hell you like."

"You can't cut me out like this. I won't have it. Just because you were a call girl, don't think you know everything. I'm pretty sexy stuff myself, as I'm sure Jamie will agree."

"Then come on along." Iris smiled slyly. "I'll show you both what the Black Butterfly is."

Jamie looked from one sister to the other, contemplating the prospect of shortly finding himself in bed with the two of them. It was a tantalizing thought. Their fierce rivalry was bound to be the source of much pleasure for him, as they strove to outdo each other in competitive displays of eroticism. Iris was obviously eager, which meant that Elizabeth could not back out now. If she did, it would be with the flat knowledge of leaving him to her voracious sister, a highly unlikely move, thank God. Yes, he wanted them both, and something told him that they wanted it that way too, *needed* it in order to complete their strange relationship. Then he noticed Derek's bottle of vintage champagne sitting on the round dining table, untouched.

"It's been an awfully long day," Jamie said.

"It's been an *awful* day."

"It most certainly has."

"What the three of us need to do, more than anything else," he said, "is just plain relax. Do you think a glass of champagne might help?"

"A glass of champagne sounds like a marvelous idea."

He opened the champagne bottle and poured three glasses full. "I propose a toast to—"

"The three of us," both women said in unison.

The camera came in for a closeup of their smiles, their three glasses touching, as the sound of organ music grew louder and the soap opera was off the air, to be continued the next day. . . .

Big Bestsellers from SIGNET

☐ **THE COLUMBUS TREE by Peter S. Feibleman.** Against the dazzling background of an international pleasure resort on the golden coast of Spain, the story of a lovely young American girl, her beautiful socialite mother, and the proud European aristocrat whom they both love. . . . "The Columbus Tree is a helluva read, it will certainly be a big seller. There's an atmosphere of mystery, menace, and ultimate doom . . . exceedingly well-written."— Boston Globe (#J5784—$1.95)

☐ **THE MAKING OF THE HAPPY HOOKER by Robin Moore.** Now it can be told—the hot inside story of how Xaviera Hollander switched from "hook" to "book" to become a literary sensation. And what an inside story it is, complete with the most kinky, uninhibited goings on and loads of titillating sexual adventures. (#W5662—$1.50)

☐ **CLOSE-UP by Len Deighton.** From the author of The Ipcress File comes a scorching novel about a Hollywood superstar and his world of image and evil. "A blistering novel, a scathing expose, a corker in its class!"—Saturday Review Syndicate (#W5656—$1.50)

☐ **THE PRETENDERS by Gwen Davis.** The exciting bestseller about the jet-setters is a masterful portrait of their loves, lives and fears. (#W5460—$1.50)

☐ **ELLA PRICE'S JOURNAL by Dorothy Bryant.** When a woman is in love, she wants her lover's baby . . . but what if the baby is her husband's? A soul-searching novel about a marriage, an affair, and a woman's agonizing decision. (#Y5629—$1.25)

More Big Bestsellers from SIGNET
You'll Want to Read

☐ **TO REACH A DREAM by Nathan C. Heard.** From the author of the bestselling **Howard Street** comes a seething new novel of streetcorner manhood at the bottom of a black ghetto. "Raw, brutal, memorable."—**The New York Times** (#Y5490—$1.25)

☐ **THE SEX SURROGATES by Michael Davidson.** The raw tapes of the sex clinic—a startling novel about the men and women—strangers—who find themselves partners in love. (#Y5410—$1.25)

☐ **AN OLD-FASHIONED DARLING by Charles Simmons.** Can a young man who works on a sex magazine and has a harem of sexually voracious ladies, break the sex habit? "Unrestrained delight."—**The New York Times** (#Q5355—95¢)

☐ **TO SMITHEREENS by Rosalyn Drexler.** A heartwarming love story with the kick of a karate chop. . . . "If Lenny Bruce had written a novel, this would have been it!" —**Jack Newfield** (#Q5281—95¢)

☐ **GOLDENROD by Herbert Harker. Goldenrod** is about love in its widest, deepest meaning, and like love, it is both funny and serious, joyous and sad, and very beautiful. "One of the most enchanting novels ever written. . . ."—Ross Macdonald, **New York Times Book Review** (#Y5487—$1.25)

THE NEW AMERICAN LIBRARY, INC.,
P.O. Box 999, Bergenfield, New Jersey 07621

Please send me the SIGNET BOOKS I have checked above. I am enclosing $_____(check or money order—no currency or C.O.D.'s). Please include the list price plus 25¢ a copy to cover handling and mailing costs. (Prices and numbers are subject to change without notice.)

Name_____

Address_____

City_____State_____Zip Code_____
Allow at least 3 weeks for delivery

Have You Read these Bestsellers from SIGNET?

☐ **THE CENTER by Charles Beardsley.** From the author of **The Motel** comes a torrid new novel of scorching sex and warped desires among therapists who cannot cure their own devastating lusts. (#Y5653—$1.25)

☐ **SEMI-TOUGH by Dan Jenkins.** This super bestseller is "funny . . . marvelous . . . outrageous. . . . Dan Jenkins has written a book about sports, but not about sports . . . it mocks contemporary American mores; it mocks Madison Avenue; it mocks racial attitudes; it mocks writers like me . . . Women abound . . . I loved it."— David Halberstam, **New York Times Book Review** (#E5598—$1.75)

☐ **THE SANTA CLAUS BANK ROBBERY by A. C. Greene.** A violent, ironic tale of nonstop killing in America's most bizarre bank holdup—the day that Santa decided to stuff his sack with all the dollars in the First National Bank. "Extraordinary power."—**Los Angeles Times** (#Y5565—$1.25)

☐ **CARRIAGE TRADE by Robert Thomsen.** Not since **Gone With the Wind** has there been such a big, lusty, unashamedly romantic novel of love and war. "A book to be read . . . who can fail to find interest in a combination of prostitutes and Civil War soldiers."—**Newsday** (#W5564—$1.50)

☐ **GENTLEMAN OF LEISURE: A Year in the Life of a Pimp,** text by Susan Hall; photographed by Bob Adelman. The pimp who makes more money than the president of the United States tells the shocking, intimate story of his profession—with explicit photographs of his world —and his women. (#J5524—$1.95)
